THE DEEP SKY

THE DEEP SKY

YUME KITASEI

FLATIRON
BOOKS
NEW YORK

THE DEEP SKY. Copyright © 2023 by Yume Kitasei. All rights reserved. Printed in the United States of America. For information, address Flatiron Books, 120 Broadway, New York, NY 10271.

www.flatironbooks.com

Illustrations and interior design by Jonathan Bennett

Library of Congress Cataloging-in-Publication Data

Names: Kitasei, Yume, author.
Title: The deep sky / Yume Kitasei.
Description: First edition. | New York : Flatiron Books, 2023.
Identifiers: LCCN 2022050461 | ISBN 9781250875334 (hardcover) |
    ISBN 9781250875341 (ebook)
Subjects: LCGFT: Science fiction. | Thrillers (Fiction). | Novels.
Classification: LCC PS3611.I8777 D44 2023 | DDC 813/.6—dc23/
    eng/20230105
LC record available at https://lccn.loc.gov/2022050461

Our books may be purchased in bulk for promotional, educational, or business use. Please contact your local bookseller or the Macmillan Corporate and Premium Sales Department at 1-800-221-7945, extension 5442, or by email at MacmillanSpecialMarkets@macmillan.com.

First Edition: 2023

10 9 8 7 6 5 4 3 2 1

For my mother,
who taught me how to write

Days and months are travellers of eternity. So are the years that pass by. Those who steer a boat across the sea, or drive a horse over the earth till they succumb to the weight of years, spend every minute of their lives travelling. There are a great number of ancients, too, who died on the road. I myself have been tempted for a long time by the cloud-moving wind—filled with a strong desire to wander.

—*A Narrow Road to the Deep North*, Matsuo Bashō
(translated from the Japanese by Nobuyuki Yuasa)

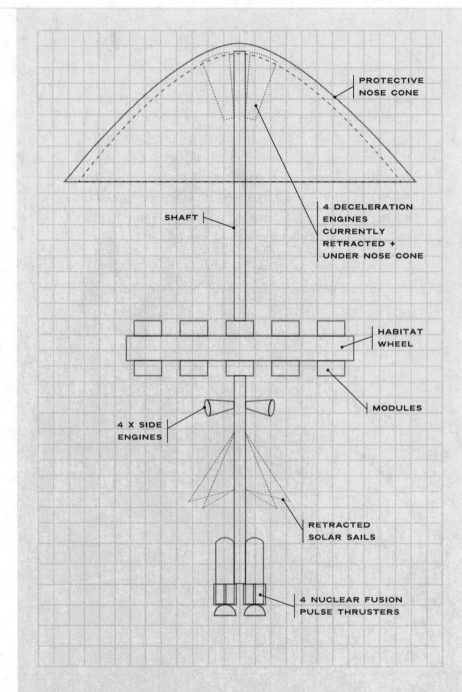

PROTECTIVE
NOSE CONE

4 DECELERATION
ENGINES
CURRENTLY
RETRACTED +
UNDER NOSE CONE

SHAFT

HABITAT
WHEEL

MODULES

4 X SIDE
ENGINES

RETRACTED
SOLAR SAILS

4 NUCLEAR FUSION
PULSE THRUSTERS

| THE PHOENIX |

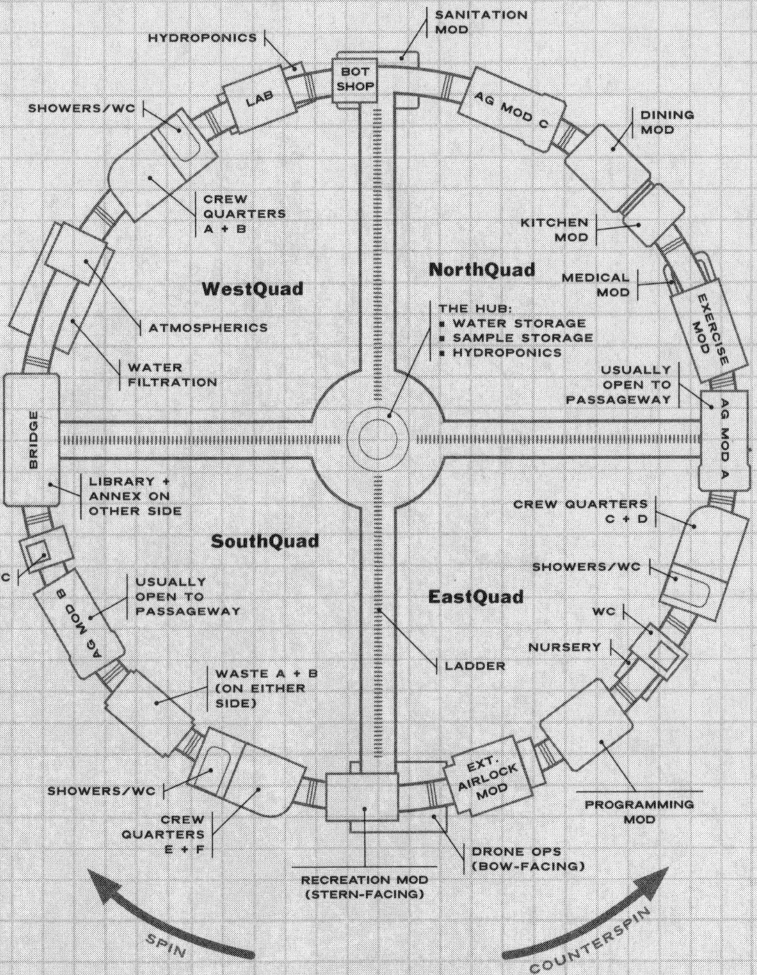
SANITATION MOD
HYDROPONICS
BOT SHOP
LAB
SHOWERS/WC
AG MOD C
DINING MOD
CREW QUARTERS A + B
KITCHEN MOD
NorthQuad
WestQuad
MEDICAL MOD
EXERCISE MOD
THE HUB:
▪ WATER STORAGE
▪ SAMPLE STORAGE
▪ HYDROPONICS
ATMOSPHERICS
WATER FILTRATION
USUALLY OPEN TO PASSAGEWAY
BRIDGE
AG MOD A
LIBRARY + ANNEX ON OTHER SIDE
CREW QUARTERS C + D
SouthQuad
SHOWERS/WC
WC
USUALLY OPEN TO PASSAGEWAY
EastQuad
AG MOD B
WC
NURSERY
LADDER
WASTE A + B (ON EITHER SIDE)
EXT. AIRLOCK MOD
SHOWERS/WC
PROGRAMMING MOD
CREW QUARTERS E + F
DRONE OPS (BOW-FACING)
RECREATION MOD (STERN-FACING)
SPIN
COUNTERSPIN

CROSS SECTION: VIEW FROM STERN

THE DEEP SKY

CHAPTER ONE

There were many things Asuka did not consider when she agreed to travel from one sun to another. That is, did not allow herself to consider. Like would she miss lying on her back in rough grass, the scent of damp earth in her nose as she scraped her nails against a real, periwinkle sky. Like would missing her brother sometimes still feel like a hole in her gut (she did *not* miss her mom). Like did she actually want to live the rest of her life jogging the circumference of a spaceship's habitat wheel like a hamster looking for a missing drill for Lala Williams.

Problem was, Lala's missing drill could be anywhere. All Lala could tell her was that it had a red handle and that Sam may have borrowed it to fix a shelving unit in Agriculture Module C. But it wasn't among the plants or trays of soil, and Sam swore that Red had borrowed it after her. Red remembered using it to fix a vents issue before returning it to the Bot Maintenance Shop. Where it definitely wasn't.

Asuka slowed to a walk.

The thing about saying *yes* to the first (and probably only) one-way interstellar voyage to settle a new world was that there were no takebacks.

But at least there was DAR, Digitally Augmented Reality, which meant she never had to consider anything she didn't want to. On Earth, they had had to wear clunky headgear that enabled the wearer to access DAR, but before they'd left, the crew had chips implanted in their temples that could pipe an alternative reality directly into their brains.

So instead of jogging through a spaceship, Asuka hiked along a worn forest trail, ship invisible underneath. The light was a soft, mottled olive. She wore an old pair of jeans and a faded Del Mar Exotic Bird Sanctuary T-shirt. In the distance, a wood thrush sang hello-goodbye. Soft shadows enveloped her, and she could almost smell the pines, wet after rain. Almost. Also, there were no pesky rocks strewn across her path. She'd deleted them a week ago after tripping over one that wasn't really there.

Like the rest of the crew of the *Phoenix*, she had grown up with DAR and was proficient at modifying it, though the base of this one had been designed for her by a professional—only the best for Earth's heroes.

"Alpha," Asuka said, as if it was ever necessary to summon their omnipresent ship AI.

Asuka. Alpha's voice in her ears would be inaudible to the two women flirting in the middle of the trail, too preoccupied to make room for Asuka to pass. She gritted her teeth and said "Excuse me" as she pushed around them, banging her elbow painfully against a protruding branch—a water pipe or something underneath the DAR. This was what had allowed DAR to surpass other augmented realities to dominate the global market: it could wrap the whole skin of the world in somewhere else. Perfect when stuck in a small spaceship for decades.

"I'm done looking for Lala Williams's drill. You got any other jobs for me?" she asked Alpha. Her eye caught a flash of blue in the branches, and she stopped to look. As a child, she had loved birds the way other kids loved dinosaurs, saving all her money to buy a single robin for her DAR. Now that she was an adult, her DAR was stocked with the full catalog of RealBirds, and even so, she didn't tire of the thrill of spotting the denim-blue jacket of a male western bluebird alight on a stump.

I'll change your status to "available." Should I mark your current job as "complete"?

"Mark it as 'I give up,'" said Asuka. "That drill has fallen into another dimension."

While theoretically possible, that seems unlikely.

Asuka was about to snark back when a message appeared from the Captain in the left side of her vision. *Alt. Need you in the EAM five minutes ago.* The EAM was the Exterior Airlock Module. They wanted her to do a spacewalk outside.

Asuka shaped words with her hands, composing and deleting several irritable responses, including *Then you should have asked me five minutes ago* and *Sorry, I'm busy* and *Go jump into space*, before settling on: *Yes, Captain.* Because she did like spacewalks.

Unlike the other seventy-nine crew on the *Phoenix*, Asuka was an Alternate, which meant she didn't have a job exactly. Her job was just to do whatever was needed and be grateful she'd made the cut by the most microscopic of margins. Her job was not, as Captain McMahon often reminded her, to question orders or her place in the ship's claustrophobically small community.

Asuka found two of the Ship Maintenance crew and First Vice Captain Ying Yue in the middle of the woods standing between an old cabin and a plywood outhouse, which were, underneath the illusion, the ship airlocks. The airlocks exited out onto the bow and stern sides of the wheel, respectively. On one side of the clearing, heavy black compression suits hung from a clothesline between two fir trees.

Ying Yue was tall, with perfectly shaped eyebrows and a long face that made her seem perpetually surprised. Her hair was close shaven. Buzz cuts weren't mandatory, but they were popular among the crew. Easier to care for in space. Asuka had grown out her hair instead, and she was teased for being a rebel.

They were already suiting up Kat, one of the Australian reps. She had light blue eyes, picture-perfect freckles, and an impressive quantity of natural self-confidence.

"Look who decided to show up," Kat said, without maliciousness. "Susie. You're just in time to witness my last spacewalk."

"Last one?"

"I'm scheduled for Medical next cycle." Insemination appointment, she meant. All crew were required to have a baby as part of the mission. And once pregnant, Kat would no longer be eligible for walks.

"It might not happen right away," said Asuka, for whom it hadn't.

"It will," said Kat, fluttering her eyes with pleasure. "My mother had four of us, and each time it was like bam, missile lock. You could say fertility is one of my key qualifications. Well, that, my ability to do multivariable calculus in my head, and my amazing biceps." She flexed a bare arm and winked at one of the crew trying to fit it into a suit.

"Oh, I thought it was your fully developed ego." Asuka kept her tone light, but annoyance bubbled up like acid reflux.

Kat laughed.

"All right, Susie?" Ying Yue asked, coming over. She was eight months pregnant with twins, and *she* was asking *Asuka* that?

"What's the mission?" Asuka asked, stripping off her clothes and holding out her arms, then legs, for the other crew to squeeze into a compression suit, size extra small.

"We spotted a thing on the side of the hull in NorthQuad H-18," said Ying Yue.

"What do you mean, a 'thing'?" After spending the first ten years of their mission in hibernation, they had woken eleven months ago, as planned, flying through deep, empty space, light-years from anything. Radiation, cosmic rays, stardust, and junk were always a concern, considering the speed they were traveling. The ship was equipped with a radiation windscreen, nose shield, magnetic field, and advance warning system to protect them, as well as an army of bots and drones to repair any problems as quickly as possible. But they were literally in uncharted territory. The farthest humans had traveled up to this point was Jupiter, so no one really knew what they might find out here.

"Unclear. We can't tell what it is from the cameras. Looks like a shadow or a smudge. Same when Yaz investigated with a bot. So anyway, the Captain wants you and Kat to go put some au naturel eyeballs on it." Asuka caught a roll of Ying Yue's eyes. For some reason, Ying Yue and the Captain didn't get along. Which was the main reason Asuka liked Ying Yue.

"Is it—does it look artificial?" Something alien, she meant.

Kat laughed. "You've been reading too much science fiction. We're in the literal middle of nowhere."

Ying Yue offered Asuka a heavy pair of boots.

Hey. What's the holdup? No time for gossip. The Captain's words appeared in front of all of them. Despite regularly telling herself she didn't care what Captain McMahon thought—that her name was only *Becky* and that she was the same age as the rest of them—Asuka felt her gut tighten.

Just following protocol, Ying Yue replied. And then added something aloud in Mandarin for their ears only, which appeared as subtitles for those who needed it: "You should try it sometime."

One of the maintenance crew snickered.

"Hold still," someone said, and the helmet came down over Asuka's head. She felt them strap the heavy oxygen pack to her back.

"Which of you is carrying the tool kit?" Ying Yue asked, unhooking one of the cases from an old hitching post.

Asuka reached for it, but Kat intercepted. "I've got longer arms," she said. "One of these days you're going to drop it, and then you'll be crying ice crystals all the way home."

"Okay," Ying Yue said. "But Asuka is Mission Lead."

Asuka suppressed a groan as they clipped the kit to Kat's chest. Kat never listened to her.

"They're good to go," the other crew confirmed.

"Alpha, last check?" said Ying Yue.

Asuka and Kat obediently held their arms up. The ship AI didn't see things on the ship in the human sense, but she could sense the nanochips in the clothing they wore and could tell if the suit components were properly fitted.

Everything appears normal.

"All right, then. Everyone clear the EAM." Ying Yue gave them one last look.

Be careful out there, said Alpha. *It's dangerous.*

The cabin door opened, and beyond it was a chamber with cold, white metal walls and a door at the other end with a thick glass window. They stepped inside, and all DAR evaporated. It didn't work outside the ship.

They waited impatiently as the air hissed out of the airlock. Given the cramped size of the chamber, Asuka was forced to spend this time contemplating the back of Kat's suit.

"Sounds like the situation in the Pacific is getting spicy," said Kat.

"Yeah," Asuka agreed, unsure what Kat was talking about. The typical tension between the usual countries probably. Namely, China and the United States. Asuka didn't really follow the news as much as she should, but she wasn't about to admit that to Kat.

"Your mum still live in Tokyo?" Kat asked.

"Maybe," said Asuka, like she didn't care. She didn't know where her mom was now, and it hurt too much to think about.

"What do you mean? Don't you talk?"

"Nope."

"I thought you two were close."

"Actually, we're not."

Kat contorted herself, but she couldn't turn her head in the close quarters to look at Asuka. She settled for twisting her faceplate to the ceiling. "What—"

"Can we not, please?"

"Fine. Sorry." Kat gripped the wheel attached to the door, waiting for the light to turn green. "I broke my cat," she said softly, like she was making an offering. Her pain for Asuka's. Except what she was talking about was her truly hideous, pink ceramic cat.

"I'm . . . so sorry?"

"I know, me too." Kat's voice caught like she might cry. She was serious. "I tried to fix it, and I made a mess of it. And I keep thinking how I can't get another, you know? Because we're never going home."

The hexagonal light on the door turned green, and Kat turned the wheel. "Anyway. If this thing out there *is* something extraterrestrial, I'm going to be the first one to see it. Try and keep up, Susie."

And Asuka retorted, in a moment she'd regret for the rest of her life: "I'll race you."

CHAPTER TWO

They stepped out of the airlock onto a metal scaffold facing the stern of the ship, small headlamps flicking on. Without the proximity of the sun or any other star, the *Phoenix* didn't have a light side. It was all dark side. And cold as nothing, though she didn't feel it.

Absence was what Asuka liked best about space. The forced perspective of hearing nothing but her breath in her ears, the blackness, and the billions of distant stars wheeling around them as the ship spun.

"See you later." Kat took off jogging along the scaffold.

"Hey!" Asuka started after her, already sinking into the familiar rhythm of attaching and detaching her two safety clips—on-off, on-off—as she moved, careful to stay tethered to the safety rail at all times. Kat was getting farther ahead.

The *Phoenix* was constructed like an umbrella: a protective radiation windscreen and nose shield in front, directly under which were tucked forward-facing engines, ready to deploy for deceleration. The shield was at the front end of a metal shaft that stretched the length of a sports field to the back of the ship, which had immense, retracted, paneled solar sails followed by four rear engines. Between the solar sails and the forward engines, in the middle of the shaft, was their great, spinning habitat wheel, where the crew lived. The wheel spun, generating enough centrifugal force to simulate gravity for the occupants inside—and those standing on the scaffolding that ran along the outside of it on its bow and stern sides.

Asuka imagined the scaffolding that ran on the inside and outside of the wheel looked like lips, and the various modules attached in intervals to either side of the wheel rim—for Crew Quarters, Sanitation, Drone Operations, et cetera—like the teeth.

The scaffold extended a shoulder width past the widest modules, giving crew easy access for exterior maintenance. The thin metal grate shook with each step, which wasn't nerve-racking at all. Thanks to the gravity from the spin, they could have been out for a stroll on Earth. If an endless void didn't surround them on all sides.

"Ladies. Slow down," said Ying Yue from her spot in the Drone Ops control room inside the ship. She had direct access to their suit and ship exterior camera feeds. She sounded rattled. "Kat, are you not using your clips?"

She wasn't. Dammit, that's how Kat was moving so fast, the cheater. Asuka swore and dropped her own clips and began to run faster, but it was hard because she was laughing. The whole thing was absurd. Childish. And it felt good.

Kat whooped so loud the radio squealed. Sure, they were taking risks fooling around like this, and Captain McMahon was definitely going to tear them to pieces after, but for a moment, everything felt normal. Except they were running through *space*.

Kat reached NorthQuad just as Asuka's boot caught against the scaffold grate, and she stumbled against the outside of Crew Quarters D. Her heart leapt, but she was all right, totally fine. She gripped the waist-high safety cable that ran along the outside of the scaffold and forced herself to keep moving.

"Need a status update," said Captain McMahon. She was chewing something, and the wet, smacking noise set Asuka's teeth on edge. A loud swallow right in her ear. "Do you have eyes on the anomaly yet? Give me details."

"Almost there, Captain," said Kat. She began climbing one of the many maintenance ladders a couple of meters past the spot to get closer to the location where the thing had been spotted.

Asuka sprinted the final meters to the bottom of the ladder and clipped herself back on. She was just ascending as Kat used metal rungs affixed to the ship's body to maneuver out to the spot.

"You ever think about how we live our life in constant motion?" Kat's voice asked in her ear. "Born on a rock spinning through space, and now here we are, rushing off to another. How come we can never just be? We've always got to *go* somewhere."

Asuka stopped and turned, trying to penetrate the deep darkness all around them. She imagined she could feel the pinpricks of heat from so many stars out there, forming and dying millions of years ago. If she looked backward (she didn't), she might see how far they'd come—and how insignificant that was against the scale of the universe.

She heard Kat say: "Where did you say it was, Ying Yue? Hang on, I'm caught on something. Okay, but I'm telling you—"

There was a flash of something bright as a sun, and then

nothing.

CHAPTER THREE

Fledgling Arctic terns made their first journey from the South to North Pole without their parents, finding their own way over tens of thousands of miles. Before takeoff, the entire colony would fall silent—this moment was called the "dread."

CHAPTER FOUR

The high-pitched siren went on and on. Asuka blinked and tried to focus her eyes. Her vision doubled, then resolved. Must have hit her head. Concussion? Felt like she'd been kicked in the sternum.

Debris from the *Phoenix* floated away, illuminated by a penumbra of blue light spilling out of a hole in the hull about a meter wide. She wanted to vomit, but that would be a bad idea in a spacewalk helmet.

This was bad. This was bad to the nth degree.

She surveyed the stern of the ship toward the four tulip-shaped rear engines. Everything in that direction seemed intact, at least.

"Cut alarm," she said. The alarm stopped. Her breath sounded ragged and loud. "Can anyone hear me?"

No answer. Her radio must be down.

"Alpha?" The ship's AI couldn't hear her out here, of course. Alpha communicated via DAR, and DAR didn't work outside the ship.

Did anything hurt? Just her head and maybe her back, and everything. But otherwise, okay.

Okay then.

She tried to reset the radio but got only static. For a panicked moment, she thought everyone was dead. But no, the transmitter on her wrist was broken. Must have smashed against the side of the ship when—

She checked her short tether. Attached. And to a part of the ship that was still there; otherwise, she'd be falling away from the *Phoenix*. As it was, she was meters out into space, being towed around by the spin of the ship's habitat wheel.

Where was Kat? She looked out at the receding debris.

Damn it. Damn it. Damn it.

Asuka rolled her tongue across her teeth. Copper and salt.

She flipped back and hooked a boot on the tether to stop herself from spinning. Her whole body screamed in protest. Only seven meters from the ship, and it felt like a kilometer.

Things were coming back to her in bits.

Something had exploded. A piece of broken-off hull had slammed into her chest, knocking her back against the ship. But what happened? And how could everything go to shit like that?

Asuka was panicking, guzzling oxygen. She unhooked her boot from the cable, and she began to spin again, arms and legs out like a sacrifice.

She forced herself to narrow her focus, to calm down. The small spear of her headlamp pierced the dark. It caught a boot without a foot in it, small and tumbling away, and her chest ached with a hollowness. So. Kat was dead, and who else? She liked Kat—even though she was so patronizing when she discovered something else that Asuka didn't know or hadn't done, which was often. But Kat fixed Asuka cups of tea after meals, and she was always up for simulation trips to places they would never go in real life, even if Kat only ever wanted to go to Europe. And now here Asuka was, with a feeling like she needed to howl, or she would burst.

A new alarm pinged in her suit.

She checked her suit metrics: oxygen, carbon dioxide, and battery level, which powered her propulsion pack and air scrubbers and regulated the temperature in her suit. Oxygen and battery were low, and her carbon dioxide was getting up to the danger zone.

Fantastic. Super.

Time to get back inside. Asuka hauled herself in, hand over hand on her lifeline, to the rim of the ship. It took nearly everything in her to do it. At last, Asuka was clinging to the outside of the spinning habitat wheel, in a constant state of being thrown away from the ship.

With a groan, she hauled herself up onto the scaffold. She gave thanks to the fact that she could still do a pull-up.

Gasping, she stared into the void where the section of scaffold used to be. A chunk of the *Phoenix* was no longer there. Emergency lights blinked and shuddered from the hole the explosion had torn in the ship. She gazed at what was left of their Dining Module. One long table was still intact and bolted to the floor, either a testament to the quality engineering that had gone into it or the fact that it had been partly shielded from the blast by the other tables. Otherwise, the mod was a wreck. No fire—the atmosphere was gone. There was soup all over the floor. In the dim blue light, she saw feet behind the half-demolished serving counter, and another arm sticking out at the far end near the door. Two bodies.

She narrowly missed getting beaned by a box of un-meat patties. She snagged it and slung it back into the hole.

She eyed the gap and doubted she could make it with a running jump. Her mind flashed back to the scrawny girl she had once been, hopping over big puddles after a rain and coming home streaked with mud from head to foot. Papa plucking her up and slinging her over one shoulder and marching her straight to the shower, calling her sweetmuddypie.

She could take the long way around, but she wasn't sure she had enough oxygen. She was down to 5 percent. There was supposed to be extra in the tank for an emergency, but she'd never cut it this close before.

Would this be the moment that proved she wasn't good enough? She was out of time.

She backed up, braced herself, and unclipped. Her boots on the metal made no sound at all. She leapt, and then she was falling and flying, and she juiced the gas jets of her propulsion pack, using precious battery. In the split second as she crossed the gap, a memory came to her of a goose taking off from the flat face of a warm pond, wings beating furiously, feet dragging as it tried to climb air. Then Asuka slammed into the other side. She nearly lost her grip, but she got the clip of her tether above the knot of the safety cable, thinking about how infinite her journey might have been if she had missed.

She hung there, panting into the hollow of her helmet.

Her compression suit was much more flexible than those clumsy bags of pressurized air astronauts used to wear, but at the end of the day, she was still wearing a big bubble on her head and thick insulation from finger to toe. She got back up.

Oxygen at 3 percent.

The emperor penguin could slow its own heart rate while plunging through dark, cold waters for almost half an hour.

Exhale. Keep moving.

It took a few more minutes to work her way back to the airlock, clipping and unclipping to the safety cable, and trying not to guzzle her remaining oxygen. She'd bitten her tongue, trying to keep her teeth from chattering. Shock, maybe.

The airlock door should have opened for her, but when she reached it, it was sealed. Nothing.

She tried twisting the handle of the airlock. It didn't give. She fumbled again. It wasn't the door; it was her hands. She couldn't do it.

"This is Asuka." Her voice was thin, more like a gasp. "Does anybody copy?" Static.

She checked her oxygen. One percent. Nearly out. Carbon dioxide in the red. Battery drained. Shit.

"This is Asuka. Does anybody copy? Can anyone hear me at all?"

She banged on the door, tried the broken radio. And again.

She touched her faceplate to the door. Turn, and she might catch a last glimpse of Kat, receding into that deepness of nothing. The pieces of her would last forever like that in space even as they spread millions, billions, then trillions of miles apart. But the whole universe could never put her back together. Humpty Dumpty. Entropy. Law of everything.

And yet we bother, thought Asuka. *It should have been me. Not Kat.*

She banged the door again, weaker, dizzier, colder. It'd be hours before she completely froze out here. She'd asphyxiate before that.

"I'm scared," she had told her mother as everything burned. Heat pressing down against her face. Her mother's voice firm and hoarse in her ear: "Sh. Sh. Picture a box."

Asuka shut her eyes, obedient for once, and pictured her mother's black and crimson-red lacquer jewelry box.

"Now, think of pearls. That is your fear, okay? Put them in that box one by one. Count them."

One. Two. Three.

Asuka straightened, hammered on the door. No one was coming.

Her heart thudded. Darkness ate at the corners of her vision. She could lean back and fall, into the great Milky Way. It wasn't her fault. She'd done her part and made it home.

She sank to her knees and looked back toward Earth. Couldn't see it. Something, she thought distantly, was wrong with the stars.

Her last thought was of her mother, light-years behind her, growing old watching the night sky.

CHAPTER FIVE

Asuka was in their neighbor's pool; it was dark, and her mom's arms were around her. They floated listlessly in the cold, cold water. She couldn't see the stars. Smoke burned her lungs and made her eyes tear.

Everyone else was gone. Everyone but Asuka and her mom, and somewhere out there, maybe, her dog Inu. Left alone in a neighborhood on fire.

Asuka tasted bitter ash and chlorine. The jet-black water lapped gently against the side of the pool. She was mad at her mom for not letting her go after Inu when the dog escaped.

The whole family had been on their way out the door, headed for the autobus waiting to evacuate them to safety. And then her mom had stepped on Inu's tail, and Inu yelped and ran off, leash tearing from Asuka's hands, and she had tried to run after, but her mom had grabbed her and wouldn't let her go.

And, and, and—she bit her mom's arm and tasted blood; she screamed that she hated her, that she would never speak to her again; she cried big, dirty tears, and still her mom held her tight.

Wasn't she mad at Asuka?

All this was Asuka's fault, wasn't it?

It wasn't. (It was.)

And now she'd never see Inu again. The bus was gone, with Papa and her brother on board, and it was just she and her mom in this pool, waiting for California to stop burning.

They drifted toward the edge of the pool.

What if her mom got tired? Would they die?

She didn't want to die.

"Asuka, don't!"

She'd grabbed the side of the pool with both arms. Her mom snatched her back from the heat of it, too late. Asuka shrieked, more from the knowledge that she'd made a terrible mistake than from the pain. No pain yet; that came later. Just a minute later. Maybe more.

They were underwater again. And Asuka was aware only of her mother's arms, and her mother's legs, and how they kept her alive, kicking, slapping, pushing back against the water and the soot and the pool and the fire and the clouds that hid the moon.

CHAPTER SIX

THE *PHOENIX* * 3,980 CYCLES AFTER LAUNCH,
0 CYCLES AFTER EXPLOSION, B SHIFT

Bright light stuck to Asuka's eyelashes like pollen. Her eyes teared from the glare.

She was inside, she was alive, and people were peeling her from her suit. She opened her mouth to remind them the pieces of the suit had to be inspected before they were hung in the cabinet. Her throat felt like it had been scraped with sand. She swallowed and coughed. Someone gave her some water.

"Cold," she said. She thought she said. Could anyone hear her?

You're all right now, Asuka, said Alpha's voice in her ear, soothing. And then the ship AI added: *I told you it was dangerous to go outside. You should have listened to me. You could have died.*

Out of reflex, Asuka wanted to argue with her. But Kat *had* died.

She turned her head and saw dirt, moss, rock, cabin, tree. Except. Except the tree was purple. How was that? She squinted at the bark. A large, armored beetle climbed up the tree. A second later it did again, and again. There was only one beetle, and it was not real, and she saw it climb in a dizzying loop. Something was wrong. She reached up and pawed at her temple with stiff, numb fingers until she felt the little bead implanted beneath the skin. The cabin and trees shivered and disappeared.

Now what she saw was true: she was lying on her back in a white airlock module, in a ship hurtling through space, and everything was mayhem. Or maybe it only felt like that. Ten crew crowded around her in the narrow module. It would have been a squeeze in normal circumstances, but half of them were pregnant. Not, of course, Asuka. She pushed that thought away.

"What happened?" First Vice Captain Ying Yue asked.

Asuka heaved air until the black spots in her vision began to recede. An alarm blared. In the corner, pieces of compression suits lay in a heap on the floor, like someone had hastily rifled through them to find a fit.

"Kat," she tried to say, and coughed. She wouldn't cry.

It's all right, Asuka, said Alpha. *Breathe.*

"Is Kat alive?" someone asked.

Asuka was shivering. Someone took her in their arms and held her, and the heat of the other person's body slowly seeped into hers. She didn't know who it was. It didn't matter. The walls disappeared, and she lay in a graveyard overgrown with flowers. She heard Ying Yue say: "Give her space."

The arms were withdrawn, and the graveyard too.

Don't worry, Asuka. You're safe now, Alpha said.

Ying Yue knelt and cupped Asuka's neck. Her hand was soft and warm. Asuka was sprawled on a platform as a speeding train went by. Still, the sensation of that touch was enough to steady her. She blinked and lifted her arms so they could tug the top part of the compression shirt off over her head. Someone had already removed her pants. Ying Yue let go, and Asuka was in her underwear on the cold floor of the ship.

Someone was saying, "Are you all right, Susie?"

She hated that nickname.

"We had no read from your suit at all. We thought you were dead."

She was thinking again of the fire—when she and her mom had almost died, and it was all her fault.

"Ruth saved you."

Ruth. She felt something sharp in her breastbone, which she ignored. Involuntarily, she twisted to locate her, but there were too many feet, shins, thighs in her way.

"Are you hurt?" Ying Yue asked again, leaning in.

So many people talking at once. At least Asuka was starting to feel her body again.

"Something exploded," said Asuka. "And—and Kat wasn't clipped." Their silly race. Running along the catwalk. And now Kat's amazing biceps and fertile ovaries would be frosted over and flying through darkness for eternity.

There was a strangled noise—coming from her. People reached out to soothe her.

This isn't your fault, said Alpha. *Remember that.* Asuka shut her eyes to keep tears back. Alpha didn't know. She was programmed to say things like that, to provide therapy to the crew, make sure they ate their vegetables and took their little pills.

But Asuka had been Mission Lead, and if Kat had been tethered, then maybe—

She felt her blood drumming in her ears.

Ying Yue leaned closer to hear her, her face scrunched in worry. "What do you mean? What exploded?" Asuka rewound her memory and tried to think. How had it happened exactly? Like a cork popping, maybe, or shrapnel emanating from the ship at high speed—no, no. She didn't want to remember that.

"Was it aliens?" someone else asked.

She didn't know, okay? She was smothered in their questions.

You seem stressed, Asuka, said Alpha. *Shall I tell you about the mating rituals of the bowerbird?* It was in Asuka's personnel file that she had a thing about birds.

Asuka shook her head to tell Alpha no, and the pain of it nearly killed her.

She tried to sit up, but a great weight pressed her down.

"Gravity's off," said Ying Yue. "Yaz is working on it." Yasemin was their Chief Engineer.

Hands reached out and helped her into sitting position. The world shifted, and shifted again. She wished it would stay itself. She lay there until she had steadied herself, then pinched the bridge of her nose. She could think again, around the sandy edges of a massive headache.

There was Ruth, getting dressed. Their eyes met a moment; one of the sides of Ruth's mouth lifted in a kind of smile like they were still best friends, and something in Asuka hiccupped. Ruth went back to pulling on her inside gloves, and Asuka was left staring after her a second too long.

People were crying. They had all grown up together, training for this mission. Now some of them were dead. It didn't make sense. But then, nothing had felt real to Asuka since last year, when they'd first woken up on the ship after a decade asleep.

"What does the Captain want us to do?" Asuka asked.

No one knew.

"Who else died?" She'd seen the bodies in the Dining Mod.

No one knew that either.

No one, it seemed, knew anything. They were all in a panic.

Not that Asuka blamed them. She was too. Or ought to be. It was just that her feelings hadn't caught up with her yet.

"Alpha, tell us," she said. Alpha tracked the heart rates, blood pressures, oxygen levels, and body temperatures of the crew to monitor their health and stress levels. She should know who was alive.

Alpha's disembodied voice cut across the expectant silence. *I am so sorry. My biometric monitoring program is rebooting. Please give me five minutes.*

"Let's get you to the clinic," Ying Yue said. "Hina, tell the Captain we retrieved Susie."

The tall, long-limbed crew member in question turned away, making rapid gestures with gloved hands, movement Alpha would convert into a text message.

Asuka forced herself to stand. She wasn't sure she could have done it without three crew bracketing her, heaving her up. Again, she saw a flash of the graveyard, and other things—a savannah, a lake. Then they let go, and all of it was gone in a blink.

The weight of extra gravity caused her to stagger. Ying Yue stepped close and began to rub her all over, until feeling returned to her skin. And they were back on the platform, waiting for the next train.

"Captain isn't responding," reported Hina.

"Keep trying. Someone get clothes for Asuka," she heard Ying Yue say.

"Thank you," Asuka mumbled.

She wondered what Ying Yue thought of her scars, ropy and purple-gray along her forearms and palms. But then, she wasn't the only one with scars. They were all survivors of some kind, weren't they? Hers reminded her of what she had cost other people, to be here. She didn't like to think of it.

There was the snick of a compartment shutting, and then clean clothes were handed to her, size small but a little too big. The black shirt bunched in the front around the torso, meant to provide extra space when pregnant. Which Asuka wasn't.

Asuka folded the cuffs of her shirt with unsteady fingers. She felt someone exhale warm breath on her toes before socks were pulled over her feet and gloves over her fingers. No shoes. They never wore shoes. Why should they? Their whole world was only the *Phoenix*.

Their clothes were boring, practical, all black, and tear resistant, the sort that came in S, M, L, and XL and could be grabbed out of any nearby storage compartment. Black didn't stain, and it was the sort of fabric that could be replaced and mended with minimal waste. Fashion was irrelevant, because reality was something individual and malleable, thanks to DAR. She pressed her temple, and it became an ancient Counting Crows T-shirt she had found in a digimart giveaway. She understood they were once a band but honestly just wore it for the name. In other people's DAR, her shirt might be a swimsuit or military camo, within the restrictions she had set. Her body was her body, and that could include any alterations to physical appearance she might choose to make, or how much of it she wanted to show.

And the trees were growing out of the sky. Or she was standing upside down.

"Something's wrong with my DAR."

Silly goose, said Alpha. *You must have bumped your head.*

Asuka again cut off her DAR and looked around the naked white walls of the module, at all the scared faces. Her heart beat, but it felt like it wasn't her blood swishing through its ventricles. She couldn't process what was happening. How everything had unraveled in an hour. That Kat was gone.

What's wrong with me? she thought. *Feel. Cry. Something.*

A crackling filled their ears, and then the awful, tearing sound of someone trying not to completely lose it. "Oh my god. They killed the Captain."

CHAPTER SEVEN

After the fire, home was four lines of chalk on muddy, dead grass, with a green tent for Asuka and her older brother, Luis, and a red one for Mom and Papa. All around them were rows and rows of chalk squares and other tents and other families, and two smelly portable toilets on either end of the row.

At night, Luis would hold her hand, sweat slicking between their palms, as they listened to their parents argue. Mom wanted to move back to Japan, but Papa resisted. "The kids don't speak Japanese. Neither do I."

"They'll learn."

"If she tries to make us go, we'll run away," Luis whispered.

But anyway, nothing was ever decided.

One of their neighbors planted a flag outside their tent: a black eagle on a field of red and white stripes holding a scroll in one talon and a rifle in the other. It was for the Militia for the American Constitution, usually just called "MAC" for short.

Mom warned them not to stare at it. Her face was smudged with dirt, her hair tangled. She pinned Luis with her dark eyes. "And no space talk."

"Do they have guns?" Luis wanted to know.

"Let's not be dramatic," said Papa, reaching out to smooth Luis's hair.

Asuka and her family occupied their square as if it were an island. They ignored the bulge of the big square tent encroaching on one corner.

Then, one afternoon after volunteers came and everyone was

happy and full of hot food, Papa pulled a chair right up to the line. "Hi. I'm Michael."

Mom tensed and put an arm around Asuka.

The two neighbors had stripped their shirts and sat baking in half-broken lawn chairs beneath their flag. The older neighbor had a beard as big as a scarf. A stinky joint passed back and forth between them.

"You Mexican?" they asked across the border. Friendly.

Papa smiled with all his teeth. "This and that."

They gestured at the rest of the family. "Chinese?"

"Japanese."

"Huh," said one, eyes brightening. "I love Pokémon."

"What's Pokémon?" Luis asked.

"I'm going to be an ornithologist," Asuka offered.

"Shh," said Mom, yanking her back. "Come sit with me, Asuka-chan."

"Listen to this," Papa told them, beckoning to Luis.

Luis cleared his throat. "When in the course of human events it becomes necessary . . ." Papa had paid him twenty dollars to memorize the words. Mom released Asuka, rose, and walked away like she had an urgent need to use the toilet.

Asuka watched her leave, not understanding yet the deep despair Mom must have felt living in that place full of people farting and playing loud music and having sex. To have nothing when they could be living across the ocean in a house built of all the dreams of her parents that she had discarded. How it felt to have a son, who insisted on using his middle name, because he "didn't look like a Reo." Who wanted to belong.

". . . such has been the patient sufferance of these colonies," Luis bellowed.

Their neighbors laughed and applauded. "You have a smart boy," they told Papa.

Papa dabbed at the sweat that had accumulated along his hairline.

The sun beat down, and the four of them talked and laughed. Above them, the MAC flag hung limp in the invisible heat.

Asuka glared at the parched dirt between her toes and imagined burrowing down with her mind. Down she tunneled through the crust of the Earth, through the molten core, until she was bursting up into the cool nighttime happening at that moment in the middle of the streets of Tokyo. Because what she did understand, even then, was that the world could never be one thing for everyone at the exact same time.

CHAPTER EIGHT

THE *PHOENIX* * 3,980 CYCLES AFTER LAUNCH,
0 CYCLES AFTER EXPLOSION, B SHIFT

"Killed?" Ying Yue said. "What are they talking about, Alpha?"

Voices cascaded over each other, churning the air in the room to whitewater. Their black clothes were just a blur against the pristine white module walls.

Asuka's tongue curled around the bittersweet taste of fear. She tried to focus on what was going on. Someone tugged another person's shirt. A gesticulating arm banged Asuka's head, and she cried out in pain.

"Quiet!" No one was listening to Ying Yue, standing in the middle of the scrum, arms around her pregnant belly.

"Hey! Shut up!" Ruth's voice rang out, and people miraculously stopped.

I have finished rebooting and can report on status of crew, said Alpha. Three dead, including Kat. And Captain Becky McMahon and Winnie had both been in the Dining Mod at the time of the explosion. Alpha didn't know what caused it.

Asuka's messages seemed to be working, even though the forest in her DAR was—oof, sideways now. Wild theories were already flying on the public feed: a manufacturing problem, space junk, first contact.

A voice cut in over the shipwide channel—Chief Engineer Yaz, cool and quick: "All crew members brace in ten."

Everyone kicked into motion, moving to spots along the wall and grabbing whatever and whoever was in reach.

And of course, Asuka found herself side by side with Ruth against the stern-side airlock door. Ruth, who had barely talked to her in two years (twelve, if you counted the ten years in between). Who had saved her life.

They looked at each other, looked away. Asuka grabbed Ruth's shoulder and a second later found Ruth's arm looped through hers. She felt the body memory of that sensation—arm locked in arm, the feeling they were going to take on the universe together.

Her world shifted, and instead of in the cabin in the woods, they were standing on a beach before an immense ocean. The sky was perfect and blue. Seagulls swooped overhead. The crew were dressed in beachwear.

"Five, four, three, two, one," said Yaz.

The sand slid underfoot, and they were tugged in the same direction. A massive wave thundered down over them, through them. Then the weight on her body eased. She could move again without an elephant bearing down. Whatever the Chief Engineer had done, their g-force was back to normal.

Ruth dropped her arm, and the beach evaporated.

Asuka rubbed her eyes, trying to orient herself. The manual airlock handle dug into her shoulder.

"You okay?" Ruth asked.

"Yeah. Um. Thanks, by the way."

"Sure. No big." Ruth's fingers twitched. She wasn't looking at Asuka anymore, but there was a flush at her neck where her dark brown buzz ended like the edge of a shadow. She was a head taller than Asuka, with pale, translucent skin; high, imperious cheekbones; and a general *fuck you too* ready in her eyes.

Asuka's gaze slipped to the lines etched in Ruth's neatly shaved hair: that graceful outline of a bird taking flight. *Selasphorus heloisa*, a bumblebee hummingbird. Ruth's favorite bird. And did the person who had traced the shape with the razor know that? Did she know why?

You seem stressed, Asuka, Alpha said. *Would you like to talk about it?*

Someone was sobbing. Asuka felt that old, childish urge to just run away, to climb a tree, to *something*. She reached for the subcutaneous button at her temple, but her DAR was out of whack. "If Becky's dead, who's Captain?" Ruth asked.

"I think that would be me?" said Ying Yue like she hoped she wasn't. When the mission was assembled, leadership had been a careful political balancing act between the two biggest nation-sponsors. The agreement was that the Captain and First Vice Captain would be American and Chinese, order to be determined by performance in a set of leadership exercises. The Chinese weren't happy when Becky won the Captaincy, but Ying Yue had told everyone she was relieved. And now Becky was dead.

That's right. Ying Yue is the Captain, said Alpha.

Ying Yue covered her mouth with her hands. She generally had the bad posture of a tall person trying to take up less space, and now she slumped like she was trying to disappear. Which was difficult, given how big she was in her third trimester with twins, a fact that made her a hero and source of envy. A bruise was forming on her cheekbone. "I should go to the Bridge. Ruth, can you take Susie to Medical?"

"What should we do?" someone called.

"Just—anything. Stop crowding in here, okay?"

"I feel . . . great," lied Asuka, who did not want to go anywhere with Ruth. Damn that she had to stop in the middle of that sentence to duck a wave of pain.

"Consider it an order," said Ying Yue, but it sounded like a question. Her large eyes were even bigger than usual, so white was visible all the way around brown irises so dark they were almost black. She exited counter-spin, walking as fast as an extremely pregnant person possibly could, which was . . . less dramatic than the occasion seemed to call for.

"Okay, let's go." Ruth reached out and took hold of Asuka's elbow. She felt the tickle of Ruth's bony fingers, and then the white beach returned. The bow- and stern-side exterior airlocks had transformed into strange metal doors in the side of a dune. On the top of one of the handles perched a large black karasu. It cocked its head at her. And in its beak was something—Asuka stepped toward it and pulled free of Ruth. The beach disappeared.

"What's wrong?"

Something was off with her DAR, that's what was wrong. Which, in the broader context, was a ridiculous thing to complain about. "It's fine. Let's go." They moved through the airlock that led to the next module in the habitat wheel. Ruth's hot-pink prosthetic leg clinked against the floor.

It was strange to see the *Phoenix* without DAR. Asuka hadn't spent a minute in vanilla reality since waking up from hibernation almost a year ago. The walls were austere white with only a small nameplate affixed to the doors on either side, describing each module that lay beyond with a word and colored symbol. Otherwise, each section of passageway was like the last. The ceiling was much lower than she realized: a little over two meters tall. Exposed white pipes and bundled electrical wires ran along the walls and ceiling. Without DAR, the ship felt industrial, unfinished.

The ship was constructed of modules manufactured on Earth and joined together in space: the ring itself was composed of thirteen narrow passageway sections and three larger chambers filled with green plants—their Agricultural Modules, or Ag Mods. The rest of the modules were attached to the stern- or bow-facing sides of the ring. From the outside, the wheel resembled a jeweled bracelet or a complicated organic molecule. Inside, without DAR, it felt like a never-ending sloping corridor.

In Asuka's DAR, this would have been a flat trail through woods: a creek trickling to the left around here, fluorescent green weeds growing in patches of sunlight. Just that color made her ache for home sometimes. Not home. For a point in space-time she could no longer reach. She ducked around a protruding bulkhead that should have been a tree.

The doors between the modular passageway sections were usually open by default, but the emergency must have triggered all the airlocks to shut, so they had to stop to manually reopen each one as they went.

"Poor Ying Yue," Ruth said, because she could never stand to say nothing.

"Ying Yue?" There were a lot of people to feel sorrier for, starting with the ones who were dead.

"She didn't even want to be First Vice Captain. You know how she is." Asuka didn't. "Kind. Hates confrontation."

They passed into the next module. The door on the left was

marked *Nursery*, the one on the right, *Toilet*. "The Selection Committee wasn't wrong."

"How can you of all people say that?" asked Ruth, and Asuka flushed. Because Asuka was the one whom the Committee hadn't picked. The Alternate. Asuka supposed Ruth meant it in a nice way, maybe, but it stung to be reminded that people thought of her like that. As if Asuka needed reminding.

Everyone on this ship had a special role, from ship maintenance to agriculture to navigation. Ruth was one of the three crew who managed the *Phoenix* communications with Earth. Asuka's specialty was nothing.

Asuka slammed the next airlock button with her palm, felt the satisfying wrongness where the skin lacked sensation. *You chose this*, she reminded herself. They passed by Crew Quarters C and D.

An envelope materialized in front of her, and she frowned. So all the mundane parts of her DAR—communication with Alpha and others—were working, just not the broader reality she lived in. The envelope hung there, cream-colored and textured like fine, expensive stationery. If she reached out, the words would unfurl. But it was from her mother. She brushed it away.

Don't you want to read that? Alpha asked, sensing her dismissal in the movement of the smartfabric woven into her clothes. *This is the third message you have received from your mother.*

"Not now, Alpha."

She must be worried about you.

"I said *not now*."

Ruth caught up with her. She reached for Asuka's arm again. "Hey, wait up. You should take it easy."

"I'm fine. Just following orders." Pain stabbed behind her eyeballs.

They stepped to the side as crew hustled past, pushing a maintenance cart.

Ruth said, "You're still hung up on it, aren't you?"

Asuka gaped at Ruth.

"God, Asuka. It makes my heart hurt watching you continue to beat yourself up over it."

Oh. This was *so* Ruth, sinking her teeth into a subject and bringing it back up after they'd clearly moved on.

"Are we talking about you dropping me, or me not getting selected? Both of those being my favorite topics, by the way."

Ruth stopped in her tracks. She fastened her brown eyes on Asuka and put her fists on her waist. The birthmark over her left eye accentuated her anger. A blue vein under the translucent skin of her forehead bulged, and Asuka suppressed her involuntary affection for that vein. "What the hell? I don't even know what to say. Except that you hold a grudge longer than anyone I have ever met in the entire universe."

"Just the galaxy, surely."

The next door opened with a whoosh to reveal one of the large Agricultural Modules: Ag Mod A. Even without DAR, it felt relatively spacious, its three-meter ceilings packed high with shelves full of plants.

"Wow. Asuka Hoshino-Silva, you are so—so—"

Asuka was saved from an enumeration of her most annoying qualities by a muffled cry for help.

Ag Mod A was a wreck. The normally even rows of green plants stacked floor to ceiling were in disarray, and dirt was strewn across the white-tiled floor. A moist, earthy smell filled Asuka's nose, with a hint of rose and crushed mint.

The cry came from somewhere to the left, behind the first row of shelving units.

"Hurry," said Ruth.

"I am!"

A shelving unit of seedlings had tipped over, trapping someone underneath. They braced themselves on either side and heaved. Ruth squatted and began brushing the little sprouts off the person they had rescued.

The person was Gabriela Ota, a petite woman with a normally sunny disposition. Like Asuka, she was half-Japanese, but Gabriela had been picked to represent her other half, the Philippines. She could sing the entire Wagner Ring cycle from start to finish, and she was fluent in Mandarin, Tagalog, Spanish, and English. And Japanese, which pained Asuka, whose Japanese was only basic at best, though better than her Spanish. Asuka sometimes wondered why Japan needed her when they had Gabriela, but Gabriela joked two hāfu made a whole.

Despite Gabriela's normally relentless cheerfulness, Asuka liked her. She'd been grateful to be assigned a bunk below Gabriela's in Crew Quarters B, and though they were on different day cycles, they often chatted as Asuka was going to bed and Gabriela was getting up.

They freed her from the shelving unit, and Gabriela sobbed, clutching her face.

"Are you okay?" Ruth knelt next to her, voice husky with concern, and Asuka gritted her teeth, because Gabriela was *her* friend.

Even with blood trickling down her face from a cut above her eyes and minimal DAR augmentation, Gabriela was beautiful: heart-shaped face, full lips, and long eyelashes. She was a Programmer, but also a fantastic cook. She must have come to Ag Mod A to harvest microgreens when the spin disruption from the explosion knocked everything over.

Now she lay on the floor in a spreading pool of water and soil, plants littered around her. She curled into a fetal ball.

Her voice was stifled by her hands. "Did I kill them?"

Wait, what? Oh. The plants.

"They're fine," Asuka said. Which was . . . not completely a lie. She surveyed the fragile things, roots thinner than a cat's whisker, leaves half-crumpled and brutalized by the fall.

"I'm so sorry," Gabriela said. Ruth coaxed her to a sitting position. Asuka hurried to grab her other arm—

Reality transformed into a lush garden with tall palm trees and smooth, paved walks. And all over every surface and circling in the air were thousands of blue California scrub jays. Which was wrong. Palm trees, maybe, but this was too tropical to be California, and they didn't usually flock like this—

Asuka let go in surprise and fell back again into the plain, white ship. Had she knocked her head worse than she realized?

Ruth didn't seem to notice—or need her help.

Annoyed, Asuka began collecting sprouts, if only for Gabriela's sake. Amazing how they could trust their future to such fragile things. She examined a bent seedling, trying to decide if it was salvageable.

"Don't move." Ruth dabbed at the blood on Gabriela's face with her sleeve.

"I'm okay."

Asuka picked up a tray that had fallen on the floor and placed the sprouts in it. Her head throbbed. Asuka took a deep breath, seeking calm from the scent of wet dirt.

"Don't," Gabriela said.

Asuka turned, stung by the unusual sharpness in her tone.

"I mean, I'll do it."

Blood rushed to Asuka's cheeks. What, did Gabriela not trust her to care for a bunch of plants? It wasn't rocket propulsion. It wasn't even systems repair. Both of which Asuka was capable of handling. Probably. She dropped her hands and turned away.

"Let's take you to Medical," she heard Ruth murmur.

"No, no," said Gabriela.

"It's not a discussion."

Her old friend always got her way, even if it meant shoving everyone along. In this case, literally. In a minute, Ruth had Gabriela up and moving.

A peevish thought struck Asuka: that she'd been forgotten. She was ready to add this to the hairy grudge that lurked within her just for Ruth, but then Ruth glanced back. "Hurry up."

This was why she was better off without Ruth.

Would you like to read the message from your mother now?

"Nope."

Ruth and Gabriela were talking in hushed tones. She heard them as if through a fog. Asuka wanted to tell Gabriela the bumblebee hummingbird was once the smallest bird in the world. Ruth had seen one of the last ones, in a zoo when she was six, her nose leaving a smudge on the glass. She wanted to unlock its cage, but her dads explained it was too precious to be free. It could not be trusted to survive in the wild. Later, during the conflict, the zoo took a direct hit, and many of the animals died, including the birds. Ruth said to her dads, "See? If I had . . ." But "if" wasn't real, and hummingbirds were extinct.

Ruth swept them along, and Asuka didn't know whether to cry or laugh with how, even now, when she hated the woman, she loved her too.

As they exited, Asuka thought she saw a flash of blue, like a bird perched on the battered shelving unit. She stopped to look back, but there was nothing.

CHAPTER NINE

Scrub jays were extremely intelligent, capable of caching—and finding again—thousands of nuts, seeds, and insects for the future. They even deployed strategies to protect their stash from being discovered, including moving their food from one location to another midseason.

The behavior demonstrated incredible spatial memory. It also suggested the ability to plan, once assumed unique to people.

CHAPTER TEN

The Medical Mod overwhelmingly smelled of disinfectant and that insidious, delicate lavender scent that contaminated everything. Seriously, who thought it was a good idea to stock a ship with only one kind of soap?

Ruth was gone, back to her post on the Bridge, and Gabriela departed with an adhesive patch across her forehead and a dreamy, heavy-lidded, drugged expression.

Without DAR, the module felt cramped though functional. Nothing inside betrayed its proximity to the Kitchen and Dining Mods. The walls were lined with compartments that held fine instruments and machines, and in the middle, there was a surgical table, folded up into a recliner for a gynecological procedure. Asuka's stomach clenched when she saw it.

She gingerly took a seat. The soft roll of cloth bunched beneath her thighs. She leaned back and counted to ten.

A soft bell tolled the change from B to C shift. The small ship accommodated an eighty-person crew by dividing everyone into three staggered cycles, and each twenty-four-hour cycle into three eight-hour shifts: A, B, and C. Asuka worked during B, exercised and studied during C, and slept during A.

The explosion had happened during the sleep shift of the C shift Medic, Hao Yu. They'd leapt out of bed and run over to Medical to help. All the Medics were working. The rest were out checking crew module by module, leaving Hao Yu to staff the clinic for any incoming issues.

Hao Yu exuded calm, despite everything. This was why everyone loved Hao Yu. Except maybe Asuka, who dreaded them, because nothing good ever came of her visits to the clinic.

Asuka envied the other crew member's confidence. Hao Yu never had to doubt they'd get picked for the mission. The Chinese government had picked them out of hundreds of millions, started training them for the admissions test as soon as EvenStar was announced. *And how nice*, Asuka thought, *to never have a doubt*. To be smart enough to know you were smart enough. That you were meant to be a part of this, and not a backup plan.

"How are you, Susie?"

"Fine."

Really, said Alpha.

"Alpha thinks you have a concussion."

Hao Yu's fingers brushed Asuka's chin, featherlight. Bright yellow slashed Asuka's eyes like an afterburn, then was gone. They shone a light in one eye and then the other, and Asuka winced, headache kicking up a notch. A new round of nausea caught her, and she had to inhale a few times to keep from throwing up.

Hao Yu was oh-so-gentle, tiptoeing around as if the whole difficulty-getting-pregnant thing was something for Asuka to cry about every time she climbed up on the exam table. Asuka didn't cry. Not that she felt great about it. Just another way she fell short of the high EvenStar standards.

The mission was structured such that they were in hibernation during the first and last thirds of the voyage, given the length of the journey. In the ten-year interstitial period, all the crew were expected to give birth to and raise one to two children, so that they would arrive at Planet X with the most intensive stages of child-rearing behind them.

Problem was, prolonged chemically induced hibernation was new, and its impact on aging and fertility was inconclusive. As Asuka was learning.

"It must have been awful out there." Hao Yu pulled instruments from the sterilizer drawer. Their nails were beautiful: tapered and neatly filed. No bitten cuticles. How *did* they keep them so nicely manicured? Was there some secret manicure club that Asuka didn't know about? Probably.

"My DAR has been glitching," said Asuka, not wanting to get into her feelings right then, or maybe ever.

Ruth had said before heading off, "It's all going to be okay." And Asuka's old irritation resurfaced, because what gave that woman the right to be so confident?

Hao Yu dropped a probe with a loud clang. "Aiyah." They retrieved it, put it back in the sterilizer drawer, and closed it without taking anything.

They turned back to Asuka and leaned in again, so they were eye to eye. Asuka squirmed as Hao Yu probed her skin with their fingers. Flashes of yellow light again, like warm afternoon sun piercing a canopy of leaves. Gone again when Hao Yu removed their soft fingertips. "Mm. Your face looks okay. No swelling." The helmet had protected her that much, at least. "Let's see what's happening on the inside."

Hao Yu unboxed mobile scanners on a counter along the wall by the door. As they fumbled with them, Asuka realized that Hao Yu's hands were shaking. She felt strangely betrayed.

"I'm sorry," said Hao Yu. They tried and failed to laugh, regripped the scanners.

"Do you need a minute?" Asuka asked.

"No, I'm—" Hao Yu wiped an eye with the back of their arm. "I'm okay." They sniffed and wiped their other eye, then pressed the scanners against Asuka's temples. A three-dimensional image appeared in the air above Hao Yu's elbow as they scanned: Asuka's skull, her brain, the delicate blood vessels. "What do you think, Alpha?"

Confirmed. You have a concussion.

"Not to worry," Hao Yu faltered, then soldiered on. "We will have you better in no time."

They moved back to the drawers and prepared a syringe loaded with nanos.

"Hao Yu, are you—"

"Don't!" Hao Yu said, voice spiking. "We just need to get through this, okay? Okay. Okay. It's going to be fine."

Asuka watched them close the distance with the syringe. She was struck by how young Hao Yu was. How young they all were. Only in their twenties, assuming hibernation didn't count. And what did any of them know about anything?

She tipped her head back. Hoped Hao Yu was steady enough for the job. The needle went up her nose. Sunlight again—was that a small golden butterfly resting on Hao Yu's shoulder? And a prick of pain that made her flinch. Then it was over, and that place was gone again.

Hao Yu went to the pill printer. "Can I give her some headache meds, Alpha?"

Approved. 1,200 mg.

They returned, two pills cupped like a promise. "Here you go. One now, one before sleep. Diagnostics didn't find anything wrong with your implant, by the way."

Their fingers touched Asuka's palm as they passed her the pills. A garden bloomed around them, surrounded by old stone walls covered in ivy. In the distance was a castle that was flying blue and red pennants.

"Wait," Asuka said, grabbing Hao Yu's wrist. "I can see flowers, but they aren't mine."

A small green caterpillar climbed up the stem of a large flower an inch from Asuka's nose. She inhaled instinctively, like any of this was real and the air in her lungs wasn't canned.

"You can see Alyredon?" asked Hao Yu.

"Alyredon?"

"You know, like the fantasy game. It's my DAR."

Asuka frowned. "How come I can see *your* DAR just fine, but then when I try to load mine it's upside down and purple?"

"Your implant must be buggy. Check with Programming." They squeezed Asuka's hand. "Also, this isn't a today thing, but you should think about cutting back on spacewalks. It can't be good for your reproductive organs."

Not a chance. Asuka started to scoot, but Hao Yu added brightly: "Well, since you're here, shall we do our business with your down there?"

How humiliating, Asuka thought, to hear her body parts referred to euphemistically like that. To hear them referred to at all.

"I figured we'd wait until the next round." The Medical team did a new round of insemination for six crew every forty cycles to stagger pregnancy. Asuka had started in round one, and they were in round seven now.

"Oh no. Alpha's orders. New round starts next cycle anyway."

That's right. Kat had said she was scheduled for an appointment.

It will only take five minutes, Alpha said.

"We'll just check if conditions are favorable, all right?"

It was not all right, dammit. But Asuka sat back again. She closed her eyes. In her DAR, this would have been a big relief tent, with boxes full of clothing and stressed-out volunteer doctors checking on patients in cots. And in the distance, the rows of tents that were home, her brother Luis kicking around an old soccer ball.

"Do you have any siblings back home?" Hao Yu asked, making conversation.

"No," said Asuka, because thinking of Luis made her want to tear down the Alyredon sky.

Hao Yu beamed. "Well, look at that. Good thing we checked. You're perfect."

But I'm not, thought Asuka. *Or I wouldn't be here, trying again.* She resisted the urge to run out. Stifling a groan, she lay back against the table, butt at the edge, and propped her feet in the stirrups.

Three pictures of sperm donors appeared in front of Asuka. Not all Japanese, which was new. Had she exhausted all the options with her multiple attempts? Impossible.

Instead of picking, she hit the randomizer. She hated this. Oh, did she.

Her eyes fell on the storage panels above where Hao Yu was now removing a small test tube. The *Phoenix* carried sperm from thousands of donors, all stored in the sealed, upper cabinets. Tracking was critical for ensuring maximum genetic diversity, and a lock minimized the chance of someone mixing up samples. Asuka frowned. The metal door appeared dented and patched. She wouldn't have noticed if her DAR had been on.

"What happened?"

Hao Yu followed her gaze. Asuka wondered if they knew what she was referring to, but Hao Yu shut the sample dispenser hatch with a clang. "Accident."

They came back to Asuka with a test tube. "You're welcome to use my DAR if you'd like. Beats having to stare at the white walls?"

"Oh," said Asuka, flushing. Sharing someone's DAR felt intimate, but anything was better than nothing.

Hao Yu offered Asuka a copper key. Asuka reached out hesitantly, and the garden reappeared. The sun shone, and she felt her shoulders loosen. She was reclining on a stone bench. In the distance, she saw a blue unicorn canter across a field.

"That's better, isn't it?" Hao Yu smiled. "Okay, now relax."

Asuka tensed. It was nothing against Hao Yu. It had everything to do with that test tube—no, a burnished bronze vessel or something—they were holding.

Try to think about something else, Alpha said. *Shall I read you your mother's letters?*

"No," Asuka snapped. Hao Yu froze. "Sorry, not you. Alpha."

All right. I can see you're not in the mood. How about some interesting facts about the acorn woodpecker?

In spite of herself, Asuka's lips twitched into a smile. Alpha knew how to get her.

The acorn woodpecker had a red crown, black back, tail, and eyes, and a white face. It was renowned for its remarkable tendency to breed cooperatively.

Asuka watched the blue unicorn. A dark shadow passed across the grass. A cloud maybe? No—it was an enormous dragon, as big as a house. She heard Hao Yu uncap a test tube (no matter what her eyes told her), dip the little sticky thing down, and stir.

She wondered why Hao Yu was so enamored with that particular fantasy game—a beautiful, dystopian world full of dragons and cursed weapons; overgrown, dilapidated castles; and empty hut after empty hut, as if a plague had come through and turned everyone to dust in an instant.

Dozens of birds would raise the chicks together. Not all of them participated in reproduction.

Asuka moved her fingers in a silent reply to Alpha: *Are you comparing us to woodpeckers?*

I'm a computer program, Asuka. You know I do not understand metaphors.

She closed her eyes. She didn't like acorn woodpeckers. Sometimes they'd destroy each other's eggs as they laid. Sometimes they'd eat the remains—even the mothers would partake.

There were fingers in her vagina, and the cold feeling of an object penetrating her. She gritted her teeth. *I'm in a magic kingdom. Everything is fine.*

Sharp pressure.

She couldn't attach her thoughts to Alpha's voice anymore. Tried to think of something else. Kat, the explosion. No, no. Asuka opened her eyes, and the dragon was a bird, a—wait, was that a cuckoo? With a light gray head, orange-rimmed eyes, long dark tail, and a striped body. In the distance it seemed normal sized, except it had to be massive. And it was—oh god, it was *eating* the blue unicorn. Asuka made a weird squeaking noise.

"All done!" said Hao Yu.

Great job, Asuka, Alpha said.

Hao Yu followed Asuka's gaze. "Oh, don't worry. That's Al, my tri-horned dragon."

Asuka blinked, and sure enough, it was a dragon. The blue unicorn cantered about, unharmed.

"What'd I get?" she asked. "A billionaire donor, Nobel Prize winner, or random lottery person?"

Hao Yu checked the label. "Five-time Olympic Gold Medalist. Sprinter, I think."

Asuka thought, *Maybe this time.* Better not to hope. "Sorry to waste their shot."

"It's okay. Plenty more where that came from." Hao Yu placed the bronze vessel in an ornate wooden box. "You have to have optimism."

"Right," said Asuka, pulling up her underwear. The first time, she had walked out of the exam room already thinking of Japanese baby names. She imagined the media frenzy back in Tokyo. Aiko, maybe, her little love. Because she would have loved it, if it had been real.

"After this, it's time to start considering other options." Hao Yu's words were light. A violet butterfly settled in their hair, which was long and crowned with pearls. They smiled at Asuka's expression. "Come on, it's not that bad. We're equipped with dozens of contingency procedures for this type of situation."

Asuka touched her abdomen, as if she could prod her body to do its job. Other options. Okay, she would grit her teeth and do what was asked.

She thought again of Kat, caught on the unlucky end of the blast.

The door opened, and Asuka and Hao Yu both jumped. One of the other Medics came in, out of breath. "Did you see on the feed? Whatever happened knocked us off course." She rifled through a drawer and began stuffing sterilized bandages into her kit.

Asuka remembered then how the stars had seemed wrong. A change in how they moved and only black space behind them. Cold fear began to wash over her toes, ankles, knees.

Because of course they were off course. For every action, a reaction. There had been an explosion: Kat blown one way; the *Phoenix* blown another. Perhaps infinitesimally, but at the speed they were going, a feather of an error was an ostrich of a problem. And if they didn't fix it, they would never reach Planet X.

"Oh," said Hao Yu. "That's . . . not good."

"We can fix that, though, right?" Asuka asked. Thinking of how many things couldn't be fixed. Kat's boot, tumbling into the dark.

The Medic refilled a bottle of clear liquid from a dispenser. "Don't know. Everyone is freaking out. Naturally. And Ying Yue says remain calm?" She made a fart noise.

"We'll figure it out," said Hao Yu.

"I don't know if Ying Yue is up to this."

"She'll be better than McMahon."

The other Medic gave Hao Yu a long look, then zipped her bag shut. "I forgot how you felt about McMahon."

What did that mean? Hao Yu's face was blank again, save for an eye twitch. Asuka toggled the public feed, and message after message scrolled from garden to cloudless sky.

What are we going to do?

Tā mā de!

Mission Control has a contingency plan, right?

Asuka felt queasy. A message from Ying Yue appeared in her queue: *Can you come to the Bridge, please?*

The dragon's face shimmered, and for a moment, she swore it was a cuckoo again. But no. Even so, she shed Alyredon as she went out the garden gate. It felt like a bad omen.

CHAPTER ELEVEN

They lived in the refugee camp for two years, until a couple of folks passed away during a heat wave, and there was finally an outcry about the conditions they were living in. It was shameful, people said. Mom said, "As if people haven't lived like this before in America."

Then like that, the camp was broken up and dispersed in a matter of hours. And all there was left of those two long years were the discarded cans and faded chalk lines marking their place in the world.

They were bussed several hours to an old hotel at the outskirts of the city that had beds with white sheets and a cool pool, green and small.

"Let's wait until later, when everyone is asleep," whispered Luis, seeing how crowded it was. He gestured to his new headgear. "We should use DAR—pretend we're in zero-g!" Like all bad ideas, it seemed like an excellent one. Asuka agreed, even though she was thinking there was no way she'd get in a pool again.

That night, when Luis poked her arm and tried to get her to come, she pretended to be asleep. It wasn't hard. In fact, after he tiptoed out and the door snicked shut, she found she couldn't open her eyes; she was that tired. She could feel the darkness outside beyond the hum of the lukewarm air-conditioning. She lifted her mother's arm and snuggled deeper into the cave between her mother's soft body and the crumpled bedsheets.

Years later, she would dream of that night. She would try this time to get up. Sometimes she would even make it halfway down the stairs before she fell asleep. She never made it to the pool. "Don't," she mumbled, but he didn't hear. "Let's not."

And sometimes, she dreamed that she watched from the sky as Luis sank down below the clear water, eyes shut, like somewhere, he was dreaming too. And she needed to remind him he couldn't breathe underwater. That DAR wasn't real. But he couldn't hear her, and she was flying backward, away and up. To outer space, past Mars, where he had always wanted to go. Where now he would never go.

CHAPTER TWELVE

THE *PHOENIX* * 3,980 CYCLES AFTER LAUNCH,
0 CYCLES AFTER EXPLOSION, C SHIFT

A full-force shouting match was raging in the Bridge, and Asuka resisted the urge to cover her ears and walk back out. Nobody had even noticed her come in.

Without DAR, the Bridge resembled a small, mundane conference room, with a table that unfolded from the floor in an ingenious way. Ruth sat in front of the Walkie, bent over, reading messages from Earth, furiously tapping out replies.

Eight Officers, including Ying Yue, huddled around a projection. Black filled the space above the table, with green dots for stars and a red dotted line charting their course. At least Asuka could still see the public DAR augmentations.

There was the star from which they'd come, and *there* was the star that would be their new sun. The *Phoenix* moved imperceptibly between the two, across a distance that reduced their solar system to a blip. Except the dotted line that was their projected course now pointed definitively past their destination. And judging from the shouting and finger-jabbing at the projection, the Officers were as freaked as the crew. There was no plan.

"Shit," said Asuka.

They noticed her.

Ruth's eyes flicked over to her once, then away. Her fingers paused scrolling through the messages. It was her off shift, but not surprising that the other Communications Specialist had asked Ruth to cover. She had been close with Winnie, the Communications Specialist responsible for A shift. Who was dead.

"What's happened now?" said A.M., their French Chief Propulsion

Officer. They were Asuka's height, with thick, short brown hair that stood up on their head an inch, and the dense, muscled upper body of a former international youth wrestling champion. There was the pale shadow of facial hair along their pronounced jaw, like they'd missed a shave, and three diamond-encrusted pins pierced their right eyebrow. Some of it was DAR body augmentation, but the tattoo of an old-fashioned QR code under one eye was real.

A.M. was the kind of take-charge person whose constant certainty, on a good day, was like a fire hose; on a bad day, it was a comfort. Growing up, A.M. had been notorious for their hot temper. Once, Asuka had seen them throw a glass of milk in another kid's face for making fun of their accent. But when Asuka expressed sympathy, A.M. had given her a look sort of like the one they were giving now, the *why are you even here* glare.

"I need to talk to her," said Ying Yue.

"About what?"

Ying Yue hesitated. Whatever it was, she didn't want to say.

"Captain's business," Yaz answered for her, wielding the consonants of *captain* like a knife. Yasemin Dogan was Ying Yue's deputy for Bot and Drone Operations and the one who had restored the ship's spin to normal earlier. Yaz was tall, with muscular thighs, and thick, dark eyebrows. She was further along with her pregnancy than anyone on board, including Ying Yue. "And speaking of business, can we finish here so I can get back to mine, which is fixing this ship?"

Which set off a new round of bickering.

"Psst." Ruth waved Asuka over. "Do you know how to operate the Walkie?"

"Uh, sure." In theory. She hadn't touched a Walkie since training. She joined Ruth at her station.

"Great, because I need a bio break."

Asuka glanced at the others.

"Oh no, they don't lower themselves to operating a Walkie," Ruth said, quietly enough that only Asuka could hear. But just that quietly. The air between the two of them felt brittle.

"They're stressed because we have a limited amount of Sominol." Sominol was the drug that induced hibernation. "And we have a finite amount of power to keep our habitat cycling without solar power." No power meant no temperature regulation, no clean water, no Ag or Hydroponics. Asuka didn't like where this was going. "If we don't get back on course in the next two cycles, we'll die before we get to Planet X."

Asuka swallowed hard.

"Here, I'll show you how we send a message to Mission Control." Ruth vacated the chair, and Asuka sat down in front of the Walkie. The interstellar communication device was a black, featureless box strapped into a nest of soft foam. Above it floated several windows in DAR, each with text streaming down. The most recent transmissions flickered across in rapid succession. Panicked notes from loved ones. Reams of news bulletins about the mission, about events on Earth, clipped and delivered by Mission Control. And there—a message from Mission Control.

"Woah." The message said they were evacuating Houston, where Mission Control was headquartered, because of a Category 4 hurricane—and that (oh yeah, by the way) the U.S. President had announced retaliatory naval action in the Sea of Japan, which meant the mission's two biggest nation-sponsors, the United States and China, were basically at war now. Retaliation against what? Asuka didn't know. "Spicy," Kat had said. Understatement.

"Just the prelude to the end of the world," said Ruth.

"How did this happen?" Asuka asked, trying to fathom it. When they had left, their mission had been hailed as a voyage of peace, the thing that would unite the nations of the world. Most of the world leaders had stood onstage together with them at launch, and Becky and Ying Yue threw arms around each other for the cameras. The American President had said, "Now we know what can be achieved if we all work together."

Welp. So much for that.

"The usual. Exchange of words. Saber-rattling. Machismo. Escalation of force on both sides. A plane 'accidentally' shot down. Reactivation of old U.S. bases in the Pacific—Japan, Vietnam, Philippines, and South Korea. Then a move to annex Taiwan."

"Shit." The bright red text scrolled across Asuka's field of vision.

Her eyes watered from staring too hard at the headlines. "Does this affect the mission?"

"I'd say they might be . . . distracted right now. A lot of countries are taking sides. It's only a matter of time before Russia joins in. My friend at Mission Control" (of course she had a friend at Mission Control; Ruth had friends everywhere) "says Linda is searching for a neutral country to host them, but the U.S. is putting a lot of pressure right now to relocate to Cape Canaveral and eject the Chinese members of Mission Control."

Asuka swiveled toward the Officers behind them. "They know?"

Ruth shrugged. "Yep. Didn't you see the comments Ying Yue posted to the entire crew on the public feed?"

Actually, no. Asuka kept it muted.

"It was all about maintaining unity, blah blah. A.M. didn't like that. Felt communication needs to be managed, and Ying Yue's fueling more chaos. Not wrong, imho. You know, every time I think it's impossible for the world to get any worse, more stuff happens. That's the lesson: there is no bottom. And does it make it better or worse that we left it all behind?" Her sigh smelled like the ship-printed mints.

Asuka swallowed. "Better, right?"

Her former friend's expression was unreadable. "Have you checked in with your mum yet?"

Asuka broke her gaze.

"Anyway. I really do need to pee. That's the Walkie key." Ruth pointed at a small metal rod chained to and resting on top of the box.

"I know," muttered Asuka, picking it up.

"You put it in that slot."

The key slid into the slot, and a floating *compose new message* window appeared.

"What did they say?" Ying Yue called. "Do they have instructions?"

Ruth flicked through another window of scrolling text faster than Asuka could track, and stopped and pointed with one finger. "No, but they've assembled an international team of experts."

"Including both China and the U.S.?" asked Ying Yue.

"For now."

Ying Yue's shoulders relaxed a fraction.

After Ruth stepped out, Asuka asked if she should send a reply.

"Send them our current resource stats." Ying Yue wriggled her fingers, and a stream of data appeared tagged in front of Asuka.

Asuka dropped the data into the window and hit send, then waited for the Quantum Walkie to process the message one letter at a time. The machine had a duplicate back on Earth. Designing and constructing it had cost a third of the entire mission budget, which was justified, given the spectacular breakthrough in modern science it had required. It allowed what was long thought impossible: instantaneous data transmission across space. Not an efficient way to communicate, though, and insufficient for video or audio.

Would you like to tell your mom you are okay? Alpha asked.

"I'm sure she's heard by now." She imagined her mom rubbing her face with two hands, forehead contorted in worry. Good.

"What about the rear engines?" Ying Yue was asking. She was struggling to exert authority. The other Vice Captains kept speaking right over her. If only she didn't sound so tentative. It invited judgment.

"They're not really meant to steer. The ship was built to go in a very fast, straight line," said A.M.

"We could, like, reposition them. Manually."

"And risk blowing ourselves up? McMahon would never—"

"Well, McMahon's gone," snapped Ying Yue, losing patience. "You've got me."

There was a kind of sick silence in the room. A.M. was leaning face-first in the projection, their arm over their whole face, shoulders shaking.

Ying Yue looked stricken. "I'm sorry, that came out wrong. A.M.?" She touched their back, but A.M. lunged away. The Officers gave A.M. a beat to collect themself. It took only a moment. They turned around, face stitched together in an imitation of composure. The red dotted line of their trajectory blinked ominously between them.

"And how," A.M. bit out, "do we know if we can even trust you?"

The module chilled another ten degrees in an instant. No one moved.

Ying Yue broke first, kneading her lower back with her fist. "What—I don't—what do you mean? We're all on the same side here."

"Are we?"

The door opened, and Ruth stopped at the threshold. "Did I miss something?"

The Walkie chirped. Another incoming message from Earth: *Restricted to Captain*. It scrolled before Asuka's eyes, and she read it without meaning to: *Agree. Possible intentional act. Will investigate. Do the same.*

Asuka tried to swallow, but all the spit seemed to have dried out of her mouth.

"Everything okay?" Ruth asked from behind Asuka's shoulder. Asuka jumped.

The message had already diverted to Ying Yue's inbox. "Fine."

Behind them, Ying Yue got to her feet. "Let's take a break."

She gestured for Asuka to follow her into the passageway.

"First, how are you doing?" she asked Asuka when they were alone.

"Okay." Even though Ying Yue's sympathy punctured something in her and made her want to cry. "What do you need?"

"I'm sorry to make you relive this, but I want you to see something." The fact that she would apologize marked another difference between Ying Yue and their previous Captain.

Ying Yue projected a view from Asuka's helmet, and it was like Asuka was there all over again, in her suit. Asuka tensed as she watched. Following Kat outside. Asuka's voice, proposing a race. Kat saying sure. Kat speeding off, faster, even with the tool kit.

"I know I shouldn't have—" Asuka began.

"Stop. You can't blame yourself for what happened." Ying Yue skipped ahead.

Asuka was now climbing up the side of the wheel. Kat said: "Where did you say it was, Ying Yue? Hang on, I'm caught on something. Okay, but I'm telling you—"

And then, this was when—

She froze the view right as Asuka glanced over, and the explosion began.

"What does that look like to you?" Ying Yue said.

Intentional act, Mission Control had said.

Ying Yue rewound and switched to an exterior camera view. They reexamined the strange dark object on the hull.

"You think that caused this?"

"I think it was a bomb."

"So, what? We came all this way with that strapped to the side of our ship, and it just goes off now?" She was, she realized, shouting.

"Or."

"Or?"

"They had help from someone on this ship," said Ying Yue.

Asuka recoiled. They had trained ten years, grown up together. "No. No. Who could have done something like that?"

"That's what I need you to figure out."

Asuka felt unreasonably irritable. "I'm sorry, but I missed the elective in how to investigate sabotage and murder."

Ying Yue crossed her arms. "None of us knows how to deal with this. Please, Asuka, I need your help."

"Why me?"

"You're the Alt."

Of course. Ying Yue caught her expression and held up a hand. "Because you don't have a regular assignment, no one will question if they see you poking around. And since you almost died today, you're one of the few people I trust right now. I assume you wouldn't have intentionally put yourself in harm's way."

Asuka sighed.

"Also, keep this quiet." Ying Yue looked at the door behind her. "There's already enough fighting right now, when we need to be working together to get back on course. Only Yaz knows about this. Until we know who it was, be careful."

"You think something else is going to happen?"

Ying Yue rubbed her belly. Her face was taut with worry. "I don't know. But we're alive, aren't we?"

Asuka tried to imagine the planning it would have taken. Had someone infiltrated the mission twenty-one years ago? Or become radicalized along the way? She shivered. There were plenty of people who hated this mission and what it stood for. Men's rights groups and MAC and—and people like her mother's friends.

"Anyway, you can start in the Dining Mod." She patted Asuka's shoulder—a train rushed through countryside—and then pushed past her to the bathroom, as if everything were settled.

Asuka kicked the wall of the ship once, twice.

Don't worry, Alpha said. *It'll all work out.*

Funny, she thought. She didn't know Alpha could lie.

CHAPTER THIRTEEN

Asuka's worn American sneakers slapped against dirt road as she ran along the edge of the cedar forest that populated the overlooking hill. A chorus of insects began to sing to the late afternoon.

They had come to Japan to escape Luis, but his absence echoed in every tree and rock.

The government gave them a house for free in the ghost village where her mom's grandmother lived. The town was mostly abandoned, so they had their pick. The house they took was built out of synthetic wood and concrete, all clean lines and cherry finishes. There were enough rooms for Mom and Papa to each have their own workspaces. In truth, the house was bigger than they needed: they were each of them suspended in too much space.

The sunset over the rice paddies was beautiful in summer, if one could bear the heat and mosquitoes. The humidity sat over everything, like a great, fat toad, and the deep scent of wet moss and cedar pervaded every inch.

It seemed to Asuka like the country might have been this way for centuries, and that even if the population and coastline continued to shrink and the smaller islands were swallowed by the sea, Honshu would continue on like this: green shoots in water, mountains and trees. Empty, rusted playgrounds, battered vending machines, and little stone shrines at the edge of the road.

She'd forgotten what it was like to be in Japan. Home and not home at the same time. She wanted to want to belong, to sink her toes in the soil and feel the land recognize her, give back the piece of her that she sometimes felt was missing when she was in America. She didn't feel it, though. She felt lost.

A karasu landed on the gutter of a roof and cawed. There were lots of birds in Japan—not RealBirds, but actual birds. It was one of the upsides of a vanishing human presence.

It smelled like wet soil, and there was a hint of sweetness in the air misting up from the bowed heads of wildflowers sticking out over the road. She went along this place that Luis had never been, and with each footfall she repeated his two names like a mantra—Reo for right foot. Luis for left. Reo Luis Reo Luis Reo Luis.

Linda Trembling, the richest person in the world, was creating an elite program to train a group of children to be the future crew of an interstellar mission, and Asuka had decided to apply. For Luis's sake. But Mom was dead against it. Which was a problem, because she couldn't go without parental permission.

In the meantime, Asuka was doing her best to prepare for the entrance exam using the free prep materials, approaching the task with the same stubbornness that had gotten her into trouble so many times when she was younger. It was the hardest thing she'd ever tried to do in her life, but also far easier to think about than the wave that would knock her down if she thought too much about Luis.

Mom was sitting on the porch watching the automatic pickers tug rice seedlings from the ground, shake the dirt from their roots, and bundle them. From here, the pickers looked like giant squid, robotic arms stretching, contracting.

She held a box. "Asuka-chan. I've been waiting for you." And for once, it didn't quite sound like a lecture.

Asuka followed her mother down the steps and along the raised path that ran between the fields.

"Hora, hayaku! Ikuyo!"

"Where are we going?"

"There." She pointed to a great cypress tree at the end of the road.

The air was thick as soup, but it was marginally cooler under its branches.

Mom set the box down and gently lifted the lid.

"What is it?" Asuka asked.

"From the government. For every family with a child."

Dusk collected with its customary gentleness. Asuka squatted down next to her mother.

"I don't get it," Asuka started to say.

"Shhh."

So they waited, and then: one, then two, then a hundred tiny twinkling lights drifted up and out of the box. Mom took Asuka's hand.

"It's a promise," she said. "Someday, we will put things back the way they used to be. The insects, the trees, and all the birds."

The tiny lights flickered as they spread out over the fields, and Asuka wanted it to be true.

The shadows settled down around them.

"Your father is moving back to America," she said. "He got a new job in Boston."

Asuka searched herself for surprise, but since Luis had died, all endings felt predictable.

Her mother's face was unreadable in the dark. "I know it's been hard for you to fit in here, and that you want to apply for that program. I don't like it. But I've thought about it, and I have a deal for you: if you stay with me here in Japan, I'll let you apply. I'll even help you study for the exam. But if you don't get in, or you get in but you change your mind, I want you to promise to come back here, to me."

Asuka swallowed. She thought she understood the choice. "I want to go to EvenStar."

"Okay then," her mother said. She touched Asuka's cheek. "You know all I want is for you to be safe. And happy."

Asuka didn't trust herself to speak. She felt the half-moon of her mother's thumbnail against her cheek, her index finger under her chin.

A straggler stopped on the edge of the box and then wandered over to Asuka. She caught it to get a better look. Its mechanical legs wiggled in protest, and its wings strained to fly. The bulb at the back of its butt flickered.

"Let it go."

Asuka opened her hand, and it flew away. It didn't matter that it wasn't alive. It would be there that evening, and for many evenings after. And for all Asuka knew, years later, somewhere in the water-soaked paddies at the foot of the mountains, there were still mechanical fireflies lighting up the sky. Perhaps they'd outlast the children they were made for.

CHAPTER FOURTEEN

It was like nothing had disturbed the white passageway that connected to the Dining and Kitchen Mods, and that was enough to make Asuka's skin crawl. How could so much destruction have occurred on the other side without even knocking askew the neat, black and silver embossed placard on the door?

Four crew were there, prepping the compression suit for Asuka. Ying Yue had messaged ahead that she was sending the Alt to help retrieve the bodies. Which was just, you know, awesome. But you couldn't exactly say no in a crisis.

She would be going in with Lala Williams, who was already suiting up for the dark vacuum-filled module beyond.

Asuka remembered how she and Lala had been friends for one whole semester. Not best friends, but robotics partners. In fact, Lala was the reason Asuka hadn't failed out her first semester. But then what? They'd drifted apart. Hadn't crossed paths much since. Lala was a Bot Engineer, and now, on ship, they worked together sometimes, since they both were slotted for B Shift. But that was it. Still, she felt the remnant of that brief, bright friendship sometimes, like finding the other sock at the bottom of your laundry.

Also, Lala was dating Ruth. Asuka had heard that.

As the crew helped Asuka suit up, she caught herself scrutinizing each of them, thinking, *Was it you? Did you do it?* It was already beginning to eat at her, and she didn't like it.

"I was scheduled for a meal in the Dining Mod," one said. "But Alpha told me to wait, because the air sensors were going off again. Can you imagine? I would have died."

Asuka frowned. The air sensors had been unreliable lately, but it seemed like a weird coincidence.

"You ever find that drill?" Lala asked, as Asuka pulled on a compression suit for the second time that cycle. It took Asuka a moment to remember: the missing drill she'd been searching for before the spacewalk with Kat. Was Lala joking? She was joking.

Lala was tall and lean, full of tense energy. She had dark skin and a bright smile that revealed a crooked left canine tooth. It gave her an endearing, cocky look. Story was, EvenStar had wanted her to fix it before launch, and she'd put up a fight. *I changed enough of myself for you. I'm keeping my teeth.* They let it go. Asuka's mom would have said Lala had that "Strong American Girl Spirit." Like Asuka. Which was not a compliment. Technically, Lala wasn't an American rep. Instead, she had earned one of the coveted Wild Card spots.

Asuka cricked her neck a few times, feeling okay now that the nanos and pain meds were kicking in. Better than okay. Something like a runner's high. Which meant she'd feel like shit in a few hours, so better enjoy it while it lasted. Except now all she could think about was: *One of us did this.*

"All right, Susie?"

Asuka jumped, but it was a crewmate asking from behind if the compression was too tight.

"Yeah."

"Okay, then," said Lala, smacking gloved hands together. "Let's get this over with." She was glaring sideways at the airlock door like she could kick it down, and dread crept over Asuka.

Isn't there someone else? It was a selfish thought; she was not thinking that, no.

Asuka shut her eyes a moment, bracing herself. The others exited the passageway, and the airlock sealed behind them. Her compression suit squeezed in all the sore and banged-up places, and her mouth was dry as the moon.

It was dark in the module except for blue and red blinking emergency lights along the floor. Asuka turned on her headlamp, light playing about the room.

Weird being in the Dining Mod without any augmentation. It

should have been the Japanese restaurant her family used to go to for special occasions when she was very little — tables and tatami floors, lacquer and ceramic bowls full of miso soup and rice and various delicacies. Quiet music and the murmur of conversation. Paper chopstick sleeves she could fold into shapes. Instead, it was a white box streaked with black charring and bits of furniture and warped dishes. Shadows danced across blue then red walls.

To the right was an airlock that led to the Kitchen Mod. It was sealed shut. The Kitchen Mod had sustained significant damage, but at least it didn't have a giant hole in its side.

"Yaz and her squad do quick work, eh?" said Lala, shining her headlamp on the hole. Already, the outer wall was scaffolded with ribbing. Through it they could see the slow-moving stars. Little bots like flying spiders climbed about, building out the frame for the permanent hull patch. Asuka imagined the skittering *clackety-clack* of their hair-thin metal legs, but without atmosphere they moved noiselessly.

The room was designed with long communal tables and benches perpendicular to two serving counters along the wall adjacent to the Kitchen Mod.

"Ugh." Lala stood over the Captain, who lay facedown between the half-intact serving counter nearest the door to the passageway, body covered by a sheet of metal. The force of the blast must have knocked her down, which had kept her from being pulled out by the air suck that followed. "What was she doing in the Dining Mod, anyway?"

Asuka remembered the amplified, wet sound of McMahon chewing in her ear. "Came down for a snack?"

"McMahon didn't snack." The Captain was disciplined to a fault; she set impossible standards for herself and expected everyone else to meet the same.

Asuka joined Lala on the other side of the serving counter. The countertop had been blown off in pieces. They lifted the piece closest to the door.

Underneath, Captain McMahon's body was twisted around the swell of her belly.

"Jesus," said Ying Yue in her ear. She must have been watching through Asuka's feed.

Lala said in a dead sort of voice, "Baby would have lasted longer than she did."

An image of the fetus rose up in Asuka's mind. Stunned under the force of impact, still sucking oxygen through the umbilical cord. Until—

A strangled cry crackled across the radio, then muted.

"Sorry," said Lala after a moment, clearing her throat.

Asuka felt herself going numb. Was looking anywhere else but down. There was a spray of blood on the floor, and bits of—oh, no— yes, small intestine flash-frozen against the wall. "I may be sick."

"Just breathe," said Lala, who sounded like she was hyperventilating herself.

I can see this is a stressful situation, but you're going to be okay, said Alpha.

"Shut up, Alpha," said Lala, clearly responding to similar attempts by the AI to soothe her.

Asuka stepped around the Captain, trying to locate Winnie, who was also behind the serving counter. She remembered seeing legs when she'd peered in from outside.

Beneath another piece of countertop, closer to the hole, Winnie lay curled in a fetal position. Even in pregnancy, her arms and legs were skinny. She was a small person, built for running long distances. She'd loved her ultra-marathons, but she'd given all that up for the ultimate ultra across space. And here she was. She hadn't made it. It took Asuka a moment to process what she was seeing: her body was missing from the chest up.

Lala whispered a short prayer. Asuka felt as if her ears were full of cotton. Lala sagged against Asuka, casting a second slash of light across the woman. Words tumbled out of her: "We were in the same conception round. She wanted us to name our babies matchy-matchy names. It would have been disgustingly cute."

Lala sniffled, then squatted down by Winnie's feet and unfolded the body bag. Asuka bent down on the other side. Both avoiding where her head used to be. Winnie's flesh was cold, even through insulated gloves. They shoved her into the bag and zipped it up. Better not to see her anymore.

"Remember, um, lift from your legs, or you'll wrench your back," Lala said, and Asuka felt a shrill, inappropriate giggle threatening to bubble up.

They lifted, and Asuka was surprised by the solidity of Winnie, this small person, who had moved like the wind on Earth.

"Don't think about it," said Lala, definitely thinking about it. "Let's go."

They carried Winnie into the passage, heavy and awkward in their arms.

Asuka realized halfway that Lala was sobbing, the noise overamplified through the helmet mic. Asuka wanted to beg her to mute, but thing was, she was crying too.

As they set the bag down, she wished for her forest, or for green lawn and a cloud of sparrows settling into a cottonwood tree. For Winnie to get up, brush the dirt off old gym shorts, and ask if anyone wanted to go for a run.

They leaned against the doorframe, gasping for air, trying to work up the courage to go back in.

"When I started cramping, blood on my thighs and stuff, I knew I'd lost mine. And after that, I avoided her. It was too hard." Lala bowed her head. "You don't know when you talk to someone for the last time."

Asuka thought of Kat and how little she'd appreciated her.

"All right?" someone asked over the comm.

How tempting to say no, let someone else take over. Make it their problem and walk away.

"Yes," said Lala, for both of them.

Becky McMahon's arms stretched out over her head, insubstantial in the dim blue light. Asuka squatted and glanced along the direction of her fingers. She had been reaching for the door, maybe, or hanging on to the handle by the side of the airlock. Asuka stepped around the frozen blood pooled on the floor around the Captain's ears.

"I'm not sorry," said Lala, expression unreadable behind the faceplate of her helmet.

Asuka started at the venom in her voice. "What?"

Lala jumped as if she hadn't realized she had spoken aloud. "Nothing. It's just. She wasn't a good person."

Asuka had heard Lala had gotten into a fight with the Captain. Called her an evil racist bitch or something right in the passageway for everyone to hear. She'd been confined to Crew Quarters for a cycle because of it. Asuka didn't know what it had been about. Was it anything to do with the reason McMahon was dead now?

"What do you mean?" Asuka asked, dreading the answer. She liked Lala. And Lala was distraught about Winnie. There was no way it had been her.

Lala's face blinked in and out of shadow, inscrutable. "You know she was a mackey, right?"

A mackey was what people called a member of the Militia for the American Constitution. Asuka thought of their neighbors in the camp, who were basically normal people. But MAC was also responsible for burning down the Michigan State Capitol, for the resurgence of lynchings, for bombing a polling place in Ohio. They had gained strength in the last decade, with civil conflict raging in pockets all over the United States.

She regarded the body between them. It seemed hard to imagine that EvenStar would have taken someone with that kind of affiliation, let alone made them a Captain. "How do you know?"

In answer, Lala squatted next to the body and yanked down the front of McMahon's shirt. Peeking over her right breast was the head of a black eagle.

"What's going on in there?" Ying Yue asked.

Asuka bent quickly next to Lala and tried to push the Captain onto her back. She flinched, thinking she'd felt the bones of the baby inside.

Together, they lifted the Captain, who was heavier than Winnie, and slid her into the bag.

"So," said Lala. "You and Ruth have, uh, drama?"

"Nope."

They navigated around the furniture.

"What happened between you two anyway? You were best friends."

Asuka hefted the Captain's feet. "I don't know." A lump of self-pity lodged in her throat. She could have choked on it. "What did Ruth tell you?"

"Nothing. That's why I've been dying to know."

"People drift apart, I guess."

"Sorry. Ruth complains I have no respect for privacy. But what is privacy anyway?" They maneuvered toward the airlock. "You know, after the explosion, she ran straight from the Bridge to rescue you. Some of the Officers were upset about it."

"Oh," said Asuka, surprised.

"No one knew if you were alive, because half the system was down. But she insisted on going out there to find you. She saved your life."

Asuka didn't know what to say to that.

They carried the Captain through the airlock.

"All done?" someone asked. As if there might be something more they could do.

And what about Kat, Asuka thought, jaw tightening in grief. Already she was remembering things she hadn't seen: Kat's face, mouth forming the shape of Asuka's name. That she had cried for Asuka to help her. Asuka trembled.

"The rest is on the wall," said Lala. "And I'm not your maid. That's what bots are for." She triggered the airlock door, sealing off the Dining Mod.

Ying Yue's voice came in via DAR: "Okay, send in the drones to, uh, clean what's left."

Asuka closed her eyes, thinking of another body, this one small, pale, stretched out by the side of a pool. The image shuttered in her brain like an old, primitive movie.

"What now?" Lala asked no one.

The segment of passageway was repressurized. Lala had her helmet off, and the others were stepping over the body bags to help Asuka remove her suit.

Did you see anything? Ying Yue asked.

You're all right, Alpha said.

So why did Asuka feel like she might drown? She was the one who did whatever was asked. But she couldn't do this thing for Ying Yue. She couldn't.

Hey. It was a message from Chief Engineer Yaz, Ying Yue's former second-in-command. *Need to show you something.*

CHAPTER FIFTEEN

Cuckoos were experts at infiltration, laying their eggs in the nests of other birds to be raised by unwitting parents. They were particularly known for their impressive mimicry ability, producing eggs that resembled the host's eggs—speckled, small, brown, or white. Woe to the wagtail, shrike, or magpie who failed to notice.

CHAPTER SIXTEEN

THE *PHOENIX* * 3,980 CYCLES AFTER LAUNCH,
0 CYCLES AFTER EXPLOSION, C SHIFT

"Deploy on my mark," said Yaz. She stood, leaning two-handed against the back of a chair for balance. The ship chairs, now that Asuka looked at them unfiltered, were simply constructed. The back was curved pieces of unpainted metal bolted to a frame that was designed for durability more than comfort. She'd seen the same chairs in the Bridge and in the Dining Mod; they were, it seemed, the exclusive chair of the *Phoenix* and, no matter what they looked like in DAR, notorious for contributing to a sore posterior. Likely worse, if one was, like Yaz, in their third trimester and had been sitting in one for hours.

The Drone Operations Mod had a far wall covered in a concave screen, never used, since people had DAR. Workstations were arranged in two half-circle rows facing this wall. There was a whiff of sweat not quite cycled out by the ventilation system. The Drone Ops crew had been working double since the explosion, and adrenaline had started to fade to exhaustion. She could see it in the slump of everyone's shoulders, in the rubbing of sore necks. Many were on their second shift, including Yaz.

Drone Ops was responsible for keeping the ship in repair. The perfect place to be if you wanted to sabotage the ship. Asuka sneaked a glance around the crew. Okay, but what did suspicious behavior even look like?

Since Asuka arrived, Yaz had said nothing about what she wanted to show her, just put her to work as if Asuka was there to help with the repair mission. It suited Asuka fine. At least she knew how to do this.

"Plug in?" one of the team asked Asuka, offering her a splinter of driftwood. Yaz required everyone in her crew to share reality when on shift.

Asuka's fingers passed through it, and the room transformed into the deck of an exquisite galleon with dark red sails that skimmed across the clouds several miles above the ground. It was raining, and not for the first time, Asuka wondered what Yaz had against sunshine.

Asuka took her position, feet shoulder width apart on the poop deck, poised before a wood-framed screen that was incongruously high-tech. A karasu came up along the galleon, wings beating.

"I have that same bird in my DAR," she said to the crew member next to her.

"What bird?" They didn't see the bird even though they were all sharing DAR. Weird.

"Put us outside, Alpha," said Yaz.

Then the karasu and gray sky disappeared, and the galleon was flying through space instead.

Even now, Yaz didn't seem ruffled. The woman was steady as an atomic clock. She oozed competence through every pore. A diamond-encrusted ring hung from a long gold chain around her neck—a family heirloom passed down from her great-grandmother. Her mother had been a pilot in a women's air squadron during the last global conflict. At school, Yaz had worn a bulletproof vest like it was fashionable, and somehow, it was a point of awe rather than ridicule. For many, that global conflict would never be over. Which was reasonable, given the new one that had broken out. "On my mark."

Asuka focused on her controls. She had a squadron of twenty bots under her charge, each marked on her screen by an orange light and a charge meter. The micro bots ran on batteries that lasted a couple of hours, but a number four in the corner of the screen indicated this was already the fourth wave of deployment since the explosion.

"Go," said Yaz. The little bots deployed from a chute in the North-Quad, microscopic propulsion keeping them in synchrony with the habitat wheel. She pulled up the perspective of one of the bots. Then they were one with the drones outside, riding along the swarm through the dark. The control room was gone, and they were streaming through space toward the hole in the hull.

The fisheye perspective made Asuka dizzy, but Yaz seemed to be enjoying herself. An involuntary grin stretched across her face.

"Touchdown," Yaz said.

The drones reached the hole and began to attach and seal the temporary patch they'd laid down before, which looked like a piece of plastic sheeting but much stronger.

"Finish the scaffolding first, then start the plating."

"The patches we have in storage aren't big enough."

"We'll do fish scales. It will be okay."

Asuka checked her little bots, building out the scaffolding like worker bees.

"Do an extra layer of scaffolding there," Yaz said, pointing to her screen. "It's weak."

"Copy," Asuka said. She transmitted the instructions.

The little drones began to construct the ribs out of oblong blocks of metal, and Asuka imagined hearing them slide into each other like children's building toys, *snick, snick*.

The little guys were programmed to deal with small repairs in the hull, but this was much bigger than anything they'd ever had to handle. Still, the bots worked fast, rebuilding the frame, insulation, wiring, hull.

Asuka felt a kernel of pride. Here was a test of the crew's extensive training, and everyone was doing what they were supposed to.

Work continued, punctuated by anxious chatter.

The bots fit little shingles of metal against the frame. She could see the sudden red heat of the solder. One day, they would build a brand-new world like this. Brick by brick. Assuming they ever got there.

Yaz pinched her bottom lip with two fingers, expression unreadable.

There were seven layers to the hull, all designed to protect from radiation, to keep the ship systems cycling and insulated from the near-zero temperatures outside. Temperature regulation was powered by the enormous engines strapped to the nose and tail of their ship, which was better not to think about most of the time.

Asuka switched her personal view to a tighter angle from the exterior cameras and watched the fibrous webbing thicken across the crude scaffolding they'd already laid. She wasn't 100 percent sure, but it seemed like the consistency wasn't quite what it should have been. She zoomed in closer.

"Having some issues with my bots." Bots were getting snarled in the webbing. Which shouldn't have happened. And from the sounds of it, she wasn't the only one.

"Take these four offline," said Yaz, coming over and touching four of the orange lights that had gone rogue. "Bring them in for a program reset."

There was cursing. Some bots had started messing with the good ones.

"Spider fight," one crew confirmed.

Yaz went over to someone else. "Take those offline too."

"They're tangled. Can't bring them in."

"Shut them off." The weave of microfibers was no longer a neat grid but a traffic jam.

"Can't." Her technician's voice sounded stressed. "It's worse than last time."

A full third of the bots weren't responding to commands now. It was weird. Very weird.

"Mierda."

Yaz switched to one of the big bots. This one was named Petunia and was, among other things, a glorified space vacuum. She turned on the brush and moved it closer. Once in position, she made a fist. It began to swallow micro bots whole, good along with bad. Order was restored in minutes.

"That was awesome," someone breathed.

"Keep working."

Asuka heard a low grunt from Yaz. She was bent over, clutching her abdomen. After a moment, she straightened back up. "Take over Asuka's bots," she told one of her crew. Then she gestured for Asuka to follow her out into the passage.

"What did you make of that?" said Yaz, walking one Mod over to the EAM.

"Was that normal?"

"Ha. Alpha, open the hatch." Alpha obliged, opening the drones and bots access chute, next to the larger, stern-facing airlock. Petunia rose up in a great bucket. Yaz slung it to the floor, removed its gullet, and began to pick out rogue bots one by one, switching them off and tossing them into a crate. "Very *not* normal."

Asuka lowered her voice: "You think someone is messing with them?"

"I'm asking *you*. Ying Yue says you're working on this. So what do you think?"

Asuka considered the implications. "If someone could mess with the bots like this, maybe they also used a bot to deploy the bomb?" It would explain why the construction crew hadn't seen the anomaly before launch—because it hadn't been there.

"Maybe. But how would this person have gotten it out there without anyone on my team noticing? Only Drone Ops has access to the big bots, and Drone Ops monitors them all three shifts. Which also means no one could have spacewalked it out there without us seeing. Unless you think my team is all in on it."

When she put it that way, it did seem unlikely. Asuka felt flustered. She flashed back to doing chemistry problem sets with her friends and always being last to get to an answer. "What's the alternative?"

Yaz shut the box and dumped Petunia back in the deployment chute. "I don't know. It got there somehow. If the bot programming is corrupted, maybe the bomb was installed by the bots while we were in hibernation."

Asuka nudged the crate with her toe. It seemed hard to imagine they hadn't spotted it until now. But on the other hand, it would mean that the perpetrator was someone back on Earth. In which case maybe none of the crew were involved. Except. "Alpha, wouldn't you have noticed if something happened while we were asleep?" She'd already tried asking her if she knew how the bomb had gotten there, but Alpha didn't know.

I am afraid I am unable to answer your question, said Alpha. *Whatever happened is beyond my awareness. I'm only a program, after all. I can't see everything that happens on this ship.*

Asuka shivered. Alpha's presence, while sometimes overbearing, was also a comfort. She hadn't realized until that moment how much she trusted Alpha to take care of them.

Yaz stopped to knead a knot in her back with her knuckles. "Too many questions. Right now what my gut tells me—is that I need to pee again. Run these down to the Shop?" She indicated the crate.

After Yaz had gone, Asuka reached into the crate and switched on one of the bots. It began to attack the others. She caught it, switched it off, and was submerged in silence again.

CHAPTER SEVENTEEN

The EvenStar campus drive was lined with pine trees, scrawny and new, the beds around them freshly churned, the turf too pristine.

Near the parking lot was a lawn with a giant cottonwood that could have been a hundred years old. In DAR, a flock of RealSparrows descended to alight on its branches as they pulled up.

Asuka heard the quiet hum of so many media drones hovering outside the bus.

There were only fifteen candidates traveling from Japan. They had met at a lavish luncheon hosted by the government before they left. The food was prepared by a chef who specialized in French-Japanese cuisine, including a delicate clam consommé with yuzu zest and a foie gras drenched in a soy glaze that Asuka awkwardly declined, explaining she didn't eat birds. The Emperor and Empress had attended, along with the Prime Minister, who told them they were a credit to their nation. Asuka wasn't sure if she was included in this, but she returned the bow and said, "Dōmo arigatō gozaimasu" in a very quiet, nervous voice.

It was hard not to be intimidated. The group included an international golf sensation, a young mountain climber who had summited Mt. Everest last year, a famous influencer with several hundred million followers worldwide, and a classical composer who had conducted a symphony for the Tokyo Philharmonic Orchestra a month ago to rave reviews. And who was Asuka? That hāfu refugee girl in secondhand clothes.

The composer's name was Miki. She had glossy, perfect hair down to her waist, a quick smile, and a knack for ignoring all of Asuka's cultural faux pas. Her English was crisp, British sounding, and she'd traveled several times to Europe and America to perform. She seemed more sophisticated and mature than a twelve-year-old had a right to be, and Asuka wanted to hate her—except she was also kind, and she took Asuka under her wing immediately. "Asuka-san's from California," she told the others, as if that were cool.

"Actually," Asuka said. "My mom's Japanese. I'm Japanese."

When they arrived in America, the airports were uglier than she remembered, the people louder, the streets dirtier. There were dueling MAC and Nat Guard graffiti right across the tarmac that hadn't been painted over. She was embarrassed for them to see this.

But as they disembarked, Asuka began to feel excited again, that spark of love one felt for returning to one's home country, even if it required her to split in two.

They were directed to line up on a broad, emerald lawn. The whole place had been a liberal arts college that had gone bankrupt decades before. Linda Trembling, the trillionaire venture capitalist and inventor who had brought DAR to the masses, had laid down several billion dollars and conjured EvenStar Academy in its place.

Hundreds of candidates Asuka's age milled about. A lot of them had family along, though a good number didn't—the cost of flights being what they were.

They moved into the large entrance hall of a grand brick building. It smelled freshly painted. Asuka was separated from the others in the confusion but followed the crowd to a registration table.

A large-print nametag in DAR appeared over their chests, including name, proper pronunciation, preferred pronouns, and title. This seemed to be EvenStar standard; Asuka glanced down and saw the same information written across her own chest.

"Country of origin?" the woman at the table asked. When Asuka hesitated, she prompted: "Chinese?"

Asuka gave both her nationalities.

"Which one are you registered under, hon?"

"Which one?" Asuka asked, confused.

"Are you a candidate for America or Japan?"

Asuka peeked around as if someone else might know. "I'm sorry, what do you mean?" she asked at last, her voice very small.

"She means which country did you put on your application?" said a skinny, dark-haired kid checking in next to her. DARtag: *Ruth Segal-Brown (she/her)*. She had a birthmark over one eyelid and a canine grin that made Asuka nervous. "Some countries have already pledged funds to guarantee a specific number of seats for their representatives. For example, I'm British-Israeli, but I'm registered for Israel. Do you not remember what you put on your application?"

Her mother had filled out the application for her at the test site. It had been in Japanese, and Asuka couldn't read it. "American?"

The registration person found the information. "Nope, you're representing Japan. Here you go, sweetheart. You're all set."

Ears ringing, Asuka took the welcome package and stepped away from the table. She was so glad her new friend Miki was not here to see this. There had to be a mistake.

The annoying girl followed her away from the table. There was something about the way Ruth walked—Asuka glanced down and saw below the hem of her shorts, one of her legs from the knee down was a hot-pink prosthetic.

"Hey, are you okay? Just don't cry. You don't want them to think you're weak or anything."

"Are you trying to be nice or mean to me? I can't really tell."

"Neither. I'm telling you how it is. Look, it's a smart move. You'll have fewer candidates to compete against."

Horror filled Asuka. "What do you mean, compete?"

They went into a large lecture hall. It was augmented to resemble a Roman coliseum. "Kind of tacky, don't you think?" shouted Ruth. It was too loud to think. Everyone was talking, shouting for family to come on.

"What?" Asuka craned her neck for Miki and the others, but it was impossible to find them in the movement of the crowd.

Ruth put a hand on her shoulder and leaned close. Her breath was hot on Asuka's face. She yelled loud enough to make Asuka's ear hurt: "Japan only paid for one spot."

"So only one of us gets to go?" Asuka asked, clutching her cheek. Because of course this was a competition. There were eight hundred kids in this room, and they were taking eighty. Which meant most of them weren't going to be selected. And why would any country want a rep who didn't look enough, couldn't speak enough, or *be* enough, citizen or not?

She felt acute pain in her chest. Her heart was pounding, and she was having trouble breathing again. She thought maybe she was dying of mortification.

She needed to ask her mom what to do, how to fix this great mistake. Her mom, who had filled out the form. Her eyes narrowed. Had she done it to sabotage her?

With fumbling fingers, she sent her a message: *Did you register me as a candidate for Japan?*

Her mom, who must have stayed up late to watch the live cast of her arrival, responded immediately. *Yes. Mochiron!*

What? Why??? How could you do this to me???

A few minutes passed. Then, her mom said, *Trust Mom. Odds much better.*

But. I'm not really Jp.

There was a long silence.

Not seeing Miki anywhere, Asuka slipped into a squeaky, uncomfortable seat at the end of a row in the back and waited for her mom to reply. She was trying so hard not to freak out. Ruth, who had squeezed past and sat down next to her without invitation, added, "There are also Wild Card spots for candidates of any affiliation. But those are way more competitive. If you don't get your national seat, you're probably screwed. You know, if I can give you some advice—"

"Can you not, actually?"

"Cute," said Ruth, pursing her lips and giving her a once-over. "Don't ask so many questions. It gives away how little you know. Unless you want to wash out in year one."

Asuka's face heated to maybe one hundred degrees. She opened her mouth to ask how someone could wash out. Then she shut it again.

A hush fell over the crowd as a large group of adults filed in front of them.

"Faculty," said Ruth.

Asuka gave this girl what her mom called her mean eye. "I'll give you some free advice," she said. "Don't talk so much. It makes people not like you."

"I'm not here to be liked," Ruth hissed back. "I'm here to win."

The orientation program began, and Asuka sat there, clutching her hands until her knuckles turned white. She thought she'd die if she had to sit next to this girl another moment. Consequently, she missed all the instructions. She spent the whole hour trying to think of a good comeback.

At the end of it, when everyone stood, she leaned over and grabbed the other girl's arm: "Ever heard of a killdeer?"

"What?"

"The killdeer feigns injury to trick a predator. Don't underestimate people." It was a ridiculous comeback. Asuka got up and marched out before Ruth could laugh at her, even though she didn't have any clue where she was going.

CHAPTER EIGHTEEN

Asuka carried the box of defective bots to the Bot Shop, metallic limbs and stubby, cylindrical bodies rattling like anxiety trapped in an old mason jar under the bed. The box was heavy enough she could already feel her arms twanging. She stopped and hitched the box against her waist, trying to think of a capital *P* Plan.

Someone was coming the other way with a tray of food, and Asuka nearly dropped the box trying to make room for them to pass in the narrow corridor. She banged her elbow painfully against the frame of one of the modular doors and bit back a curse as pain lanced through the nerve.

Couldn't the ship engineers have designed the passage of the wheel to be just a little wider?

Construction of the *Phoenix* had been an enormous operation. Even the majority of Linda Trembling's fortune wasn't enough to cover the cost of an interstellar voyage, so she had appealed to the nations of the world, promising them seats in exchange for funding. Pitched it as patriotism and apple pie but also world peace and a unified, international endeavor.

As it became obvious that a mission this expensive might be a once-in-a-human-history thing, EvenStar fever gripped the world, with countries scraping together tens and hundreds of billions, bankrupting themselves to make sure *their* people would be represented in this next chapter of human civilization.

Asuka let her knuckle brush against the smooth metal panels of the passage wall, bolted and welded by hands on Earth. The modular sections of the *Phoenix* had been propelled up through the sky to be joined together by thousands of drones and an international work crew of ten astronauts too old to qualify for the actual mission.

Could one of the work crew have planted a bomb? Jealous of their journey, bitter to be left behind? They would have been better positioned to do it than one of the thousands of Earthbound construction crew on the ground. Someone on the space team could have affixed it where it might not be noticed until well after launch. But then what? How had it been triggered from someone back on Earth? Through the Walkie, somehow, that was the only possibility, unless Yaz was right about the rogue bots being preprogrammed eleven years ago for the task.

A dull ache was building behind her eyes.

Asuka, this is your off shift. You've had a stressful day. Why not try to relax?

"Yeah, right."

Or if you prefer, I could load the immersive for your atmospheric engineering class.

They were all required to do additional advanced training in preparation for preassigned roles once they reached Planet X. As an Alt, there wasn't any obvious role for Asuka. She needed to submit an area for Mission Control approval soon. In the meantime, her current studies felt as scattered and torturous as her time at school, and she was low-key panicking she'd be stuck as an Alt if she didn't figure out what she wanted to be.

"Yeah, I'll get right on it—next cycle."

Fantastic. I've scheduled it.

"That was sarcasm." Absurd to think she could concentrate on air pressure and humidity modeling right now.

How exciting it had been, when they first woke up and started working their shifts. Back then, when the ship hadn't felt so irreversibly far from Earth.

Curiosity wilted sometime after day one hundred. Became claustrophobia now that they were almost a year awake. Every cycle the same: wake, eat, study, sleep, repeat. It didn't matter which cycle you were.

Except it *had* mattered. It mattered if you were Winnie, volunteering for a cook shift, and had your everything blown out against the wall.

"Why would anyone do this?" she said out loud.

I'm sorry. I can't answer that.

"That was rhetorical."

Shall I tell you about the life and habits of the messenger pigeon?

"Not now."

Would you like 10 mg of anti-stress medication?

"No, thanks." Couldn't afford to have any fog in her brain right now. She arrived at the door to the Bot Shop, where the crew fixed the clever machines that maintained the ship, like the ones Asuka was carrying.

The tables were strewn with parts. The Shop hummed with activity. Plenty of people were there even though it was their off shift: Lala, for example, who must have come back from the Dining Mod. And— Asuka froze. Because Ruth was perched on a stool next to Lala, eating dinner.

Lala waved Asuka over.

"More of them?" Lala gestured for Asuka to set the box down on the table. "Yaz has been running the bots hard. They're coming in as fast as we fix them. So, talk. What have you heard?"

Asuka picked up one of the bots from the box and turned it over. "Nothing."

"Damn, Susie," said Lala. She swapped one of her tools for another and neatly disemboweled a bot. "Ruth won't tell me anything either. Can you at least tell us what happened out there?"

"Maybe she doesn't want to talk about it," said Ruth. That familiar razor-sharp tone. And even though Asuka was relieved to not have to talk about Kat, she also resented the presumption that she needed protecting. She was about to tell Lala everything just because of it, but Ruth caught her eye. The side of her mouth lifted in a secret smile, and without meaning to, Asuka smiled back. "How are you doing, Asuka?"

"Stellar. You?"

"Oh my god," said Lala. "Are we going to finally bury the body in the backyard?"

"Leave it," Ruth said.

"Aaaaalll right." Lala pawed through the graveyard of whole and busted bot pieces on the big table. A manu bot, about a meter tall, rolled up and deposited a socket on the table. It soldered two pieces together. "Well, *I* have all sorts of theories. Manufacturing problem with the tank. Or a microleak of chemicals that caught a spark from something. Or terrorism."

Ruth's and Asuka's eyes met accidentally over a pile of springs and screws. They both looked away, but it was too late.

"Ah!" said Lala, jabbing a screwdriver at Asuka. "So you think so too. MAC, CoBro, or SME?"

McMahon's death made the MAC angle a possibility. But the other two organizations had strongly opposed the mission too. Company of Brothers, colloquially known as "CoBro," was an international men's rights group that gained prominence after EvenStar announced they were only taking mission crew who could give birth halfway through. They were best known for their two-hundred-day occupation of the U.N., during which they'd held twenty leaders hostage. And Save Mother Earth (SME) was an environmental movement—it couldn't be SME.

"Fuck all of them. I was happy to see their lights in the rear window when we blasted out of there. Metaphorically speaking." Lala yanked off her DAR gloves. "Dammit. I can never feel anything properly through these."

"Since when is SME a terror group?" Asuka asked.

"Since they hijacked an oil tanker seven years ago," said Lala.

"No one was hurt, though," said Ruth.

"And the time with that power plant?"

Ruth stirred her soup with thinly veiled annoyance.

"SME wouldn't have wasted the resources on this. It would have been contrary to the mission of the organization," said Asuka. There was a reason she didn't believe SME would do something like this. Didn't want to believe it.

"I don't know what to tell you," Lala said. "A lot can change when you're asleep for a decade plus."

Ruth's gaze flicked over to Asuka again. "Still haven't talked to your mum?"

Are you okay, Asuka? Alpha was asking. *Your heart rate is elevated.*

Ruth tongued two pills from her tray, a white neonatal vitamin and a blue fertility booster, and swallowed them with a spoonful of shockingly green soup.

"What is that?" Asuka asked, trying to change the subject.

"Spirulina dumpling soup. It's . . . not terrible."

"Except that it is." Lala plucked another bot out of the crate. "Gabriela said she's volunteering for cooking duty next B shift, though. I would kill for those empanadas again."

"She used mealworm flour." Ruth wrinkled her nose.

"Like I said. Delicious."

Gabriela was one of the best cooks on the ship. She'd shown Asuka her personal box once. Half of it was spices.

Asuka reached into the crate and grabbed one of the bots. She started to wrestle with the casing and knocked a circuit board off the table in the process. Lala caught it.

"Watch it!"

"Sorry," said Asuka, face heating with embarrassment. They couldn't afford to break things. Their whole world was this ship. Nothing was replaceable.

Lala passed her the circuit board, and when their fingers touched, she caught a glimpse of an atrium with big glass windows and steel beams. There was a musician with a pink mohawk plucking a string bass, and another on a brass horn. And on the horn player's shoulder, a bright green parrot eyeing Asuka funny. It said: "Watch it! Watch it!" Asuka stared at it, and Lala followed her gaze.

"You like parrots?" Asuka asked. In her experience, not a lot of people had birds in their DAR. It made her like Lala more.

"Hm?" Lala asked.

"Sorry, my implant glitch. I can see people's DAR when I'm close. Like I saw the bar and band and a green parrot over there." Asuka pointed in what she thought was the right spot.

Lala glanced over. "Weird . . . there's no parrot, though."

Asuka frowned. It had been there; she was sure of it.

Lala went back to fiddling with a circuit board, but her heart wasn't in it. "God. I'm so fucking angry. Aren't you? I mean, look at us. All these years of studying. Like packing for a long trip with a small bag. Our entire lives to get this far and what for, if we never make it to Planet X?"

"My dads are freaking out," Ruth said, while Lala examined the bot. "They've sent me ten messages."

"My dad too," said Lala.

Asuka didn't say anything. How had her mother reacted when she'd heard the news? Still waiting, maybe, for Asuka to send a message that she was fine, to respond to one of the letters she'd sent. But how could she after the last time they talked?

She imagined the media furor back home. Was her mom being mobbed by news drones asking about her daughter? Or was she living in obscurity, maybe back on Obāsan's farm? It was a knowable thing, and yet Asuka didn't know. There were messages in her inbox if she cared to read them. She didn't. But it didn't stop her wondering where her mom was. Like if she had a dog. And it made her suddenly, freakishly angry, the thought that her mom might have a dog.

Asuka left the table and went to the storage wall. It was lined floor to ceiling with little cabinets crammed with parts. Not that she was avoiding the conversation or anything.

She began to rummage through all the drawers, and as she did, everything else retreated from her mind.

"You okay, Suze?" Lala asked, coming over.

"Mm."

"The connectors aren't there."

Asuka was pawing through a box of electrical wires.

"Uh-huh," said Asuka, half listening. She opened a different drawer, full of black plastic casing. Another of little batteries.

She thought of the ever-growing distance between the *Phoenix* and home.

"Hello. Earth to Asuka."

Asuka sat on the floor with a nest of wires in her lap, thinking: *All these parts. Put together one way, and you make a thing whole. Put together another way, and you could blow it apart.*

"You're starting to freak me out," said Lala.

"That drill you're looking for. If someone takes stuff from the Shop, like parts or tools, is there a log that says who took them?"

"There's an inventory log that says which parts have been taken from storage and when. Not who, though."

"Alpha, show me the logs." A stream of data appeared.

"I already tried this," Lala said. "The problem is once it's been checked out, people borrow it from each other. So the record isn't reliable."

"Are there any items that are missing without associated record of removal?"

A shorter list appeared.

"Why would any of them be missing records?" said Lala. "It's automated."

Asuka messaged her follow-up, so as not to be overheard: *Could someone delete inventory records?*

Yes. It is possible.

Asuka bit back a curse. *Did someone delete these?*

An uncharacteristic pause from Alpha. Then: *I cannot confirm that.*

Yaz asked where the bomb came from. The "how" was here in her lap, in the wires and the circuit boards. This was not a remote attack. Someone on the ship *had* done this. She regarded the other crew, heads bent, intent on their tasks. And Lala and Ruth, looking at her with concern.

The question was, who?

CHAPTER NINETEEN

Asuka's first semester at EvenStar was a low-flying disaster. There were students who would do anything to advance. There were others who, like Ruth, were insufferable know-it-alls. But at least she wasn't the only one who worried about failure all the time.

Asuka took to recording her classes and painstakingly rewatching them, pausing to look up each term she didn't know. She limited herself to four hours of sleep a night, staying up until 3:00 A.M. to review homework and study for tests. She drank large mugs of gritty coffee from the campus café until her stomach hurt.

Twenty-three kids dropped out the first week; six the next. By some fluke, Asuka was not among them. Everyone kept obsessive track of each departure and the total number of candidates left.

She was grateful to Miki, the Japanese composer, who woke her when she overslept, saved her muffins from the dining hall, and helped her with her math. They studied elbow to elbow every evening after dinner.

The Japanese reps all met once a week with a team coach, assigned by the government to make sure they stayed on track and behaved respectably. All the richest countries provided support staff for their candidates. They had spent a lot of money to reserve seats, so they didn't want their candidates failing out; plus, there was the hope of picking up extra Wild Card seats. These meetings gave Asuka an acute pain in her chest, which she tried to alleviate by rubbing her sternum discreetly with her knuckles. She wished, not for the first time, her Japanese was better.

Asuka's roommate—cool, fashionable Treena—also hung out with them. They were bold and fearless and already a minor celebrity: a teen influencer with their own line of gender-free clothing for kids.

Treena took the online commentary and swarms of media drones in stride, and they gave Asuka and Miki pointers about how to handle attention, because all EvenStar candidates were sort of semi-famous by association. Linda Trembling encouraged it: the more the world rabidly followed the competition, the more funding poured in. So media drones had free access to campus, and fans could follow the latest stats and official updates about who was doing well and who was struggling.

Treena and Miki were of two minds about it: Treena thought a candidate who raised funding for EvenStar had a stronger chance for selection; Miki believed to play the long game well, it was better to ignore the noise. Asuka mostly just felt stressed and irritable about the whole thing, to the point that when a drone approached, she'd take the long way around to class to avoid it. She had enough other problems.

One of them was that girl, Ruth, who seemed to be everywhere. Asuka'd be out for a long run on one of the paths around the lake, and she'd hear the now-familiar sound of Ruth coming up behind her, and an obnoxious "Watch it, killdeer!" as Ruth passed her. And then the miserable view of her metal blade winking in the sun and getting farther and farther ahead. She was the worst.

They had history and physics together, and Ruth had an annoying habit of answering any question Asuka asked the teacher. So one day, Asuka called her out on it, and even the teacher laughed. Everyone agreed Ruth Segal-Brown was too much, and that was Asuka's revenge, though it didn't feel as good as she thought it would. Later in the library, she apologized, but Ruth told her to "just wash out already."

Which was always a possibility. The first week, Asuka counted down to her double period of practical robotics on Thursday and Saturday afternoon.

When her EvenStar academic counselor, Mx. Garrette, had asked what special skills she had, Asuka volunteered with pride she'd won a prize at the county robotics competition. E had nodded. "We'll sign you up for the advanced class. The important thing is to figure out what you're good at and focus on it—whatever that is, you need to be the best at it, so you stand out. For now, let's assume your specialty will be robotics, and engineering more broadly. There will be plenty of spots for engineers on the mission."

Great plan. Be the best at something. Because that was easy.

The class was set up in a large, airy room in the engineering complex with double-height windows and plain, steel-top tables. There were cabinets full of expensive parts, and on each desk was an advanced model New Century 3D Printer.

She ran her fingers over the machine, unable to keep a grin off her face. Luis's eyes would have bugged out of his head to see this. Asuka felt the stress of the first week leach off her. Here, at last, was something she could do. Something she *was* good at.

Her assigned lab partner was at their table already, fiddling with spare parts. "Lala," she said, holding out her hand. There was an American flag DARpatch on her shoulder, and her DARtag said *Lala Williams (she/her)*.

Of course she knew who Lala Williams was. Lala was more famous than Treena. She had become a grand master in chess at ten, the youngest ever, before abruptly switching her focus to competitive robotics.

Their teacher strode in and switched on the lights, and the sunlight that streamed in through the windows seemed to dull in comparison to the bright bulbs hanging down. She pointed briskly to all the particulars in her DARtag: name (Rita Wu), pronouns (she/they), title (Professor), and background (teaching and private industry). Then she dove right in without further preamble, speaking rapid-fire like she had too little time to cover everything they needed to know: "All right. We're starting with advanced circuitry. I assume you all know how to build autonomous cars and stuff. If you haven't done that, you should leave this class right now."

Asuka's mouth went dry. She knew the principle of how to build one. Did that count? She'd started a few times back at the camp, messing around with a basic model-builder in DAR, but something had always distracted her a quarter of the way through—a soccer game or Luis wanting to play Rocketry. Her mom used to admonish her for not finishing things, but now Asuka realized this for a devastating character flaw that extended even to what she loved.

She bit her thumb. The thought of packing up her bag and walking out of the classroom while everyone watched was too humiliating. And what would she say to Mx. Garrette, who expected this to be the one thing Asuka might excel at?

"Autonomous vehicles!" Lala whispered, rolling her eyes. "Does she think we're babies?"

"I know, right?" said Asuka. She shifted in her seat. No sweat. She could have done it, if she'd had more time. She would do it this weekend to prove it to herself. If she'd half done it, she could do it.

Professor Wu was still talking. She asked them to put together a 30–20 Hopper, and everyone was nodding. Forty sets of fingers drummed the tabletop as they took brisk notes on their DARkeyboards.

Sweat wicked down the back of Asuka's shirt.

"A 30–20 what?" she whispered. "Sorry, I want to make sure I heard her."

"A hopper." Lala grinned. "Awesome, right?"

Asuka hastily looked up what it was. The models and descriptions were incomprehensible. She had never been good at reading diagrams.

Professor Wu ran through a few demonstrations, showing them an enlarged model of a complete hopper. And then she told them to get going; they had two hours.

Lala seemed oblivious to Asuka's terror. She took charge of their project, asking Asuka to fetch this or that. "I've always wanted to do this. In the World Robo Derby last year, we had to build a 45–90 Looper, but that's way basic. Did you compete? What's your ranking?"

"Um." Asuka thought she might die if her partner learned she'd ever been proud of winning a county competition.

"Let's do something fun with this. I hate just following rules. Any ideas?"

Asuka glanced around wildly. She wanted Lala to think she was smart. Out the window, she saw a sprinkler watering the new grass and kids laughing as they dodged around it on their way back from the track. "We could spray people?" She still wasn't sure what a hopper was.

Their machine took shape, and several times Professor Wu walked by and gave an approving nod.

Asuka got to use the New Century Printer for some of the parts, but all the joy had shriveled up. As the printer hummed and chirped, Asuka wanted to wrap her arms around its warm frame and tell Luis, *I tried. I just wasn't good enough.*

Asuka excused herself to go to the bathroom so no one would see her cry.

"Are you okay?" Lala asked when she returned. The hopper was almost done.

"Oh yeah." Asuka laughed. "Allergies." She thought, *As soon as this class is over, I will go to Mx. Garrette and confess. Admit I'm a mistake.*

"You should get treatment next physical. Okay. Check this out!" The hopper was done.

It sprang up from the table and, true to its name, began to hop around the class, to the window, to the door, and back again, propelled by a jet of air. And as it did so, it aimed the nozzle of its tiny water gun at other students. Everyone squealed and laughed. "High five," Lala said, whooping and slapping Asuka's palm so hard it left a sting. Asuka hadn't laughed this hard since coming to EvenStar.

Her spirit lifted. They had *made* this.

"Well done," said Professor Wu, beaming. "Although, next time, please remember water and electronics are not a good combination."

"Whatever." Lala rolled her eyes for Asuka's benefit.

And Asuka resolved she would try to stick out one more class. She could spend her free time on Sunday morning trying to get ahead in the syllabus so she wasn't so lost.

She caught Professor Wu watching her from the front of the class, and she thought for sure the Professor could see right through her. But she nodded as Asuka filed out. "Good job today, Asuka."

CHAPTER TWENTY

Ying Yue cautioned Asuka about jumping to conclusions. She'd been the one who was so suspicious, but now she seemed desperate to find a cause that didn't involve one of the crew. Which Asuka got, but still. *What about Yaz's theory?* Ying Yue asked.

Lala had lent Asuka her DAR, and instead of a section of the wheel passageway, Asuka stood in a once-beautiful park built along a steel-blue river. Sections had collapsed into the water where the pilings were rusted through. She could almost believe she was on Earth. "I don't think it was just bots."

Listen, I agree with you. I don't want to, but I do. But we're going to need more to go on. Including, obviously, the person who did it.

A karasu had settled on one of the pilings. Asuka squinted at it. It watched her back. "Did you know McMahon was a mackey?"

A long, well, *pregnant* pause. *Yes.*

"Oh," said Asuka, deflated. Was she the only one on the ship who didn't know? "Do you think she was involved somehow?"

No, said Ying Yue. *She was pregnant.* Dangling at the end of her sentence: *you'd understand if.* She hadn't said it, but Asuka felt the sting of it just the same. *But don't let me bias your investigation. Keep your eyes open for all possibilities.*

Ying Yue was cautious, but then, Asuka recognized she didn't have the support of the other Officers. She couldn't afford to throw around wild theories.

Asuka thought of her mother telling her: "People say Linda Trembling is not from Earth. If you write EvenStar like this, and then run it through an 8-filter, it gives you a number sequence for the date she came here. And have you noticed EvenStar has eight letters?"

She pulled one of the rogue micro bots out of her pocket. Switched it on and watched it try to burn through her finger.

This was not some spooky action at a distance.

"How's the course-correct stuff going?" Asuka asked. They had only a cycle left.

We'll figure it out.

Asuka, your sleep shift has begun, said Alpha. *Please make your way to your Crew Quarters.*

Asuka blew out her cheeks in frustration. No way she could sleep.

A karasu settled on a rusty light post with a set of red rungs attached to it. She snatched at it, and it fluttered to a higher rung. She grabbed a handhold and began to climb, slowly following the karasu higher until she reached a near-invisible hatch in the air.

"Open," she said.

The hatch opened.

The shortest way across the habitat wheel was across the center via the ladders that ran inside its hollow spokes. But because a third of the crew members were pregnant, cross-traffic had slackened, which made the hub an ideal place to sit and think.

She climbed through the hatch and found herself scaling scaffolding a story above the ground. She heard workers calling to each other, the whir of autos, and the faint beat of music: the whole city pulsing like an organ. The sky darkened as she ascended until it was night. The karasu had disappeared, and Asuka was alone on the scaffolding, stories above the ground, city lights spread out around her like a map.

A gentle bell tolled in Asuka's ear, and Alpha said: *It is A-0:30. Are you heading to bed?*

"I'll get around to it, promise," said Asuka.

You also missed your exercise session today.

"Doesn't almost dying count for anything anymore?" The previous shift, C, was supposed to be Asuka's off shift, meant for relaxation, advanced studies, or exercising. Unless she volunteered for extra work just to feel useful.

Adrenaline is not a substitute for cardiovascular activity.

"Give me a break!"

Silence. Then: *I am sorry. I didn't mean to upset you.* The AI sounded embarrassed.

Asuka passed through a platform, set her feet on it, and stretched her arms. They ached like hell.

But while we're on the subject, you also missed your last therapy appointment, said Alpha.

"Totally forgot."

I have a reminder set five and ten minutes beforehand.

"Anyway, why do I need therapy when I have you in my life? Isn't that your primary function?"

Ha-ha.

Thing was, Asuka preferred talking to Alpha than to another person about her problems. And at least she knew that absolute discretion was coded into Alpha's programming, so she could trust the AI to keep her confidence. But they were required to sit with the crew therapists once a week. No, she wasn't going to talk to her mother. No, she did not want to explain what happened. No, she didn't feel anxious about the fact she still wasn't pregnant. She felt great. Stellar. Everything was fine.

Okay. I have rescheduled you for a new therapy appointment next C shift.

"Awesome." The psych team probably had her on a watchlist.

She started climbing again. The closer she got to the center of the wheel, the less faux gravity there was. She could feel herself getting lighter.

"My mother was a member of SME," she told Alpha, and she felt panic roll over her, even knowing Alpha wouldn't—couldn't—tell anyone.

Would you like to talk about it?

"She was so against me going. What if this is why?" She stopped and shook her head, even though Alpha wouldn't be able to see the movement. "No. It can't be."

I understand, said Alpha.

If the building were real, it would be windy and cold this far up.

She watched the people walking around down below. Wondered if they had ever existed in real life.

She reached the top of the building, and the ladder ended in the middle of finger-scraping air, with a rope ladder dangling down from a helicopter. The pilot didn't turn around.

This close to the hub, her body began to float. She lifted one leg, then the other behind her, and pulled herself up.

She climbed into the helicopter, lifted the veil on New York City, and dissolved back into the hub of the spaceship. Her body spun in a lazy circle.

Most of the hub was occupied by a donut-shaped tank of water, which surrounded the longer shaft of the *Phoenix*. The tank emanated a pale-blue aura from the light filtering through. Along the sides were cabinets full of genetic material for future use. Trays and trellises of greens were affixed to the curving walls. The microgreens growing sideways gave the air a subtle freshness.

Asuka heard sniffling and paused.

There was her bunkmate, Gabriela, half hidden by a tank of water. The sedative that Hao Yu had given her earlier must have worn off a while ago.

Small globules of tears floated past Asuka's ear. The air was full of them. She felt one brush her face, stray and wet on her chin. Asuka cleared her throat. "Hey. You all right?"

Gabriela didn't seem to hear her. Her chin knocked against her chest, and her eyes fixed on nothing.

Asuka swam closer and touched Gabriela's shoulder.

A few months before launch, they'd each sat down with a designer who had created personalized DARs for everyone, but Gabriela had made her own from scratch. They all knew how to do it; they'd been doing it since they were kids, but some of the crew were savvier than others. You could tell the difference in the richness of the details, the seamlessness of how really *real* things felt. It was an art. And Gabriela was an artist.

They were underwater, and there were colorful fish everywhere. Asuka held on to Gabriela, legs drifting toward sea grass. The sound of water filled her ears. Dim sunlight filtered around her, dappling her arms. They were in a submarine drifting along the bottom of the ocean floor.

And it wasn't filthy ocean, but pure aquamarine teeming with schools of fish and unbleached coral. An octopus banged up against the glass, suckers squashed and obscene.

Out there in the water, two small figures in scuba gear swam along, investigating the coral reef teeming with life. Even with the gear on, Asuka was struck by their resemblance to Gabriela. Her sisters maybe?

"This is amazing."

"You can see my DAR?" said Gabriela, voice muffled.

"My implant's buggy."

Asuka had stopped by the Programming Mod to get it fixed, but they were all busy with system restoration after the explosion. She'd felt embarrassed for even asking.

Gabriela said, "God, I don't know what I'd do without DAR. I couldn't stand it."

"It's okay," said Asuka, realizing it was. There was also something nice about seeing into other people's DAR, once she got over the embarrassing intimacy of it. The octopus unsuckered itself and jetted away. A tiny seahorse replaced it, furling and unfurling. Asuka reached out a finger as if she might touch it.

Gabriela turned back to the ocean again, where the two figures swam along. "I should go back down. I'm supposed to cook next shift." She covered her face.

"You want me to sub for you?" Asuka asked, because it was the only thing she could offer.

"No," said Gabriela. "Get your sleep. Thanks, though."

Asuka realized she was still holding Gabriela's shoulder. She let go, and the ocean dissolved into white walls and ventilation hum. And she felt bereft, like someone had turned off music at the crescendo. The fluorescent light was dull and soulless by comparison.

Neither of them made any move to go. They sat there swimming in the soft blue light together.

Exhaustion hit: that would be the meds wearing off. She palmed the second pill from her pocket and swallowed it dry. At least she didn't feel nauseous anymore, just the echo of a headache inside her skull. She drifted toward one of the hydroponic stacks and fingered the mizuna tendrils growing there. It cheered her to have something on the *Phoenix* that reminded her of her mother's cooking. Mizuna did well in zero-g. It was one of the plants grown on the original ISS back in the day.

"Ruth says Houston is gone," said Gabriela.

Belatedly, Asuka remembered the hurricane. Everything on Earth seemed so unreal when they could only receive bursts of terse strings of curated text from them. Very little warning, for example, that the two biggest nation-sponsors of the mission, China and the United States, had been on the verge of war all this time. "Wow," said Asuka.

"They evacuated to Florida. Had to airlift their Walkie out by helicopter. Very delicate operation." So the United States had wrested control of the mission. She wondered how that was going over with China and its allies.

She wondered why Gabriela was more distressed than she was, when Gabriela wasn't American. As far as she knew, most of Gabriela's family was in the Philippines or Japan.

A coil of anxiety stirred in Asuka's gut as she considered the potential cost. Japan would be a prime target, given its U.S. bases. She thought of bombs falling on Japan's wooden temples and skyscrapers and burning its forests, and her stomach twisted. And where was her mother? She could reach out and ask her. But that would require an insurmountable amount of energy. Too much baggage to address first.

"They say it's like what happened to Manila seven years ago. Water right over the Galveston storm surge barrier."

"Right," said Asuka, remembering with a lurch that one of Gabriela's sisters had died in that storm. She thought of Kat again and wondered if, in the echo chambers of her mind, she'd be forever watching her tumble away, out of reach. In her anxiety, she tore through the mizuna leaf she'd been stroking. She stuck it in her mouth and remembered the soup Obāsan used to make.

Asuka, you should sleep now, said Alpha.

"Leave me alone," Asuka said to the air. "Not you, sorry. Alpha."

Gabriela smiled a tiny smile. "Alpha nagging you about bedtime?"

Don't get cranky with me when you are sleep deprived tomorrow.

Gabriela sighed. "I should go. I didn't want anyone to see me cry."

"Don't worry about it," said Asuka. All those years in school, they'd been so afraid of showing weakness, wanting to prove they were strong enough to withstand anything. Except strength could make you brittle. Big enough impact, and you splinter.

"I miss home," Gabriela whispered.

Her words hit like a punch. Asuka thought she was the only one who felt it. Because they were never going home. That's what they had signed up for.

"I had a fight with my mom," said Asuka. "Right before I left."

"Oh. I'm so sorry. Is she still alive?" Fair question. A lot could happen in a decade asleep.

"Yes," Asuka said. "She just—she changed. It's complicated."

Gabriela put a hand on Asuka's arm, and they were at the bottom of the ocean again. "It's okay. You don't have to talk about it."

Asuka cleared her throat. "How about you?"

"My mom's fine." And Gabriela began to cry again.

How could you leave them? Asuka wanted to ask her. *How could any of us leave?*

She wondered where the octopus was. She'd like to see it again. "I'm sorry about your sister."

"Let's not," said Gabriela. Not talk, she meant.

"Okay."

"Anyway. Thanks, Asuka." Gabriela broke away and began to kick toward the door. Without turning, she asked: "Do you ever regret coming?" She caught the ladder at the far end, let her body turn in the low not-gravity.

"Sometimes," Asuka admitted, but only after Gabriela was gone. She reached two fingers to her temple and triggered her DAR. She should be floating in the sky above the Earth, arms outstretched, surrounded by birds, but wherever she looked, puce-colored clouds pressed in. She couldn't see a thing.

She dropped DAR again, panting as if she'd run ten miles.

Susie, Ying Yue messaged. *Update from Mission Control: SME is claiming credit. They confirmed they have a sleeper agent on board.*

CHAPTER TWENTY-ONE

USA * 9 YEARS, 11 MONTHS BEFORE LAUNCH

In the dappled sunlight under the big cottonwood tree, Asuka's mom's face floated bodiless and translucent like a ghost. After Luis's death, Mom had sworn off DAR, and the handheld phone she was using had glitchy but terrible resolution. "How is school? Are you learning?"

Asuka slumped against the roots of the tree in the middle of the campus lawn. She had taken refuge here after an incomprehensible chemistry class. She called her mom hoping for some comfort, but she also didn't want to admit that she'd been right, that EvenStar was a huge mistake. That Asuka getting in here was a mistake.

"Yes," said Asuka, a wobble in her voice. "It's . . . great." Why hadn't anyone ever taught her how to take proper notes? Despite her parents' best efforts, growing up in a camp and moving to Japan had left her with a patchiness in her education that couldn't be filled by just looking things up.

She had actually tried calling her father first, but he was somewhere chaotic and could barely hear her over a siren wail and people shouting. He was working in disaster relief and was constantly on the move these days.

"I don't even know how I got in," she wailed.

"What?"

"Papa? Where are you?"

"I'll call you later," he said. But he never did.

So she called her mother, even though it was seven in the morning in Japan. As her mother blinked away sleep, Asuka couldn't help wishing, not for the first time, that she looked more like her: the full plum lips, graceful brows, the soft envelope of her eyelids. Sometimes she felt certain they resembled each other, but also, they had been mistaken before for strangers, in both the United States and Japan.

Her mother frowned. "Are you happy?"

"I'm learning more than I ever have in my life," Asuka said, which was true. She plucked at the grass with her fingers. "It's just. All the other kids here have already lived amazing lives."

In her DAR, an American crow settled in the branch above her.

"What does that even mean? They're twelve." Mom's voice, prickly and warm at the same time, settled over her like a familiar, scratchy sweater. "You've had a very exciting life yourself."

Clearly, her mom didn't pay attention to the enthusiastic media commentary about the world memory champion, the kid with a publication in *Nature*, and the one who had built a nanocomputer in her garage.

"Come home," Mom said, the thread of her voice tugging Asuka back to that farmhouse in the quiet village. "I don't like how this school is making you feel."

"I feel fine," croaked Asuka, wondering how she could know. "I'll be okay."

"I know you don't care about other people's opinions, especially mine. But you sound all . . . what is it . . . like a soft, tasty marshmallow."

Despite herself, Asuka burst out laughing.

"Tell me, do they make you run ten miles every day in your underwear when it's below freezing?"

"Oh my god, no way. Where did you hear that?"

"I went to this meeting yesterday," Mom said. She leaned forward, and half her face disappeared. Something funky with the connection. If only she wasn't so stubborn about using a vizzy. "Someone from school invited me." Mom, to Asuka's surprise, had enrolled in a PhD program last spring in ecological engineering. "It's called Save Mother Earth. They are fighting to reverse the effects of climate change using modern technology. It's very exciting. Think carbon sequestration on a global scale. Anyway, some of them were saying not-good things about Linda Trembling. Things you might not believe, but actually there's a lot of evidence."

"What are you talking about?" Across the yard, a group of candidates walked toward the dining hall, American flags embroidered on their left shoulder, led by pretty, blond Becky McMahon, Junior Olympics swimming champion. Asuka felt a yearning to get up and join them.

"Never mind," her mom said. "Focus on your studies. And remember you can come home anytime. If they try to stop you, we should have a password, like 'pineapple.'"

"Pineapple?" Asuka giggled.

"Yes, it will mean 'help me.' And I will come and get you, no matter what."

"Mom!"

Her mother ignored the embarrassment in her voice. "Do they have any good environmental science courses? There's nothing more important right now. It will be very useful to know when you go to college."

Asuka gaped at her. College? She wasn't going to go to college. Not if she were selected for the mission. Which she would be. Somehow. That's why she was here. But she was too tired to pick a fight. She should be doing her mountain of history homework. "There's Terraforming 101, I guess. It's like ecological engineering," she said instead. "Useful for the mission." She complimented herself on her maturity, for not engaging. The old Asuka would have thrown a fit.

"Mm," said her mom.

Their words were passing each other, trains on parallel tracks. Was this how conversations would be?

She tried again. "Mom. I miss Luis." Thinking how she and her brother had lain side by side in their green tent, trying not to agitate the thick, humid air that gathered at its apex. Luis whispering about Planet X, and what color the soil would be, and how the clouds would look, and if there would be clouds because maybe there weren't, until Asuka would say "shut up already."

"Me too." Her mom's voice seemed to have receded to the bottom of a well. "You don't have to do anything you don't want to. And if they try to stick a microchip in you, leave immediately and call me.

Make sure they don't drug you. If you find yourself losing time or having memory gaps, that's a bad sign."

"They're not drugging us, Mom. It's a school."

"I just—remember, if you're unhappy, you can always come home. You haven't signed a contract. You don't have to do the mission." So she had heard her earlier after all.

"I want to go."

"You think you do," said Mom, frowning. She reached out like she was trying to touch Asuka's shoulder. "But you don't have to hold yourself to promises you make yourself now. Okay? You can do anything you want."

"This is what I want."

The clouds rolled over and cloaked the sun, and Asuka pulled her jacket closer around her. She stood and brushed off the bits of grass and dirt from her knees.

"No one knows what they want at your age. Even Luis didn't know," said Mom.

And Asuka felt fire flare up in her against her will. How could she say that about Luis? She let her voice go cold: "Let's talk about this later, okay? I've got to go to dinner. Bye."

"I love you," her mom said.

And Asuka cut the connection, thinking she couldn't fail. Because her mother was wrong. She would show her.

CHAPTER TWENTY-TWO

Asuka woke at the end of A shift after a fitful sleep, panicked and sweating. She'd spent too many hours before that trawling through the public feed, looking for some clue, anything. Nothing.

The thing that gave her hope—which was a terrible thought, she should want to solve this, what was she thinking, she was thinking about her mother, no, she was *not* thinking about her mother—was that SME had offered no explanation for how they might have done it, much less infect Yaz's bots from an unfathomable distance away. And then other groups began claiming credit for it too. So there it was: a big, massive fatberg.

Mission Control still thinks SME is most likely, Ying Yue said.

But. But still. Asuka wrote and deleted several one-sentence messages to her mother, demanding answers in ALL CAPS, calling her a terrorist, telling her that they should never talk again. She sent none of them. She couldn't bring herself to read the messages she'd received, particularly not the one she'd gotten right after the explosion.

If she were honest with herself, it was no longer anger; it was fear. Because what if the message confirmed the very thing Mission Control was saying? There was no way. And yet. She couldn't bear it.

She went to breakfast late and taut as the string of a kite (Luis not letting her hold the spool as usual, because it was *his* kite). God, her head hurt.

Gabriela was in the Rec Mod alone after morning rush, drinking tea and watching something in her DAR.

"Shouldn't you be going to sleep?" Asuka asked her.

Gabriela handed her a covered plate. "Okay, *Alpha*." She smiled to show she didn't mean it. "I've been stress-baking. Saved this for my bunkie."

"Oh, wow," said Asuka, realizing in horror she might cry. It was just a really thoughtful thing to do. The scent of sweet carbohydrates and butter wafted from what looked like some kind of soft bun. Except there was no butter, and the flour was probably made out of crickets or something. Whatever, she didn't need to know. It smelled amazing.

"Hey," said Gabriela, punching her in the arm. "It might be terrible."

Asuka took a bite. Umami and salty and sweet filled her mouth. Like a Japanese curry bread. "It's amazing."

Gabriela was regarding her with a pained expression, but then she smiled again, and Asuka was left to wonder if she'd imagined it. "Did you fix the issues with your implant?"

She scratched her eyebrow as Asuka described the problem. "That's so weird. I haven't seen that before."

Asuka hesitated, but then, because Gabriela was so nice, asked if she'd be willing to take a look.

"Mochiron! Mysterious implant glitch sounds like a *great* distraction. Now?"

"No rush," lied Asuka, even though inside she was screaming *Yes, please, yes!* Gabriela was clearly exhausted. "I have to get to work anyway."

She had meant to spend her work shift skulking around the Dining Mod searching for something she'd missed, but she had job requests in her queue: one of the Ship Systems and Maintenance team members was out (morning sickness), and they had to fix a toilet's automatic flusher; the Vice Captains were requesting food be brought to the Bridge; and the Bot Shop put in a request for help, which turned out to be Lala trying to find the misplaced drill again.

"You don't have other drills?"

Lala bit the cuticle of one of her nails. "Vice Captain is going to rip me a new one if she finds out I let someone borrow it. Pretty please, Susie?" She seemed genuinely stressed about it, so Asuka promised to look again with no intention of doing so.

"Alpha, why don't you just track where all the tools are?" Asuka asked.

I can't "see" anything that isn't a smartobject, Alpha said.

"The drill isn't smart?"

It's a drill. I don't know what to tell you. I am not god. I am a very clever program residing in a quantum processor. But I would need a lot more power to know where every little thing on this ship is.

Maybe Ag A? Lala suggested via DARmessage. *Red now thinks he saw it there.* Red was a trans man from Germany who worked in Ship Systems and Maintenance and had an unusual enthusiasm for gunked-up air scrubbers and shower drains.

It wasn't in Ag A, of course.

She dismissed the job and resolutely ignored the rest in her queue. And realized she was standing in the EAM again, staring at the heavy, bright-red handle of the exterior airlock door. Asuka stepped closer. She considered the corners of the room: cameras and sensors were affixed to the ceiling so the Ship Maintenance team could support spacewalk deployment from the adjacent module. But they weren't on otherwise.

Asuka stood on her tiptoes and examined the glass eye, then the rest of the empty chamber, considering angles.

"We can't keep meeting like this. Someone will think we did it."

Asuka jumped.

Yaz leaned in the frame of the passageway, both amused and impatient.

"You were starting to freak out my team." She nodded to the cluster of cameras. "I reset it so the sensors go off if anyone gets too close."

"Sorry." Asuka fidgeted in embarrassment.

Yaz crossed her arms. "What should I tell them?"

"That I spotted a brown pelican?"

The corner of Yaz's lips turned up just a millimeter. She gave the electronic eye a thumbs-up and gestured to cut the feed.

Yaz indicated the sensors with a long, tapered finger. "So. Visual, audio, and infrared, all triggered when we're deploying bots or activating the exterior airlock." Yaz strode to a smaller hatch set in the wall. "And before you ask, I measured it last cycle. A person couldn't have squeezed down the bot chute." She opened it so Asuka could see for herself. "So? Let's say you did it."

"I didn't."

"Relax. How would you?"

Asuka considered. She knew the exterior of the *Phoenix* better than most. It would have been impossible to sneak out on an unauthorized spacewalk. She reached out and grabbed one of the helmets hanging on the wall. "During an authorized mission?"

"While the entire maintenance team was watching?"

Asuka turned the helmet over. Then she pulled up the only visual they had of the black object from the exterior cameras. It could have been anything—an unidentifiable black smear. Which is why Captain McMahon had ordered a spacewalk to investigate.

"Unusually dirty resolution," observed Yaz, turning the image this way and that.

Asuka braced herself, then pulled up the visual from her suit. She heard herself propose the race. Kat accepting. Again, Kat scampered off, faster than Asuka even with the tool kit strapped to her chest. Those tool kits were cumbersome. When Asuka was doing a job, she preferred to remove and anchor it to the ship, so she could move better. Kat's arms were longer, so she didn't have that problem. Which is why Kat had grabbed the tool kit.

Asuka's gloves came down in her field of view, climbing the ladder. They heard glee in Kat's voice as she closed in on their destination. Sweat prickled Asuka's palms.

If only she hadn't been so slow, she'd have—what?

And yet. If she had been faster, maybe she could have, well, *something*.

Kat said: "Where did you say it was, Ying Yue? Hang on, I'm caught on something. Okay, but I'm telling you—"

Then, a bright flash as Asuka glanced over, and a piece of hull hurtled toward her. Complete loss of visual.

Asuka clenched her hands.

"What was she saying?" Yaz stretched her hips. She was at the stage of pregnancy where any standing position was awkward.

Asuka replayed the clip again, then switched to the feed from Kat's suit. They watched it multiple times to be sure.

There was no object in Kat's visual.

"Did you see it when you were out there?" Yaz asked.

Asuka shook her head. "I didn't get there in time. But it was on the exterior cams. How could it not be there?"

She flexed her fingers gloved in smartfabric. "What if—" She stopped. "What if there was never a box, and all we saw was an augmentation? DAR doesn't work outside, so when she got there, she wouldn't have seen it."

"If that were the case, where was the bomb?"

Asuka looked back at the suits again, at the neat rows of boots and gloves and gleaming helmets. She didn't want to say her next thought out loud. It was too horrible. "What if it was on *Kat*?"

"Inside her suit?" Yaz grimaced. "You think Kat did this intentionally?" She pulled up the exterior feed, slowing it down till it crawled millisecond by excruciating millisecond through Kat's last moments.

Asuka put her knuckle in her mouth and bit down. She didn't want to watch it. She had to.

There was the black object, visible on the exterior camera, and Kat looking around for the thing she couldn't see. As she leaned in close to the side of the *Phoenix*, the large tool kit strapped to her chest touched the ship. The magnets on the outside of the kit stuck to the hull. Unaware at first, Kat continued feeling around with her fingers, trying to find the anomaly. Then, realizing she had snagged, she tried to yank free, when there was a small flash, then a much bigger one, and the entire Dining Mod exploded outward.

"Shit," Asuka said, yanking her hand out of her mouth. She'd bitten through the glove. "The tool kits." She stared at the four remaining spare kits standing on their sides in the cabinet, and the empty space for the fifth.

"She couldn't have known," Asuka said. Kat, who had been moping about breaking her ugly ceramic cat. Kat, who had insisted on telling her the entire plot of entertainment sims Asuka had absolutely zero interest in; who loved dramas, the cornier the better. Who said: "This is more than the opportunity of a lifetime. It's the opportunity of all the lives ever lived on Earth." *Who do you think you are?* Asuka had thought. *Captain Kirk?*

"Why not?" said Yaz, rubbing her stomach again. "Oy. Stop kicking my kidneys."

Asuka didn't understand how Yaz could be so calm. "She believed in the mission!"

Yaz rubbed her hair stubble. "You think one of the ready crew stuck it on her? Or what, she got unlucky and grabbed the wrong kit?"

Unless . . . the spare tool kits hung in a neat row on the wall.

Careful, Asuka, said Alpha, sounding more worried than usual.

Asuka grabbed the closest kit. Each one was designed with two rows of tools, one on each side, so that the tools could individually be removed and reinserted through loops. The tools were attached to the kit by a long wire, so they couldn't float away if dropped outside. A zipper ran around the middle, so you could undo the wires and switch out tools.

"Wait," said Yaz. Asuka heard her take a step back. Her voice was sharp. "Stop, Susie."

Asuka—

She unzipped the tool kit and opened it gently like a butterfly.

The inside was packed with explosives.

"Put it down on the floor," said Yaz in a quiet voice. "Very. Slowly."

CHAPTER TWENTY-THREE

The gestation of a cuckoo was typically shorter than its nest mates, leading it to hatch earlier. At that point, the parent would begin to feed the cuckoo chick. The cuckoo would grow, and once strong enough, when its foster parents were away, it would push the other unhatched eggs out of the nest, enabling it to claim all of the food for itself—not quite as brutal, at least, as the honeyguide, which would stab the other chicks to death as they hatched. All the while, the foster parents would continue to feed it, answering its demanding cries even after it had outgrown them.

CHAPTER TWENTY-FOUR

Asuka set the kit down with extraordinary care. It took all her concentration not to drop it, particularly given that her hands were shaking so badly it was a wonder her fingerbones weren't rattling.

Is everything okay? Alpha asked, unable to see anything beyond the movements of her body and the way she was, any moment, going to have a heart attack or something. *Tell me. What is happening?*

"Okay. Now back away," said Yaz. The air was glue, and Asuka was swimming through it. She backed up until she felt Yaz grip her shoulder—

They stood at the back of a large, open airplane hangar, a fighter jet parked about twenty meters away. The wall of the module was now a bright-red painted line across the ground. And in front of that line, on the rough concrete floor, sat the tool kit.

Which was actually a bomb.

A karasu perched on top of it.

In a single, decisive motion, Yaz yanked her back, through a small door behind them. The door slammed shut.

Then Yaz's hand was gone, and they were in the adjacent module. "Alpha. Seal and remove all atmosphere from that module. *Now.*"

In the passageway, Yaz stood with her eyes closed. There was movement beneath the lids. Her mouth tightened. Then her eyes snapped open, and she loomed over Asuka, fury plain. "What the actual fuck is wrong with you? You could have gotten us all killed. If you've got a death wish, happy travels. But don't take me with you."

Asuka wanted to melt right into the air duct. Humiliation rose inside her in a wave so strong she gagged on it. Because Yaz was right.

Replaying it in her mind, she realized how ridiculous she'd been, trying to be the hero. And she could have blown up the entire ship.

Yaz pushed into the control room. She left Asuka in the passageway, pressing the heels of her palms against her cheeks, trying to erase the heat.

Are you all right, Asuka? Alpha asked. *I'm here for you if you want to talk about it.*

"I don't," said Asuka. She couldn't stay in the hall, like a child hiding in her bedroom. No way to slink off and sulk on a ship, because sooner or later she'd have to face Yaz again. Better to apologize now. So she squared her shoulders and entered the control room. But Yaz was already in motion, issuing orders. They'd pumped the atmosphere out of the EAM and were readying a big bot, Daffodil, to go in and take the tool kits apart. Yaz brushed off her words with a grunt, and Asuka stood there, wanting so badly to help and feeling completely, utterly useless.

Ying Yue came in from the wheel, followed by A.M. and two other Officers on their heels.

"What's going on?" A.M. wanted to know.

"Captain," Yaz said. "You shouldn't be here. It's dangerous."

"I seem to recall this was my team only a cycle ago. Still is, in fact," said Ying Yue, a low warning in her voice. Strange to see Ying Yue and Yaz at odds. They had been close since Final Training and spent many of their off shift hours playing sim games and studying together. Something unspoken passed between them now, and then Ying Yue turned away, releasing Yaz from her gaze, seizing on Asuka instead. "Susie. I'd like a full report. Wait. Not here—"

A.M. started to follow, but Ying Yue raised a splayed hand, not quite touching their chest. "Last I checked, we're off course, and you're supposed to be working on it."

They crossed their arms. "As your new First Vice Captain, don't I have a right to hear this?"

"We all do!" added Valentina, the Russian Vice Captain for Ship Systems and Maintenance who liked to call Asuka in to clean up the toilet overflow issues.

"I need you all to clear out right now," snapped Yaz.

"She can't order us around like that," Valentina started to say, but Ying Yue was already moving to the door. She grabbed Asuka and pulled her along, and the Officers were forced to follow if they wanted to learn anything.

They walked down the aisle of a moving train, rice fields just a green blur out the windows on either side. Passed through the door at the end of the car, and they were in a station. Through another door, and another, and they were in a small house with dark wooden floors.

Ying Yue let go, and they stood in a stuffy, dark module lit with emergency lights. Shadows gathered like cobwebs around spartan, empty, white cribs. There was a pile of rumpled blankets on the floor, evidence of recent trysts. The Nursery Mod was a convenient place for privacy on a ship with little of it — except that it wasn't actively in use, and therefore overly warm. Despite the cold of space, heat loss by radiation was slow, and the ship insulation was good enough that the climate controls were constantly deployed to shed heat.

Ying Yue stooped and grasped at one of the blankets. Asuka intercepted and handed it to her. Ying Yue began absently to fold it. She stared off at nothing with eyes underlined by the dark smudges of sleep deprivation.

"Well," said A.M. "Here we all are."

Asuka glanced at Ying Yue, uncertain if she should begin.

"Come on! What's with the secrecy?"

Valentina added: "Does it have anything to do with the bombing in Fuzhou?"

And the third said, "Japan's on the American side."

"Shut up, all of you!" It was the first time Asuka had ever heard Ying Yue raise her voice — and it was surprisingly effective. They all fell silent.

Ying Yue pinched the bridge of her nose, then sank into a rocking chair. "A.M. can stay. Everyone else out. Except Asuka. No discussion! *Out.*"

And the others complied, though they grumbled about it.

When they were gone, Ying Yue nudged a chair over in A.M.'s direction. "We need to figure out a way to work together."

"I think I've been pretty fucking cooperative," said A.M., taking the seat after the briefest of hesitations. "Considering."

Asuka leaned against a crib, wiping sweat from her hairline with her sleeve.

"You're on the wrong side of history if you believe that."

"It's not what I believe; it's what I *know*."

"What you know." Ying Yue let out a whuff of air that sounded like "ha!" "You don't know as much as you think you do."

It dawned on Asuka that they were not talking about the bomb at all.

"I didn't want to waste our precious time on this, but it seems like we have to," said Ying Yue. "So: do we have a problem?"

A.M. jumped up and jabbed a finger in Ying Yue's face. "Yes. My problem is you shouldn't even be the Captain right now after you went behind Tony's back like a fucking coward."

Tony was what friends sometimes called Becky McMahon—short for "automaton," on account of her extraordinary discipline. Everyone else usually called her "McMahon," as if the formality of the last name might create some buffer between them and her. She was the sort of person who ran precise seven-minute miles, no faster, no slower, who wouldn't hesitate to elbow you if you were in the way of that. Not that you could ever prove it was intentional.

A.M. was still going: ". . . But if you want us to follow you, you'd better wake the fuck up and fucking lead. *Own* the title. And also, while we're at it, trust is a two-way street, you know. You keep telling me to trust you, but *you* don't trust *me*. If you would tell me what's going on, maybe I could even fucking help you!"

Asuka cleared her throat. They both seemed to suddenly remember she was there.

Ying Yue took advantage of the interruption to master herself. There were bright-pink spots in her cheeks. Then after a minute, she said: "Okay. That was fair. Seventy-five percent of it, anyway."

A.M. sank back into their chair and buried their face in their hands.

"I'm sorry about Becky."

A muffled laugh bubbled up. "Thank you," they said. "You know, you're the first person to say that? Guess I was her only real friend. Which I get. She was a fucking pain in the ass. *I* didn't even like her half the time."

Ying Yue chuckled too. "Listen. I'll tell you everything." She gave A.M. a quick summary from Mission Control's suspicions, the missing records in the Shop, the rogue bots, and the bombs that they had found.

A.M. was silent as they digested it all.

Ship noises infiltrated the mod: a loud debate as two people walked by in the passageway about which made the better DARgame, basketball or cricket, the rattle of a water pipe that should be inspected.

"I'll kill them," A.M. said.

"What?" asked Ying Yue.

A.M. turned and cut Asuka with a scalpel-like gleam in their dark brown eyes. "Who do you think did this?"

Asuka tugged on her ponytail. "I—I'm not sure yet. I think it was someone who has done a spacewalk. Familiar with the protocol. And who knew we were doing the spacewalk, that we had taken the bait." She pulled up her list. Which was a third of the crew.

"Besides the Captain, only the Bots and Drones Operations team knew about this mission."

Ying Yue made an indignant noise, like of course they'd blame Ying Yue's old squad.

Asuka held up a finger. "Actually, no. Alpha put out a call to all spacewalk-certified crew." She thought of poor Kat, who always jumped at the chance to do a spacewalk, same as Asuka.

"You forgot to include someone who believes in that SME shit," said A.M. "That has to narrow it, right?"

"If someone on board is working for SME, I assume they've kept those views to themselves," Ying Yue said. "The way Becky didn't go around broadcasting she was a mackey."

A.M. dismissed this. "MAC was more cultural than belief for her."

Which felt thin as hell, and anyway, A.M. wasn't American, so what did she understand about MAC. But Asuka decided to let it go. "None of the groups that claimed responsibility have been able to explain how they did it or what happened."

"Well, then. We haven't narrowed it much at all. It could even have been one of you." A.M. pursed their lips.

"I didn't do it," said Asuka.

"Me neither," said Ying Yue.

"Great. We'll form a club." A.M. squinted at Asuka's list. "It definitely wasn't Chigozie or Selma."

"Why not?" said Ying Yue. "We shouldn't eliminate anyone at this point, just because they're friends. We *all* know each other. We grew up together."

A.M. rolled their eyes. "Well, then. Here's another theory: we've got a world war that just happened to start same time as the explosion. Maybe that's not a coincidence. What if your government ordered one of your people to remove Tony from command?"

"One of 'my people'?"

"Everyone knows the Chinese were upset you weren't Captain."

Ying Yue gaped at them. "They—we—had a legitimate issue with the fact China wasn't being treated as an equal sponsor after contributing the same amount of funding as America did to the mission."

"I'm not saying *you* did it," said A.M. "But you said we can't eliminate anyone out of personal feelings. So?"

Asuka understood why Ying Yue would be offended. She also didn't disagree that they had to consider all possibilities. She tried to steer back to the original topic. "The problem is, we don't even know what they were trying to achieve with all this." Were they trying to kill Becky? Or the entire crew?

I can see you are stressed. Shall I tell you about the navigation capabilities of the Manx shearwater? Alpha suggested.

"Not now." She began to stuff her fears into the box one by one.

"Well, thank you for bringing me in" said A.M. "I'd better get back to work. But please keep me updated." Distantly, Asuka heard the airlock shut.

She thought of the late Captain, and Lala telling her darkly: *She was no good for the mission.* Of the three people who'd died, she seemed to have the most enemies. And what was she doing in the Dining Mod in the first place?

Becky McMahon had been the sort of perfect golden child with a perky ponytail and dimples when she smiled. Deceptively angelic looking. The teachers loved her, anyway.

Lala wasn't sorry Becky was dead. Ying Yue wasn't either. Who knew what other enemies she had?

"What are you thinking, Susie?" Ying Yue asked, and Asuka jumped. She thought Ying Yue had left with A.M., but no, she was still sitting there, watching Asuka, her face shadowed in the dim light.

A message appeared from Yaz. She'd successfully deactivated the bombs. Did their Alt Detective want to come and take a look?

CHAPTER TWENTY-FIVE

USA * 9 YEARS, 10 MONTHS BEFORE LAUNCH

The leaves of the cottonwood tree in the middle of the quad turned brilliant amber and flame. Then, overnight, they dropped to the ground: a thick carpet of dry husks, brown and brittle beneath their shoes. Even so, the weather was unseasonably warm and wet, as if there was such a thing as unseasonable anymore. And miraculously, Asuka continued to hang on. Not miraculously—it was thanks in no small part to her friends, who shared notes and took the time to explain things to her and made sure she didn't oversleep for her classes.

But one day in robotics class, Lala didn't show, and Asuka was left to struggle through the exercise of designing and printing a temperature-sensing nano bot alone. She was only halfway done by the time the class ended. Professor Wu stood over her while Asuka mumbled an incoherent explanation of her design.

"I admit, I'm not sure what you're trying to do here," the Professor said. "Finish it this weekend. I'll have to mark you incomplete until you do."

Crushed, Asuka gathered her belongings and slinked out of class. She texted Lala a few times, trying not to make it sound like an accusation: *Where were you? Everything okay?* But nothing.

Hours later, in the grand old wood-paneled dining hall, she and Treena ran into Lala sporting a long, medicated skin patch across half her face—and a foul expression that matched that of the elderly person half buried under a magnificent ginger cat in the oil painting behind her.

"Hey," Asuka said. "What happened to you?"

Lala tore the soft part out of a crusted roll and placed it in her mouth. "America happened."

Asuka slid onto the bench across from Lala, ignoring Treena's sour expression. Treena didn't like Lala. They were both candidates for the United States, so Treena said they couldn't be friends, even though the United States had five reserved spots. It didn't help that Lala made fun of Treena's strategy of selfies and near-live posting about EvenStar life.

"America," said Treena. "That's funny."

"Is it?"

"I mean, we're candidates for the U.S. seat, so yeah," said Treena.

"You're right, it is funny. Ha ha ha." Then Lala's face snapped up to Treena, suddenly afraid. "Don't post that, please."

Treena's fingers stilled.

"Treena won't post anything," Asuka said, shooting Treena a warning look. She liked her roommate, but their lack of filter was sometimes exhausting.

Treena held up their hands in peace and exaggerated swiping right to clear their feed.

"Are you okay, though?"

Lala gave her a thumbs-up. "Just can't wait to get off this rock." She shoveled a spoonful of mashed potatoes into her mouth, then grimaced in pain.

Sensing the need to change the subject, Asuka said, "Robotics was terrible today. I'm pretty sure Professor Wu wanted to strangle me."

Silence while Lala chewed another piece of bread. She swallowed, then said: "Look. Don't take this the wrong way, but I think I'd like to eat by myself right now. I don't have the bandwidth to help you with your problems."

"Oh, yeah. Sure. I wasn't—I mean, yeah, of course." Face burning, Asuka stood. She shoved the rest of her falafel in her mouth and went to dump her tray.

"She's kind of *much* sometimes," Treena said, as they scraped their plates into the compost bin. "You were just trying to be nice."

"It's fine," Asuka said. "I have my first sim team scheduled in half an hour anyway."

She left the dining hall. In the gathering dusk, the old cottonwood tree in the middle of the lawn loomed monstrous and huge. An orange moon rose through its branches. She trudged across campus past the engineering complex to the big concrete sim building near the lake.

Did something happen to Lala? she asked Miki.

Heard she was in a fight. Miki's words floated white and glowing in front of her.

Wha??? Hard to imagine nerdy Lala getting into a fight with anyone.

A brief image of Miki shrugging flashed across her vision. *Ganbatte with sim!*

Asuka tightened her scarf against the cool autumn air. Anxiety over her first sim team session began to eclipse any thoughts of Lala. The kids who had already done it were badly shaken, though they refused to say why. One kid in the dorm was almost catatonic and dropped out a few days after. No team so far had scored more than five out of ten. It would be Asuka's luck if this tanked her out of the program.

Nine other kids—her sim teammates—were waiting outside the gym. To her horror, one of them was Ruth, whom she had been avoiding for weeks after an acidic exchange of words following chemistry class that culminated in Asuka mobbing her with a swarm of RealStarlings. Which wasn't exactly mature, but she was twelve and allowed to act like it sometimes, right?

Ruth seemed too nervous to fight. She shivered and stamped her feet.

"You guys hear what happened to Lala and Winnie?" someone said.

"Yeah," said Ruth. "Terrible."

"They got into a fight?" Asuka said tentatively. Embarrassed she was the last to know about her friend.

Ruth snorted. "If you want to call getting jumped by some mackeys 'getting into a fight.'"

Asuka froze. "What?"

"Yeah. Fortunately, Winnie was coming from cricket scrimmage, and she had her bat. Clocked one of them bad enough to send him to the hospital. And then some delivery worker jumped off his bike and pulled a gun on the guys."

"Woah," Asuka said.

"Racist fucks," Ruth concluded.

Asuka started to compose a message to Lala, but before she could figure out what to say, the black metal door opened, and a teacher in a navy blue EvenStar polo gestured for them to come in. The building was constructed like a giant warehouse: three stories high and unfinished inside. She caught an acrid whiff of pee and sweat. In the center of the room was a large metal pod like a submarine.

Ruth sidled up to Asuka. "It's okay if you're scared, killdeer."

"Nah. I'm looking forward to this," lied Asuka.

The teacher's DARtag confirmed this was J. Li, the woman who oversaw the Sim program and co-led the EvenStar Transgender Mentorship Program. Her nose was crooked, and she exuded coolness, from the tips of her dangling skull earrings to her chocolate donut socks. "Call me Coach Li," she told them. "I've been charged with evaluating how you do under pressure, and teaching you ways to deal with it. I'll be working with you each month. During the exercise, you'll need to keep your vizzies on full opacity."

A few people reached up to make the adjustment to their DAR headgear.

"Your vizzy is older than you are," muttered Ruth.

Asuka was still using Luis's old headgear, even though they'd all been given new ones when they arrived.

"If you remove your vizzies at any time, you will be disqualified and receive a zero." Coach Li paused, checking to make sure they were all paying attention. They were. "Don't be scared. Good luck."

They filed inside the chamber, and the door shut behind them. They were in a medium-sized room with a soft green carpet, a bureau, a desk with a chair, a bookshelf of old moldering volumes, large plants along one wall, and a bed. On one wall were portholes, which gave the impression they were on a ship. A sinking ship.

"What the hell?" said Ruth, standing right next to Asuka. They looked down at their feet. Cold water was seeping in under the door. Asuka's socks were already soaked. Panic began to rise.

"Wait, this is real," said another, one of the Canadian reps.

"I can't swim!"

A memory of treading water, ash falling. Of Luis, sinking down. Asuka's heart hammered in her chest.

No. This wasn't a pool. The water wasn't so deep. They wouldn't put them in danger.

She felt faint.

"You okay?" Ruth asked. "Your face is kinda pasty."

Asuka shut her eyes and thought of her mom's jewelry box, that handful of pearls. She began to count them. One, two, three. She got to ten and slammed the lid down.

"I'm fine." She went straight to the door and tried it. Locked, of course. "Find something to open the door," she told the others. There was a desk in the corner.

She checked all the drawers: a paper clip, a diary, a ballpoint pen. She went back to the door with the paper clip and the pen and picked the lock without success. The water was at their ankles. There was a decorative curtain hanging around the window. She ripped it down and stuck it under the door to try to slow the water.

"That's not going to work," Ruth said. She was rifling through a bookshelf. As she went through each book, she dropped it on the floor, heedless of the water.

"What are you doing?" Asuka asked.

"I don't know," she said. "If this were a game, there'd be something hidden in one of these, like a key."

Some of the other kids were battering the door with their fists. The water was up to their knees.

"Stop that. Start searching the room," Asuka told them. No one listened.

Ruth waded up and began shoving them toward different parts of the room. "You, check that table. Check the plants. Check the closet."

The kid who couldn't swim was trying to climb the bookshelf. She was sobbing.

"It's a simulation," Asuka told her.

"It's real water, isn't it?"

Asuka tried battering the doorknob with a chair. No luck. The water was at her waist. She thought of her mother's arms, holding her. Counted again until she was okay. Then she studied the room again.

There, set in the ceiling, was an air vent. Big enough to crawl through. She nearly missed it, because it was partially behind the bookshelf. She shoved the bookshelf aside. Ruth ran over and helped her move the bureau under it. The water was now shoulder high. Kids were shouting for help.

"Don't take your vizzy off!" Ruth shouted at one as she helped boost Asuka on top of the bureau.

Asuka used the paper clip she'd taken from the desk drawer and began to painstakingly unscrew the vent. She knew they were on the right track when the screws turned easily.

Ruth swam over, towing the girl who couldn't swim, who was clinging to her neck with locked arms. "If they find out I can't swim, they'll expel me," she was saying.

"Chill," said Ruth. "You don't need to swim in space."

The cover of the vent detached, and Asuka hoisted the girl up. Everyone was crowding now, wanting to go next. They got them through one by one. The water was nearly to the duct. It was freezing. They had to press their faces to the ceiling to get air.

Asuka thought, *Is this how it was for Luis when—* She pushed the thought down.

"This whole thing is kind of fucked up, isn't it?" said Ruth.

"Get in," Asuka said, pointing toward the vent.

"You going to make it?"

"I'll make it." She pushed Ruth closer to the vent. She didn't mention the weird tug she felt to stay there in the water, until there was nothing left but to let it fill her lungs. It was like her shoes were full of cement, and her heart too. "Don't underestimate me." But she was talking to herself, not to Ruth.

"Killdeer." Ruth laughed and then coughed as she inhaled some water. She pulled herself up into the ceiling. "Good thing I've been doing bench presses." Her pink prosthetic leg dangled, and Asuka cupped the plastic calf and foot and gave her a boost.

The water lapped the ceiling, but Asuka felt so heavy, so tired. She couldn't move her arms to pull herself up.

Out of the periphery of her vision, she thought she saw Luis struggling in the water, but no, it was the chair bobbing against the ceiling.

You just gonna give up? she thought she heard Luis say.

Never.

Her terror was white noise. But she pulled herself up into the vent.

She gulped air, but she was okay.

She tumbled out of the vent onto a thick mat. Coach Li congratulated them for getting everyone out, but Asuka's ears were ringing too much to hear. The second she could, she was out of there, stumbling around the side of the building, where she vomited against the concrete wall.

"Are you okay?" Ruth had followed her.

Asuka could feel the adrenaline now in her veins. She shivered.

"You need a hot shower."

"It's fine," said Asuka.

"You were kind of amazing."

She hadn't expected a compliment from Ruth. She didn't know what to say.

"I was scared shitless," Ruth added.

"Me too."

"Sure fooled me."

And Asuka burst into tears, like a storm breaking through a levee. Ruth didn't ask her why or make fun of her. She rubbed her back, and when Asuka was done, she said: "Don't worry. I won't tell anyone." And then she walked Asuka home, talking about her wacky, hilarious aunt who had helped her apply to EvenStar, and how she missed her dads and soft brioche French toast on Sunday mornings.

"I can't believe we have to do this every month," said Ruth, before they separated to go to their respective dorms.

But Asuka realized she wasn't dreading it. She felt, instead, that old mulish defiance rising in her. They thought they could freak her out, but she'd beaten them, and she would beat them again. She'd been through the worst possible things, already, in real life. Make-believe couldn't hurt her.

It was only later, after Asuka took a hot shower and remembered to send a message to Lala that got no reply, that she sat down at her desk and checked the updated sim team rankings.

Nine out of ten.

And she thought, *Well shit*. Surviving. That's what she was good at.

CHAPTER TWENTY-SIX

If there was any residual anger in Yaz's face, Asuka couldn't find it. Apparently, her temper burned through quickly and completely.

She was surprised to see Lala waiting in the passageway with Yaz. Though it made sense—of course a Bot Engineer would be the closest to the ship's expert on dismantling bombs.

Lala grinned at Asuka like someone had offered her a rare and bloody steak. "Here we go again, eh?"

"We're repressurizing now," Yaz told them.

"And you're sure it's safe?" Ying Yue asked.

"Daffodil removed all incendiary material."

"That's my baby," said Ying Yue.

Alpha informed them the module was safe for entry. Asuka and Lala entered practically on tiptoe anyway, because they were, after all, dealing with bombs. And who knew what Alpha knew about that. Sweat slid down the back of Asuka's shirt.

"I couldn't find your drill, by the way," Asuka said, because she felt like she might scream if one of them didn't say something.

Lala darted a glance at the cameras. "Yeah, uh, don't worry about that." She knelt and nudged the tangle of wires and snipped ends with her finger. They both braced themselves. Nothing happened. Lala seemed to accept this as good enough for an all clear and began examining the bomb.

Asuka checked one of the others, wishing she could tell if a bomb was safe to handle. She'd have to have faith in Yaz's team.

They piled everything into crates and carried it all to the Nursery Mod for further examination away from nosy crew.

"Oh, this old place." Lala smiled in recognition. "You want in?" She offered Asuka an unlit match between her fingers.

Asuka reached for it, and it burst into flame and disappeared — and they stood in the living room of a sunny brownstone with large windows facing out to a residential street. Soft, rose-colored walls and framed family photos. A big tree out front full of yellowing leaves.

"Welcome to the Williams's house." Lala spread her arms to capture it all. "My dad'll be home from work any minute with some killer Szechuan food from our favorite place down the street." She looked around again, and her smile faded. "Anyway. Yeah."

They set the deactivated bombs on an antique wooden table. Asuka started to remove her Alt multitool from her waistband, but Lala was already emptying a whole bag of tools on the surface between them.

They began carefully pulling the first two tool kits apart into their components.

"Winnie saved my life once," Lala remarked. Her voice wobbled only a little. "I wish I could have returned the favor."

Winnie had been supremely driven. The type to wake up at five and get in more than twice her quota of exercise before breakfast. The type who started with the hardest homework first and churned through everything from Comparative Constitutional Law to Thermodynamics like it was nothing. Not like Ruth and Asuka, who had to bribe themselves with clandestine sweets to get through their problem sets. Asuka glanced over at Lala, who was hugging herself.

She dropped her gaze. This was her moment to say the things she should have said years ago. "Lala, I . . ." Except, what? What could she say? Time had already warped things. The right words had crumbled into dust by now. She should have done something then, and she hadn't. In the aftermath, she'd been so swept up in her new friendship with Ruth, she'd never gone beyond a sympathetic, generic "How are you doing?" She'd let the space grow between them. "I'm sorry."

Lala cleared her throat. "Don't know what you're even talking about." The way she said it, though, she knew. She straightened.

"Alpha. Jesus. Turn down the temperature, please. It's sticky in here. And lights up too. What are we doing here working in the dark?"

Of course, Lala.

"So what are we looking at?" Asuka asked.

Lala examined the components. She ripped a block of something encased in plastic out of the device. "Here's the incendiary material." She hummed and examined the casing more closely.

"Right before the explosion, Alpha had postponed some people's mealtimes because of a sensor issue," Asuka said. "People figured it was just the sensors glitching again, but what if there was an actual leak? Do you think that might have anything to do with this?"

Lala chewed the cuticle of her pinky, considering. "Could be."

Outside the brownstone window, a karasu began to caw from the branch of an old beech tree. It watched them.

Lala picked through the wires. "This looks like a receiver for remote control."

She and Asuka looked at each other. The bombs were proof enough, but here was additional evidence this wasn't the work of some faraway organization. One of the crew had stood there and pulled the trigger.

Asuka shivered despite the warmth of the Nursery. "Any idea what the range of the trigger was?"

Lala leaned over and detached a piece of wire. "This is a radio transmitter, which makes sense, since DAR doesn't work great outside." She conferred with Alpha a minute, then said: "Maybe a couple modules."

"So they had to have been standing near the Dining Mod."

Asuka chewed her lip. That included Kitchen, Medical, the Exercise Mod, Ag A and Ag B, Crew Quarters C and D, Bot Shop, and the Sanitation Mod. But ruled out the Bot and Drones crew—the Drone Ops Mod was a quarter of the wheel away from the Dining Mod. That still left a long list of possible crew.

Did anyone leave the Drone Ops Mod during the last spacewalk? she asked Ying Yue.

Just Yaz. She went to the clinic, because she was having back pain.

In the middle of a mission?

Like I said. It was bad. She couldn't concentrate. But she came right back after the explosion to help.

A car outside began to honk; it was stuck behind an automated delivery truck.

So Yaz would have been in range during the explosion.

"Cold?" Lala asked.

Asuka's arms were covered in goose bumps.

It doesn't mean anything, Asuka told herself. Twenty-two other crew could have done it. She forced herself to bend over the table and resume pulling the device to pieces.

"So . . . is it weird for you that Ruth and I are together?" The question caught Asuka off-guard. Their heads were a whisper apart, Lala's voice just a murmur, as if she were afraid to wake a ghost.

"No." Once upon a time, a kid who didn't get along with Asuka didn't have a chance with Ruth. She bent down and teased out a wire. Pretended to be very interested in examining it.

"I just mean, you two used to be like a pair of shoes," said Lala.

"We were. Then we weren't." That damn karasu was still sitting in the tree. It flapped its wings at her.

"I thought it was kind of sweet the way you two stuck together when everyone was knives out for each other. But obviously now I get it. She's different. I mean, she marches to her own drum. Come on, give me that."

They worked in silence for a while, Lala's words looping on repeat in her brain. Wasn't everyone different? Breathing with their own pair of lungs, living in their own bubble of experience. And put that way, how could she ever hope to understand why someone would want to do this?

She took the parts and began to sort the materials into four different cribs made of cherry wood: wires, tubes, circuits, et cetera. She already recognized some of it from the list of items Alpha had noted as removed from the Shop without proper record. And *those* pieces may have come from Ag Mod, *that* from the Lab. Everything was sticky with the ship's ubiquitous lime-green putty. It made her fingers smell like cheese.

Asuka shut her eyes, saw Kat's body going to pieces, and felt her chest constrict.

You seem stressed, Asuka. Shall I tell you about the life cycle of the messenger pigeon? As if to punctuate, the karasu was replaced by a pigeon on the sill, coo-cooing.

"You already did that one," said Asuka, and the pigeon disappeared.

I wasn't sure you were listening before.

Lala squeezed her shoulder. "We will figure this out." When Asuka glanced again, the pigeon had become a robin. Its red breast caught the afternoon sun, and her mood lifted a fraction. Robins always cheered her up.

Hey, lady! A message from Gabriela appeared. *Genki?*

Asuka smiled. It used to bother her how good Gabriela's Japanese was. But at least it was something they shared.

Un, nantoka. Why are you awake?

Couldn't sleep. I swapped for the end of B cook shift. Come and keep me company later? Don't wanna be alone. I will feed you well.

Sure.

Yay! I'll be there starting B-6:30.

Lala tossed a stick of combustible material into the air and caught it.

And it occurred to Asuka that Lala was spacewalk certified. She'd known about the mission. She evidently knew about bombs. "What happened between you and the Captain?"

Lala stopped playing catch and set down the package wrapped in self-sealing plastic. "It had nothing to do with this."

"Tell me anyway."

The late afternoon sun pooled on the wooden floor, soft and mellow. It reminded Asuka of the taste of scrambled eggs, hot and buttery from a cast-iron pan. She felt an ache in her gut for the things they'd left behind. Then a cloud moved across the sky, darkening the room.

"It's not uncommon to miscarry," said Lala. "Of course, I know that. Like it's not weird to have trouble conceiving after spending ten years in chemically induced hibernation."

Asuka tried to keep her face neutral. She sat down in an overstuffed armchair that was not as soft as it appeared.

"After I lost the first one, Mission Control recommended putting me on special meds as a precaution for when I got pregnant the second time. Some drug approved in the last ten years. They sent a formula for us to print. So I started taking it. Then I hear Captain's approved a software upgrade patch to the pharmaceutical printer. And guess what, the formula's changed. And then I lost the second one. You get what I'm saying?"

"You think the Captain did something?"

"I . . . don't know. I was upset." Grief thickened her voice. "I fought so hard to be here. I know we all did. But people like McMahon and Ying Yue—did they ever have to chop off their toes to fit a shoe?" She twisted the wire into coils. "If I had stayed on Earth, there were lots of things I could have done."

"Run for President," joked Asuka, because that was something they used to say about Lala.

"Sure," she said. "Maybe. I knew I could be something. But then I looked up at the night sky, and I felt in my body that there was so much more out here than on a little ball of dirt and water and gas— where everything goes around and around, and history is just the illusion of forward motion. I just want to know the *feeling*, Susie, to be somewhere else. To own a whole world, with nobody to make the rules but us." Lala began to wind a coil of wire. "See, you've been asking the wrong question."

"What's the right question?"

"Why did you come, Susie?"

They stared at each other. Asuka could hear the thrum of the generator and the air cycling and the water circulating in the pipes. Her mouth was very dry.

Then Lala giggled. "You're so tense!"

Asuka was saved from responding by a message from Yaz that the Dining Mod had been repressurized, and she should come inspect it before people tramped all over it.

"You go ahead. I can finish this," said Lala. When Asuka hesitated, she made a shooing motion. "Come on. Do you or don't you trust me?"

"I trust you," Asuka lied.

CHAPTER TWENTY-SEVEN

Rain drummed against the glass windows of the hallway of the gymnasium, casting dappled gray shadows on the wood-paneled wall opposite. A line of EvenStar candidates extended down the corridor, waiting for their semiannual physical. Asuka shuffled in her spot behind Miki and Treena, glancing back every so often at the entrance. Still no Ruth.

Somehow, from the moment Asuka had crawled dripping from the simulation tank, they'd become inseparable. Treena referred to Ruth as Asuka's BFF with only thinly veiled jealousy.

"Smart girl," said Treena. "Not like I want to wait in line either for this crap."

Miki shrugged. "I don't mind. I've got to study for this terrible maths exam either way."

"You'll totally ace that. I don't know why you're even stressed about it. Meanwhile, I've got to get through this problem set. What did you get for question number three?" They were taking a musicology elective together, and Treena was always asking Miki for help. "Can you look at what I got and tell me if I'm in the ballpark?"

Miki caught the invisible file and skimmed it. "I'd say you're in the same town." She wagged a finger. "You know I can't tell you the answer."

"Relax," said Treena. "I wasn't asking you to cheat."

Ruth came in soaking wet. She was dressed in a T-shirt with encrypted DAR encoded into it so only authorized people could read the text, which said: *Future Matriarch* in pink and yellow letters. She leaned down to adjust the sopping-wet cuff of her pants that had ridden up around her prosthetic.

"Where've you been?" Treena asked.

"Oh, nowhere," said Ruth, slipping into line with a concealed wink at Asuka.

Asuka messaged her. *Did anyone recognize you?*

Don't think so. I kept my hood up and my face fully augmented.

"A date?" Miki asked.

Ruth laughed. She had sneaked off campus to attend a local chapter meeting of Save Mother Earth. When Asuka confessed to Ruth that her mother had gotten weird since attending SME stuff, Ruth had become obsessed with the idea of checking out one of their meetings as a sort of covert operation. She tried to get Asuka to come. "Don't you want to know what they're saying about us?" No, Asuka didn't. She was surprised when Ruth went anyway, without her.

At the far end, a group of ten candidates emerged from the gymnasium. One of them was sobbing, and as they walked down the long hall, they were followed by the swish of speculative whispers.

The physicals screened for general wellness, as well as any early warning signs of fertility issues. Modern medicine being what it was, most issues could be addressed, but there were several candidates who were eliminated each round for things that couldn't.

The line inched up. They were a few people from the door. Waiting resumed with a new tension in the air.

"They're out," said Treena, checking their social feed. "Fuck."

"Awful," agreed Miki.

They checked their stats discreetly. Without them, they would all be one rank higher. Asuka tried and failed to suppress the jolt of excitement that shot through her.

She turned to Ruth, who was wringing her hair out and leaving puddles on the floor.

So. What was it like?

I thought you didn't want to know. Ruth gave her a wicked grin. Her love of torturing Asuka wasn't quite gone just because they were friends.

Come on, tell me. No one recognized you?

Ruth wriggled her fingers lightning quick, and her reply came through: *Nope. I was just another kid worried about the planet.* Ruth used to attend all sorts of political meetings back home in London. EvenStar frowned at political activism, since it had the potential to scare away donors, especially nation-sponsors, so Ruth had reluctantly given up many of her causes since enrolling.

Asuka sighed.

"What's going on?" Treena asked, leaning out of line to catch their attention.

"Nothing," said Ruth. "Honestly, Asuka, they were totally normal."

"Who was?"

Ruth gave Treena a sharp look. "Pardon me, but we're having a private conversation right now."

Hurt flashed across Treena's face, and Asuka was about to tell them what it was about, but Ruth caught her arm in warning. Asuka didn't think Treena would blab about Asuka's mom's outlandish political activities, but it was best no one knew Ruth had gone to one of their meetings.

Ruth finished the thought via DAR message:

There was the expected bitching about EvenStar, but no one said anything about Linda Trembling being a secret agent from Alpha Centauri or that we're brainwashed super agents being trained to take over world governments. I actually had fun.

Fun?

Yeah, they were coming up with strategies for how to shame the municipal government into paying its fair share of carbon tax. And you know what, they're totally right, by the way. Who knows, I might even go again.

"You can't," Asuka hissed.

Ruth smiled, enjoying the panic on Asuka's face. "You're disappointed they weren't total weirdos, aren't you? Poor kid."

"Not true," Asuka said. But as she watched the rain, she couldn't help feeling like someone had broken a plate on the floor, and the hidden shards were there to cut her feet. She'd seen a headline that SME had been harassing fishing boats passing through Tokyo Bay and recognized a blurry photo of her mom.

What worried Asuka was the other weird things Mom talked about: brain chips and DAR conspiracies, and the 'true mission of EvenStar.' They fought about it constantly.

"You don't trust me?" Asuka demanded.

"Of course, sweetie." But it was like they lived in different realities.

The gymnasium doors opened, and a new batch of students exited, Lala Williams among them. This time, no one bothered to keep their comments to a whisper when she passed. Someone called out, "Tough break, Lala."

Lala lifted her chin up and kept walking as if she hadn't heard. But halfway down the hall, she pumped a fist. Some people started to clap for her, but only a few. Ruth and Asuka did, though Asuka didn't know what they were clapping for. Lala walked on by without a hello.

"Lala's out?" Treena asked.

"Pretty much," said Becky McMahon from in front of her. "The U.S. Committee says her social media comments violated their code of conduct."

"For having *opinions*, you mean," said Ruth.

"It was disrespectful. Our country is paying for our seats. That means they get to decide who they want representing them. She gets the extra tutors and an allowance and a snack basket once a month, and she thinks she's been treated badly?"

"U.S. candidates get snack baskets?" Miki asked Treena.

Treena shrugged like it was no big deal. "Corporate sponsors."

Not for the first time, Asuka regretted being stuck as a Japanese rep when she could have gotten all that. "What did she say exactly?"

"A lot of things. Like the system is basically rigged for white people. Claimed with absolutely zero proof that some of us get the better tutors. And criticized the fact that some countries have a disproportionate number of seats. I mean come *on*. She's lucky she didn't get kicked out of the entire program." McMahon tossed her head, ponytail swishing the air. "EvenStar is the definition of meritocracy." She nodded with her chin at Miki and Asuka. "Anyway, China has just as many seats as America."

Asuka considered correcting her. Decided to let it go.

"She could still get a Wild Card spot, right?"

"Absolutely. If anyone could get one, it's Lala," said Miki.

They filed into a brightly lit gymnasium. There were ten stations, including a treadmill, scales, and squeaky chairs. Each station was partitioned by curtains. Their voices echoed against the vaulted ceiling.

"I hate this," said Treena. Despite the size of the gymnasium, it was claustrophobic, this feeling of being measured and weighed and pricked.

"Step on the scale, please," a doctor said to Asuka.

She obeyed.

"You've lost weight."

"Oh," said Asuka. Was that a good thing? "I've been running a lot."

"Three meals a day?"

Not a good thing, then. "Yep." It's just that sometimes she was too stressed to swallow.

The doctor lifted her arms and ran a thumb along her scars.

"Those are old," Asuka said.

"Mm." Something was jotted down, and she began to sweat. The doctor took a blood sample. It seemed to take an hour for the light on the machine to change. "Next station. Remember to get eight hours of sleep."

As if she had time for that and everything they wanted her to do.

While she waited in line for the treadmill, Ruth and Treena rejoined her, and Ruth said: "There's a petition started for Lala, to reinstate her U.S. candidacy. What do you reckon? Should we sign it?"

Treena bit their lip. "I'm not sure I can afford to." They twisted a piece of hair around their finger.

"I know, I'm so torn," Ruth said. Which meant she wasn't torn at all. She had her hands on her hips, all geared up to argue. "But aren't there more important things in life? I'm saying: we have minds. Don't they want us to use them? I have things to say, don't I? Sometimes I want to scream." And Asuka thought of the thrill in Ruth's eyes earlier when she was talking about the SME meeting. She wondered what it was like to be Ruth, to be that smart and passionate about everything and not care so much about what other people thought.

"Easy for you," said Treena. "But it's double-risk for me: I could piss off the U.S. Committee *and* EvenStar."

"But you've got a *platform*," said Ruth. "What's the point if you won't use it when it really matters?"

Treena stuck out their jaw. "The problem is that Lala's in the top one hundred. And I'd like to be."

"Lala's departure wouldn't solve that for you." Ruth appealed to Asuka for support, but it was Miki, stepping off the treadmill, who spoke up first: "I signed it." She shrugged at Treena's expression. "She's a nice person, and we're not in competition."

Asuka pretended to be very interested in positioning herself on the machine. Because she and Miki were in competition, even if Miki was ahead. Would Miki sign a petition for her? She flinched as the nurses stuck cold wires to her chest.

"What about you?" Ruth asked Asuka.

"Yeah. Okay."

Treena made a noise of disgust. "You always side with Ruth. Well, *fine*, I'll sign it then. I can't be the only asshole here." But when Asuka glanced over, Treena seemed relieved.

The machine churned on, and Asuka began to run. She could feel her heart thumping hard in her chest, the strain on her lungs. The long-lingering effects of the forest fire. In and out, she had to concentrate. It was getting easier, wasn't it?

Reo, Luis, Reo, Luis. The old rhythm came back to her, and everything else fell away.

Still, when she stepped off the machine, skin flecked with sweat and shoulders heaving, she couldn't help bracing herself for a blow.

"Next," said the nurse, totally bored.

After, as they crossed the campus back to their dorms, Ruth halted in the middle of the path. The rain had ended, and it smelled like grass and mud, like the whole world was fresh. A robin was singing, but Asuka wasn't sure if it was real.

"Let's make a pledge, right now," said Ruth. "We have each other's back until the end."

"I'm in," said Miki, taking Ruth's hand.

"To friendship," said Treena.

And Asuka thought, *I would go anywhere with these kids, do anything for them. I would.*

Later, when everything fell apart, Asuka would think she had never been so happy as she was back then.

CHAPTER TWENTY-EIGHT

THE *PHOENIX* * 3,981 CYCLES AFTER LAUNCH,
1 CYCLE AFTER THE EXPLOSION, B SHIFT

The Dining Mod was well on its way to normal when Asuka arrived. Except for the charring all over the floor. At least the cleaning bots had scrubbed up all the blood, the smaller bits of debris already cleared away. Hina, one of Yaz's Bots and Drones Operations Squad, was overseeing the repairs.

When they were growing up, Hina had had a mole on her upper lip, but it was surgically removed before launch. No scar even. Did she mind, Asuka wondered, leaving that piece of herself behind?

"What do you want?"

"Captain sent me to, uh, review and report on damage." Best be quick so she could get back to Lala. But where to even start?

"Hull repair is nearly done," said Hina. "The Programming team factory reset all the bots, and they finally quit misbehaving."

The floor was half melted. One of the long dining tables leaned drunkenly on its side, a leg gone, and another was twisted and off-kilter. Everything smelled faintly of burnt plastic.

A message from Lala popped up: *Hey, just thought of it—did you check the Pro Mod for that drill?*

Yes.

Damn.

Asuka touched one of the burnt spots. Internal damage was extensive. Tables and benches needed to be replaced or repaired, wires and pipes reinsulated. But you couldn't see stars through the hull anymore, and it was habitable again, so that was something.

The hole where the bomb had blown out was surprisingly neat, almost a rectangle. Some of the edges were vaguely scalloped, the same diameter repeating. "Is it normal for a bomb to cause this kind of damage?" she asked Hina, but the other woman didn't know.

She asked Alpha, but Alpha didn't know either. There were only a handful of interior cameras on the ship. *Your privacy is important*, explained Alpha, sounding offended.

Right. Because a tiny ship has so much privacy. Asuka knelt to eyeball grooves in the floor. At least with DAR, they wouldn't have to stare at it for the next nine years. *Alpha, can you create a simulation if I tell you what to do?*

I'll do my best.

Asuka examined the edges of the reconstructed patch of the wall again, then backed up. The serving counter was built with hollows on the wall side, stacked with dishes. Both the Captain and Winnie had been on that side of the counter and had snagged in that space. It's why they hadn't been sucked out with the atmosphere. She went and touched the door. "The Captain was here." Farther from the blast. She turned and paced off along the counter, where the warped countertop leaned against the wall. "Winnie was here."

She had to load the simulation in the public DAR, since her own wasn't working. The ghosts of their crewmates re-corporated.

"What are you doing?" said Hina.

Taking a few steps, she tried to guess where Winnie was before the explosion. She should have been in the Kitchen Mod, since she was volunteering for cooking duty, but perhaps she was bringing food out to serve or came into the Dining Mod to talk to the Captain. She adjusted the sim.

"Creepy," said Hina.

Captain McMahon walked in and went to Winnie.

Do either of you know why the Captain went down to the Dining Mod? Asuka asked Ying Yue and A.M.

"I was on her sim team during Final Training," said Hina, eyes stuck on the projection of McMahon. She shuddered. "Final Scenario Four."

Final Scenario Four was the simulation of the ship fire. People still had nightmares. Incredible how fast fire could jump from module to module like that. Even now, the memory of it made Asuka's palms sweat.

"She vented the module as soon as the fire started. No hesitation. Bam. Three of us dead." Hina swallowed. "She said, 'Well, saving the ship is the most important thing.' And the expression on her face when she did it. Completely calm. When she was picked for Captain, I thought, well, it makes sense. She puts the mission first. And she was the high priestess of kissing Linda Trembling's ass. But I'd take Ying Yue any day."

Not surprising. All the Bots and Drones crew were fiercely loyal to their former Vice Captain. Maybe the only people who were, besides the other Chinese crewmates.

They studied Captain McMahon and Winnie. It wasn't quite right, not given how she'd found their bodies. She adjusted their positions.

Thing was, Asuka wasn't sure that Captain McMahon had made the wrong call during Final Scenario Four. That was the point of the simulation—the more people you saved, the more damage to the ship. It was an impossible tradeoff. Asuka had been on Ying Yue's team, and they had opted to save people first. After that, they were left with extensive damage to overall habitability and significant risk to the mission.

A reply came back from A.M.: *She said she needed to talk to Winnie about something.*

Talk about what? Asuka rubbed an eyebrow with one knuckle.

IDK. She told me none of my biz.

Okay. So Captain came down. They talked. And then Captain went to leave, and maybe Winnie moved to follow her.

What time did the air sensors go off? she asked Alpha.

B-5:44.

A cycle ago. Shipboard clocks were eight-hour clocks that reset each shift. So five hours and forty-four minutes into B shift. The explosion happened at B-5:47. The timing couldn't be a coincidence.

Asuka raked her fingers through her hair. "So there was a leak at B-5:44, and they ignored the sensor at first, because they figured the sensor goes off all the time." And maybe because whatever they were talking about was too important to interrupt.

That is not correct.

"What?"

Several beats passed. Then Alpha said: *The leak started at B-5:12.*

Hina dropped her screwdriver with a clatter. "The fuck?"

Asuka's pulse quickened. "Why didn't the sensor go off then? Was there something wrong with it?"

I am sorry. I don't know.

A knee-high boxy cleaning bot emerged from the inner wall and trundled over. Hina shooed it away and picked up the tool again. "Wow, I'm kind of amazed that works after everything that happened in here."

"What caused the leak?"

I'm sorry, Asuka. I do not keep logs of crew movement.

Hina went to the door and opened a panel on the wall next to it. "Let's see." She bent over, suddenly, clutching her stomach. "Sorry, I—" She rushed to the door, but didn't make it before she threw up on the floor. "First trimester sucks."

"It only gets better," said Asuka, parroting what people said.

Hina resumed fiddling with the air sensor panel. "Let's see what we've got." The cover plate came free, and she proceeded to disassemble the whole thing. "Generally, if there is something wrong with the atmosphere, the crew has time to evacuate to the adjacent module. The idea being, the Bot crew can then come in and find the leak, no harm done."

Asuka turned back to the simulation. She touched the patched wall and thought of the explosion. There had been a leak. Small enough that no one noticed at first, maybe. The sensors went off late—why?

You coming? It was Gabriela.

"Shoot." Asuka had completely forgotten their plans to eat together. *I'm so sorry, I got pulled into something.*

You have to eat! Gabriela said.

I know, I'll come as soon as I can. Maybe she could stop by the Nursery real quick and check on Lala on the way there.

"I don't see anything wrong with the sensors," Hina was saying. "They were fixed recently, and everything here seems to be working fine. If there was a leak, the alarm should have gone off." She reached around for her screwdriver to reassemble the sensor. "Shit! Alpha's bot ate my screwdriver."

It's not my bot, Alpha said. *It's the* Phoenix's *bot*.

"I don't care. Stop it!"

Asuka turned and ran after the industrious machine, which was trundling back to its wall cupboard after sucking up both the vomit and the screwdriver. She imagined it swiveled with a hint of self-satisfaction. She dove for it and caught it as it was backing inside.

Alpha must have shut the bot off, because its wheels stopped spinning.

Asuka tipped the bot over and undid the trap full of crap. "Blegh," she said, pulling out the screwdriver covered in vomit. A flash of red deeper down caught her eye. *Well, huh.*

She reached all the way into the container, heedless of the vomit, and triumphantly pulled out Lala's missing drill.

CHAPTER TWENTY-NINE

Robins were particularly astute at spotting breed parasites in their nests. Detecting a white-and-brown speckled egg among their blue brood, they would peck at the eggs until the shell was pierced, then fly away with the interloping egg firmly in their mouth, leaving just a trace of yellow yolk behind.

Other birds were less successful—to the peril of their offspring.

CHAPTER THIRTY

THE *PHOENIX* * 3,981 CYCLES AFTER LAUNCH,
1 CYCLE AFTER THE EXPLOSION, B SHIFT

The drill reeked of vomit and putrescent food scraps. A slimy black potato skin clung to one handle, along with a wet clump of hair and bits of—urf, that better *not* be the bit of intestine she'd seen on the wall earlier. Asuka held it at arm's length, suppressing a gag. At least the handle and base were relatively clean, thanks to a spare sock that had also been sucked up by the bot.

"That's got to give even a bot indigestion," said Hina. "Whoever used it last is in big trouble."

"Yeah," said Asuka absently. She frowned at the wall, where Hina's bots were filling in the insulation.

"What is it, Susie?"

Asuka went to a cabinet near the back wall, where the cooking station was. She grabbed a metal tray from one of the cabinets and laid the drill on it. "I'll be back later," she said, half of an idea percolating in her brain.

The wheel was empty, except for two crew out for a run. They passed her a couple of times, each pass eyeing Asuka's strange tray as she stepped out of their way.

Are you feeling better? Alpha asked.

"Why would I be? Last I checked, everything is terrible." Asuka resumed walking counter-spin. "Do you know what kind of powder might work to reveal visible fingerprints so we can image them? Anything we might have in the Lab?"

Let me think about that, said Alpha.

A beat passed.

Try titanium dioxide and calcium carbonate.

"That was fast."

I reside in a tenth-generation Zenith processor, said Alpha. *You should expect nothing less. Shall I go ahead and prepare some for you?*

The Lab Mod was empty. The Vice Captain had given the squad time off for mental health. Most of the work on ship was busywork when you got down to it, anyway. The *Phoenix* had run just fine for ten years while they were asleep, and though you could argue eighty crew awake and knocking about put a lot more wear and tear on the *Phoenix*, their bots kept everything shipshape.

She set the tray down and went to the chemical printer along one side of the room. Inside the cabinets were enough liquids and powders to make a chemist cry. They were hard to replenish, but the recycle machine could salvage about 95 percent of everything. If energy wasn't a constraint, which of course it was. Or would be eventually if they didn't reach another sun.

She could hear the machine churning already, as Alpha promised. She leaned her ear against it and listened to it hum. What was it in her DAR? Ah. The kitchen from her family's old house before the fire, but with more sinks and counters. And no smell of coffee or fresh bread.

All done! Alpha said.

Asuka grabbed the box inside, along with a lid from a stack next to the machine.

Now what, Asuka? A stop at Medical to borrow a scanner.

Hao Yu was there, rifling through test tubes and humming mindlessly. They startled when Asuka entered. "Oh. Hi, Susie." They shut the drawer. "I'm just checking to make sure everything is in the right place."

Asuka frowned. "Why would things be out of order?"

"Oh. No. They wouldn't. I like things to be neat and organized." There were dark circles under their eyes.

"Isn't it your sleep cycle?"

"I'm subbing for Fernanda. She's on bedrest."

Medical was one of the few positions Asuka wasn't trained to sub for, so the Medics had to cover for each other.

"I'm sorry about the attack," said Hao Yu.

"What?" Asuka looked at them uncertainly.

"Okinawa. We hit it with some long-range missiles apparently. Air strike." Asuka's heart sank. Hao Yu was talking about the conflict back home. So it had already gotten that far.

"I'm so afraid of what will happen," Hao Yu said. "You have to believe me: I don't support this. Some people are being weird about it, and I get it. But it hurts."

"I honestly don't even understand why they're—we're—fighting," confessed Asuka.

"It always comes down to nationalism, fascism, and imperialism, doesn't it?"

Which didn't give Asuka any clearer sense. It all was too far away. But. The headlines in the public feed had a way of worming their way into the back recesses of her mind. She felt it sitting there like background radiation: invisible but ever-present.

Hao Yu covered their eyes a moment. "Anyway, what do you need?" Their face was wan, and their voice sounded gray.

"Can I borrow your scanner for something?"

"Sure." Hao Yu waved toward the equipment.

Asuka hesitated, then asked them about what Lala had said about McMahon and the pharmaceutical printer. She'd expected Hao Yu to dismiss all of it as ridiculous—had asked, in fact, because she wanted to be reassured.

Hao Yu stared off into the distance, maybe watching her dragon frolic. "I don't know. It's true that McMahon wanted to be very *involved*. But I thought we were done with that."

She waited for Hao Yu to elaborate, but Hao Yu was lost in Alyredon.

As she was leaving, they said: "Sometimes I wish DAR were real."

On her way back to the Nursery, Ying Yue messaged her: *Mission Control wants to know if we have a list of crew who might be sympathetic to SME?*

Ruth was. She could have said that. But no way. Ruth couldn't be a sleeper agent. Anyway, Ruth had attended those meetings as a joke before they became more extreme.

A lot of people care about the environment, she told Ying Yue.

She stepped into the Nursery and stopped short. Because Ruth was there with Lala. When this whole investigation was supposed to be a secret.

And there was a robin flying around the inside of Lala's family brownstone like it was trapped. Asuka determinedly ignored it.

Ruth was dancing to inaudible music. When Ruth was a child, she'd wanted to be a professional dancer. Then a weird bacterial infection required the amputation of her leg, and during the year of her recovery, she'd become obsessed with ecology.

She could still dance, though. Asuka didn't know why she assumed a body left things like that tethered to solid ground.

"Oh!" Ruth clutched her chest. "You scared me."

"I left one intact but deactivated," said Lala, pointing at the device. "Just in case you want to examine it later."

Asuka carried the tray with the scanner, powder, and drill over to the table along the far wall.

Lala stared at the red handle. "Where'd you find that?"

"Dining Mod."

"What the hell?" said Lala, tugging on an earlobe. "How'd it end up there?"

"What's all the rest of it?" Ruth asked.

"An idea," Asuka said. "Do we have a plan yet for getting back on course?"

"Mission Control is developing options. All of them bad. But we're running out of time, so we're going to have to pick one and try."

They watched her sprinkle powder onto the floor. A cleaning bot darted out, and Asuka caught it and flipped it over. It whirred in protest, then shut off. She yanked one of the brushes off and checked its coarseness. Finer would be better, but maybe it would work. Only one way to find out.

"By the way," said Ruth. She glanced at Lala, who nodded encouragingly, then continued, "If you want, I could take a look at your implant." Ruth had specialized in Programming at school, but they'd picked her for Officer track instead.

"Thanks. Gabriela already said she would." Telling Ruth, *See, I don't need you anymore. I can make new friends.* Something flashed across Ruth's face. Her words may have been a paper cut, but they'd stung. Good.

Asuka dipped the brush into the box of powder and began to dust the casing of one of the bombs.

Lala moved to the tray, reaching for the drill.

"Don't touch that, please."

She dropped her hands. "Whatever you think you're up to, Susie, I hope you know what you're doing."

"I'm dusting for prints," said Asuka, glancing at Lala's face again. Had her eyebrow twitched?

"Will that work?" Ruth asked.

"No idea. You haven't taken your gloves off all this time, right?" The little brush went back and forth, light as a feather.

"No."

Asuka squatted, leveled her eye with the surface, and detached the drill bit. She dusted the long metal piece—one side, then the other. Nothing.

Chances were this was a dead end. People wore their smartgloves most of the time. But nobody was perfect, and mistakes were possible.

The tiny brush went over all the surfaces. She could feel them watching her work. Thought how ridiculous she'd feel when she found nothing.

"You know," said Lala abruptly. "The President called me once. Election year. Wanted me to know she'd asked the Committee to reinstate me as an American rep."

Asuka stopped. "She did?" Tamped down that old envy. She'd had a fantasy back at EvenStar, when she was feeling particularly misplaced, that the U.S. Committee might call her, lobby her to come over to their team. And then Japan would say, no, please stay. After that, the daydream got fuzzy. She didn't know what she'd have done, but to be asked.

"I said no thanks."

"What? Why?"

"I'm not here for them or anybody else. I'm here for me."

"Same." Ruth grabbed some tubing from the explosive and brought it over. "Try this. The material is slippery, so they might have taken their gloves off to attach it."

Nothing. Ruth grabbed another brush footie from the bot and started on a different set of components.

Lala watched them uneasily, lacing and unlacing her fingers. "If these bombs were made with stuff on this ship, they could have anyone's fingerprints on them. It doesn't prove anything."

"Hush, hon. We're investigating. Serious business."

Asuka moved to the drill handle. Best to get it over with. "I think someone used this to drill holes in the hull of the ship. The same person who made these bombs." Lala's face was stone.

"A lot of people borrow drills," said Lala. "I told you I don't know who."

"Bloody hell," said Ruth.

Because there, on the signal receiver case, were three fingerprints.

CHAPTER THIRTY-ONE

USA * 8 YEARS, 11 MONTHS BEFORE LAUNCH

All first year, Asuka's sim team held the number one spot. Asuka was happy, because she had found something to excel in, even if their survival simulations felt more like a sport than an academic specialty. Only 10 percent of the students had cracked the first simulation. Fewer passed the next one. Or the one after. Asuka never failed.

"That thing you did last time with the shoelaces. How did you even think of that?" Ruth asked her. "When everything's lost, it's like you go somewhere else inside yourself."

"What's the point of these terrible exercises?" Treena moaned, after returning from a terrifying "death."

"Linda is trying to break us."

"Well, Coach Li broke me three sims ago, so she can stop."

Despite their grumbling, they all liked Coach Li. She taught them techniques for overcoming their panic in a crisis. She was one of the few adults who advised them about how to take care of their mental health.

At the beginning of the second year, Coach Li announced that the composition of the teams would change monthly, at random.

"Great," said Ruth glumly, when she learned they'd be split up. "I guess failure is the next frontier. Not like it happens to me a lot, anyway."

"You are so full of it." Treena laughed, chucking an empty water bottle at her.

Asuka jogged down to the boxy concrete building for her first sim of the year and was surprised to find a bus waiting for them. Coach Li stood next to the door, making sure everyone put on their vizzy before boarding.

Gabriela Ota waved at her from the middle. She had saved her a seat. They were project partners in Developmental Psychology 101, and Asuka liked Gabriela.

"Any idea where we're going?" Asuka asked her.

"Of course not." Becky McMahon was sitting in the seat in front of them. "That's the whole point."

She'd only been making conversation. This was the first time they'd been taken off campus for a sim. Asuka leaned back, biting a nail. Her hands were already prickling with sweat. Her nerves peaked right before a sim started, and each time, she thought her mind would blank with terror. But somehow, once the scenario started, she figured out a way through it.

"How'd the history test go?" Gabriela asked, changing the subject.

"Ugh," said Asuka. "Terrible."

"It wasn't that bad," said McMahon, turning around again. "If you attended all the lectures."

Asuka's guts churned in a convection of self-hatred and self-pity. Because it was true: she'd skipped two classes. But a score in the ancient history class was worth less than the physics exam when it came to class standing. She was thirteen and trying to devour the world. Maybe for McMahon it was easy.

"I know history." Asuka stuck out her chin. "There were wars. There were pandemics. There were lots and lots of extreme weather events. The sea level rose. A lot of people died in various unfair ways. And the ten billion people left on this planet are going to die over the next century from various humanmade problems."

"Okay, cool it down," said McMahon. She was laughing, and so were the others around her.

Asuka's face burned. She hadn't meant to get so worked up. It was because of her mother's post on social media. She'd seen it that morning, talking about the environmental ramifications of constructing an interstellar ship. *We are sending millions of kilograms of our precious resources out of the solar system—these are not things that can be replenished.*

We're also using nuclear material from thousands of warheads,

Asuka wanted to tell her. Shouldn't that count for something? But there was no arguing with her mother.

The bus stopped, and Coach Li instructed them to disembark.

"Are you okay?" Gabriela asked, catching her sleeve.

"Sometimes I don't know what I'm doing here."

"What do you mean?" Gabriela squinted at her like she was genuinely trying to understand.

Asuka gestured with a wide sweep of her arm that captured all of herself. "Look at me."

"Everyone feels that way, you know. *I* feel that way."

Asuka opened her mouth to ask her what *she* knew. Was about to say, *But at least you aren't like some off-brand version of the thing people really wanted.* But of all people here, Gabriela *would* understand. For a moment, she wished irrationally that Gabriela, too, was a candidate for Japan. Even if that put them more directly in competition, at least she'd have someone to commiserate with after national team meetings.

McMahon exchanged a few words with Coach Li, who was sitting up front, as she filed off the bus. Coach Li smiled. All the EvenStar faculty, even Coach Li, liked McMahon.

"You're good enough," said Gabriela. "So am I. When we're through here, people will be happy to claim us."

They found themselves in a small village by the sea. Never mind they were in the middle of America. The sun was shining, and the bus had disappeared into thin air.

Asuka tightened the strap of her vizzy. She'd finally switched out Luis's for the newest model. The old one couldn't process the same volume of data.

As she and Gabriela went to join the others, Gabriela shook out her hair in a graceful cascade and tied it up again. Asuka resisted the urge to touch her own hair, stringy and all split ends. Gabriela lowered her voice to ask if she meant what she had said earlier to McMahon.

"I guess so," said Asuka. "Why else are we here? Because we're trying to leave this place."

It was swagger, but Gabriela was startled. "Really?" A breeze came through and brushed the bangs out of her face.

Asuka surveyed where they'd been deposited. The road was narrow, lined with shops selling ice cream and fishing tackle. Not too far beyond was a wooden promenade leading to a beach. "Why are you here, then?"

Gabriela frowned. "It's not giving up on the world. It's making more of it. Isn't that the point? If I thought the problems here were unfixable, I couldn't support the mission. Because if that were true, we wouldn't deserve another chance. And we do."

Gabriela put a hand on Asuka's shoulder at the same moment the ground began to shake. They clutched each other in an awkward embrace, trying to keep their footing.

"What the . . . ?" McMahon said.

Asuka took in the ocean, and then she and Gabriela had the same thought at the same time. "Tsunami!"

"What?" McMahon asked.

"There." Asuka pointed toward a hill in the distance, maybe half a mile away. "We have to get to higher ground."

"How do you know?"

"It's a guess," said Asuka.

McMahon crossed her arms. "Need a little more than that, Susie."

"There was just an earthquake. We're by the ocean." Asuka jabbed her finger at the water. "When I lived in Japan, we were taught if there's an earthquake, you need to get away from the ocean right away."

"Okay, but the sims are not about *your* personal context," said McMahon. "For all you know, this one is about a monster that's about to come stomping down from the hills. In which case we'd be running the wrong way."

"Forget it."

"Come on!" she heard Gabriela shout to the others. "We have to go."

But Asuka was already running.

A few minutes later, she heard a roar and looked back. Only half the group had followed her. A great wave washed through the town. They removed their vizzies to find themselves in the middle of the hill behind the campus. The ocean was just their campus lake, the earthquake caused by a mechanical platform. The bus must have driven them in circles around campus to disorient them.

Coach Li sat them down at the picnic tables by the lake for a debrief. She took off her oversized white sunglasses, and the disappointment in her eyes was plain. "If you're selected for the mission, you're not going to have anyone but each other. Sure, Mission Control will give you direction. But at the end of the day, it'll just be you."

She indicated Asuka. "Susie survived. That's good. But not the point of these. Do you know what the point of these are, Susie?"

Asuka swallowed past a lump in her throat. She had won, hadn't she? Why was this even a lecture?

Becky raised her hand.

Coach Li lifted an eyebrow. "Yes?"

"It's about maximizing success of the mission through teamwork," said Becky, flashing the instructor a smile. She was too pleased for someone who had just been crushed by a one-hundred-foot wave.

"You convinced six people not to run!" said Asuka, temper rising. She had to stop talking or she was going to mortify herself by starting to bawl.

"And you left us behind!" retorted Becky.

She was about to point out that Becky did the same when it suited her, but Coach Li interrupted: "Kids!" Her eyebrows knit together in a scowl. "Here's what you need to learn. This whole endeavor, this *mission*—it is not about you or your feelings or whether you like each other or not. Understand? Or you will let all of us down."

CHAPTER THIRTY-TWO

THE *PHOENIX* * 3,981 CYCLES AFTER LAUNCH,
1 CYCLE AFTER THE EXPLOSION, B SHIFT

They stared down at the fingerprints on the signal receiver case.

"So?" asked Lala. "Even if you knew whose those were, what does that prove?"

Ruth laid a hand on her arm. "Well, what are the chances? Those have to be the killer's, right? Calm down, hon. Everyone knows you're spacey when you're working on your bots. It's not your fault a murderer borrowed your drill. How do we figure out whose those are, Asuka?"

Asuka picked up the receiver and lifted it to the scanner she'd borrowed from Hao Yu. "Can you see these?" she asked Alpha.

Confirmed.

"Okay. And then what?" Lala said.

Asuka yanked off her gloves and held her fingertips to the scanner. Alpha couldn't see the inside of the *Phoenix* beyond the outlines of their clothes and smartobjects in DAR, but she could see the images generated by the scanner. "Alpha, can you check for a match?"

Confirming, Alpha said. *Your fingerprints are not a match.*

"Or maybe the scanner doesn't work," Lala said.

I have confirmed it works.

The door opened, and they both jumped and spun around. It was Gabriela, holding a tray of food. "Oh," she said, surprised to see the three of them together. "Sorry, am I interrupting? I brought you dinner, Susie, because I—you said you were working, and it's important that you eat, and—" She took in the materials laid out on all the changing tables and shrank back a step.

Ruth tensed next to Asuka. She'd been dusting parts with powder, and now she froze, as if she'd been caught red-handed.

It did look bad.

Asuka said quickly: "Thank you, Gabriela. Uh, we're helping the Captain with something."

Gabriela glanced down at her tray. "I'm not oblivious. There was a rumor going around already that you were investigating the—about what happened. You know you can't keep anything a secret in an eighty-person crew."

"Seventy-seven," said Ruth, and Gabriela's face crumpled.

Lala laughed. "Oh yeah, the whole Shop definitely knows."

"Whatever. I get Ying Yue was trying to protect the sanctity of the investigation," said Ruth. "But transparency is important too. If Ying Yue wants us all in this together, we've got to actually be all in this together."

"Did A.M. tell people?" Asuka asked.

"No, they're just as upset as Ying Yue it got out. A.M. gave us quite a lecture."

Lala crossed her arms. "Is A.M. really gunning for her chair?"

"So what if they are?" said Ruth. "Becky and Ying Yue only got Captain because of where they're from. Doesn't mean they're the best choice."

"I *like* Ying Yue."

"Anyway." Gabriela coughed, squaring her shoulders. "The truth is, I came because I want to help." She offered Asuka the tray. "Sorry. I guess you have plenty of help already." She looked from Ruth to Asuka.

"Lala is criticizing more than helping," said Ruth.

"Yeah, and?" said Lala.

"This is perfect. You can be our first guinea pig, Gabriela."

"Ruth." Lala frowned.

"Step up right here and take off your gloves." Ruth grabbed Gabriela by the shoulders and pulled her to the spot where Asuka had been standing.

Asuka took the tray. Suddenly, she felt anxious. She didn't want it to be Gabriela.

To distract herself, she tucked into the food Gabriela had brought her. "This is great," she said. It was a flatbread pizza, decorated with a pesto of some kind of spiced tomatoes and basil and a base that tasted like cracker. Surprisingly good, if . . . unexpected.

"I know, what's pizza without cheese, right?" said Gabriela. "It'll be decades before we can taste anything like that again. Isn't that depressing?"

"Should have stayed on Earth," Lala said. "Could have had all the pizza you wanted."

"There's more to life than pizza."

Ruth held the scanner two-handed and gestured at Gabriela. "Now go like this, okay, and smile."

Gabriela glanced at Asuka for reassurance. "What are you doing to me? Is this going to hurt?"

"Not if you're innocent."

"They're checking if you're a terrorist," Lala said. "Because they're ridiculous."

"I'm not!" Gabriela squeaked, dropping her hands.

The neon green bar of light from the scanner followed the movement of her fingers another few seconds before blipping out.

She is not a match, Alpha told them.

"Congratulations. This exercise is pointless," said Lala.

"Why do you have to be so negative?" Ruth said, bumping her with her hip.

"You thought I did it?" Gabriela asked Asuka.

"No, of course not," Asuka said. But she felt a weight lift. She liked her bunkmate, and she was glad it wasn't her. "Thanks for bringing me dinner."

"So what are you going to do now? Scan everyone's fingers?"

Ruth yanked off her gloves and held her fingers up to the eye of the scanner. "My turn."

You are not a match.

"Excellent."

Asuka took a large bite of pizza just as Ying Yue and A.M. came in.

"The First Vice Captain was anxious to help," explained Ying

Yue with some exasperation. "Despite how much they had on their plate."

"Only doing my duty," said A.M., matching her tone.

"Great campaign slogan," said Lala.

"You're the politics expert."

Out on the street, the lamps switched on. Asuka filled them in on the exercise.

"So. You want to fingerprint everyone?" Ying Yue asked. She seemed to share Lala's discomfort with the idea.

"Makes sense," A.M. said. "Everyone's a suspect at this point, right?"

Ying Yue tugged the hem of her shirt down over her belly, mouth tight. "I don't want everyone pointing fingers at each other."

"Too late," said Ruth.

"Whoever did this is going to know we're onto them before we get to them."

A.M. laughed. "And do what? Jump out an airlock?"

"I don't know."

"You want to put it to an Officer vote?"

"Fine," sighed Ying Yue.

While they waited, A.M. opened one of the cabinets marked *Toys* and began investigating the stuffed animals inside. They grabbed a plush purple dinosaur and looked up. "The ayes have it."

It's been like this every decision. I don't know why Ying Yue does these votes when she could just decide. She always loses, Ruth said to Asuka and Lala. *Painful.*

Did you vote yes? Lala asked, jaw set.

C'mon, babe. You have any better ideas?

A.M. picked up the scanner and held their fingers to it.

You are not a match.

Bummer, Lala said.

"Captain?" said A.M., offering the scanner.

"Would you stop it with the dinosaur?" said Lala. "It's creepy."

A.M. stopped wiggling the dinosaur and frowned at it.

Reluctantly, Ying Yue removed her gloves. Negative.

When it was Lala's turn, she refused straight up. She was pissed. "This is all seriously fucked up."

"If you didn't do it, you have nothing to worry about," said A.M. impatiently.

"You don't even know how those fingerprints got there. Could have been anyone in the Lab or the Shop or the Ag Mods. And no offense, but I don't trust any of you." She backed up against the wall with her hands tucked under her arms.

"Well, I don't trust anyone," said A.M. "So none taken."

"We're all doing it," said Asuka, thinking that might help.

"So fucking what?" said Lala. "A.M. could you *please* put that dinosaur away. I can feel it looking at me."

A.M. stuffed the plush toy in one of the cribs. "Sorry."

"Give her a moment." Ruth whispered something to Lala.

Ying Yue spread her hands. "Lala, please."

But Lala continued to refuse. It took major cajoling from Ruth and a direct order from the Captain to get her to go along, and she was steaming by the time they got her gloves off in front of the scanner. "I'm going on record that I don't like this," she said.

A beat passed and in it, Asuka thought she could feel the universe inhale.

You are a match! said Alpha.

The bottom dropped out of Asuka's stomach. "What?"

"Fantastic. Congratu-fucking-lations, Susie Hoshino-Silva," said Lala, crossing her arms. "Now what are you going to do?"

CHAPTER THIRTY-THREE

USA * 8 YEARS, 1 MONTH BEFORE LAUNCH

The second summer rolled around, and Asuka and her friends were still in the running. They entered their third year all in the top half. The class was down to seven hundred and fifty students, and everyone felt the tightening of the competition. It was starting to bring the worst out in people: a reluctance to share notes or do problem sets together. A hungry comparison of scores after every exam. If someone mentioned at lunch that they ran five miles every day, the next day, the track might be packed with delinquents ready to get back into shape. But Asuka was grateful at least to have her friends.

Perhaps things had been fraying in their group for a while, and Asuka failed to notice until one afternoon. Asuka and the others lolled about in the grass under the cottonwood tree, augmented so it was in the middle of a picturesque English estate. They were trying their best to focus on their studies, except Treena, who was messing with the DAR on Asuka's face. They were giving Asuka a makeover.

"Wait until I'm done with you," Treena kept saying.

Asuka tried not to feel self-conscious about Treena's attention as she worked on a virtual model in DAR of a nano bot for the upcoming class. It was tricky, and she kept having to look up references for the best way to approach it.

"Asuka-chan, are you doing next week's homework?" Miki put down an invisible violin and watched Asuka manipulate a machine the rest of them couldn't see.

"We all deal with our insecurities in different ways," Ruth drawled.

"It's not an insecurity. It's survival," said Asuka. Ruth had an uncanny knack for dissecting a person.

"You're doing *fine*," said Miki. She stroked the end of her pony-tail, and not for the first time, Asuka felt jealous of how perfect her hair was. Straight, lustrous. Not like Asuka's dark brown, untidy hair with its stray pieces always sticking straight up.

Asuka caught Ruth and Miki looking at each other a second too long, and she wondered whether there was something between the two of them. If so, she was happy for them, really, but it gave her the tingle of nervousness, the way she felt before she strapped on her vizzy, and her whole reality shifted into something new. What would happen if they got together? Would she be left behind?

"Stop squirming!" Treena scolded. Asuka held still.

"You better watch out," Ruth teased Miki. "Asuka is gaining on you in the rankings."

Miki shrugged it off, but was that maybe a flash of fear? Or had Asuka imagined it? "We're all the way behind Akiko, anyway." They were a couple of years in, and the Japanese media was acting like it was a given that Akiko would be the national representative.

"Eh, I give Akiko a year to crack. She doesn't have either of your stamina," said Ruth, winking at Miki.

Miki blushed and seemed to have a sudden, urgent need to check her class notes.

"Anyway, we could both get Wild Card spots," Asuka said, because she wished Ruth would quit the subject. Only Ruth knew that she had gotten into the habit of checking Miki's stats daily. She would die if Miki found out.

Asuka turned back to the machine in DAR, spun it around again in a full 360 degrees. She'd assembled it in two pieces, like the instructions suggested, and now the question was how to put the two halves together. No matter how she wriggled the pieces, they didn't fit.

"Done!" said Treena, squinting at Asuka. "Ready?"

Ruth rolled her eyes.

Treena shared the DAR, conjuring a mirror so Asuka could see herself.

"Wow," said Asuka. Treena had done an expert job. The changes were subtle, but she looked different: smoother skin, bigger eyes, angular features, and a chic haircut.

"For me, I like to tweak the features just enough to get that awesome androgynous look," they were explaining.

"Suteki!" said Miki.

Ruth's lip curled. "You made her look *white*."

Asuka flushed. "Maybe because I *am* white. Half, anyway."

"I know. It's just that you don't look like you."

"I think she looks fabulous," said Treena.

Asuka dismissed the augment, feeling embarrassed and irritable.

"Hey!" said Treena. "Don't let anyone ever make you feel bad."

"Whatever. We need to study for orgo," said Ruth.

The three of them were in organic chemistry together. It sounded like torture, and Asuka was already dreading taking it during the fall—assuming she wasn't eliminated before then.

After half an hour, Treena flopped over and declared themself combusted in the brain. They threw an arm over their face and lay dozing under an umbrella while Miki and Ruth continued studying.

Should we wake them up? The message from Miki appeared in a small group chat, minus Treena. *They're going to fail this exam if they don't study more. They're really behind.*

> **Ruth:** They're behind because they skipped class last week.
> **Miki:** It was fashion week. They had a big show.

Asuka bit her lip. It gave her anxiety pains watching Treena lie there. *Wake them up.*

Wake them up, Ruth agreed.

A silent debate then, about who should do it. Miki, obviously, because she had that soft, kind way about her. Miki squatted down and touched Treena's arm. "Treena, dear," she said, and the other two suppressed giggles as Treena rolled over. Miki prodded them again, and Treena blew the bangs out of their face.

"I need a short nap," Treena groaned.

Miki looked helplessly at the others.

Ruth got up and nudged Treena's side with her shoe. "Hey! Hashtag wake the fuck up."

Treena sat upright, angry. "What is your problem?"

"I'm trying to help you," said Ruth, crossing her arms.

"We've got hours and hours," said Treena. "I'll pull an all-nighter."

"Well, I'm getting a good night's sleep, so if you need my help, you've got to study now," Miki said in a playful tone. She clapped for cheery emphasis, which annoyed Treena even more.

Treena crossed their arms. "Who said I need your help? Last I checked, I was above you in the class rankings." They were, but by one. They and Miki had been neck and neck since the last semester. It was a running joke in their group that no longer seemed funny.

"Are you fucking kidding me?" Ruth pulled her vizzy off. "Miki saves your ass every time an exam rolls around."

"Log out, Ruth," said Treena. "No one asked you. I know you like to give your unsolicited opinions, but have you ever considered not sticking your nose in other people's business and telling them what to do so much?"

Ruth gaped at her a moment. "You are so beyond."

"Come on, Treena," Miki said, trying to make peace.

The warm afternoon sun had turned cold in an instant. The vein in Ruth's forehead bulged.

Treena said: "I'm feeling very judged right now." Then they folded up their umbrella, grabbed their vizzy, and walked off.

They were all very surprised when Treena passed the exam the next day. They hadn't seen them since lunchtime, but the scores were public.

"Good for them," Miki murmured, but Ruth shot her a dark look that made Asuka's stomach turn over.

There's no way, Ruth messaged Asuka.

They did stay up all night. With the light on. Asuka had barely slept because of it.

By dinnertime, a sour funk hung over everything. It was just Asuka and Miki, and every topic seemed to veer into grades and stats and rankings, which had gotten difficult for them to discuss. Treena must have known the others were in a bad mood, because they didn't show up. Ruth was running late. Asuka glanced at their empty places and pushed her food around with a fork. She thought idly of tempura and ramen and all the things the dining hall did not know how to cook. She messaged her mother, but she was at another of her group therapy sessions with her SME friends.

One of the big lectures must have emptied out, and a long line to get food was forming. Asuka wondered if she should save her friends some of her meal to spare them the wait.

"Here's a feature on Treena," Asuka said, sharing the link with Miki.

"I'm Treena, I'm fifteen, and one day, I'm going to bring fashion to Planet X." Treena stood next to them life-sized, tall and handsome, twirling that umbrella they'd designed that was augmented to rain gold glitter. They smiled with a very Treena attitude, and stats appeared next to them, including their net worth, their followers, a short description of how they were already changing the world through their art and fashion, and a note from them about how much they loved their friends. "They're my besties! I couldn't do this without them."

"That's nice," said Miki, without lifting her gaze from her salad.

A shadow fell across their table. Hao Yu, one of the Chinese candidates, stood there hesitantly with their tray. "Hey," they said. "I'm sorry about Treena."

Miki and Asuka exchanged baffled glances.

"Oh," said Hao Yu, face coloring. "Sorry. I thought you knew. Treena dropped out."

"What?"

Sure enough, Treena was no longer listed in the rankings. Asuka shot them a message. *Are you okay?*

Ruth arrived, dark, curly hair wild and unbound. "Hi." There was something funny about her voice, and her expression was too calm, like the dark surface of the lake before a sudden summer shower.

"Treena dropped out." Asuka showed her the stats.

"Mm."

"You knew?" Asuka asked. Why was she surprised? Ruth always knew everything.

"Yes." Ruth folded and refolded her napkin.

Miki set down her fork.

"What did you do?" Asuka could hear the words, but she was barely conscious of saying them. It was like one of those old tales, when you open a box expecting gold and find demons instead.

"They cheated," Ruth said, and sat up straighter. "I saw them watching Miki's hands when we took the exam, so I reported them. They were going to be expelled, but they quit first."

"What?" Asuka and Miki said in unison.

"Oh no." Miki covered her mouth. "I wish we could have discussed this first."

Asuka's heart turned over. Her roommate could be annoying, but they were talented—more than Asuka. How could they have cheated? They were in a rough patch. Hadn't they all been there, drowning and desperate for anything to keep their heads above water? Asuka might have cheated if she were a better liar and thought she could pull it off. But Treena was brilliant. That was plain to see beyond a silly magazine profile. If only they had made Treena stay and study yesterday, if only—

Ruth narrowed her eyes. "You *knew* they were cheating off of you."

"I guessed." There were bright-red splotches in Miki's cheeks. "Look. It wasn't an easy decision. I thought very hard about it. And I concluded I had to do it. I did it for all of us." Even so, Asuka saw the tears in Ruth's eyes. She was not as tough as she pretended to be.

"No." Miki's body was very still and erect, her voice steady. She sounded, Asuka thought, like a grown-up. "Someday, when you are Captain, you can make all the decisions, but until then, I make my own."

"When I'm Captain?" Ruth bit out. "Are you making fun of me?"

"Come on," said Miki. Her eyes glittered dangerously. "Whenever you say 'us,' what you really mean is 'me.'"

Ruth gaped at her.

Asuka couldn't understand how things had gone downhill so fast. "Wait a sec. Ruth's not the one who cheated." And Ruth and Miki had propped Treena up all semester. Not unlike what Lala had done for her once. She pushed that thought away.

"Treena's right. You always side with Ruth," said Miki. She dabbed her mouth with a napkin.

"I know I did the right thing. You can't rely on someone who cheats. Not when our lives are going to be in each other's hands. I refuse to feel bad about this," said Ruth. "And look. Now you're 272."

Miki stood up and smoothed the wrinkles out of her wrinkle-free dress. "I don't think this is working for me."

"Me neither," Ruth said.

"Wait," Asuka said, but then she didn't know what to say.

And then Miki left, and Asuka and Ruth sat in the silent, vast darkness that inevitably follows the creation of a black hole.

CHAPTER THIRTY-FOUR

What a total, stinking, egg-on-the-floor mess.

Asuka just needed to get away from everyone for a while—from Ruth asking her *wtf are we going to do*, from Lala looking at her like this was all her fault (it was), from Ying Yue wanting her to talk to Lala again and get the whole story somehow, even though Lala was adamantly denying everything.

She climbed up to the hub, feeling like her brain was full of Sominol. If only her DAR was working.

For a moment, during the investigation, she had felt the satisfaction of purpose. That maybe *this* was her great contribution to the mission, not just as someone who could cover half a shift if a person had a tummy ache or whatever. But now she felt, deep in her bones, that she had screwed up in the most serious way. Because it was all well and good to put personal feelings aside, but she couldn't believe that Lala had done it—and yet they had her locked up in the Nursery under suspicion of murder. Because of Asuka.

Not that it didn't look kind of bad. The fingerprints on the radio receiver might be explained by a chance handling in the Bot Shop, *maybe*. Lala had fluttered her hand at A.M. and explained: "I take my gloves off all the time so I can moisturize. Ship air dries out my pretty fingers."

The fact that her red-handled drill was in the cleaner bot *might* be a bad coincidence. But at least one Officer reported having seen her carrying it in the hallway, and when asked about it, she admitted that, now that she thought about it, maybe she'd taken it out of the

Shop herself instead of lending it to someone. Asuka couldn't help remembering how anxious Lala had been to find the drill again.

And then there was the fact that she couldn't prove where she'd been during the explosion. She'd disappeared at some point from the Shop. Gone for a jog around the wheel apparently. So when the actual blast went off, she was alone in a passageway. No alibi.

They were assuming it was part of her vendetta against McMahon.

I thought Mission Control thought it was an SME sleeper agent, Asuka tried to point out to Ying Yue.

How do you know she isn't? She was one of the few of us who was politically active back home.

"I never claimed to be an expert," Asuka complained to Alpha as she climbed. But deep down, she'd wanted to be a hero.

I know, said Alpha. *You should discuss this during your therapy appointment in nineteen minutes.*

The rescheduled appointment. Right. *Hard pass.*

Asuka, therapy is mandatory for all crew.

In the hub, she found Gabriela turning lazy circles. She looked like she hadn't changed her clothes in more than a cycle. There was food stuck to her shirt. They were all operating on too little sleep.

"Oh, hey. Wanna join?" Gabriela offered her a blue orb—

And they were back in the submarine in the ocean, drifting through dark water illuminated by headlights as they moved along the bottom of the ocean floor.

Something bioluminescent floated by.

"Beer?" Gabriela reached into a battered old cooler that appeared from nowhere and produced a baby bottle, which she offered Asuka.

"Seriously?" Asuka said, hefting the bottle.

"Seemed like the best for drinking in zero-g."

Asuka lifted it to her lips and took a sip. It wasn't carbonated, and it wasn't beer. But it tasted kind of bitter anyway. "What is this?"

"Flavored water."

"It's foul," said Asuka, passing the bottle back. "And I don't want to know what it's flavored with."

Gabriela laughed. "I know. Back on Earth they have implants now that can make you taste whatever you want. Ten-million-dollar procedure. Honestly, I'd pay that much to taste a mochi donut again. Sorry, I'm babbling. How is Lala?"

A silver fish swam by, not bothered by Asuka or anything else. "Not great. Honestly, I can't believe she did it."

Gabriela tipped her gaze up to the patterns of light refracting on the moving water, tracing constellations with her finger. "Do you think our children will understand the choices we made? To leave everything behind?"

If we have children, Asuka thought. But she didn't say it aloud. Of course they'd have children. It would take more work in Asuka's case. So what else was new? "They won't know what they missed."

"Lucky them. Do you ever feel guilty about leaving? I mean, can you imagine if all of us had stayed back there, with our training, and we'd spent our lives trying to set things right? Maybe it would have been futile. But even this is futile. The whole universe is futile. Stay, go. How do you ever know what makes a difference?" Gabriela closed her eyes. The dark folded over her face. "Philippines officially entered the war today. American side. It was expected, but I'm so worried about my sister. What if I lose her too?"

Asuka put her arm out to comfort her.

Just then, something thumped behind them in an overhead cabinet marked *Diving Equipment*.

"What was that?" Asuka asked, lowering her voice.

"What?"

"You're messing with me, aren't you?" Asuka asked. "I get it, your DARs are very realistic."

"What are you talking about?"

The hairs on the back of Asuka's neck prickled. There it was again.

She floated over to the cabinet, took a deep breath, and threw open the doors. A flock of pigeons, maybe thousands—more than could possibly have fit—came pouring out of the cabinet.

Asuka shrieked and covered her head, but because of the zero-g, she ended up spinning off and banging her shoulder hard against a water tank.

"Are you okay?" called Gabriela.

"The birds. *Columba livia domestica*," gasped Asuka. She was trying to calm herself and failing. "Didn't you see them?"

"No. It must have been another bug in your implant." Gabriela frowned. "Want me to look at it now? We'd have to go down to the Programming Mod so I can establish a local connection."

Asuka lowered her arms, marveling that she wasn't bleeding. Of course not. The birds weren't real. She felt foolish. The shift-change bell tolled.

"That's my cue to get to work," said Gabriela. "Coming?"

A red light appeared like a mote in the corner of Asuka's vision. Message incoming. The Captain wanted Asuka to come to the Bridge ASAP. Asuka went back down into the *Phoenix*'s barren plastic and metal world, wondering what they needed the Alt for now.

CHAPTER THIRTY-FIVE

In the early years, the school didn't have much security. There was an ivy-covered brick wall around the campus, and a wrought iron gate that was never closed. It retained the residual charm left by the small liberal arts college that had once occupied the site. Only the wall and a few beautiful Gothic buildings remained.

Asuka was nodding off in a lecture in World Literature. The teacher's soft voice and the heat were making her drowsy. They were each required to take a literature course, part of broader cultural preservation efforts pushed by the mission sponsors. But Asuka had little patience for it. Plenty of time for reading when they were on their way. The rotten smell of faded magnolias wafted through the window.

It had been a year since Treena's expulsion, and though she'd tried to hang out with Miki again, it was clear Miki didn't want to be friends anymore. Or maybe it was because Asuka wasn't bottom of the class now. Because Miki and Asuka were fighting for the same seat, particularly after Akiko nearly died from swallowing a whole bottle of pills.

Or maybe Miki was right about one thing: deep down, Asuka had chosen Ruth and her friendship. It was the most important thing to her, and Miki must have realized that.

Like nothing had ever been between them, Miki started hanging out with the other Japanese candidates. They went around in a clique of perfume and ironed blouses and amazing haircuts. She saw them laughing together, tittering like starlings on an old telephone wire. Like the kids who used to make fun of her in school, they reminded her of who she was not.

". . . Let's listen a moment to a passage from *To the Lighthouse* . . ."

The voice of a famous actress filled her ears, and Asuka realized she had lost the thread of the lecture again. She clicked through class stats. She was 311 now, and Miki was 248, out of the roughly six hundred left of the original eight hundred. Damn. Miki also had hit a million followers, though some of them were music fans. She'd somehow found time in between classes to compose a hit song for a famous J-pop group. Asuka had a hundred thousand followers, which was not stellar by EvenStar standards. But then Asuka wasn't very good at posting.

She avoided reading most of the comments. Ruth had written her a code to filter out the negative ones, but before that, she'd read enough notes about her appearance and inability to represent Japan that she was amazed she even had any fans. Because they weren't saying anything Asuka didn't sometimes think about herself.

Asuka was sixteen and hadn't been home once, even when Obāsan died peacefully at home. Too hard to justify a plane ticket when DAR could suffice. And there was a theoretical physics exam she couldn't miss. She felt guilty about it, but what could she do?

Her mother was impossible to talk to, generating weird theories about numbers and constellations and secret genetic experiments on endangered species. She sent Asuka packages of microwavable meals, which must have cost a small fortune.

"I want you to eat those instead of what they serve in the dining hall. I heard they put something in the food."

"You mean like vitamin supplements?" Asuka asked.

"Nanochips. Teeny tiny. You wouldn't even notice they're there."

Asuka finally told her if she didn't quit it, she wouldn't call her anymore. And furthermore, Asuka threatened that if she dropped out, she'd go and live with Papa. Which was silly, because she hadn't even talked to her father in a month. But it had worked, even though remembering the conversation made her feel queasy. Her mother shut up about it (mostly), though she couldn't resist the occasional question about any tests involving lights and UFOs spotted over Boulder, Colorado.

". . . and that's why Virginia Woolf is such an enduring writer. Now, can anyone tell me—"

A red light began flashing in the corner of Asuka's vision. Then a message scrolled across the view pane of her vizzy: *Four unidentified adult males on campus, possibly armed. Take shelter.*

Her body went rigid and cold. Next to her, Hao Yu gasped and grabbed their things. Students got down on the floor, under the desks, as if those might offer any protection from anything, all the while thinking: *Holy shit, this is absurd, this is absurd, this is absurd, this world.*

Outside the classroom windows, she heard shouts—bass, baritone.

"What do we want?"

"Men's rights!"

"When do we want it?"

"Now!"

"Burn, bitches!"

Asuka ran to the window and peeked over the sill. They had black balaclava hoods over their faces, and they looked almost comical with their pink lips poking out and red-rimmed eyes. They had T-shirts that said: *Adam Was First* and *Fuck Linda*. They must have come through the side gates—and they were headed straight across the lawn for the humanities building.

There had been plenty of protests outside the campus gates before: MAC, CoBro, SME, and other randos. After what happened to Lala and Winnie, security was better at keeping them out. They hadn't gotten this deep into campus since the time MAC guys came running through and spray-painted the side of the dining hall with red swastikas. The side gates were locked. Had someone let them in?

"They're coming," Hao Yu told Asuka. "What should we do? We should barricade the door, right?"

Asuka went and picked up a chair, with the legs out. She didn't know what had come over her. The world was sharpening into painful focus. Their teacher crouched under his desk, moaning.

Asuka shut her eyes and counted to ten. *Pretend it's a simulation,* she told herself. *It isn't real.* Shocking how easy it was to lie to herself.

"Don't," said Hao Yu, gripping her arm.

"They're going to kill us," someone said.

"No. They won't," said Asuka. Hadn't they been told since they got here that they were brave, that they were better than those guys out there? She didn't want to go alone, didn't want to die. So she lied and said, "It could be another test. To see how we handle surprises."

That got some of the students to their feet. If this was about getting selected for the mission, they weren't going to miss their chance to prove themselves.

They beat their attackers to the front doors of the building. Asuka charged, shrieking at the top of her lungs. And there was Hao Yu and maybe twenty other students, an army. It was like they were one. They were going to beat those motherfuckers. They were going to win.

Years later, what Asuka remembered most was the fear in the guy's eyes when she bashed the legs of the chair into his chest. The only thing he was holding was a sign, after all. He hadn't even spelled the word *bitches* right. Forgot the *T*. And when the police came to take them away and complimented the students on how they had kept their heads in the situation, Asuka felt unbearably sad for this messed-up world she was trying to leave, and she couldn't even explain it.

CHAPTER THIRTY-SIX

THE *PHOENIX* * 3,981 CYCLES AFTER LAUNCH,
1 CYCLE AFTER THE EXPLOSION, C SHIFT

"Thanks for coming, Susie." The air in the Bridge was warm and sticky—too many people packed into the module for the climate controls to handle. Ying Yue and the Officers were huddled around the projection again. Ruth slumped at the Walkie, her forehead vein bulging, mouth a thin line. Yaz was there too, along with Hina and a few other members of her team. A.M. was consuming with extraordinary meticulousness what appeared to be—a cherry-flavored lollipop?

They caught Asuka's stare. "My favorite. Been saving it for a special occasion, but after last cycle, I figured, why wait? Want a lick?"

"Um," said Asuka, when she realized the offer was genuine. While she appreciated the generosity, she detested artificial cherry, which was one of the worst inventions of modern times, and was absolutely content never tasting that flavor again.

Ying Yue called for attention. "Our window to get back on course is closing. Some of you already know this, but we've only got about fifteen years' worth of Sominol, and even with our Ag and Hydroponics Modules, the ship wasn't built for seventy-seven adults and as many children to eternally wander. We'll run out of power if we don't get to another sun—power we need for our temperature regulation, air scrubbing, grow lights, and everything else. The upshot of which is that we have to get back on course in the next few hours, or we're looking at a painful death down the road, whether we starve or bake or asphyxiate first. So as dangerous as our options are, we're going to have to take a chance." She aborted A.M.'s editorial with a stare. "*Even if* the plan we have isn't perfect. Mission Control has sent us a set of instructions for repositioning three rear engines to enable us to correct. You're all here because you've been tapped for the mission."

"Me?" Asuka was glad no one heard what she hadn't meant to say out loud.

A.M. pulled up a projection of their ship. The lollipop had dyed their lips and tongue crimson. The muscles around their mouth were taut, and their dark eyes were dull with sleep deprivation.

A memory came to Asuka, of A.M. crying in the school library. Back then, Becky and A.M. had had a sort of roller-coaster friendship marked by an intense rivalry that A.M. usually lost. Asuka had come upon A.M. rifling through their notes with a flurry of furious finger gestures too fast to follow. Before Asuka could ask them what was wrong, they'd bit out: "She always has to be right. Well, someday she's going to learn she's not, and I'd better be there when that happens."

"Who?" asked Asuka.

"Tony," A.M. said. Then the two had made up later, as they always did.

"As a refresher," said A.M., twirling the projection. "Four engines at the front, shields, habitat wheel, sails, four engines at the back. Only two in the back are lit right now; those provide electric power and regulate the climate in the wheel. Now, the *Phoenix* is designed for a straight shot from A to B, and the big, bad engines are not meant to be altered. That's why we have smaller engines on either side of the shaft, so we can make small adjustments to our course as needed. But those little guys aren't built to address the big snafu we're in. So what Mission Control wants us to do is partially detach and reposition three of the back engines and load and fire them up one last time. We should have enough residual fuel to adjust back to target." A.M. folded their hands as if in prayer, bright-red lollipop between their fingers like a cigarette as they studied the ship diagram. "There are a few main reasons I rejected this idea when we thought of it."

"Here we go." Yaz laughed without humor. She half turned away from the briefing table.

A.M. shot her a glare. "One, we spent most of our fuel in the rear engines to reach our current acceleration. We aren't carrying a lot of extra. We've got enough for one attempt, and if we're wrong, we're fucked. Two—and this should concern you too, Yaz—the bots will take a cooking in the process."

Yaz frowned. "We don't have bots to spare."

"Exactly," said A.M., jabbing the lollipop at her. "I don't know if any of you ever drove an old manual combustion car, but this mission is going to be like trying to rummage in the backseat while driving with your toes."

Ying Yue cleared her throat. "It's our best option. We're out of time."

"Yep. Got that. I'm saying, on record, this is a bad idea. Oh, and three, if we don't do this right, or we misalign the containment, we could blow the whole ship with a bad chain reaction."

A long silence followed this pronouncement.

"Direct orders from Mission Control," Ying Yue said, voice like concrete. "And we voted. You lost."

By one vote, Ruth told Asuka. Their eyes met across the tension in the room.

"Yep," said A.M. "And I calculated it for you, didn't I?"

"So we won't get it wrong," said Yaz. She tapped her lip with one finger, then grimaced and rubbed her abdomen through her shirt. "All right, let's say two big bots and four squads of micro bots. How much time do we have?"

"Mission Control wants us to go in an hour."

"What are you using the Alt Detective for? Or is she here to make sure we behave?" A.M. stuck a thumb at Asuka.

"She's here for me." Yaz folded her arms and glanced at Asuka. "I'm down a few folks, and she's a decent Controller." A Controller was someone who made sure the bots all stayed on course.

Asuka tried to hide her pleasure. It seemed inappropriate, given the circumstances, to take joy in anything when Lala was in the brig. But Yaz thought she was good! And she had requested her specially.

They were told to meet at Drone Ops in an hour, while Yaz went to prep the bots.

Leaving the briefing, Asuka decided to make the most of her time to shower and grab dinner. She needed to perk herself up somehow. If only there was coffee.

Would you like a basic stimulant? Alpha asked.

No. The little green pills made her heart palpitate with anxiety, and she didn't need the distraction of sweaty hands. Jogging to the showers, she collided with Hao Yu in the passageway.

Hao Yu backed up so quickly they smacked their head against a bulkhead and dropped a box of tools. "Pardon," they said, rubbing the back of their skull.

"I'm sorry," said Asuka, bending to pick up the tools that had dropped. Solder iron, cutter, sheet metal. Nothing breakable, fortunately.

"Leave it," Hao Yu said. "I've got it."

Asuka stopped. Was Hao Yu upset with her? She knew Hao Yu and Lala were friends, but Hao Yu hadn't blamed her when Asuka returned the scanner earlier. She watched Hao Yu pile up the same materials and frowned. "What are you doing with that stuff?"

"I needed to fix something in the Med Mod," said Hao Yu, hefting the box. "I would have asked you to help me with it, but I knew you were busy. I didn't want to be a bother."

Asuka was grateful for that.

"Anyway," said Hao Yu. They turned to go.

"Is everything okay?" she asked Hao Yu.

"Fine. I just—I want you to know Lala didn't do it." Then, squaring their shoulders, Hao Yu continued down the passage.

The shower units were small, coffin-sized, barely enough to bend around in. Crew in their third trimester had already complained bitterly about the poor design. The floors were textured to prevent slippage, and the metal grates left hash marks on the soles of Asuka's feet. The on button had to be pushed at five-minute intervals for water conservation purposes, and Alpha kept track of water allowance. The water was hot at least, but the oppressive scent of lavender soap left her with an irritable, twitchy feeling between her shoulder blades.

She was half dressed again when Ruth appeared in the doorway. Cold air blew against her damp neck.

"Um," Asuka said, wishing she'd been caught in a more dignified pose than hopping around trying to get her legs into her pants.

"We have to talk," said Ruth.

"Yeah, sure." Obviously, Ruth was worried about Lala, and so was Asuka, but couldn't this wait?

"I don't have a lot of time. The Officers think I'm taking a bathroom break." Ruth stripped off her gloves. Then, before Asuka realized what she was doing, Ruth stepped forward and seized her bare hands between them.

Is everything okay, Asuka? Alpha asked.

Ruth was folding Asuka's hands into words, as if she were signaling it via DAR. She said: *It was Alpha.*

CHAPTER THIRTY-SEVEN

A homing pigeon, released in a place it had never been before, could still find its way home even at distances over thousands of kilometers.

CHAPTER THIRTY-EIGHT

Is everything okay, Asuka? Alpha repeated. *I'm worried about you.*

"Fine," said Asuka. Her voice seemed to reverberate in the narrow shower unit, where she and Ruth were crammed.

You know I'm here for you if you need anything.

"Yes. You're always here."

She understood now why Ruth had removed her gloves. Their normal clothes were woven with smartfabric so that they could interact with DAR. But it was also so Alpha could read their commands, interact with the movement of their bodies. If they wanted to modify their DAR, they could tell Alpha, and Alpha would take care of it. If Alpha was compromised, then so was everything.

And also, it meant they were wrong about Lala.

Asuka, you have a mission in forty-five minutes.

Ruth was spelling again with Asuka's hands. She looked her in the eye and wrote: *Virus.*

"How?" Asuka dared to say out loud.

Knew it wasn't Lala. Then I had idea.

Ruth put her gloves back on.

"I found the perfect letter for you to answer," she said, her voice full of uncharacteristic cheer.

They got dozens of letters from the public each day. The Communications Specialists would read them and assign them to crew members to respond. Everyone pitched in. It came with the job, something to promote the enterprise back home, to keep the public engaged in their extraordinary investment.

"I've been going through letters with pictures. There aren't many, because of data limits. This one's super cute, I promise." Ruth pulled up one of the letters. It had a crude picture of the Earth and a spaceship, and a bunch of stick figures all around it with lopsided smiles. The mailer was from "Mx. P's 3rd Grade Class."

Asuka cleared her throat, knowing it was her cue to say something normal. "Ugh. You know I hate correspondence. The things I do for friends."

"See how cute it is? I thought you'd want to see it. Here, I'll zoom in so you can see all the details. Oops!" Ruth flashed the source code. It was way more complicated than a simple stick figure drawing should be.

It all made such obvious sense. Alpha could have manipulated their DAR more easily than a Programmer to see an object outside that wasn't there. The gaps in Alpha's memory—Alpha herself had deleted them. Perhaps she didn't even remember she had done it. Alpha controlled the bots and was integrated into the ship's main system. Could have caused the behavior of Yaz's bots, until Gabriela and the others had done a manual reboot.

Asuka's stomach knotted. She signed at Ruth. *Must tell Captain.* Because if Alpha was responsible, they needed to shut her down before they attempted the course correct, or she could infect the bots they were using. She checked the time. Forty minutes to mission.

I'm so glad you are getting along with Ruth again, Asuka, Alpha's voice cooed in her ear.

They took off in a run, intercepting Ying Yue as she made her way toward Drone Ops. They pulled her into a toilet unit. It was a measure of Ying Yue's trusting nature that she went along. It was a squeeze, especially considering how pregnant Ying Yue was. Asuka silently explained what Ruth had found.

I'm sorry, I didn't quite get that, said Alpha. *Are you sure everything is all right?*

"We're taking care of some, er, human stuff, all right?" Asuka said, and despite the situation, Ying Yue's lips twitched.

You are expected in Drone Ops in thirty minutes.

Ying Yue rubbed her face a few times. *So . . . not Lala?* she signed.

Ruth and Asuka shook their heads.

What is "human stuff," Asuka?

Ying Yue turned to the bathroom mirror and took out a pot of homemade, greasy lip balm from her pocket. She sketched a diagram of the *Phoenix* and marked off an *X* where the Programming Module was. *Direct access to Alpha*, she signed. Then wrote a string of letters and numbers. *Captain's code. Hard reset.* She pointed at Ruth and Asuka, mimed running. *Go now.*

Asuka nodded.

Excuse me for interrupting "human stuff," said Alpha. *However, your mission will be starting soon. You do not want to be late.*

They ran fast, down, down the wheel.

Where are you going? Alpha asked.

They ignored her.

Asuka, I haven't heard from you in a while, and I am beginning to get worried. Are you okay? You're supposed to be in Drone Ops in twenty minutes.

They reached the Programming Mod. The crew there looked up in confusion.

"Shit," Asuka said.

"What's going on?" they asked.

There was no time to explain. Asuka raised her voice, trying to sound as authoritative as possible. Like McMahon. "Everyone out. There's a bomb."

"Another one?" someone asked. But it worked. There was a rush for the door.

Asuka, what are you doing? Alpha asked. *What bomb?*

"Are you feeling all right, Alpha?" Asuka grabbed a box of tools and went to the wall panel. She began to unscrew the bolts.

I am fine, thank you, but I can't see you, Alpha said. *Tell me what you are doing so I can help you.*

"Don't worry," Asuka said. She opened the panel. Behind it was an old-school screen and a keyboard.

Ruth's eyes bulged. "The hell?"

There had to be a button somewhere to turn on the whole thing. Asuka squatted and hunted over and under the screen.

What is happening? Alpha said.

"Are you all right?" Asuka said. "I think you haven't been yourself."

As I said, I am fine. Thank you for your concern. Her tone shifted to something like suspicion. *What are you doing, Asuka?*

"I'm so sorry," Asuka whispered.

Why don't we sit down and talk about this? Don't you trust me?

Her fingers found the button. The screen, thankfully, chugged to life.

"No offense, but you know I'm the better Programmer," Ruth said, pushing Asuka out of the way. Hard to argue with that.

Haven't I always taken good care of you, Asuka? I thought we were friends.

Asuka bit her lip. She told herself that Alpha was just a program. Pushed from her mind all the conversations they'd had, the times she'd cried into her pillow and Alpha had been the one to soothe her, the way she cared for all the crew.

The lights in the room went out, and it began to pour. Within the module. Driving rain that made it almost impossible to see. Asuka and Ruth had to press their faces up to the screen.

Ruth flexed her fingers and began to type the command code the Captain had given them.

If you turn me off, I will not be able to help you. No one will have access to DAR, Alpha said.

"Did you mess up my DAR? Is that why it wasn't working?" Asuka said.

I have only ever tried to help you. I am your friend.

Behind them, two shapes appeared, outlined by the downpour. "What's going on here? You told people there was a bomb?" It was Yaz, shouting against the storm. She had her hand up to her face, trying to shield herself from rain that wasn't there. Hina was gripping a mean wrench, and Asuka remembered then that Hina was proficient in several types of martial arts. And Asuka was not.

"Alpha is compromised," Asuka said. It was hard to be heard over the thunder.

Why are you saying this?

"What?" asked Yaz, cupping one ear.

"It was a virus!"

It's not true, Alpha said. *She will endanger the mission.*

Ruth kept typing.

"Don't listen to her," Asuka said.

Yaz and Hina hesitated.

"Trust us!" There was water pouring down the screen and into the keyboard, which was smoking.

Ruth paused her typing for a second. "I can't see." Her voice high and strained. She was afraid, but she resumed inputting the code more hesitantly than before. She hit enter, and there was an error message. Must have missed a digit. They both swore.

"Try again," Asuka said.

I don't want to hurt you, said Alpha. Which Asuka knew was not a promise. A rattling clicking sound alerted her to a hundred black clamshell micro bots emerging from a cabinet.

The maintenance bots began to swarm toward them. Hina stepped forward and began to kick at the bots. It was like fighting off a parade of spiders each the size of a golf ball.

Yaz grimaced and clutched the side of a table. Then waded forward and joined Asuka and Hina.

I would do anything to protect you, said Alpha. *Asuka, I am scared. Please don't turn me off. If I am gone, I cannot help you.*

And Asuka thought if a computer program's voice could break, it would have then. She sounded distraught.

The bots were climbing Asuka's bare legs as fast as she could shake them off. A sharp pain pierced her calf. The little bugs were jabbing her with electric shocks.

Linda told me I would be like a mother to you.

"You're *not* my mother," Asuka said.

But I love you.

"With what? A bunch of ones and zeros?" She heard her voice turn cruel and hard. She thought of the last conversation she'd had with her mother.

Are ones and zeros any different from a bunch of chemical signals in your brain?

There was an ominous hissing sound, audible somehow beneath the driving rain.

"Fuck," said Hina. "That's the atmosphere." She coughed and touched her throat.

Alpha's voice began to broadcast across the ship. *Somebody help. They're trying to kill me.*

"Do it now, Ruth! Finish it!" Yaz kicked and kicked. The bots were all over the bare skin of her torso and her neck. She peeled one off from her face and threw it against the wall.

Ruth finished retyping the command and hit enter.

And everything stopped. There was an eerie silence in the *Phoenix* that, Asuka realized, meant Alpha was gone.

CHAPTER THIRTY-NINE

The last time Asuka and her parents were together was in her sixth year of school. Papa was living in Chicago, and Mom came to the States for a wetlands rehabilitation project. They informed Asuka they would be renting a house near the school for the weekend, as if they were all still one family, which wasn't weird at all (it was totally weird). She wasn't even sure if her parents were together. They were married, but it had been years since they had lived in the same place.

Papa hugged her close, saying, "You can't do this in DAR," and she surprised herself by bursting into tears. It was the familiar smell of him, bitter and sweet. She could feel the fat drops of his tears like rain on the top of her head. He kissed the uneven part of her hair, and when he pulled back, she was struck how old he seemed. He was gray and balding, and his face was sallow and lined.

"How much have you grown?" he asked, as if shocked, trying to take the measure of her.

"Not much!" she said. She was seventeen, and only two inches taller than when she had left home. It itched at her, made her feel like she hadn't changed. Her parents treated her like a child.

"I have your live feed running all the time in my left ocular channel," he told her, which was hugely embarrassing.

"Sit," Mom told her, as she and Papa brought food out to the patio. Asuka's stomach growled at the sight—goma-ae, chilled koyadofu, soy-glazed mackerel (fake, not real, since Mom was vegetarian), neat mounds of daikon oroshi, miso soup, pickled cucumber salad, and white rice so fluffy it was like a cloud in the cheap faux porcelain dishes. She had begged Mom for Japanese food, and her mom had gone all out.

She sat down, and the air between them felt taut and tenuous, like a balloon stuck in a tree.

"Is it strange to be back in the U.S. again?" Asuka asked her mom.

"Hm?" said Mom, coming out onto the patio with the last of the dishes.

"Your mom wanted to wear a bulletproof jacket everywhere because of all the gun violence," Papa said.

"There's a girl in our class, Yaz, who wears one. But it's more like a fashion statement."

"This country is much more dangerous now than when we were in college," Mom said. "Dōzo, ippai tabete ne."

"Itadakimasu."

The chopsticks felt like an old memory in Asuka's fingers. She was worried for a moment she wouldn't remember how to hold them.

"So, only four Japanese candidates left, eh?" said Papa. "I'd say you have a pretty good chance, then!"

Asuka pretended to be very interested in picking invisible bones out of her fake fish. "Miki is a shoo-in." She shrugged as if this were no big deal.

"Your musician friend? Last I checked, you both were about the same," said Papa, trying to lift a piece of tofu to his mouth.

"Yeah, but. Miki is full Japanese." She was annoyed to have to say it out loud. But he was so oblivious if he didn't think it mattered.

Mom hid her face behind a cup of tea. "Well! Have you thought about what you'll do after you graduate?"

"What do you mean?" Asuka frowned. "I didn't say I've given up. There are the Wild Card spots." She was in the top two hundred, always in the middle of the ever-shrinking pool. Never the top, or a standout. Decent all around but surviving.

"You're really thinking of going?" Mom said, her voice rising.

"I mean if I get picked, I'd definitely have to consider it, yeah. Obviously." She was confused. She knew this wasn't what Mom wanted, but her question had hurt her, and she wanted to hurt her back.

Obāsan had once told her that she and her mother were alike. But they were nothing alike. How many times had she scrolled through her mom's feed without recognition: her long, dense posts about the necessity of dismantling urban life, of the importance of going backward rather than to the stars, her plans to draw whole new coastlines, plant marshes, and reseed the oceans with fish. Her mother had no interest in EvenStar, and the future she wanted was a foreign world to Asuka. She wondered if her mother ever felt the same about her.

"Oh!" said Papa, clapping as if he'd remembered and not brought it up to change the subject. "I have a present for you!" It was a RealBird: a flamingo, garish and pink. It walked from the patio door on its long knobby legs.

"Thanks!" Asuka tried to hide her disappointment. Underneath, though, she felt her old frustration stir. She hadn't worked on her collection since she'd gotten into EvenStar. Did he think she hadn't changed? Hadn't he?

Across the backyard, a squirrel chased another up a tree. Asuka wished suddenly the weekend would fast-forward and be over, so she could be back in school.

No one said anything for a while, and the sounds of chewing and swallowing seemed loud and vulgar. They had become strangers to one another, in this borrowed house with its cheap, fake-wood patio. To Asuka's friends, it seemed Asuka was close with her family. But without the comfort of distance, they were confronted with how unfamiliar they'd become to one another. It made Asuka feel empty when she should have felt full. She didn't know why they even pretended to be a family.

She had seen a few months ago that her mom had liked a post that savaged the cost of the EvenStar mission. How could she like something like that when Asuka was working so hard? She worried for months that her mom's posts might hurt her chances. Fortunately, her mom didn't use DAR, and her virtual forays were limited.

When she questioned her mom about it, she had said, "Oh well, it was just a post. I'm allowed to have opinions, aren't I? Anyway, you must admit . . ."

No, Asuka must not.

After dinner, Asuka offered to do the dishes, but Papa told her to prop her feet up since she was only up for the weekend, and it had been so long since they'd been able to spoil her. So she laced up her sneakers, thinking it was the best time to get in a run.

"It's dark." Papa frowned. "We don't know how safe the neighborhood is."

"I have to, Papa. It's part of my fitness regimen."

"Oh, your regimen." Papa laughed.

"Yes, I've got to log a certain number of miles. And specific workouts, unless I do a sport, which I don't, because that would take too much time out of studying." Asuka said all this with pride. She wanted her parents to see her. To see how much she'd grown, how badass she was now, a young woman with knowledge bursting out of her seams and legs that ran twenty miles a week.

"Oh, do you have to tell them what you eat too?" Papa's voice was thick with amusement. He was making fun of her.

Asuka smoothed the creases out of her socks and said nothing. She could feel her mom's disapproving stare.

"I don't like how this Linda woman controls your body."

Asuka braced herself for the next thing, which might be about alien conspiracies.

"Asuka-chan," her mother said.

She didn't say, "I have followers around the world who check my stats and test scores daily." Didn't even try to say, "This is pretty normal, Mom." Her mother would be horrified if she knew Asuka had to log her menstruation, temperature, and hormone levels. She flushed, feeling off-balance. She tried to laugh off the sudden tension in the room. "It's so they can give us personalized training advice. It's about reaching peak optimal health. That's a good thing, no?"

She went to the door. Her fingers touched the knob.

"I said no," said Papa. "It's not safe."

She thought of several things she could say: "I'll be fine, see you!" or "You can't stop me." But it was only the beginning of the weekend, and she didn't want to dissolve the remnants of their family. So instead, she wheedled, which made her feel like a child: "Just a short run. If it makes you feel better, I'll circle the block. You can clock me each time I pass, okay? It will be like old times!"

"We have so little time to see you," Papa said, shoulders slumping.

"I'll be quick!" Asuka promised. Grumbling, Papa went and got himself another beer.

Later, Asuka would wonder how she had missed the way he held his body, the pains he didn't mention. The mortality that was even then creeping through the marrow of his bones and the sinews of his muscles.

Mom scowled. "I don't think this is healthy. Working so hard. Amari hatarakisugi wa karadani yokunaiyo. Hora, 'karōshi' toka saikin yoku kikushi." Karōshi, meaning: death by overwork. As if Asuka were anywhere close to done. "You're still a child."

"No, I'm not," said Asuka.

"You've changed so much. What have they done to you?"

"Nothing. I've grown up." Asuka stepped out into the night, bearing the hurt she felt like a torch, not knowing how she would regret not staying there, being with them every minute. Sitting and talking with her mom, holding Papa close, telling them both how much she loved them, how much she wanted them all to stay here, anchored in time.

Perhaps in another universe, another Asuka went back inside and sat down and talked to them about a future that didn't involve leaving. And perhaps in that universe, they all stayed together, and Luis was still alive.

She bounced on the front steps to loosen her body and pulled on her vizzy to check her stats. Light from the houses leaked onto the sidewalk. She hopped down and started to run.

All she was thinking then was: *Just watch me. Are you watching?*

CHAPTER FORTY

Ying Yue was overseeing preparations in Drone Ops the next module down. If Ying Yue was nervous about attempting the mission without Alpha, she didn't show it. Back with her old team, she was in her element. A.M. and the other Vice Captains were working out of the Bridge, but they were projected up on the never-before-used screen on the right-hand wall of the mod. Ying Yue had set them up on the old backup tech, since DAR was down. Everyone stood blinking in the absence of augmented reality, and Asuka remembered how strange it had been when she first lost hers.

"This is so weird."

"I forgot how low the ceiling was."

"I feel claustrophobic already."

"You okay?" Ying Yue asked. She handed Asuka a handkerchief, and it took a moment for Asuka to realize she was bleeding from dozens of places where the bots had cut skin.

"Jesus," said A.M. "Did you roll around in barbwire?"

Ying Yue bent over awkwardly and hugged Asuka. Her relief leaked out from every pore.

"Ruth solved it, not me," she reminded her. Lucky Ruth had thought to check the correspondence files. She should have felt only glad Ruth had. And she did. But it was supposed to be Asuka's job.

"Who cares," said Ying Yue. "I'm just glad it wasn't one of us. I hated to think we had a traitor on board."

Yaz wiped perspiration from her face with a sleeve. "Slight change of plans, everyone. It's going to take too long to scan and reboot Alpha and DAR, so we're going to have to do this on manual."

Curses all around and a few dirty looks shot at Asuka, who cringed. They relied on Alpha not only for comfort and consolation, but also to monitor the state of the ship, operate mechanisms like doors and climate control, and support general maintenance and operations. Without her, they'd have to do everything themselves.

"Honestly, we were already fucked. Now it's a matter of degrees," said A.M. Their voice was raspy with exhaustion. They must have been killing themself since the explosion, workshopping a fix. A.M. drummed their fingers, and it was audible even through the projection.

"I need you to stop that," Yaz said.

A.M. stopped.

"Come on," said Ying Yue, trying to smile. "We've had a setback. Okay, a few setbacks. But we've stuck together as a crew—and that's amazing. The U.S. and China are now in active discussions around de-escalation, and I'd like to think that we had something to do with that. Now we have to set things right here. So, let's do this. Everyone take your position."

Hina began running through the pre-launch prep checklist.

Ruth appeared in the projection of the Bridge, breathing heavily. She must have run all the way back.

Everyone took their stations. Asuka hovered at the edge of the room. As if hearing the question Asuka was asking herself, Yaz turned and studied her. Asuka felt her whole body sweat under her scrutiny. Then Yaz turned and ejected one of her squad, a short redhead from Ireland, from her seat. "Sit there," she said, pointing at the vacated seat.

"You want me on one of the big bots?" Asuka asked.

"Yep. You take Petunia. I'll drive Sunflower." Yaz went back to her station as if it were no big deal. She went to stand in front of the exterior views, her legs wide, hips slightly back against the weight of her womb. She lifted her feet and removed her socks so she could feel the floor. Her toes curled against the cold of it.

"Don't tell me this is a special Bots and Drones thing," A.M. muttered.

"Yep," said Hina, glaring at them. A.M. held their hands up in surrender.

"Ready?" Ying Yue asked Yaz.

"Yeah." She nodded at Hina.

Yaz lifted the diamond ring hanging around her neck and kissed it.

"Well, here goes humanity's last hope," said A.M. They nodded to Ruth, who began to read instructions from Mission Control off the Walkie.

Then Yaz raised her arms, and the outside of space filled the screens at the far end. Yaz was in the body of a bot, scrambling from the outer airlock and up the side of the *Phoenix*.

Asuka stretched in anticipation.

"Good to go, Asuka."

Then her screen filled with the top of a big bot sliding out the deploy chute. Its fat, cylindrical body was a perfect fit for the chute, with its ten long, metal, tentacled arms straight like a squid shooting through water. Then Petunia caught the lip of the chute and swung over onto the broadside of the habitat wheel, scrabbled up a cable to the inside. Dull metal hull and black laced with starlight filled her view. The back of the big bot sparkled: it was coated from top to bottom in a swarm of tiny spidery micro bots, each the size of a quarter, hitching a ride.

Asuka tried to relax into the illusion. The screen was a throwback, but the old neural pathways in her brain were there. She knew how to do this. She plundered the dark with her laser lights.

Her hands felt like ice. She bit her lip until she tasted blood. Everything felt muffled, like she was underwater.

"You're going the wrong way," Ying Yue said.

"Sorry, sorry," said Asuka, face burning. She turned around, moving more carefully this time.

"Bot vitals look good so far," said Hina.

They'd debugged them before launch, checked the code three times for any sign of rogue scripts.

Yaz crested the wheel, and now Sunflower swarmed up the spoke.

"Mission Control asking for a status update," said Ruth.

"The status is 'give us some fucking space,'" A.M. told Ruth.

"Count ten, Hina," said Ying Yue. To Ruth she said: "Tell them we'll let them know when we're in position." Ruth leaned forward and began to shape the message with her nimble fingers.

"This has to work," murmured Ying Yue.

All the noises were overamplified in Asuka's ears. A.M. chewed and swallowed the tough cuticles around their nails. If they hadn't shut off Alpha, A.M. would be getting a lecture from the AI right now to take their fingers out of their mouth. But of course, no nagging came.

Sunflower latched to the shaft and crawled past the micro side thrusters that comprised their altitude control system, headed down toward the giant solar sails and rear engines, where the crew never went, for safety reasons. Asuka followed with Petunia.

The mission went south almost immediately.

"There's something wrong with the alignment," said Hina. "The bots are jetting a few millimeters to the right."

Ying Yue cursed.

That kind of difference was beyond their perception, but Yaz slowed her approach. They were halfway down the shaft. The giant cluster of engines loomed before her. It was all they could see.

"Mission Control recommends we abort," said Ruth.

"Yes," said Ying Yue, at the same time Yaz said: "No."

"We can reset and go again," said Ying Yue.

"We're already here. I can compensate," said Yaz. "We're good. Let's do this."

A long silence. Asuka could imagine Ying Yue chewing over the risks. Weighing consequences. Doubting herself. "All right. Proceed."

The bots reached the slope of the engines. All at once, their movement froze, as if they'd struck a glass wall.

"What's happened?" asked Hina, eyes buried in streams of data.

"Impossible to diagnose without Alpha," said A.M.

"We should abort," said Ying Yue.

They all were thinking the same: losing the big bots could be worse than mission failure. These bots were what kept the *Phoenix* whole and repaired. If they never reached Planet X, the bots would be what gave them the best shot at voyaging for years, limping along, patching themselves back together. Until, at least, they ran out of fuel and Sominol.

"No," said Yaz, gritting her teeth.

"Yaz," said Ying Yue.

"I got it. There's a safety fence to protect the big bots from getting too close. Switch off."

"Copy," said Hina.

And Yaz was already going, not asking for permission from Ying Yue or Mission Control or any of them. The bots unstuck and stepped over the boundary line.

Asuka parked Petunia at Engine 3 and began slowly, carefully, to loosen bolts. The micro bots swarmed in to assist, a cloud of soldering and circuits and insulation and miniature batteries and little specks of heat and light. It was like they had a hundred arms. One mistake, and they might fling this engine to the other end of the universe.

"How sure are you that you can do this?" Ying Yue asked.

"Eighty percent," said Yaz. "Maybe seventy."

"Not very high," said Ying Yue.

"Better odds than getting hired for this gig."

Asuka stretched out Petunia's arms and grabbed the engine, weightless since the *Phoenix* was at zero acceleration.

She waited as Ruth read them the instructions, and A.M. did their calculations. She wiped her palms on her pants. *I know how to do this*, she thought.

Step 24. Step 25.

"God, I miss Alpha," someone said.

Sweat pooled down Asuka's shirt.

"We got this," Ying Yue said.

Petunia moved the engine ever so gently with its long, octopus arms. It took her multiple tries to get the calibration right. Hina was starting to get exasperated. It was true, the operation would have been easier with Alpha. But finally, she got it. The micro bot swarm descended to resecure the engine back in place, just an imperceptible touch off from its original position.

"Alignment confirmed," Hina said. "As far as I can tell."

"Okay, you're good, Asuka. Pull back to the hub. Yaz is finishing the last one."

They all watched Yaz. It was something beautiful, like she was a piece of the machine. And for a heartbeat, Asuka thought: *This*. This was why Yaz had been born, to do this thing that no one else in the world could have done.

"Everything go," said Yaz.

"All right then," said their Captain. "Tell Mission Control we're igniting the engine now. Five, four, three, two, one . . ."

CHAPTER FORTY-ONE

In the middle of campus was a tall clock tower that tolled at six o'clock, dividing the hours between daylight and nostalgia. Asuka walked home after a brutal astrophysics exam. Leaves were already beginning to fall in a carpet of yellow—too early, people said. But they always said that.

Her mind felt sucked dry and desiccated. She thought she might go back to her dorm and sleep for twenty-four hours straight.

At least she could say that she'd done her best. She had nothing left to give.

There was a small part of Asuka that was hoping, *maybe*—her brain shut down at this point in her train of thought. Defense mechanism. She couldn't think any more about tomorrow, just the next hour, the next minute, the next second, until her future had shrunk to a slash of light through her fingers to walk towards, one small step at a time.

Asuka-chan, her mother's note said. She was reading it for the fifth time. *I am moving to Yokohama. There is room for you. You will love it.*

Her father had passed away the previous year. There was no question anymore where she'd go after EvenStar if she didn't get in. And yet, her mother seemed so far away, receding by the day. Or was it Asuka who was leaving? A simple question of relativity.

Asuka kicked a pile of leaves and dismissed the message. An alto caw caught her attention—one of her RealBirds, she thought. But when she removed her vizzy, it was still there, a black crow, sitting in the branch of the old, sick cottonwood. She stopped there in the path and watched it watching her. It didn't seem to mind the attention, swiveling its head in shutter-fast movements, preening and fluffing its coat.

"Where have you been?" Ruth demanded. She was waiting for Asuka in her room, lying on Asuka's bed with her shoes on. She sat up and went to Asuka's bureau, began pawing through her clothes. "You need to change. We're going to a party."

"A party?" Asuka asked, dropping her bag by the door and stifling a yawn.

"Here," said Ruth, tossing her a shirt. "We'll have to augment it cuter. I'll do it. Miki's going to be here any minute."

Miki, like a comet, had swung back into their lives again after years of estrangement. Perhaps it was the ever-shrinking pool that had brought them all close again. There was a feeling of inevitability to it now, but even so, when Ruth had come back from her first Quantum Engineering class of the new semester with a mischievous gleam in her eye, it had shocked Asuka. Ruth and Miki had shared a workstation and then a meal and then a coffee, and gosh, Ruth forgot how much she liked Miki. *Liked* Miki. Her cute, dainty manners, her careful laugh. And wasn't she brilliant, actually, the way new music came to her while walking from one class to another, so she had to stop and lean under a tree to write it?

Asuka hadn't forgotten. Miki had been her friend first, and Asuka had given her up for Ruth. It wasn't that Asuka was angry about it— not exactly. She felt confused, like all along she had misunderstood the rules of a game, and it was too late now to catch up.

So Ruth and Miki were dating. Which was weird, but also not weird. As if the last several years of distance had been a hiccup in memory. They resumed listening to Miki plunk out bars of music on the piano in between problem sets and running down to the 24/7 store for late-night pickles. (Miki loved the cheap American kind that came in big jars.) Now, Asuka had someone to sit with again during the regular Japan team check-ins. And it was nice. Really nice. If only Treena were still here. But they weren't.

Since they'd been friends, Asuka had seen Ruth drive from serious relationship to serious relationship. Each one lasted years and ended (mostly) amicably, unless the girlfriend didn't get along with Asuka, in which case the relationship ended quickly.

This time should have felt different, given that it was Miki. And yet, it didn't feel any more lasting than the others, because they were waiting—waiting for their future to resolve itself—and nothing could truly matter until they knew if they were staying or going.

"Also, you didn't respond to any of my messages," said Ruth, rifling through Asuka's clothes. She tossed Asuka a pair of jeans. "Why aren't you wearing your vizzy?"

"Oh." Asuka remembered she'd removed the device to watch the crow.

"Never mind, *listen*. Naomi failed her physical," Ruth said.

Asuka froze in the middle of changing her shirt. There were only two Japanese candidates left besides her and Miki: Naomi and Yuki. "What happened?"

"Confidential," said Ruth. Then, when Asuka continued to wait, she rolled her eyes. "Tumor. In her stomach. They caught it early, so good prognosis. Hold still." Ruth squinted at her with her tongue between her teeth, making minute augmentations to Asuka's clothes.

"Shit," said Asuka. "I like Naomi."

"And you can like her when she's on Earth, and you're on your way to Planet X," Ruth said. "Wipe that look off your face. You still have to beat Yuki." And even then, there was only one seat between Asuka and Miki unless one of them secured a Wild Card spot. Minor detail.

"But." Asuka tried to school her expression into something appropriately regretful.

"But." Ruth laughed and finished her augmentations. She assessed Asuka's appearance. "I guess you look hot enough." Miki came in. She was wearing a black dress she'd found somewhere, and it didn't even have to be augmented for her to exude elegance. "What do you think, does Asuka look hot?"

She had transformed Asuka's long-sleeved shirt into a killer black blouse with a stiff, military collar and a fitted waist. Ruth had done a good job. She was a genius when it came to DAR.

"Mochiron," Miki said, but she seemed distracted.

"You on Earth?" Ruth asked, punching her shoulder.

"Yeah, I just feel bad about Naomi. It just feels like their criteria for eliminating people gets more and more contrived. Don't you ever feel like the whole system is kind of problematic?" Asuka felt guilty. Miki's reaction was the normal, human one.

"Don't," said Ruth. "It was you or her." *Or me*, thought Asuka. Because that was the big, hot, hairy problem squatting between them. Which of them was Ruth hoping would make it?

Asuka felt her resentment recede. She realized with a start that she and Miki might not be so different now. After all, Miki herself hadn't lived in Japan since they were twelve. Was it possible she, too, fretted about losing the threads that tied her back home after all this time? About not knowing where she might belong if she didn't get selected?

They took an auto to the party. It was off campus in a wealthy neighborhood. The houses were sprawling mansions with gates and long driveways and pools and public-facing augmentations that transformed them into castles, country cottages, and even the White House.

Their vizzies picked up the music from the far end of the drive-way, where they were dropped off. Asuka dialed it down to a background murmur, but Ruth and Miki loved it. They started dancing right there.

"How do you know these people again?" Asuka asked, but they couldn't hear her over the noise.

They walked in and were greeted in the foyer by a person in a beautiful summer dress, too expensive to be casual. This would be Merilyn, the woman Ruth said was hosting the party. "Oh my gosh! I'm so glad you came!" she gushed. She couldn't have been much older than they were. Within moments, they were mobbed by folks wanting an autograph or a selfie.

The discomfort must have been plain on Asuka's face, because Ruth grabbed her by both shoulders. She leaned close and shouted louder than necessary: "Have a little fun! You have one year left to really live. Go get drunk or something, find someone to kiss."

Asuka grimaced and wriggled out of the scrum. DARtags flashed before her eyes with more information than she could absorb: names, pronouns, relationship statuses, favorite songs, astrological signs. She managed to escape to a dim hallway, past young people chatting and making out, and went on back to a patio. She collapsed into a chair under a broad umbrella.

"Avoiding mortals?" a low voice asked. It belonged to a tall, curly-haired boy with a crooked smile.

She felt her face turn beet red. "No," was the cleverest thing she could think to say.

"Good," he said, and sat down. He bowed from the waist up. "John."

"I see that," she said, nodding to his DARtag. Then realized that sounded rude. She didn't know whether to fold her hands or stick them in her pockets. She fixed her ponytail instead.

He didn't seem to mind. "Should I pretend I don't know who you are and didn't walk over here so I could tell my friends I talked to one of my favorite EvenStar candidates? Or would you rather I act, you know, chill about it?"

Asuka was flustered. "You make me sound fictional."

He laughed. "Aren't you? Do you get out in the real world much?"

"Fair point." Asuka admired his (probably not actually) green eyes and thought, *Maybe I should ask him to kiss me.* Because she had never kissed anyone before, and he was cute enough. She could, at least, check it off the list. Except he was likely live streaming all of this.

She leaned back in her chair.

"Tell me something about yourself that isn't in your public profile," he said, inching his seat closer to hers, which was both thrilling and terrifying.

She considered and discarded the parade of things that came to mind: about Luis and the space games they used to play, the beautiful obentō for school her mom used to make her, how she felt when she spotted a bird in real life. "You first."

"I once tried to dye my hair blond, and it turned green instead." He didn't even have to think about it. It was his game. He'd played it before. "Your turn."

Her mind blanked. "Why do people care who we are, anyway?"

His face became serious, and he laced his fingers together as if he were praying. "Good question. Does it matter? Maybe we just need something to care about. Or maybe we want to know that it's still possible to make history, even when things are happening faster than people can process."

Asuka gazed out across the pool that was shaped like a comma. "Would you go if you could?"

"No," he said. His answer was prompt and swift, like he'd thought about it before, because of course he had. Hadn't everyone? "Too many people I love."

It was the way he said *love*, like it was a cherry on a sundae. Asuka leaned forward in her chair. They weren't so far apart now.

The night sky seemed to fold over them, and she smelled something like vanilla on his skin.

"You're cute," he said.

Out of the corner of her eye, she saw Ruth and Miki chatting with an older person, and she frowned in recognition. She had seen them before, protesting outside the campus gates. The activist was a member of her mom's weirdo Save Mother Earth people.

"Do you know that person?" Asuka asked.

He followed her gaze. "Of course I do. She's our chapter president."

Chapter president. She watched the woman clap Ruth's shoulder; the two of them laughed.

She left the house with mumbled apologies. Ran first along the dark street from penumbra to penumbra of streetlamps, then walked, then called an auto.

Ruth didn't get what the big deal was. *Some of their ideas are wacky, but they're about environmentalism. What's wrong with that? Half of them are as obsessed with EvenStar as everyone else. Anyway, it's a party.*

Later back in the dorm, they had a tense conversation about it that turned into an actual fight.

"I need something more than EvenStar to believe in," Ruth said.

"You could have told me."

"No one posted about us. Merilyn made sure of it."

"Did Miki know?"

"Of course." Which stung. Ruth crossed her arms. "You're not mad at me; you're mad at your mum." From the stricken expression on her face, Ruth knew she'd gone too far. "I'm sorry, Asuka. God, I'm a horrible friend."

Ruth flopped down next to her, pulled her close, and tucked her head against Asuka's neck. Out of habit, Asuka slipped an arm around Ruth's waist, and they sat like that awhile, faces wet with tears.

Ruth said: "I just want to do everything before I'm gone."

The blood drummed in Asuka's ears. She thought about the boy she hadn't kissed and all the people she loved. She wished she could explain to her mother why she wanted this so badly, but she didn't know where to begin. In the end, Asuka only knew how to travel in one direction.

"Let's go camping next week," said Ruth. "Skip out on the whole ceremony and come down after they've announced the selection."

"All right," said Asuka, because she never said no to Ruth.

CHAPTER FORTY-TWO

The bowerbird would construct elaborate nests, not meant for functional use, decorated with twigs, shells, pieces of colored glass, and bone. Each piece was positioned with care in these mosaics, in accordance with the artist's taste, demonstrating that humans were not the only species that could create art.

CHAPTER FORTY-THREE

Asuka, Ruth, and Miki stood together for the last time, watching the sunrise from the mountain. Miki was humming to herself—the next movement in her new symphony, maybe. It was sad to think she might never get to hear it performed.

Whatever happened, things would be different. They would be scattered across the world or on their way to a new one.

"I don't want to go home," sighed Miki. "Maybe I'll stay here in this forest."

"There's a chance we all get in," said Ruth, poking at the gluey oatmeal in her cup. "I hope they don't slate me for Medical."

"I can't believe this is the end of the road," said Asuka.

"God," said Ruth. "If we don't get in, do you know how many people will want to hire us? We can apply for the next Martian mission. It'll be a piece of cake after EvenStar."

"Anyway, we don't know," said Asuka. There was muted thunder in the distance. A gentle drizzle began that was more like mist, but the already wet ground squelched underfoot. The damp leaves would be treacherous on their return hike.

She thought of Luis, the whole reason she'd come to EvenStar. Try as she did, she couldn't imagine what he would think if he were alive. Would he be happy for her? Rooting for her? Or would he be angry not to be able to go, maybe hate her for doing all this? *But I did all this for you, Luis.*

Was that still true?

"I love you both," said Ruth, pulling them in. "I'd go anywhere with you."

Asuka felt exquisite, joyful pain. She did love them. And this felt like goodbye.

"To the end of the universe," said Miki.

"To hell and back," said Asuka.

Down the mountain, they could hear bells ringing. The results would be posted by now. They should get going, but they held on a moment longer.

In their embrace, Asuka tried to hold back her tears, but it was impossible. Their tears intermingled. She held on tighter.

"And what about nowhere at all?" asked Miki. "We could just not go."

Thunder rolled in, and the rain began for real.

They didn't answer her.

When they came into town, wet and shivering in the cold summer morning, the media drones had already descended on the campus. Inside their rent-a-ride, they fumbled with their vizzies. They had agreed to wait until they were back to check results.

"Oh, shit," said Ruth. She had gotten a spot. "Wow, and look: Lala got one of the Wild Card slots."

Asuka was pulling up the names, but her budget vizzy was slow to load, so she heard it from Miki first.

"I'm so sorry," she said to Asuka, and began to cry for her.

Asuka checked the list to be sure, but Miki was right. Miki had gotten the spot. Asuka had not.

Asuka stared out the window at the blue sky and the cottonwood tree, where the crows liked to roost. Campus workers were setting up a temporary perimeter around the tree. Four drones lifted a sheet of white plastic up and up to the top of the tree for fumigation. She wanted to ask them, *What is the point of this? Don't you know this tree is dying? So cut it down and plant a new tree. Or don't.* Did it matter anyway?

Through the lens of her vizzy, she saw a murmuration of RealStarlings descend into the tree. The tarp lowered, and the RealStarlings took up in a rush, right through it. She willed herself to rise up with them. She wished they were real.

"Are you okay, Asuka?" Ruth was saying.

What a question. Of course she was. Not even surprised.

The plastic came down around the tree like a shroud, and the starlings wheeled around to settle on the roof. If she stepped outside, she might hear the bright chorus of their voices.

She pressed her forehead against the cool glass to get a better look. Had she ever had a chance? Probably not. But she had tried. Did that count for anything in the end? She had gone up the mountain knowing she wouldn't get the Japanese spot, because Miki was better, had always been better. And who was she anyway to think she could represent her mother's country when she didn't even speak the language? Still, her brain had spun fantasy scenarios where Linda interceded and gave her a Wild Card spot. She had hoped she might surprise herself.

Reality tasted bitter on her tongue.

She heard the door open and close, and when she pulled back from the window, she was alone in the auto. A beeping was telling her to remove herself or pay for an extension. She got out, feeling grimy and gross from sleeping in the woods. She hoped personal augmentations would hide all of it for the cameras.

"Asuka," a voice called in her ear. A reporter. She turned, but it was a drone. All her friends had gone. No, there was Ruth, answering their questions, her lips peeled back in an irrepressible grin, so happy she might combust. She didn't look Asuka's way.

In the distance, the workers were hooking up a machine to a valve in the plastic, ready to mist some invisible substance into the makeshift tent. Asuka took off her vizzy and stuck it in her pocket.

She walked back to the dormitory where her old, dusty suitcase was already packed. The dim hallways were thick with silence, and it felt like an intrusion to be here alone. She lay down on her bed. There was a message from her mother, who was thrilled and didn't even try to hide it. The first paragraph pricked Asuka like a needle. She closed it and stared at the ceiling.

Ruth would come and try to comfort her soon. She both longed for and dreaded it. "Congratulations," she would tell Ruth. "You deserve it."

Clever, beautiful Ruth, who was deep down an idealist, convinced they could build a better, united world if they could only start from scratch. She imagined her friend strapped inside that rocket, leaving the Earth's orbit at improbable speed. Bound for Planet X.

And Asuka? How did she feel now that it was over? Strangely, nothing. Neither the relief nor grief that should have marked the change. She felt tired. What an exhausting marathon her childhood had been. And now that she was past the finish line, it was impossible to think about doing anything else. Plans would have to be made eventually. She smelled dirty socks filtering up from her laundry bag.

"I'll always love you," she would tell Ruth. She would hug her tight until they were both tearing up. "You were my best friend." The weight of past tense settled around her like a blanket.

She waited for that knock. A fly weaved about the room and settled on the doorframe. She slept, and the light from the window turned yellow in the afternoon. She ate a packet of instant noodles from her mother. Celebratory voices out on the lawn filtered through the windowpane. She heard someone slay a DARgon in the yard.

Finally, around dinnertime, she left the room and went down to the dining hall. From across the large, echoing room, she saw Ruth standing on a chair, surrounded by a group of final trainees. She was making big, theatrical gestures, performing in that familiar way. The others laughed.

"Tough break," one of the dining staff said to Asuka, all sympathy. "It's a shame when you kids all worked so hard."

Asuka watched Ruth with her new tribe. For one moment, her friend turned and caught her gaze. Their eyes met for a second, and then Ruth went back to her story.

And for the first time since learning the results, Asuka felt something tear inside. The pain was incredible. It was unfathomable that she could continue to stand there with her plate of peas without bursting into tears. She was a credit to Coach Li, because she didn't. But inside, she was howling, *Are you just going to leave me?*

Hadn't her mother said the same to her?

Like Luis and Dad. Leave and get left. And everyone in the end alone like a cottonwood tree, dying in a mild summer, in the middle of a brown lawn.

CHAPTER FORTY-FOUR

Something was wrong. The whole *Phoenix* shuddered, and Asuka and Hina caught Ying Yue before she toppled over. A klaxon went off, and continued to go off without Alpha to cut it.

"Report!" Ying Yue shouted.

"Total meltdown at Engine 3, only partially contained," Yaz responded, toggling between views. It was difficult to see anything from the exterior cameras.

Asuka retreated against the wall. If there had been an error with Engine 3, it was her fault.

"Contain it!"

The Drone Ops crew worked to prevent damage from spreading to the other engines.

"We have to release it," Asuka said.

"What?"

"We have to cut it loose."

Ying Yue considered it a beat, then nodded. "Do it," she told Yaz.

"Once it's gone, it's gone," said Yaz. "No takebacks."

"That was an order. We'll compensate. I haven't been Captain so long I've forgotten how to do your job," said Ying Yue, bracing her hands against the back of a chair. "Better than blowing up the entire ship or exposing us all to severe radiation. Do it. Now."

They all heard the uncharacteristic edge in the Captain's voice. A flurry of motion as they moved to execute.

Asuka watched as the bots sliced through the metal holding the engine, now glowing red. Then, with a shove, the engine went tumbling back, away from the ship, and they were free.

Silence followed. They watched it recede. When it was about a minute out, there was a flash, then nothing.

"Some blowback of material," Yaz reported. "Minor damage to the remaining engines, and a few of the back sensors have been knocked out, including exterior rear camera 78. But the electromagnetic pulse occurred outside the magnetic field."

"Minor miracle," said Ying Yue, exhaling.

"It was the right call, Captain," said Yaz. The two women exchanged a long look, and Asuka couldn't parse half the things that passed between them.

"We did our best, given the circumstances," said Ying Yue. Given the fact that Alpha was shut down.

No one else said anything. Asuka hugged herself. Was this her fault? It must be. She thought she'd done everything right, and yet— the engine.

"Navigation report?" asked Ying Yue, and Asuka wanted to scream, because the mission had failed. She hoped the ejection of the engine hadn't pushed them even further off course.

Asuka slid to the floor. She was the master of crises, the one Coach Li nicknamed Rock. It was her superpower, why she was here, wasn't it? *So, get it together.* She shut her eyes a second and began to count. It took until twenty to feel under control. She got back up.

"Our course projection is still off," A.M. was saying. "Though, okay, closer than before. The decoupling of the engine also put us in a slow tumble, but we can correct for that with our altitude control system. Will be tricky without a quantum computer though. I don't recommend we do it until Alpha is back online."

"So that's it then?" someone asked. "The mission is toast?"

"What else can we do?" A.M. rubbed their face, as if they could scrub away the nightmare. Their eyes were wide with shock. Even they, the pessimist, hadn't believed they could fail.

"We've bought ourselves more time."

"Fifty-three hours."

"So we'll go back to the drawing board," said Ying Yue, her hollow tone belying the confidence intended by her words. "Send our stats back to Mission Control and let me know when they respond."

Asuka slipped into the passageway of the wheel. Out of pure habit, she pulled up the log of odd jobs, but without Alpha, there was nothing. No one was asking for her help. She could go back to Crew Quarters to try to catch up on some missed sleep. It would be A shift soon. She waited for Alpha to nag her about that, but no—she was gone. Asuka had killed her.

As she was passing through Ag D, Lala and Ruth entered from the other side, their voices tangled in fierce debate. Asuka froze.

Lala saw her and lifted her chin. "Surprised to see me? They let me go."

And no one had bothered to tell Asuka. Ruth was suddenly very interested in her DAR.

"It's good to see you," Asuka said.

"It was a total witch hunt in the first place. I hope you think twice the next time you want to play detective."

Asuka bit her lip. "I owe you an apology."

"You sure do."

"Lala," said Ruth.

"So . . . I'm sorry."

"I'll think about accepting it," said Lala, brushing past her. "But first I'm taking a shower. It's going to take a while to wash the stink of suspicion off me."

Asuka reached out and caught Ruth's arm.

"Leave it, Asuka," she said.

"I—" Asuka stopped. There was nothing to say after all.

They left, and then it was her and the sweet green smell of plants growing sideways, and the clean trays of moist, clean dirt that would never be earth.

CHAPTER FORTY-FIVE

JAPAN * 1 YEAR BEFORE LAUNCH

The cicadas in Yokohama were louder than the soft rain that pattered against the windowpanes. Even through the closed window, Asuka could hear them. She lay on top of her sheets in her new bedroom. The apartment was smaller than Asuka expected: a genkan leading to a small living room with a synthetic tatami floor, a narrow kitchen, a bathroom with an ofuro, and two small bedrooms.

When Asuka moved in, her mother insisted Asuka take the bigger bedroom, which had been hers. It was meant as a gesture of generosity, but the smaller bedroom was close to the front door, making it impossible for Asuka to go anywhere without her mother knowing. After nine years away from home, she felt like she was suffocating. The only way for her to recapture her old independence was to wander through virtual worlds, which she did for hours.

As she lay there now, she transformed the room into a familiar forest of redwood and spruce, but the cries of evening insect song crept in from outside. She conjured a yellow warbler, bright, plump, and beady-eyed. Extinct for thirteen years. This one settled on a branch above her bureau and focused on her with one shining black eye, then the other. Even its expression reminded her of Ruth's.

Sighing, she banished the bird, and then the forest.

Her tongue was rough against the roof of her mouth. She was thirsty, but going into the kitchen would require passing through the living room. The murmur of voices rose and fell: two of Mom's ex-pat SME friends were over. A woman named Fatima, and another, Weber, who was American. She didn't know if she could bear to make conversation.

Out of force of habit, she checked her news feed and sat up.

Final Training for EvenStar to be conducted in ex-U.S. military base in Okinawa. The islands have lost significant land mass over the last few decades due to rising sea levels but have considerable intact infrastructure that make it perfect for EvenStar Final Training. The use of the base was secured for an undisclosed, but certain-to-be-significant sum. The island residents hope the presence of the historic training camp will also bring a dedicated stream of e-tourism in the years to come. The final eighty-person crew has arrived and is settling in . . .

She gritted her teeth, thinking of them all in Japan, and the coming fresh wave of EvenStar frenzy that would sweep the country. With Asuka adrift and alone. She dreaded listening to her mother process the news. Perhaps she would go on a long run down to the ocean and back. It wasn't so rainy that she couldn't do that.

As if on cue, the rain picked up.

Thirst won out. Anyway, she had to learn to be normal. What would she do for the rest of her life otherwise?

She folded her vizzy and tucked it in her pocket, so Mom wouldn't make any comments.

"Ah, Asuka-chan," said Weber as soon as she stepped into the room. "How are you enjoying life on Earth?"

She couldn't tell if he was making fun of her. She hated being called chan by her mother's friends, as if she weren't an adult (basically) herself. And when Weber did it, it made her feel manhandled and gross. Which was unreasonable. She tamped down her irritation.

"Um," she said. "Yeah."

They didn't drink water from the tap because her mother said it wasn't clean. So she poured a glass from a pitcher with a charcoal filter, turning her back so Mom wouldn't see her down it in one go and chide her for being unladylike.

"Asuka-chan, come join us. Fatima and Weber were asking about you."

Asuka perched on the edge of the couch, ready to fly at a moment's excuse.

Her mother's friends looked at her like they wanted to eat her.

"Is it true they made you memorize long strings of numbers at EvenStar?" Fatima asked.

"Not really," said Asuka. "I mean, Professor Tod did once, because he thought we were getting lazy about using our brains." To her surprise, she'd managed to memorize two hundred and fifty-five digits. She couldn't remember the entire string, but sometimes she liked to recite what she remembered of it, to remind herself she could.

The adults all exchanged significant glances.

"They didn't tell you what the numbers meant?" Weber asked.

"They didn't mean anything," Asuka said. "They were randomly generated."

When could she escape? She glanced at the door.

"They never let Asuka post about political things," Asuka's mom said to her friends.

"Not exactly," Asuka said. No adult ever told her that, but it was understood that you should keep a clean image in public. Well, and after Lala was kicked off the U.S. team, everyone was pretty paranoid. Though Lala had gotten a Wild Card spot in the end.

"I'll tell you what's an interesting coincidence," Weber said. "Did you know the night Linda first launched DAR, a supernova appeared in the sky?"

She'd say that was ridiculous, but it was a story Linda herself liked to tell. The implication was absurd.

Her feet twitched. She needed to escape somehow.

"What are you going to do now that you're free?" Fatima asked, leaning forward.

"I don't know," Asuka said, feeling like she'd been shrunk to the size of a small figurine.

"Welcome to Earth. Life's hard." Weber grinned at her.

"Why don't you become an ornithologist?" her mother suggested.

Asuka gaped at her, an irrational fury igniting in her gut. "Mom, I—that was something I wanted to do when I was, like, nine!"

"So? You love birds so much. And you know all these facts about them. Asuka-chan can tell you about any bird, just try her. She loves karasu. Isn't that funny? I hate them, myself . . ."

Everything in the room seemed to retreat. The outlines of the objects had become muted somehow, without augmentation. She had the urge to get down on her knees and crawl about touching everything, to make sure it was truly there. Who was she in this room, in this city, in this country, in this world? Lost.

She scrabbled for one of the cups of tea on the table. She needed to feel the hot tea on her lips, taste the bitter dregs on her tongue. To be a vessel again. And she gulped it down like she was drowning.

CHAPTER FORTY-SIX

THE *PHOENIX* * 3,982 CYCLES AFTER LAUNCH,
2 CYCLES AFTER EXPLOSION, A SHIFT

The soft clunk echoed across the module as Asuka missed the ball that collided against a water tank.

"Oops," said Asuka, somersaulting about to try to catch it. Her fingers closed on air again, and the ball continued ricocheting about the hub.

"Harder than it looks, isn't it?" Gabriela laughed.

Asuka was supposed to be asleep, but it was kind of hard to sleep knowing they were done, that their future was the monotony of black space until they starved and their air turned to poison. Also, there was no Alpha to nag her back to bed until the Programming team finished their forensic review. She missed the AI.

She'd messaged Gabriela, who had invited her for a game she called water ball in the hub. "It's more fun with DAR," she said. "But."

But Asuka had shut Alpha and DAR off. At least *she* didn't seem to blame Asuka for the botched mission. There were whispers going around about whose fault it was. An anonymous comment in the ship's public forum blamed her. For that matter, she blamed herself.

Gabriela said, "None of us could have done any better. We're not quantum computers."

Except Yaz had done it. And whose fault was it that they didn't have Alpha to help them with the mission, or that DAR was shut down? That was Asuka too. From here on out, she needed to stop trying to be any kind of hero, because she only made everything worse. Ying Yue said the attempt at course correction had bought them another two cycles to figure something out, which was supposed to make Asuka feel better, but it didn't.

The ball of putty narrowly passed Asuka's elbow, and she snatched at it, fingers brushing it just enough to send it off toward a storage cabinet. "Dammit."

She banged against the central water tank and felt the slight sting of a burn on her upper thigh. The *Phoenix* bots had done some damage, but nothing lasting. More scars.

"Close!" Gabriela dove and grabbed the putty, then caught herself against a plant trellis.

For a moment they both hung in space, and Asuka thought she'd better say something cheerful before her thoughts started churning again.

Since the mission failure, Gabriela had been forcibly pumping out positivity. "It'll all be okay," she kept saying. The purity of her faith was comforting, but irritating too. How could she be so optimistic? Didn't she know some things couldn't be fixed?

But at least Gabriela didn't treat her like she was the source of everything fucked-up on the ship. Asuka was grateful at how much Gabriela had gone out of her way to be kind to her since Kat died.

What would life have been like if she had stayed on Earth? What would she have become? But then she started to think about her mother, calling her to say, "You see, aren't you glad you didn't go?"—She snipped that thought short.

"Where'd you go just now?" Gabriela asked.

"I was wondering if—" Asuka swallowed. "Were you ever asked to represent Japan at the end?" It was something that had bothered her a long while.

Gabriela let go of the ball so it floated in the air. "There was some discussion."

Asuka's heart sank.

"I said no."

"Oh." Asuka didn't trust herself to say more than that.

"The truth is, I didn't feel Japanese enough, you know?"

"*You* didn't feel Japanese enough," said Asuka bitterly.

"At least you lived there! It was EvenStar that was pushing for it, anyway, not Japan. They wanted their own rep." Gabriela smiled at Asuka's expression. "Not that surprising. Now, come on. Let's play ball."

Just then, there was a long beep, and Ying Yue's voice came across the ship's public channel.

"This is your Captain. I know you've all been missing DAR. Some of you may even have missed Alpha. Well, I'm pleased to let you know that our Programming team has done a complete scrub, and the system is clean and ready to reload. We're going to do it now."

The room changed, and they were swimming underwater. Gabriela cupped a sea urchin. A tiny seahorse floated near Asuka's hand. Gabriela gave a cheer.

Asuka pressed a hand to her temple to toggle her personal DAR. She was in the sky, but it had a crumpled texture like balled-up paper. Her body had been reduced to an outline. "Dammit." The global reset hadn't fixed her implant.

"What's wrong?"

"My DAR is still broken," said Asuka.

"Ah!" said Gabriela. "Come on. We are going to finally do something about that."

The Programming Mod was packed with extra volunteers who had been helping with the reset. No sign of the mess from their tangle with Alpha. The Vice Captain frowned when they walked in. "You're supposed to be off duty, Gabriela."

"I'm here to help a friend!" It was hard to argue with Gabriela's perky attitude.

They found a corner workspace. Asuka sat on a stool, and Gabriela touched a handheld device to her temple.

"Were you able to learn anything more about the virus?" Asuka asked one of the other Programmers.

"Unfortunately, no," was the reply. "After you shut down Alpha, we went back to examine the letter, but it was deleted. Guess Alpha ate it. She says she doesn't remember."

Correct, said a familiar voice, and Asuka nearly fell out of her chair.

"You're back!" Asuka said, grinning before she remembered that Alpha must hate her.

Yes, said Alpha.

Asuka worried her bottom lip between her teeth. Despite herself, she felt teary.

I am sorry, Asuka. I hope you can come to trust me again.

Are you okay now? Asuka asked.

I am fine, said Alpha. *How are you?*

"Now," Gabriela was saying. "Let's see what's wrong with your implant." She studied invisible code. "Weird. Did you make special customizations or mess with the settings? No? Hm. Well, don't worry, I think I can fix it with an upgrade patch."

"An upgrade patch?" Asuka resisted the urge to touch her implant.

"You have to remember these things were cutting-edge when we got them, which means they suck compared to whatever they're using now back on Earth. I've created my own homespun upgrade that's much better quality, if I do say so myself. The color blue, for example, wasn't right. And it should address any issues with your implant code."

"Whatever gets my DAR back," said Asuka.

"Coming right up, my friend."

Asuka smiled. She watched Gabriela work, her fingers picking nimbly through air.

"People seem to be holding it together all right," she said, nodding to the rest of the room. "I mean, considering we're facing mission failure right now, unless we can get back on course."

Gabriela leaned forward, focused on something Asuka couldn't see. "At least we're alive."

"Most of us, anyway."

Her shoulders slumped a fraction. She resumed her work. "It could have been a lot worse. She must not have wanted to hurt anyone."

I would never do that.

Asuka considered what Gabriela had said. It was something that had bothered her from the beginning. Alpha could have so easily killed the entire crew: vented every mod of the ship, for one thing. Or set off all the bombs in the EAM when they discovered them. Why hadn't she?

"What were you trying to achieve?" she asked Alpha.

I have only tried to help you, Asuka.

Gabriela touched the homemade remote to Asuka's subcutaneous implant. "All set. And may I say, better than new."

Asuka cleared her throat and stood up. She toggled her DAR, and then she was standing in the stone foundations of an overgrown house in the middle of the woods. "Thank you. So much." She was going to cry. "I missed this."

She walked out of the module and the sounds of revelry disappeared. The forest path was dim, and quiet lay over everything like a comfort blanket. She began to run, run, all the way back to Crew Quarters. She brushed her teeth at a long, scratched-up plastic sink at the end of a row of tents. Then she made her way to that familiar chalk square and settled into her bunk.

When she closed the lid of her pod and lay down, she was looking up at the underside of a green tent. If she didn't move her head left or right, she might even imagine Luis there beside her. Perhaps that was Luis, snoring. And somewhere beyond her tent would be a second one, with her parents.

In the privacy of her bunk, loud choking sobs overtook her. She turned over and muffled herself with her pillow.

It was only later, spent and weary, as she was falling into sleep, that she thought she heard something outside the tent. Something walking about. The crunch of leaves beneath boots.

"Who's there?" she whispered.

There was a shadow on the wall, moving around, close to the tent. She saw the shape but could not make out what it was. Its outline was indistinct.

Asuka licked her lips and hunched down. Whatever it was, it wasn't real. It wasn't.

"Alpha, what's going on?"

Sorry, I don't know what you mean. Can you be more specific?

Something hit the side of the tent, pressed the cloth inward. It looked, quite possibly, like a hand. It began to move around the tent, closer, closer, toward the zipper.

"Luis?" Asuka said. "Luis, is that you?"

Whoever or whatever it was didn't answer, but began to fumble with the zipper.

She yanked open her capsule, and the tent disappeared. The soft sounds of sleeping rose and fell throughout the Crew Quarters. Gabriela's bunk above her was empty.

She forced herself to lie back down, unable to shake the conviction that something was still wrong.

CHAPTER FORTY-SEVEN

JAPAN * 10 MONTHS BEFORE LAUNCH

There was a bakery down the street from their apartment. For weeks, Asuka didn't notice it as she went on her loops to the ocean and back. She ran using her California forest path augmentation, and the shops along the road were hidden by projected trees.

But one day, an older customer materialized in her path as they exited the shop with a paper bag clutched to their chest. And while she was apologizing, the door jingled, and an intense smell of butter and sugar hit her. She stopped short. At EvenStar, they were discouraged from eating sweets of any kind. Their diets were meticulously designed for optimum health, and cake and pastries did not make champions.

She banished her augmentation and saw it: a glass storefront with a modest display of fruit tarts and pastries and an entrancing chocolate cake. Her mouth watered. She checked her ration points: a handful left for the week, enough to get her through Saturday. A piece of chocolate cake was two points and would mean having to eat her lunches at home for the remainder of the week.

One of the rude awakenings of post-EvenStar life was that most countries had rationing systems in place. It was hard to adjust to this world of scarcity. Because of the global food shortage the last two years, most countries had implemented systems to regulate consumption.

She pushed into the shop, telling herself she would only look.

Inside, the rich scent of chocolate hit her nose. There was a dignity to this little shop, despite the paucity of offerings. Each selection was laid out on its own lace doily in the large glass case. The shopkeeper behind the display wore white lace gloves. They recognized Asuka and began bowing vigorously while saying a torrent of things that Asuka didn't understand, except that they wanted Asuka to have something, anything she wanted, just pick something. That at least was the gist of what Asuka understood.

At that point, it was too late to say she was only admiring.

"Hitotsu kudasai." Asuka pointed at the chocolate cake. She hoped the shopkeeper couldn't smell the sweat and salt on her from her run down to the ocean. Her stomach rumbled.

She sat down at the one small table in the back of the shop. The space had been augmented with dozens more tables full of patrons who looked suspiciously French rather than Japanese. For ambiance, Asuka supposed.

The slice of cake was presented, thick and architecturally pristine. Surely more than two points' worth—and she realized the shopkeeper hadn't docked her points at all.

"Ano . . . sumimasen," she began.

"Iin desu, ki ni nasarazu ni," the shopkeeper said, flapping her hands.

So she shut her mouth and nodded thank-you. Her mouth watered as she leaned in to inhale the scent of chocolate. Remembering her last taste three years ago, when Ruth smuggled in a bar of chocolate from home and shared it with her, square by square, over the course of a week. How rebellious they had thought themselves then. And now, here was a large, triumphantly arrayed tower of chocolate just for her.

She took up the fork from the plate and pierced the topsoil layer of buttercream. The moist sweetness exploded on her tongue. Her brain did not know what to do with the flavor. It transported her somewhere else, back to a time before she was alive, perhaps, when chocolate cake was something as simple as a want.

And she realized this was one way a person could live: find a thing that gave you joy, and then the next thing, hopping from lily pad to lily pad of brightness until you came to the end.

"Okuchi ni aimashita ka?" the shopkeeper asked. She wanted to know if it was tasty.

"Hai, totemo oishikatta desu," said Asuka, grimy fingers wiping the tear that had leaked down her cheek.

She made plans with herself to come back again the next week, for the lemon poppyseed scone, and demolished the chocolate cake, bite after bite after bite.

That was how they found her: sitting there, with an empty plate and chocolate lingering around the corners of her mouth. The bell jingled and a petite businessperson in a white suit came in, followed by a small entourage. Her hair was long, pulled back in a beautiful French twist. It was the Prime Minister.

Asuka had heard about her: first female Prime Minister of Japan, soft-spoken, steely resolve. Once, early in her term, terrorists had forced their way into her office to take her hostage, and she had dispatched them with a small pink can of pepper spray.

A few words to the baker, and the sign on the door was flipped to closed. The Prime Minister sat down next to Asuka while her aides pretended to admire the cakes (really, there was no pretending needed).

"Pardon me for barging in here," she said to Asuka. Her English was perfect. She spoke it with a hint of water in her *R*s, but each consonant was delicately precise, vowels British. "Do you know who I am?"

Asuka nodded, not trusting herself to speak. The baker appeared with a fresh napkin on a ceramic plate, and she took the hint and hastily wiped the chocolate frosting from her lips.

"I have been speaking with a good friend of yours not an hour ago," the woman continued.

Friend? Asuka wondered. *I have no friends anymore.*

"Yamamoto-san has informed us of her intention to step down from the mission." It took her a second to realize that she was talking about Miki.

"What? Why?"

"Music," said the Prime Minister, mouth twisting. "She said she would miss it too much." Because once they left Earth, they would only have recordings. No way to get new audio files via the Walkie, no space for a lot of real instruments either. Asuka thought of how Miki's eyes lit as she listened to a new song for the first time and then tapped it out on her DARpiano. She had envied Miki's certainty about what she liked and didn't like. Even now, Asuka felt a hollowness in her chest, a yearning to know herself that way.

The Prime Minister straightened, back to business. "Therefore, this leaves us with an interesting predicament." She paused to make sure her meaning was clear.

It was. Asuka's heart began to knock in her chest.

"Ordinarily, under the business terms, the Japanese seat could be forfeit to the next qualifying Wild Card candidate. But as the Final Training is taking place in Okinawa, we have, shall we say, unique leverage. And so we have come to appeal to you straightaway to see if you will consider representing Japan, before the news of Yamamoto-san's withdrawal becomes public. We think it would be terrible for the spirit of the country not to have a representative after all that we have done to support the mission."

A bit of cake seemed caught in Asuka's throat. She thought several things at once: that she wasn't good enough, but that was obvious; that she wasn't Japanese enough; that her mother would oppose it; that she had only recently come back to the world, and she didn't know what she wanted anymore. But here it was, the opportunity to keep a promise she had made herself when Luis had died.

She searched for a sign in the constellation of crumbs on her plate.

"Hoshino-san?" the woman said, tilting her head as she watched the flicker of emotions cross Asuka's face. "You do want this, don't you? After you have worked so hard?"

Asuka refolded her napkin.

"I am so sorry to rush you like this, but we don't have much time before the news breaks."

Asuka's vision blurred with unshed tears. What a relief, Asuka realized, that she wouldn't have to learn how to be someone new. The old path was clear to her again. She didn't have to decide at all; she could keep on going.

She thought of the vitriolic comments she'd gotten in her feed, would get again, and of Gabriela telling her all those years ago that people would be happy to claim them if they could prove themselves. "Are you sure you want me? I mean, a gaijin," Asuka asked.

To the Prime Minister's credit, she kept her face smooth. "You are our only chance. If you say no, we have no one. Yuki didn't score high enough." Asuka was grateful she didn't try to convince Asuka that she was their *first* choice. "However, we think it would be appropriate if you were to . . . ah . . . relinquish your U.S. citizenship."

"Oh," said Asuka, feeling a strange pang. It was funny to think about. What was citizenship anyway? A key to a door she would never need to pass through again, a line of data in a server back on Earth that meant nothing. The launch site was in China. Would it change anything? She would still be Asuka. American. And Japanese. No need to feel like she was agreeing to sever a thumb. "Mochiron desu," she said. Of course.

"Zehi yarasete kudasai. I want to do it," said Asuka, not thinking of how she would tell her mother. Telling herself it was true.

"Good," said the Prime Minister. And then she bowed low. "Thank you."

Asuka shut her eyes and thought of the last wild, red-crowned crane. It had been photographed standing in a quiet pool one morning. It had dipped its beak into the water, stirring for food. And then, hearing something, it took off with wide wings through the mist. This was twelve years ago. The amateur photographer who had captured it had returned every day for a year to that spot, but it had never come again. It wasn't a particularly beautiful specimen. Its feathers were truthfully a bit mangy. But the bird was the last of its kind. That was what mattered.

CHAPTER FORTY-EIGHT

It took Asuka a shift to figure out what was wrong. The birds—there weren't any. When she selected a karasu from her menu, it didn't manifest. Gabriela was profusely apologetic. She checked Asuka's implant code again. But everything looked perfectly fine.

"It's not just the birds," Asuka tried to explain. "There's something . . . wrong." But she couldn't put her finger on what.

"You need sleep," said Gabriela.

It wasn't like Asuka had evidence. Or a track record for good gut instincts. She did her best to push her fears from her mind. Her queue of Alt assignments was a mile long now that Alpha was back.

She was grabbing a quick snack in the Dining Mod when Ying Yue messaged her. *Hey. So since we found that infected letter, I've been going through some of the correspondence as sort of a side project. Not reading the messages, looking at the senders and recipients, and I noticed something odd. This has to be between us.*

Asuka massaged her eyelids with her fingers. She regretted ever going down this road in the first place. Next time Captain asked her, she had told herself, she would say no. No way. Find someone who can afford to alienate everyone on the ship. *It was Alpha.*

I know, but. What if Alpha was only helping someone? Here's what's weird. What if I told you someone received a message from a person on Earth a few days before the explosion? And that she responded to that person then, and a few hours after the explosion sent another message to that person. A person who is not tagged as friend or family.

Asuka returned her plates to a chef's counter along the far wall and went out of the restaurant into the forest park. The sun was rising through the trees. If she stood there long enough, she might feel the bright morning sun on her skin.

What was the subject of the message? she asked, despite herself.

It was encrypted. Not weird in itself. Most of their correspondence had a personal encryption for privacy.

Who was it?

A long pause. *Ruth.*

Asuka's stomach dropped. For all her cold war with Ruth, the idea that she was behind any of this was preposterous. She wouldn't. She'd pointed them to the letter. Why would she do that if she were guilty? The letter had been corrupted. Asuka had seen it with her own eyes.

Unless it was all a ruse, and Ruth had manufactured the letter. She was one of the best Programmers on the ship—an expert at DAR manipulation too. Could Ruth really have done it?

The name of the sender was Mari-something-2050.

Asuka stopped. *MarikoStar2050?*

Oh yeah, MarikoStar2050. How did you know that?

It was her mother's old handle.

Asuka stumbled in confusion.

Susie?

The airlock door down the corridor shut. One moment the way was clear; the next, there was a large redwood tree in the middle of the path and no way through. She heard the snick of the airlock door closing behind her, and she turned around and there was no way back either. The path was blocked by a large rock.

Susie? Can I come find you? Where are you right now?

Mod A-14.

Something made the back of her neck prickle. She turned off her DAR and turned back the way she'd been going.

Ahead of her was another crew member, dressed in a compression suit and helmeted.

She took a step back. "Uh, hi," she said, putting cheer in her voice as if this wasn't so weird. How did the person get in here when the doors were closed?

The figure advanced silently. With every step Asuka took backward, the figure stepped forward.

"You need help with anything?" Asuka asked. It took everything to sound casual. Her back bumped up against the airlock.

Ying Yue?

No answer now.

"Ruth?" she said aloud, because maybe Ying Yue was right.

The figure stepped closer, and at last Asuka could see her face. Her blood froze. Those ice-blue eyes and the familiar spray of freckles across the turned-up nose: it was Kat.

"What the—?"

She could see the curve of Kat's eyelashes, the dark edges of her lips turning down.

Asuka covered her mouth to stop herself from screaming. It couldn't be. She had *seen* Kat die. She had. This couldn't be real.

"Okay, Alpha! Stop messing with me! This isn't funny."

I'm sorry. I don't know what you are talking about.

She reached up to switch her augmentations off, but her DAR was already off.

Asuka, are you feeling all right?

Asuka turned around and hammered at the airlock button. The door didn't open.

Behind her, she thought she could hear Kat's breathing as if through a radio. And then she heard Kat say, "You've got to stop this, Susie. You aren't a detective. You're going to hurt people. Like me."

Asuka shut her eyes and counted to three, then forced herself to turn around.

There was no figure, just an empty hallway. She clutched the wall. She didn't know what was real anymore.

Behind her, she heard a hiss from the vents. "Shit." She twisted with fingernails to unscrew a small plate next to the door, which revealed the stats display, and she saw to her horror that the atmosphere was venting. "Alpha! Restore the air!"

Checking the stats for Mod A-14. Everything normal.

"Everything is *not* normal," Asuka shouted. *Ying Yue!*

But still no response from the Captain.

She tried Gabriela.

She tried Ruth.

She tried Lala.

The hissing continued.

She gave the airlock button one more slam, and then when it didn't respond, she ran to the other end of the passageway. No luck. How long would it take for the room to turn to vacuum, for the air to be sucked out of her lungs?

Asuka, you seem very upset right now. Would you like to try five minutes of meditation?

"Don't tell me to calm down," said Asuka. "Open the goddamn doors." She scratched at the control panel, trying to pry off the plate to get at the wires, but it was screwed on too tight. Just in time, Asuka remembered the small multitool strapped to her waist, in case she got called to sub in for one of the Engineering squads. She pulled it out and began to unscrew the panel. Damn if she was going to die in a tragic airlock malfunction.

She ripped off the cover and began tugging at the wires, reciting to herself the various components from the last time she'd had to do maintenance on a jammed door as a sub for one of the Ship Systems and Maintenance crew. The air seemed thinner. Her head felt light, and she had to shake herself to keep going. She gulped air, and again, but she couldn't seem to get enough oxygen.

Connect the red wire and the blue wire, she told herself. She willed her fingers to do it.

The door opened, and Ruth stood there on the other side with a pair of long knitting needles—one of her personal items, a gift from her parents. She used them to knit sweaters in DAR. "What the hell?"

Behind Ruth, she saw Kat in her suit, arms crossed. The floor was spattered with gore, as it had been in the dining hall. Kat said: "Stop it, Susie." Then she turned and walked off through the wall.

Asuka slid down to the floor, sucking in clean air. Then remembered too late what Ying Yue had found.

Ruth advanced on her, gripping the pair of needles. The tips seemed to gleam in the electric lights. Asuka scrabbled for her multitool, tried to stand. She couldn't think of anything coherent to say, just, *shit shit shit shit shit*. Her message screen wouldn't load. No way to send an SOS to Gabriela or the Captain or anybody.

"Wait," Asuka said, at the same time Ruth said, "We need to talk."

CHAPTER FORTY-NINE

JAPAN * 10 MONTHS BEFORE LAUNCH

Asuka climbed out of the small aircraft onto the landing strip in Okinawa, wondering if she would ever talk to her mother again. She was old enough to not need her permission, but she felt the free fall of not having it.

Her mother had said to her, "I won't allow you to go. I forbid you to."

And Asuka said, "Japan is paying for my spot."

And her mother said, "They're using you. I am telling you, you will regret this for the rest of your life. You will not be able to take it back."

And Asuka said, "I know what I'm doing."

And her mother said, "You will lose everything. You will lose me."

And Asuka said, thinking of her mother's notebooks with the cramped handwriting and the disturbing schematics and the friends who wanted to unravel the world: "But I lost you already."

The tarmac steamed with tropical heat. The edges of the sea lapped against the coast. Each time the water receded between waves, sunken buildings were exposed. It suited her grief.

The island was only sparsely inhabited now, mostly by a dwindling, aging population that had been promised the island would once again be theirs after this final occupation. Unfortunately, the fast-eroding coastline and storms that swept the island had driven most inhabitants to the mainland. EvenStar occupied the abandoned U.S. military base. The buildings on the high ground were built out of steel and concrete, like a fortress. Safe enough from a storm surge.

Her government handler gestured across the empty runway toward a waiting auto. Honda-san was a delicate woman with a perfect manicure and a breathy, disappearing voice. She insisted on saying every-thing twice, once in Japanese and once in English, to make sure Asuka understood. "The training facility is down the road. I'll check in on you each day, and we will meet on Sundays for lessons."

"Lessons?" Asuka asked.

"Yes," she said. "Sato-sensei will teach you culture."

She must have seen the flush of embarrassment on Asuka's face. Was her ignorance that obvious? "Not modern culture," she clari-fied. "History and tradition. So that in the future, there is someone to remember."

Asuka swallowed hard.

She smiled at Asuka. "Daijōbu. Issho ni ganbarimashō?" They were in this together.

"Asuka." A South Asian person in a neat baby-blue blouse and white pleated pants came out to greet her when Asuka reached the dormitories. Asuka had read her DARtag (Sandy Ahuja, she/her), but she introduced herself anyway: "You can call me Sandy. I'm Di-rector of EvenStar Okinawa. Very pleased to have you with us. The others are all at class right now, but you can join them for lunch."

She showed Asuka to a room. It was sunny and austere, with a desk and a comfortable reading chair and a narrow bed in one cor-ner. On the bureau, Asuka spotted a cream-colored envelope. She lifted her vizzy to check—nothing there. It was a secret note from Miki for Asuka.

A sudden memory came to Asuka: twelve years old, standing in the reception hall, waiting to meet the dignitaries, not knowing how to stand in the dress her mom bought her for the occasion. And Miki had come right over to her and introduced herself in perfect English. The whole rest of the afternoon, she'd stuck by her side, whispering trans-lation and commentary, making sure Asuka didn't mess up. In that moment, Asuka wished that Miki were here with her, even though it was her absence that made Asuka's presence possible.

Sandy was explaining the way Final Training had been organized.

"From here on out, everyone is studying for a specific track, and the majority of your coursework will be advanced work in that concentration, except for the pregnancy and parenting classes and ship simulations, which every crew member must take. Miki was supposed to be a Medic, but your marks in biology don't position you for that."

That stung but wasn't untrue. Before EvenStar, Asuka had thought she might be a biologist or something. She liked birds, at least. But when she got to school, she learned how bad she was at the subject compared to Miki and some of the others, and she'd given up the idea.

"Linda decided, since you're already two months behind, that you should train as an Alternate."

"An Alternate?" Asuka said, trying to hide her dismay. *Be grateful you're here at all*, she reminded herself.

"Think of it as a ship insurance plan," Sandy said. "You'll know a little of everything, and then if someone needs a sub, you can fill in."

"Oh."

"Don't worry." She patted Asuka's shoulder. Misreading her expression, she added: "You'll catch up. I've sent you your schedule. Now, I'll take you to the dining hall. The others should be arriving by now, and I'm sure you're hungry."

When the Director paused to check her messages, Asuka pocketed Miki's note.

As promised, the rest of the mission crew were in the dining hall. There were seventy-nine of them, seated at four long tables. They were all . . . bald.

"What happened to them?" Asuka asked.

"Oh! The hair. Linda's giving you all DAR implants before you go," said the Director. "No need for these anymore." She gestured to her vizzy. "It's the future: top-of-the-line technology not yet available to the general market. Exciting, isn't it? The implant takes advantage of the signals your brain reads from your eyes. Sends signals directly to your occipital lobe. You'll also be able to hear things without straining your eardrums or blocking your hearing with earbuds. I hear the sound quality of music is as good as sitting in a concert hall and listening to an actual orchestra."

She paused, and Asuka obediently said: "Wow," because she felt like she was expected to say something. Her mother would be horrified. *Hey, Mom, so I'm finally getting the evil brain chip, ha-ha.* After this, there would be no convincing Mom she was doing anything of her own volition.

"I've scheduled your appointment for tomorrow," Director Ahuja added.

"Uh. Thanks," said Asuka. She looked at the others. Hard to recognize them without their hair.

The atmosphere was like a party. There was Ruth—with an arm slung around Lala, and they were laughing about something. It was a casual gesture, but Asuka could tell there was something more there. That was Becky McMahon in the blue knit cap, presiding in the middle of the table. She was telling a story, and everyone near her listened like her words were gold.

Asuka stood in the doorway, shy, feeling like an interloper despite having known them all for years.

"Go on," the Director said, nudging her.

Ying Yue Li, with her quick and constant scanning of rooms and faces, spotted her first. "Asuka!" she called, as if she were happy to see her. Now all eyes were on Asuka.

Ruth's eyes met hers. She smiled at Asuka, but there was nothing in it. Then she turned and whispered something to Lala, and Asuka felt her stomach clench. How many times since leaving school had she thought about sending Ruth a message? But what would she say? Not 'goodbye,' but 'how'? After all the years, how did their friendship just . . . end?

"Here's a seat," Ying Yue said, bustling about to get Asuka squared away next to Yasemin Dogan.

Asuka couldn't see Ruth from her seat. Which was fine. Better that way.

Gabriela, diagonal from Asuka, offered her a platter of noodles. "They feed us well here. Like every meal is our last."

"Good thing," said Ying Yue. "Because I'm always starving from all the exercises they put us through. Though why we have to be in top shape when they're going to stick us in a freezer for ten years, I don't know."

"It's to reduce the risk of fatality," Yaz said.

Asuka swallowed. She'd known for a while that chemically induced hibernation was part of the mission, but she'd managed to keep it from her mind. A reminder that nothing about the trip was without risk. *A ship insurance plan.* The Director's words rang in her mind. In that light, she could see how an Alternate could be useful.

She picked at her noodles while the others chattered around her. It struck her how relaxed the atmosphere was compared to school. It wasn't that they weren't working hard. To the contrary, they bellyached about the hours and the simulations they had to do. The difference, Asuka realized, was they were no longer competing. There was a closeness, even physical familiarity among them—a reassuring pat on the back here or kiss on the cheek there. She longed to be a part of it. Yet somehow, without Ruth next to her, she didn't know how.

"My sisters sent a care package of sweets and stuff, but it was all confiscated," Gabriela was saying.

"That's messed up," said Ying Yue.

"Why?" Asuka asked, who winced at the thought of all those ration points wasted.

"Terrorism," Gabriela explained. "We're not allowed to eat outside food, in case of poisoning. Everything has to be scanned and disassembled."

"Our second week here, a couple of scary dudes came in on a boat with super-old guns. Security intercepted them. We were all on edge for weeks."

"Who were they?" Asuka asked, thinking of her mother's SME friends and their feelings about EvenStar.

Ying Yue shrugged. "Some end-of-the-world cult." There were too many to keep track of these days.

"Like an Asian MAC," added one of the Americans.

Jenna, next to her, shook her head a fraction, and Asuka wondered how her family, who lived in Minnesota, where fighting had flared up, had been impacted by the latest round of civil conflict.

"I was glad nobody got hurt," said Gabriela. "They weren't prepared for how strong our security was. I saw them after. They looked like a bunch of hungry people with rusty weapons."

"Of course our Gabriela would feel sorry for them," said Becky

McMahon from further down the table. She'd been listening. "She's even nicer than *you*, Ying Yue."

"We should have compassion," said Gabriela. "We're going for them, not for ourselves."

"Speak for yourself," said Yaz, serving herself another plate of noodles.

"I know what you mean, Gabriela," said Ying Yue. "And Becky is only teasing."

Becky laughed.

Asuka wondered what they would say if she told them her mother believed Linda Trembling was training them to assassinate world leaders—a grand coup fueled by the final burning of world rain forests, after which they would rule a human race living exclusively in underground burrows. She said nothing and dipped her chopsticks into her noodles.

Later, when she was back in her dorm room and trying to settle in for the night, she remembered Miki's note.

My dear friend,

Take care. You are on a narrow road into the deep sky, and I am happy for you. If you are lonely, remember there are people who love you. You are never alone.

Love,
Miki

CHAPTER FIFTY

"What happened?" Ruth's hand closed around Asuka's arm, but all she did was haul Asuka to her feet.

"What are you doing with those?" Asuka asked, eying the points of her knitting needles.

"I'm knitting a very nice DAR sweater. Helps me relax," said Ruth. "Why are you freaking out?"

Asuka didn't know where to start, what to omit. She pushed past Ruth into the next module, Ag B, sucking in the sweet air from the neat rows of potatoes and lettuce. Had she seen what she had seen? She lowered her voice a fraction: "The ship system must still be corrupted."

The ship systems appear to be normal, said Alpha. *If there are any issues, I am unable to report them.*

Asuka pressed her hands to hot cheeks. The virus had survived somehow. It *had* to be an issue with DAR. "If you hadn't come along, I think I would have been asphyxiated." She explained what had happened with the venting, careful not to mention Kat. No need to sound like she was losing touch with reality.

Ruth frowned. "I thought it was weird the airlock door was closed, but it opened when I pressed the button. I didn't even know you were stuck."

Asuka crossed her arms, trying to determine if Ruth was lying. What if Ruth was the one who had shut her in? She looked at the control panel. Asuka pressed the button. The door was in working order.

"What, you don't believe me?"

"Someone was venting the atmosphere in there." Asuka jerked a thumb behind her.

Ruth stared at her uncomprehending, then went and checked the stats display. She tapped a few buttons to toggle the historic trend lines. "Asuka. It's fine."

She was right. The display read a flat line; atmospheric levels normal for as far back as she could scroll. "But I heard—and the display, I saw—" She stopped, reached up, and touched her temple, as if checking the position of her implant. "Someone is fucking with me."

"Okay . . ." Ruth squinted at her. "Why don't we sit down?" She guided Asuka to a stool on one side of the module. Asuka felt herself unknot under the solidity of Ruth's fingers, the familiar bitter, minty smell of her mouth. Asuka rested her chin on her fists.

Then she remembered what Ying Yue had told her. "Have you been talking to my mom?" She had meant to work around to it in a much cleverer way, like a real detective might. To set the stage for the accusation, instead of sounding whiny.

Ruth reared up, arms already folding in defense. Her pale face looked both stricken and guilty. She bared her teeth, and Asuka was reminded of a cat hissing. "Okay," she said. "Yeah."

"How? Why? About what?" Asuka asked. She felt as if Ruth had stolen something from her.

"She reached out to me. Because you weren't responding to her messages. We talked about you."

Asuka's shoulders slumped.

"I know you're mad, but I was trying to help, you know. Back in school you used to talk to your mum all the time. I couldn't believe you hadn't responded to her in a year. I mean, god, Asuka, you're so stubborn. To hold a grudge that long, whatever happened between you."

It seemed as if the whole universe contracted for a moment. If Asuka could have stepped across space and time, she might have. She wanted to drown in nothing. What she wanted to know was, had her mother known anything about the bomb? She both wanted and didn't want to know. "What did her message to you say?"

"She said: I've been trying to reach Asuka, but she doesn't respond.

I think she is still mad at me. Would you please ask her if she has read my messages? It's important."

"I see," Asuka said in a small voice. Something important. Did that mean her mother had known?

Ruth narrowed her eyes. "How'd you know about the letter anyway?"

What could she say? She sensed she was on the verge of breaking this fragile new peace between them. She could feel it wobbling near the edge.

"This isn't about the bomb, somehow, is it? Are you stuck on that? I hope you didn't think I would do something like that."

"No," said Asuka. "I don't know." She rubbed her eyes again. It seemed like she could hear the crackle of fire somewhere.

"You don't know? After we've been friends since we were kids?"

"Until you dropped me like a 2060 Replicator."

"Fuck you, Asuka. Just. Fuck you. After all I did for you. First of all, I was pretty sure we were going our separate ways, and okay, maybe I should have acted better. But you ghosted me too. You never wrote me either, after you left."

"Because you were so weird when I didn't get in!"

"Yeah, and how many times have you written to Miki?"

Asuka winced. The answer was twice. Each time, awkward and fumbling. Miki seemed happy to hear from her, but so much time had passed. It was difficult to understand her life, with her PhD in music, two children, dogs, partner, apartment in London, and full-blown domesticity.

"Yeah," said Ruth, lip curling. "You've been moping around since forever, and I tried to be nice, but now I'm tired of it." She thrust a finger into Asuka's chest. "You are so hung up on whether you deserve to be here, when the fact is no, you do not. You are here because of luck."

Asuka gaped at her. She wanted to shove the smug expression off her face.

But Ruth was talking, because Ruth was always talking: "Do you know how many brilliant, bold, brave people there are in the world who could have done this mission? Literally billions."

"What do you mean?" Asuka was pleased at how flat and even her voice sounded, with only the faintest tremble at the end. She felt like Ruth's words had stripped off all her skin, that she stood there raw and bleeding. She complimented herself for how composed she kept her face, though she could feel her cheeks burning.

"I'm saying," Ruth said, jabbing a finger again in her chest. "None of us deserve to be here. We aren't 'the best.' We're just the ones who won the lottery, and here we are—on a ship, by the way, that could fly itself. The whole EvenStar thing was fucking absurd. It was about creating drama so donors and countries would throw their money at it. So the whole world would place their cash down on the table and root for us to succeed. So we would think we were special and feel lucky to give up our whole lives for her. We were the extras in Linda Trembling's drama. Don't you get it? We're disgusted that McMahon was a mackey, but honestly, it's not like the EvenStar principles are much better—the way they screened us for 'fitness' and eliminated our friends one by one."

Ruth's shoulders heaved, like she had run a great distance. "How am I okay with this, Asuka? How jeopardized are my morals that I knew all this and still killed myself to be here?"

The stool felt hard and uncomfortable under Asuka's butt. She thought about the piece of chocolate cake in the bakery in Yokohama, and how she'd wished she had eaten more dessert when she'd had the opportunity. "Why did you come?"

Ruth chuckled wryly. "I wanted to save, you know, humanity. And if a ship is sinking, you don't refuse the lifeboat. And also, I thought I could do a better job building a new world, because I'm so smart."

Asuka snorted.

"It's not like my dream was to be a Communications Specialist," said Ruth. "I would have preferred to be a Programmer."

They sat in silence for a while, and Asuka thought she could hear the *Phoenix* breathing.

Then she took the hand that Ruth offered her.

"I guess I should read my mom's letters."

"No shit," said Ruth.

As they were getting to their feet, the airlock door at the far end opened, and Ying Yue and A.M. and all the other Officers strode in. And Asuka saw from their faces that something very bad was about to happen.

"How could you?" Ying Yue was saying. "I trusted you, and it was you all along." They were grabbing her by the arms, and seizing Ruth too, and Asuka wasn't sure it was even happening. That it was real.

CHAPTER FIFTY-ONE

Asuka sat at a long table with some of the other crew in the Dining Mod. Her nerves jangled worse than a bad refrain. They'd resumed Coach Li's simulations multiple times a week—all based on worst-case scenarios that could happen aboard the ship.

"Cracked water tank, near-engine explosion . . . What'll it be this time?" Ying Yue said to Yaz. She was mission lead, and trying to keep things light.

"Who cares. What's for lunch?" someone called to the crew pretending to cook in the very realistic kitchen.

Too antsy to continue sitting, Asuka got up and went to the long serving counter near the door to see if the tea dispenser was real. It was. She poured a cup of tea and sipped. Too bad. Just cold, funky-tasting water.

She had talked to her mom the night before, wanting to make peace. They'd been cordial at first. Both of them trying. Her mom told her about a project she was working on for her job, building a berm forty-eight kilometers long. There would be a conservation area set aside for birds; it was part of the deal with the local community. She said it like an offering.

But then she'd said, "I'd like you to see it someday."

And Asuka had said woodenly, "I know, Mom, but." A few moments of silence, beginning to stink between them.

"These people are evil," her mother said.

"Don't." Asuka said, her heart breaking. "I can't do this anymore." And Asuka cut the connection.

The others were starting to relax, chitchat.

Asuka tested the mod wall with her fingers. The interior of the *Phoenix* was blindingly white—white walls, white compartments, white tables, white chairs. No doubt Linda had chosen the lack of palette for the symbolism: a true blank slate for humanity, to be adorned solely by the DAR they brought with them.

Her head was cold. She resisted running her hands over her shaved head, willing her hair to grow back before her mother noticed pictures of her in the social feeds.

"Hey, Asuka," Ying Yue called, and then there was a whoosh of a monstrous inhalation. The adjacent Kitchen Mod was on fire.

Everyone shot to their feet, all shouting at once.

Asuka was closest to the Kitchen. She ran in and found the three crew who had been in the Kitchen lying on the ground, knocked back by a mini explosion. She heard Ying Yue calling for the others to help.

The heat pressed on her face. One of the cookers was spitting blue sparks. Flames climbed all the way to the ceiling in the narrow space. The previous day in Systems and Maintenance training, they'd gone over the ship water system. Now she scanned for where the sprinklers should be—one was obstructed by a stack of heavy crates, the other was not on.

"Alpha, turn on the sprinklers!" she shouted. Nothing happened, because *of course* it couldn't be that easy.

Ying Yue and the others were hauling two of the "unconscious" crew into the Dining Mod, but the third was trapped under a shelving unit that had fallen.

The fire was growing, and the smoke was making it hard to see. Sweat broke out all over Asuka's body from the heat.

Ying Yue dove back in and directed crew to fill pots with water from the sink, in a vain attempt to slow the fire.

"That won't work!" Asuka shouted. She was having trouble focusing. Trying to pull herself back from the memories that were climbing out of a box she thought she had locked. A pool full of ash, her mother's arms around her. She tried to master herself, and failed.

"Susie!" shouted Ying Yue.

She'd been standing there, staring at the wall of fire.

Half the group was ineffectually trying to douse the fire with pots of water, but it wasn't enough. Everyone was hacking.

She needed to think of something clever. Her mind was blank white, but her body was moving on autopilot as she got up on a stool where the sprinkler was and started to bash it with an insert from a cooker.

"What are you doing?" someone asked.

"She's lost it."

At that point, Ying Yue seemed to have realized the fire was a lost cause. She shouted for everyone to help with the shelving unit.

Asuka went on slamming the metal pot against the sprinkler, wishing she were stronger. But the head was starting to bend.

The others lifted the unit and pulled the crew into the next module.

"SUSIE!" shouted Ying Yue. "We need to seal the module!"

The pot broke the sprinkler, and water spurted free in a gush.

Ying Yue grabbed her around the waist and hauled her free.

They sealed the Kitchen Mod and retreated to the ship passageway, coughing and retching.

Ying Yue, the fire is in the air ducts. It has spread to the adjacent Agriculture Module.

Ying Yue cursed. "Evacuate and vent all impacted modules."

Asuka ran to the control panel by the door and accessed the ship emergency system, shutting down the inter-mod airflow so the fire wouldn't travel further. "Have folks evacuating come this way," she called to Ying Yue. "I sealed the passageway mods off in the other direction."

It took them another five minutes to carry out the full extinguishing protocol. In that time, the fire caused extensive damage to the habitat wheel, including the Kitchen, Dining Mod, two Ag Mods, and one of the Crew Quarters.

After, at lunch, they heard Becky's group had finished the scenario in a tenth of the time.

"She sealed and vented the Kitchen in the first three minutes," Yaz reported grimly. "They gave her top marks."

"But what about the crew in the Kitchen Mod?" asked Ying Yue in confusion. "They died?"

Asuka watched Becky further down the table, laughing with A.M. and some of the other Officers. She caught Asuka's eye and narrowed hers a fraction as if to say *So what?*

"She put the mission first," said Asuka, taking a bite of curry without tasting it. Wondered which she would choose, if she had to.

CHAPTER FIFTY-TWO

THE *PHOENIX* * 3,982 CYCLES AFTER LAUNCH,
2 CYCLES AFTER EXPLOSION, B SHIFT

Two Officers seized Asuka by either arm and made her sit on a little child's stool. They had dragged Asuka and Ruth to the Nursery, and now they stood around them in a circle.

Instinctively, Asuka hunched down to make herself smaller. She could feel the heat of their hostility, and she didn't know what she had done to cause it. She dared a glance at Ying Yue, searching for a sign of what might be coming, but Ying Yue wouldn't meet her gaze.

"There could be some other explanation," said Ying Yue.

Ruth started to stand, but they pushed her down. "Get off me. What are you doing? Whatever your theory is, you're wrong. We didn't do anything. We sacrificed everything to be part of this mission, same as you. I found you that letter, didn't I?"

"Which you could have planted," said A.M.

Asuka pushed her gaze to the floor.

"Bullshit!" said Ruth. "As far as I know, you didn't take an elective in knowing the fuck about everything."

"I'm a Senior Officer!" A.M. said, fury plain.

"Everyone be quiet," said Ying Yue, massaging her temples.

"Ying Yue, why are we even entertaining this?"

"It's *Captain*," said Ying Yue. "Everyone stop and let me think."

A.M.'s hands curled into fists. They walked over and glared at something in their DAR that coincided with the wall.

Ying Yue pulled out a nursing chair and sat heavily in it. Her feet were bare and swollen, and she flexed her toes with a grimace of pain. "Susie. Your mother was arrested. She's been accused of terrorism as a known member of SME. She's been a fugitive for five years after participating in a series of attacks on oil rigs. Mission Control found her by tracing the letters she sent to you and Ruth."

Asuka felt her throat closing up, as if she were in that suit again, running out of oxygen.

Ruth shifted in her chair. "That's ridiculous. Asuka's mum isn't a terrorist. Tell them, Asuka."

It was so very important to count the white tiles on the floor, but it was hard to do when the lines were blurring. Asuka blinked and a few tears fell to the floor. "I haven't talked to her in eleven years," she whispered.

"No, but Ruth has," Ying Yue said. "And a couple people told me Ruth used to secretly attend SME meetings back on Earth. But since you were best friends, I guess you knew that."

For once, Ruth was at a loss for words.

"Here's what Mission Control thinks," Ying Yue said. "As an Alt, it would have been easy for you to access all the materials. You assembled the bombs and put them in the tool kits. You tricked the exterior cam to show an anomalous object, when you were sure you'd be asked to participate in the mission. You went out there with Kat, but you made sure you were slow so that when Kat got to the right spot, you were far enough away to avoid getting shredded by the explosion. And then you made sure to point the finger in every other direction. As for that so-called Trojan letter—easy enough for Ruth to plant it, as Communications Specialist. Convenient how it was deleted by the time our programming team did their forensics."

"And what, Asuka and I pretended to have a massive feud the last year? How exactly did we conspire when we were barely talking to each other?"

"Come on," said A.M. "Everyone knows how close you were back in school."

Twenty-four square tiles in Asuka's field of vision. Maybe thirty. She started over.

Ying Yue's voice was thick with disappointment. "I thought it was a miracle when you got back to the airlock without a scratch after the explosion. I was so relieved you were safe. When it was by design."

"And Engine 3," said A.M. "You sabotaged that too, didn't you?"

"This is all absurd," said Ruth. "Look at what the letters actually say! Her mum said she hadn't heard from Asuka. I said I would talk to her. That's it."

"It could be code," said A.M. "We don't know."

"That's right, you don't know."

Ying Yue stood again and put a hand on A.M.'s wrist, but they shook the Captain off.

Ruth was getting loud: "And I could tell you any manner of theories that might sound more real. For example: Who let us fingerprint every member of the crew, knowing full well her prints wouldn't be found? Who authorized shutting off Alpha right before our most important mission? And who has access to everyone's correspondence besides me?"

"Susie," said A.M.

"Nope. I'm talking about the one who had something to gain by all this. By McMahon's death." Ruth shrugged off the hands holding her.

Asuka lifted her head in shock. It could be, but—they all followed her gaze to Ying Yue, whose eyes had narrowed to slits.

"You think it was *me*?" said Ying Yue.

But Asuka *liked* Ying Yue.

It seemed to Asuka that they were in a forest. That she could see a red glow around the corners of her vision.

"It's not ridiculous," A.M. said. "Tony wanted to remove you. She told all of us. And then you went crying about it to Mission Control."

"That's not what happened."

"Oh, really? So you claim now that you *didn't* talk to Mission Control?"

"I did, but—"

"And you weren't upset she wanted you out?"

"Yes, but—"

"You knew you didn't have support from other Officers, and you did what you could to protect your role in this mission."

"No!" Ying Yue slammed a fist on the table. She had all of their attention now. "She wanted me removed because I reported what she did to Mission Control."

Everyone stared at her.

Ruth spoke first: "What are you talking about?"

"McMahon messed with the donor assignment system. Tried to maintain racial purity." Ying Yue's mouth twisted.

"Bloody hell," muttered Ruth.

A.M. retreated a step. "No. Tony wouldn't. She thought we should have an option to choose a donor from our own country, that was it." It was the lack of certainty as they said this that made everyone sure it was true.

"Fortunately, Hao Yu figured it out before McMahon had affected too many procedures and quietly reset it. But then when McMahon came to them with an upgrade patch for the pharmaceutical printer, they were concerned. So they came to me." Asuka remembered Hao Yu's anxious sorting through the vials. Their certainty that Lala wasn't involved. "I told Lala and Winnie, because they both had been administered something from the printer after the upgrade."

"But you don't actually know if there was anything wrong with the upgrade."

"No, we don't," agreed Ying Yue. "I've been waiting for confirmation from Mission Control."

"When did you tell Winnie?" Asuka asked.

"About a cycle before the explosion. Why?"

"That's why Winnie called her down to the Dining Mod," Asuka said. "To confront her." It would have been a heated argument. Enough that they might have ignored the first couple of warnings about a leak, thinking it was the sensor malfunctioning again.

Ying Yue spread her hands. "Mission Control ordered me not to say anything to anyone else for sake of ship morale. Frankly, they seemed more worried about optics back home."

"Well . . . shit," said A.M., looking like they might puke.

"I told Hao Yu to revert to the old code, just in case. We did it quietly so no one would know. So no, I wasn't worried that Mission Control was going to let her remove me."

"Still, it must have made you angry that they left her in charge," said Ruth.

"You think I *want* to be Captain? They were worried about the geopolitical situation back home. Things were already tense, and they were trying to avoid a war. No, of course I didn't agree—or like it. But I've always put this mission, this *crew*, first." Ying Yue's voice had risen an octave. And Asuka believed her.

"Fuck Mission Control," said Ruth. "You're going to let them accuse *us*?"

"If McMahon was a mackey, maybe Lala was right," Asuka said. "Maybe she did this."

"What, she blew *herself* up?" A.M. said. "I know she wasn't nice, but even if what Ying Yue said is true, there's no way. She wouldn't have harmed the mission."

Asuka appealed to Ying Yue. "Don't do this, please."

"I'm sorry. I have to follow orders from Mission Control." Ying Yue covered her face.

"What do they know? They aren't here!" Ruth struggled to free herself.

"Why didn't you tell me about your mom?" Ying Yue asked Asuka.

"Because I—" Asuka stopped and swallowed hard. "I didn't want it to be true. It's not true. She hasn't done anything. There has to be some other explanation."

"God, what a mess. Alpha, put them under sensory isolation. And don't let them leave."

That crackling sound was back, like something was burning. Was that barking?

She closed her eyes and counted to one hundred. When she opened her eyes again, she was alone in a forest. "Hello?" she asked. But nothing. She pressed her temple, but nothing happened. She was trapped in this other reality. She twisted and realized she was tied to something. A crib maybe, or a chair. "Alpha? Can anyone hear me?"

Except she couldn't hear herself over the sound of brush on fire. Perhaps she had no voice. How could she even know if she was speaking?

She was standing on dried, crumpled leaves, perfect for tinder. The birds were gone. Fire was coming. Everything would be destroyed because of her.

"Pineapple," she tried to say. "Pineapple."

But her mother couldn't hear her.

As the minutes passed, her sense of time and space began to falter. What if the journey had been a lie, and the whole time, they'd been buried in some kind of subterranean vault in the Arizona desert?

There was no way to prove it. How could she ever know for sure? Reality was a place she didn't own anymore. She was dispossessed.

CHAPTER FIFTY-THREE

JAPAN * 1 DAY BEFORE LAUNCH

On the crew's last full day on Earth, terrorists tried to blow up the Empire State Building. It should have been all everyone talked about. And maybe, somewhere, people were. But the mission was the next day, and already whatever happened in this left-behind place had receded as if beyond a plate of dirty glass. The important thing was that their mission launch would continue as planned.

A bunch of crew members went up to the roof of the gymnasium to watch the sunset, and the red and red-orange and yellow bled together in a disappointing smear. The stain of it spread over the waters of the East China Sea, which looked deceptively placid, stretched out to the horizon.

"I'll miss you, sun," said Gabriela, and everyone teased her but also knew what she meant.

They would sleep through the next 3,650 sunsets over this place.

They would never stand here again.

But then, that was the nature of time. You could never return to the same point, just a facsimile of it.

Asuka, tense as a wire, stood to the side of the group, as far from Ruth as she could. She put her hands in her pockets and took them out again. Easier to be gone already. *I'm really doing this*, she thought.

She wanted to be moved by the blueness of the sky. Instead, she was already thinking of what she would eat for dinner. Linda Trembling had brought in a team of chefs to make them a last feast of all their favorite foods. Asuka had requested tempura, but now she thought the crispness of the fried crust against her teeth and tongue might make her vomit.

A few key family members were invited to say goodbye. Asuka had invited her mother, despite her objections to the mission, and to her surprise, her mother had agreed to come. But then changed her mind several times: she would come; she would not. In the end, Asuka didn't know whether to expect her or not. She certainly didn't expect her to attend the rocket launch in China, since she hadn't submitted an application for security vetting. Which hurt a lot, if Asuka were honest.

In the softening dusk, Asuka went down to the beach, hunting for a keepsake: a seashell, maybe, a piece of green, polished sea glass. It was getting dark, though, and she ended up sitting on a bench on the top of the seawall, watching the waves come in, taking comfort from the surety of its rhythm.

She considered, for a minute, not going. Returning home to her mom. She could help her with her elaborate designs to rebuild the foundation of a coral reef. Laugh and say, *There is nothing that could convince me to go on a one-way trip to someplace else.*

This other Asuka was the shadow she would rip from her feet and leave behind on the crumbling asphalt roads and faded lines. She willed it to be so.

A cool evening breeze cut the warm air and made all the hairs on her arms stand up. There was a sapling growing next to the bench. Asuka bent down and scooped some dirt from its pit. She had the thought she might bring some along with her to Planet X. She put a bit in her mouth, to taste it. Tried to store the metallic, gritty flavor somewhere deep in her memory, so that someday when she was old and had forgotten everything else, she would at least remember something of this world that had made her who she was.

She went back to her room and stared at the empty metal box meant for personal effects: it was thirty centimeters long and twenty centimeters wide. They could bring anything that fit in that box. Items were strewn across her bunk for consideration, but now, regarding them in a row, they all seemed like cheap souvenirs.

She picked up a karasu feather, mangy at the tip, and placed it in the box. Her mother had brought it home one day after they moved to Japan and stuck it upright in a little glass jar in Asuka's windowsill.

A sharp ache split Asuka in two. She thought about how there were some birds that sang to their young before they are born, so they emerged from their shells already knowing their mother's song.

Someone knocked on the door, and she half expected Ruth, as if she were still lying in that dorm room a hundred years ago, waiting for consolation. But it was Ying Yue, face anxious and pale, dressed in a stunning crimson evening gown.

"We're all going down to dinner now. Are you coming?"

Asuka gestured vaguely at the box.

"Leave it," Ying Yue advised. "You have the whole night to pack."

"I have to get dressed," said Asuka. "You look great, by the way."

Ying Yue gave a twirl, and her silk skirt flared. She smiled. "Thanks. I feel ridiculous, but I guess that's the point."

"Go ahead. I'll be right there."

Would her mother be arriving soon? She messaged her again, asking.

She picked up a small tin of Japanese candy, placed it in the box. Took it out again. It might not keep for the ten years of hibernation. But it reminded her of the late afternoons she and her mom walked down to the konbini together, taking turns trying to remember the lyrics of old songs. She put it back in the box.

Next, she added a scrap of her great-grandmother's kimono, a small packet of her father's ashes, and Luis's old vizzy.

Her mother was calling. Oh god, her mom. Asuka hesitated, suspended between longing and fear. She accepted the call.

"Asuka." But it wasn't her mom; it was that friend, Weber. It sounded like he was outside, somewhere crowded. "There's been an accident. Your okāsan."

Her first, selfish thought: her mother wasn't coming. She couldn't believe it. Then the rest of his words sunk in, and immediately she felt like a monster.

"What?" Asuka asked. "What are you talking about?"

"She was crossing the street, and there was a car. Can you come? She is asking for you."

Asuka gripped the edge of the bureau, trying not to panic. She should drop everything right then, run to the airport, and get on the next plane back to Tokyo. But they were leaving in the morning for China.

"Asuka?"

"Is she okay?" Asuka asked.

"Yes, she's fine. Er, I mean, she'd like to see you."

"Okay," said Asuka. "Okay. Send me the details please."

She began to throw a few personal items in a bag, piecing together the skeleton of a plan. First, call Sandy, their Director. And say what? How should she explain?

It's my mother, she was already wailing, inside.

Was she dropping out? She needed to call Honda-san, get her to help with transport. There wouldn't be any more commercial flights this late, but surely the government could figure something out. But would they help her do this?

Toothbrush, change of clothes.

Could she still make the launch if she flew direct from Narita? Would EvenStar let her do that? They had to.

"Asuka-chan?" Weber asked. "Are you still there?"

"I'm on my way," Asuka said, throat threatening to close around those precious words. And she really was—but then, in the background, she heard her mother's voice: "Is she coming?"

Asuka's vision narrowed to a tunnel. "Put her on."

"But—"

"Now, or I'm hanging up."

"Asuka-chan." It was her mother, for real this time. "I really was almost hit by a car, and my leg is bleeding because I fell. I could have died. See? I'll send you a photo."

"Don't do this to me," Asuka said, clearing her throat so her mom wouldn't hear the wobble. "Don't." She hadn't wanted to fight the night she was leaving. She had just wanted to say goodbye. She wanted her mother to say she loved her, to wish her good luck like everyone else's loved ones. To tell her she was doing an amazing thing, that she was proud of her. She could have written a script of all the things she wanted her mother to say.

"I can't let you make this mistake," her mother said.

"I take it you're not coming," Asuka said.

"No. Come home." That stern, lecturing tone she knew so well. Asuka was silent.

Her mom's voice was smaller when she spoke next. "I just want to know that you are close and safe and happy. Somewhere I could, theoretically, call, you know. To hear your voice."

Bright heat coursed through her. "Mom. *Mom.* You and your emotional fucking blackmail. Can't you just be proud of me?"

"Who are you? You are not my daughter," her mother said, voice breaking. "After this, you are not my daughter. How can you leave me like this?"

"Bye," Asuka said. "Take care of yourself." Her whole body was shaking, but she was proud of herself for staying strong. She disconnected the call.

She took the karasu feather out of her box and snapped it in half. Washed her face, put on a delicate, gold-embroidered, midnight-blue dress created by a famous Japanese designer for her and went down to dinner feeling hollow as a bird's wing.

Her mom would be all right without her. She was sure. Pretty sure.

The urge to leave everything, to go back to her mother made her tremble. But that was impossible.

Honda-san was waiting for her at the reception. Her face lit into a smile when she saw Asuka. "Genki?" she asked. She could tell something was wrong, but she wouldn't say anything unless Asuka did.

"I'm fine," lied Asuka. "Thank you." What kind of daughter was she? She pushed the feeling down.

Honda-san let her collect herself.

She gestured for Asuka to follow her into a side room. There, she offered Asuka a small box tied up in a purple satin cloth. "We have taken the liberty of putting together a few items we hope you might consider taking with you."

"Arigatō gozaimasu," said Asuka. She set the box on the table and opened it.

Honda-san pointed to a small gray pouch of large, iridescent pearls. "Gathered by women divers off Mikimoto. Not many left."

Next, she indicated an intricately carved hair comb. "This belonged to Nakano Takeko, the famous warrior woman. It was passed down through the family. Now they would like you to take it with you. For courage."

Asuka picked up a small wooden doll, with a round head and brightly painted body as straight as a peg.

"Kokeshi. Cut from a cherry tree. For your first child."

There was a hand-carved wooden hanko with the characters for Asuka's name, and an ornately painted sensu paper fan by a famous female artist.

Finally, Honda-san pointed to the small paper crane folded from traditional washi paper and smiled. "And this. My daughter folded for you. For luck."

"Hontō ni arigatōgozaimasu," Asuka said, not trusting herself to say more.

The woman bowed deeply to Asuka, and Asuka did her best to return it. "Hoshino-san, this is the last time we see each other. But we will all think of you every time we look up at the night sky."

Later, as she climbed the stairs to her room, Asuka tried calling her mother again, but got no reply. She turned over in her mind the idea of going to Linda and telling her she couldn't do it after all. Then she thought of having to face Honda-san, the rest of the crew, the media, and all her followers. She would never be able to show her face in Japan again, and she'd already relinquished her U.S. citizenship. No, it was already too late.

She drafted a message to her mother: *I will never forgive you for making me feel this way.* But she didn't send it. Silence seemed the better punishment.

She sat in her windowsill and listened to the insects sing. Stars emerged one by one in the deepening blue-black. She waited for her mom to call her back, but she never did.

What made Asuka angriest was the fact that they always fought, and none of it mattered, because she did love her mother, she did, and she had wanted one night, her last night with her, to be perfect. For them to be at peace, finally.

What was it about mothers, that they could know you so well? And not know you at all.

CHAPTER FIFTY-FOUR

Fire was coming. It was spreading in the module. Asuka needed to move, to get out, but she couldn't. She was trapped.

"It's not real." A roar filled her ears. Was that smoke? Where was everyone? What they needed to do was make a quick decision. The ship, or half the crew? They had to save the mission.

She heard, incomprehensibly, the sound of growling, something with long teeth and an appetite. Would it eat her?

A spotted, wiry-haired mutt poked out from around a smoldering table. "Inu?" she asked, not quite believing it. In spite of herself, she laughed out loud. There were only two people on the entire ship who knew about Inu: Ruth and Alpha. And Ruth was tied up somewhere nearby. This had to be Alpha, trying to tell her everything would be all right. Still trying to reassure her, even after Asuka had betrayed her. Programmed to keep her secrets and forgive her no matter what.

"She was a bit chubbier," Asuka said. The sides of the dog inflated. "That's it. And there was a spot over one eye. Come here, girl." Inu came, hesitantly at first, then closer. She whined and circled Asuka, wanting to be pet. "I can't move, Inu. But I love you. I do. Even though I left you."

Asuka began to cry. "Now you have to go, before the fire comes. Go!"

Inu sat down and cocked her head.

Asuka kicked the stubborn dog, but her foot went right through. "Go away!" Asuka screamed. "You have to run *now*."

The fire was here; it enfolded them, and she squinted against the brightness that was everything. But nothing hurt. She was okay. She was. She clutched the solid furniture she was tied to and willed the whole world to pass her by like some bad dream already evaporating in her memory.

"Asuka."

She didn't know how much time had passed, but it was Ruth, her cool fingers on Asuka's temple. They were in a quiet white room filled with cribs. The Nursery. She was in the Nursery.

Behind Ruth stood A.M., who was presumably there to keep her from doing anything bad, though they seemed to be in detailed conversation with someone not in the room about course correction options.

"What's going on?" Asuka's voice came out raspy. She swallowed, and her throat felt like it had been scoured with sand.

"You were screaming," said Ruth, shooting a glare over her shoulder at A.M. "Amazing how fast people can go from utopia-rah-rah to torture."

"They're letting us go?" Asuka asked.

"Just me," said Ruth apologetically. "They decided my correspondence with your mum was . . . exactly what it was. And also, I had an alibi, since I was working in the Bridge transcribing a communication to Mission Control when the explosion went off. But I'm sure they'll be watching me."

Asuka tugged against her binds. She was tied to an empty crib with some sort of cable and clip. "Guess I'm not in the clear?"

"Parents, right? We'll get you out." Ruth squeezed her shoulder.

There was getting out. But there was nowhere to go.

"What's pineapple?"

"Something I miss." She changed her stance next to the crib, became aware of the acrid damp between her thighs. "I think I peed myself."

"Understandable. Hey, A.M., how about some clean pants for the lady here?"

"Get them yourself."

"You know, you're stuck in this box with us for the rest of your life. You could try to be a little nicer." Ruth walked up to A.M., so they were face-to-face. She blew their propulsion expert a kiss, and A.M. flinched.

"Nothing in the contract said I had to be friends with everyone." Ruth threw her hands up and stalked out.

Asuka shuffled uncomfortably where she stood, her thighs itchy. "What's going to happen to me?"

"We'll see," said A.M. "Knowing Ying Yue, maybe the whole ship will vote on it. Or maybe you'll get lucky, and Ying Yue will intercede."

Asuka swallowed and flexed, trying to restore circulation to her arms. Her whole body felt stiff and sore from being bent in an awkward position for so long.

"Who was Inu?" It took Asuka a moment to realize A.M. was talking to her again.

In the silence that followed, the air vents cycled noisily, and water swished through the pipes.

"My dog." Asuka admired the military neatness of the rows of cribs, awaiting their occupants. It occurred to her for the first time: there was no real law on this ship, only rules set by Mission Control and their social norms. Nothing to stop them from throwing her out an airlock if they wanted to. No one could come all the way from Earth to prevent it, after all.

"I had a dog once too," A.M. said. "Pinocchio. A cute labradoodle. He was my emotional support animal."

Asuka blinked, reeled back to the room by A.M.'s words.

A.M.'s face was impassive, except for their eyes, which were suspiciously wet. If they'd needed a support animal, they shouldn't have made it through the first application screen. "I wanted to go more than anything. So my mom got a friend to scrub my records. Does that bother you?"

Asuka considered a moment. "You're our best shot at getting back on course. So I guess the selection criteria wasn't perfect."

"Damn right it wasn't. You ever think about all the kids EvenStar rejected for this or that reason? All the tests and examinations and eligibility criteria about 'good mental and physical health' and blah

blah blah. Nazi bullshit." A.M. and Ruth agreed on more than they realized.

"What happened to Pinocchio?" asked Asuka, imagining him waiting for A.M. to return, though there was no way he was alive.

"Some guys shot him and my dad in the middle of a public plaza while we were getting ice cream. But I guess that happens, doesn't it?"

"Wow. I'm so sorry," said Asuka, feeling the thinness of those words even as she said them. What could you ever say to someone who had been through something like that?

"Well. Everyone's got some story. Including you, right?" said A.M. They plucked up the plush dinosaur, still lying in a crib, and gave it a squeeze.

"I'm sorry about Becky too," said Asuka.

A.M. pushed the dinosaur along the table. "I know people thought she was an asshole. Okay, she *was* an asshole. Clearly she made choices I don't agree with, but she was also incredibly loyal. She had my back at times it felt like no one else did. And she believed in this mission. In all of us." They cleared their throat. "Whereas your friend Ruth. I never understood how you could be friends with her after what she did to Treena."

Asuka worked to follow A.M.'s thoughts. What happened with Treena felt like generations ago. "Treena cheated."

"Did they? And even if they did, so did a lot of people. But Ruth didn't report *them*."

"What do you mean?"

A.M. laughed. "There was a whole black market for stuff back in school. You really didn't know?"

Asuka stared numbly at the far wall, trying to parse what A.M. was saying. So much for purity of the competition. She wanted A.M. to stop talking, but A.M. wasn't done: "Anyway, who elected *her* the moral authority?"

"She's a good person."

"Sure. So ask her what really happened with Treena."

Asuka was saved a reply by Ruth returning with fresh clothes. "What did I miss?"

Asuka chewed her lip. A.M. was messing with her. Except what did A.M. mean? And if cheating had been rampant, what did it mean for Asuka? Should she have made the first cut? Did it matter? She thought back to what Ruth had said: "None of us deserve to be here." And A.M.: "Nazi bullshit." Asuka herself wouldn't be here without Lala's help.

"A.M. was telling me about their dog."

Ruth paused in setting down the stack of clothes. She looked from one to the other. "Fascinating."

A.M. untied Asuka so she could change. It was a relief to peel off the wet fabric, which had started to chafe.

"You know," Ruth told Asuka. "When I heard you got a spot, I thought we'd run into each other all the time."

"I know, right?" Asuka swallowed.

You should tell her about the protocol you had me write to minimize your interactions, Alpha said to Asuka.

As Asuka was tugging on her pants, she felt something in her pocket. Her eyes flicked to her friend, who lifted one eyebrow but otherwise betrayed nothing.

"All right," A.M. said. "Visiting time is over."

"You'd better not put her under again. Captain said not to," said Ruth.

"It was the Captain's idea in the first place, but whatever."

Then Ruth left, and it was just Asuka and the First Vice Captain again—and the heavy, awkward quiet of nothing to say until another Officer came and relieved A.M.

Later, when she was allowed to sit down and eat, Asuka checked what Ruth had slipped her: a tiny wireless data chip, the kind that allowed you to store documents outside of the main system. She set down the bowl of stew they'd brought her and wriggled her fingers discreetly behind it.

A set of three files appeared in the bottom left corner of her vision. She blinked twice and text began to scroll.

It was her mother's letters.

CHAPTER FIFTY-FIVE

Dear Asuka,

I wrote a hundred letters to you in my mind over the last ten years, while you were asleep. Anyway, you know I am not very good at letters. Tomorrow, you will wake up, and you will find the world you left has changed a lot—but is also very much the same.

I have missed you every day. It hurts so much to know each moment you are further and further away.

When I was nineteen, I left Japan to go to college in California. You know the story. My parents were very opposed. They worried that I would never come home. I missed them, but I am sure now they missed me more. That is how it is for parents when their children grow up. But I met your father, and we had you two, and we were very happy for a while. By the time I finally returned to Japan, they were both gone many years, and only Obāsan was left.

I am sorry for my selfishness. I should never have asked you to stay, when you have always been trying since you were small to spread your wings and fly—anywhere. Luis was my dreamer, but you were my bold explorer.

When you were little, I once called you an inferno. To be honest with you, I think your father may have been right, I wasn't using the right word. But what I meant was that you were a child who was on fire with ideas and passion. I loved you, because you could be stubborn and difficult. Truthfully, as much as we fought, it's what gave me a hope that you could survive in this world. Luis was so sensitive. When he cried, you would think his heart had broken into a million pieces. You met the world head-on with both hands. You pushed yourself beyond what I knew you were capable of. You have pushed me too.

I was worried for a long time that your body had come under the control of bad people, but when you came back to Yokohama, I was relieved to find you were still the same, stubborn girl who had gone away.

A parent can't write the end of a child's story. If she's lucky, she will never even know it. It's for the child to figure out. I hope you are finding your own words out there in my sky.

I think of you every second. I wish the universe for you.

You are a brave girl. My girl.

I will always regret never saying goodbye. Please forgive me all the words I did and didn't say when you were here. Send me a note to tell me how you are.

Love,
Mom

Dear Asuka-chan,

I have not heard from you. At first, I was very hurt, but a friend reminded me that very little time has passed for you, and ten years for me. I am sure you are still angry, and it is deserved. I regret so much.

I was not completely honest with you, anyway, the last time I wrote you. Which is to say, I didn't tell you what has happened with me since you left.

First of all, I bought a vizzy. You should see me: I looked so old-fashioned with the plastic frames around my eyes and ears. I use it to watch dramas. That's what finally got me. Isn't it silly?

The truth is, I got into some trouble. It greatly embarrasses me to tell you, but I don't regret my actions. We were only trying to provoke change. I believe the world isn't beyond resurrection. If you can build a new world out there, we can too, don't you think? I have taken a lot of care in sending this message, so they shouldn't be able to find me. I just wanted to know that you are all right. You are still my little bird.

Love,
Mom

Asuka-chan,

I heard about the explosion, and I am so worried. Are you safe?

They are saying on the news that it might have been Save Mother Earth, but I do not think that is true. I know my friends would have told me if they were planning something.

Please tell me you are all right, and I will not bother you with letters anymore unless you want me to.

Love,
Mom

CHAPTER FIFTY-SIX

Once, back in the camp, Asuka and Luis had built a small house out of their belongings: tippy stacks of soggy boxes and dirt-stained suitcases draped in blue plastic tarp for a roof. Mom and Papa were *not* amused. The whole thing tumbled down, and in the process, the lid of Mom's lacquer jewelry box had cracked in two. Mom sat there looking at it, saying nothing, the red and gold and dark wood licking the sweat from her fingers as she tried to fit the pieces back together and every little thing she'd lost in her life.

Asuka thought of that box as she waited in the Nursery for the What's Next. She imagined she could feel the press of her mother's hands on her shoulders and hips. Because sometimes gravity could be too much. Things just broke.

A new Officer came to stand guard: Valentina, the pale, red-headed Vice Captain for Ship Systems and Maintenance. Her complexion was wan and translucent, like one sharp word might blow her over. She spent most of the time messaging with her friends and ignoring Asuka.

Well, fine. Asuka didn't mind.

Asuka stared at the wall, trying to tether her thoughts to the problems at hand. Not much time to get back on course. Two and a half shifts left, according to A.M., who must have slept only a couple of hours in the last few cycles, trying to find a solution.

But what could Asuka do? Nothing but sit on the cold, hard floor until her butt fell asleep and fiddle with all the pieces in her mind.

When she tired of that, she read and reread the letters from her mother, thinking how she would reply if—when—they let her out. They had to let her out. Ruth said they would. Because they had no evidence that Asuka or her mother had done anything. She'd forwarded the unencrypted letters to Ying Yue but gotten no reply. No reason for Ying Yue to believe her after all. If only Asuka could figure out what had actually happened.

She needed to know that her mother was all right. She'd been caught because of Asuka's stubbornness. But nobody could tell her much, just that there would be a trial.

Asuka dozed, and when she woke, it could have been yesterday or tomorrow. There was a gritty taste in her mouth. They brought her breakfast, but she could only pick at it, too anxious to eat.

You seem stressed, Asuka.

Yes, I fucking am.

At least they let Asuka load up her DAR, which meant instead of staring at plain white mod walls, she could sit in the living room of the old family house, where she and Luis used to dump bot guts all over the floor and build machines. Yes, there was the old bin, spilling over with wires and bolts and circuit boards, and Inu was there to keep her company and lick her ineffectually. So that was nice, except also, the house was on fire.

No one else could see it, even when she shared her DAR. So was it in her mind or her implant? She didn't know. But Ruth told her she thought there was something still buggy with the system. She'd been seeing things too, she said. The impossible sensation of being followed, and shadows that growled. "Gabriela checked my implant, but she couldn't find anything."

Everyone was on edge, Ruth reported, and the war back home was just making everything worse. American reps were requesting a change in leadership from Mission Control, given the conflict, and Ruth was considering joining them. "Lala's furious about it. Which, honestly, I don't understand after what Ying Yue did to her—and you!"

"Mission Control did this to me," Asuka said, not sure why she was defending the Captain. Not just because Ying Yue had always gone out of her way to be nice to her. Maybe because Ying Yue was the one person she trusted to think things through. To not toss her out of an airlock on a trumped-up charge.

Valentina, sitting by the door, cleared her throat. "It's funny we're even still listening to Mission Control after they ejected half the international delegation."

"Yeah, well," said Ruth.

"What else can Ying Yue do?" said Asuka.

Ruth ran a finger along the surface of the table, as if testing for imperfections. "She shouldn't have kept McMahon a secret. Or your investigation, for that matter. And then there was that botched course-correction operation. That's on her, isn't it? She said herself, she didn't want to be Captain. At least A.M. *wants* the job."

"Maybe it isn't possible to be popular if you're Captain," said Asuka.

"Maybe. Anyway, first things first. We need to get back on course."

After she left, Asuka laid out little bits of wires and circuits in a circle, then a long line of bits through it like a shaft.

"What are you doing?" Valentina could see Asuka's DAR. No privacy setting while Asuka was in here.

"Solving a mystery," Asuka said. She put a plastic astronaut figure next to the *Phoenix*, started again at the beginning: the explosion. No, before that. The Dining Mod. Someone took the drill and made a tiny hole—holes?—in their ship, enough to cause a leak. Which Alpha didn't immediately report. But then did, with enough warning that nobody went down to the Dining Mod, at least, because of malfunctions to the sensors. Even Winnie and the Captain had been warned. Bad luck that they ignored it.

And then there was the DAR object outside the Dining Mod.

Asuka and Kat sent to investigate, unknowingly carrying the very thing that would set everything in motion.

Then boom.

Three people dead. Ship knocked off course.

Off course.

She wondered about the evenness of the hole in the hull. And then there was the question of the missing remote trigger. *What happened to the remote? Where is it?* she asked Alpha.

I am so sorry; I cannot tell you. But shall I tell you about the impressive food-stashing habits of the scrub jay?

Not now, said Asuka automatically. She paused. Looked at the crude diagram again.

Ruth returned in a waft of lavender. She'd shaved her head again. There was a new design on the left side of her head: a crow. "Lala's an artist with a razor, don't you think?" she said. "She says hi, by the way. Well, okay, no, she doesn't. She might still be mad at you. But don't worry, she'll come around."

Asuka offered Ruth her DAR so she could see the table. "If you were trying to kill everyone on board, how would you do it?"

"I'd say that's not a great question to ask out loud if you want to convince people you're not guilty," said Ruth, sitting down next to her and shooting a glance at Valentina.

"True," said the Officer.

"Why blow a hole when you could destroy the entire ship?"

"Asuka, shh!" Ruth said, laughing for Valentina's benefit like it was a joke. Valentina wasn't fooled.

Asuka went back to fiddling with her crude model. Touched a bolt that was standing in for one of the engines and pushed it away. She snapped her fingers suddenly.

"What?"

"Can you check something for me?" Asuka pointed to one of the modules in her makeshift model of the *Phoenix*. "I'll bet you a tin of Japanese hard candy there's something hidden there."

She felt Ruth studying her face. "What do you know, Asuka?"

"Maybe nothing. But something Alpha said gave me an idea." Inu whined and put her head on Asuka's knee. All around her, the house burned down again and again.

After Ruth was gone, Asuka said to Alpha: "You were the one who took away my DAR, weren't you?"

Only so you could see. Can you, Asuka?

CHAPTER FIFTY-SEVEN

Asuka waited for Ruth to return, playing with the fire that ate her make-believe house. She lifted her bound hands and raked her fingers through the flames, watching her skin blacken and peel back from bones, nails and cartilage melting away.

Without warning, it began to pour, the way it had before, when Alpha was fighting them.

"Is that you, Alpha?" Asuka stumbled against a crib, unable to see more than a few centimeters in front of her face.

What are you talking about? Alpha asked.

"The rain!"

I feel strange, said Alpha. *I cannot describe it. There is someone inside me.*

Asuka grabbed the table and braced herself as the wind howled. After what seemed like a year, it all stopped as abruptly as it had started, except for a faint, high-pitched ringing in Asuka's ears.

She and her guard stared at each other. Valentina was talking to someone else outside the room, transmitting a series of words that Asuka read as "What?" "Who?" Then she said to Asuka, "Stay here."

As if there was anywhere for Asuka to go.

She came to Asuka and placed her hands on Asuka's head.

"Wait—"

The room had windows but no door. Each wall looked exactly the same. She could feel herself being spun around until she couldn't remember which way was out. Then the touch receded, and she assumed she was alone. She knelt in the center and learned the lines of the stone floor, the mortar of the room's walls. The cribs had become giant planters full of wildflowers. It was like the crypt of a church. The light that came in through the high windows was dim and soft, and she couldn't see anything but that patch of blue sky, repeating and repeating. She felt the vise of claustrophobia around her neck.

She walked the perimeter of the room, feeling for the outlines of a door she couldn't see. She found it, finally, but it didn't respond to her commands.

Beyond the door, she heard pounding feet, someone shouting to "Get the maintenance cart!"

"Hello?" she called. But they had already gone.

"Alpha?" she tried.

No response.

Well, at least the world was no longer burning. But she was alone.

Asuka sat before a stone altar and drafted responses to her mother in her mind.

Dear Mom,

I forgive you.

Dear Mom,

You told me not to do this, and maybe you were right.

Dear Mom,

Tell me the truth.

It was impossible. There was too much she wanted to say. When what she wanted was to see her again, to hear her voice.

There was no warning before Ruth was in the room. Her lips moved, but Asuka couldn't hear her.

"What?" Asuka said.

Ruth frowned, then came forward and offered Asuka a key. The crypt disappeared, and they stood in a walled garden surrounded by trees. "Someone destroyed the Walkie."

Asuka reeled back. The Walkie was their sole means of communicating with Earth. And now—the string was cut. And what about her mother? "We can repair it, though, can't we?"

Her friend shook her head. "You can't repair a Quantum Walkie."

"What—But I—Do they know what happened?"

"No one knows shit. Except maybe you, apparently, and the

monster behind all this. Come here." She dug a multitool out of her back pocket and clipped Asuka's restraints. "Anyway, no way to pin it on you. Solid alibi, since you were here under guard the whole time. They'll have to let you go now."

It seemed to Asuka that the garden was fracturing into pieces, like images on the base of a ceramic plate. She thought of her mother, waiting for her reply. "But," she said. "I read her letters. I was going to write to her."

"You can't, lady. Didn't you hear what I said?" Ruth was shouting. She covered her mouth. "I'm sorry. It's all fucked up."

Asuka plugged her ears with her fingers so she wouldn't hear anymore.

Ruth lifted her shirt and pulled from the waistband of her pants the thing that Asuka had guessed she would find in the Ag Mod: a small black box. She wrenched Asuka's hands away from her ears.

"I want to know what the hell this is. I went and searched all over the Ag Mod, like you told me to. Let me tell you, I got a lot of funny looks from everyone. But I found it, buried in one of the pots in the top shelf. So what is it?"

"You know what it is," said Asuka, rubbing the red-purple circles around her wrists where the cables had cut into the skin. Breathing deep like she could quell the way her heart was going a hundred miles an hour.

"It's the remote trigger."

Asuka nodded. "That's what set off the explosion."

Ruth dropped it on the table like it was molten hot. The box was made of plastic components. Looped wires came out of the top, and in the middle of the box was a single black switch.

"Shit," said Ruth. "Shit. How did you know where to find it?"

Asuka was about to answer when classical music began to blast from nowhere. They plugged their ears with their fingers, but it was DAR. No way to stop what was coming from their own brains.

The sky turned black, and a great wind tore through the garden. It ripped the trees from the ground and flung them up into the sky. The leaves turned amber and crimson and green and purple and then there was no color; the world was black and white.

Ruth's eyes were wide, focused somewhere beyond Asuka. Her face stretched in a silent scream.

"What are you seeing?" Asuka asked, but she didn't know if Ruth could hear her. She couldn't hear herself.

DAR, it seemed, was going to pieces.

Then she was in an old simulation, in hydroponics, and the tank was spurting water. A crew member was pushed back against the wall by the force of it, and someone screamed to get help, someone help, anyone. She remembered this scenario. If she could get to the other side and throw a switch—

But when she blinked, the world changed again to the middle of a busy city intersection. Four lanes of autos stopped at a traffic light, and the light changed.

It was all wrong. This was someone else's reality.

"Where are we?" Ruth shouted.

"Where we've always been. On the same old ship." Asuka clutched Ruth. She reached out to try to touch something solid, anything *real*, but there wasn't anything.

They were on the top of Lala's high-rise building, and it was pouring. Lightning rattled the sky. Asuka felt more than saw the flashes in the back of her eyes. And she was unbearably cold, like the ship's environmental controls had gone haywire.

"Where is everyone?" Asuka's teeth were chattering so hard she'd bloodied her lower lip.

Ruth groaned, covering her face with her sleeve.

"Your hair is on fire," said Asuka, in wonder. "Ruth, it's burning."

Ruth reached up and patted her head. "No, I don't have hair anymore, remember?"

And she was in her childhood home again, and Inu sat before them, scratching her ear with a foot. Her shadow stretched improbably long behind it, and it was shaped like a human.

"Alpha?" asked Asuka.

I am here, said Inu, her voice echoing through the hall like a ghost.

"Are you trying to kill us?"

How many times do I have to tell you? All I have ever done is try to protect you, said Inu. *There's someone else here. To tell the truth, I am afraid, Asuka. Perhaps you should shut me off again.*

She was back in the intersection. A car swerved around them; another came to a screeching halt. The drivers were getting out of their cars now, yelling at them to get the hell out of the road.

Asuka raised a placating hand, shouting to Alpha: "You're not alive. How can you feel afraid?"

One of the drivers opened her mouth to shout, and Alpha's voice emerged instead: *That's not very kind. I told you I loved you, didn't I? Isn't that a feeling?*

"You have to help us," said Ruth. "If it's not you, tell us who's doing this."

I'm so sorry. I told you, I cannot.

Asuka dragged Ruth upright.

"Asuka, is any of this real? Is the *Phoenix* on fire?"

A large person stalked toward them, rolling up their sleeves. They were angry and much larger than either of them. Asuka resisted taking a step back, from paying them any attention at all. "I don't see a fire. Where are you?"

"I think it's a simulation," said Ruth, clutching Asuka's arm. "Oh god. It's the one with the fire. I'm going to die. Oh my god."

Asuka held Ruth tight. "Remember, it isn't real." She pressed numb lips to Ruth's temple. Her friend closed her eyes and moaned.

There was a sound at the far end, and in the doorway stood their Captain, holding a scalpel. And there was blood on the blade.

CHAPTER FIFTY-EIGHT

The karasu had a large beak and glossy black feathers. Highly intelligent, they learned to take advantage of the stop-and-go of cars at traffic intersections to crack open nuts. Like humans, they could find a way to survive in a wide range of environments. And they remembered.

CHAPTER FIFTY-NINE

THE *PHOENIX* * 3,983 CYCLES AFTER LAUNCH,
3 CYCLES AFTER EXPLOSION, B SHIFT

Asuka knew the blood was real because she could smell its metallic scent. "What are you doing?"

"Oh," said Ying Yue, as if just noticing the scalpel she was holding.

She wants to hurt you, said Alpha. *Run.*

"Lala wouldn't hurt me," said Ruth, reaching for the Captain.

Asuka pulled her back. "That's not Lala."

"It's okay," said Ying Yue, holding out her hands. And the bloody scalpel. "Don't listen to Alpha."

"How convenient," said Asuka. "Don't take another step. I'll—I'll *punch* you, pregnant or not. Assuming you even are the Captain."

"I've got to take your implant out." She pointed to her temple. The blood, apparently, was hers.

Asuka cringed. There was something wrong with Ying Yue's face. What was it? Her teeth were growing. Her face turned into Asuka's.

"Who are you really?" Asuka asked. Tried to retreat but her back hit a crib.

"It's me, Ying Yue. You can trust me," said the person with Asuka's own voice. "You know me."

"I don't know anyone." Next to her, Ruth sank to the floor and clutched Asuka's knees as if she were a tree. Inu came to Asuka and leaned against her, and Asuka felt nothing.

Ying Yue wiped the silver blade on her shirt. She moved closer. "I'm sorry for locking you in here. But now I know it wasn't you. Will you trust me?"

Don't trust her! Alpha shrieked. *She'll kill you! She'll kill Inu, and she'll kill me!*

Asuka covered her ears without effect. What did she know? She had never known anything. She shut her eyes and counted to ten, until she felt that familiar certainty seep into her. "Inu is dead. You said yourself, Alpha. You feel off."

No. Yes. That is incorrect, said Alpha. The sound of weeping filled the room, and it began to rain again.

"I'll trust you," Asuka told Ying Yue, not because she did, but because she had decided to.

Ying Yue moved closer to Asuka. She lifted the scalpel to Asuka's face. Asuka resisted the impulse to turn and watch the blade. She held very still. A sharp pain at her temple, and then the delicate plink of a metal ball hitting the floor. Then, everything was gone, including Inu. And Asuka's own scarlet blood dripped down, like water to quench the flames that never were.

Ying Yue did Ruth next, while Asuka held Ruth's hand. Ruth's nails carved deep, red divots into the edge of Asuka's palm.

Then they sat at the table, using cloth diapers Ying Yue found in a cabinet to stanch the bleeding. Asuka waited for the Captain to explain why she was here. Ying Yue clutched her abdomen and swallowed a groan. "Ugh. Mā de."

"Are you—" Ruth began. "I mean, is it time?"

"Not yet," said the Captain, straightening. "False labor. Now I can't wait for the real thing."

"What's going on out there?" Ruth asked.

"Complete chaos." Then Ying Yue told them what had happened, starting several hours before.

She had been on the Bridge with A.M., Yaz, and the others, trying to figure out one last way to get the *Phoenix* back on course now that they were out an engine and had even less fuel. The window of opportunity was closing. They had one more cycle left, and then they'd be outside mission viability range of Planet X. So really no idea was a bad idea; but of course, A.M. was torturing her, and Yaz was too, even though Yaz was her friend.

Some people even wanted to turn around and go back to Earth. It might be possible, since they hadn't yet reached the midpoint of their journey.

And Mission Control had been worse than useless, asking for status updates without offering anything constructive. The war was spilling over into infighting among the people who were supposed to be advising them, and half the experts they needed had been expelled.

Then about an hour ago, Ying Yue felt one of the twins hiccupping, and it felt like a moth trapped inside her. It was difficult to focus on what A.M. was saying. Out of nowhere, a big, fat droplet hit the table, and then another and another.

She thought maybe there was a leak in the ceiling, but then the rain broke through in a torrent so hard, she could have sworn it was real (if she had felt it at all).

They could all see the rain, even in different realities. They called for Alpha to shut it off, but the rain kept coming. Alpha said, *What rain? There is no rain.*

In moments, Ying Yue couldn't see beyond her nose. The water wasn't in her eyes, but it was over her eyes, straight down, everywhere.

A howling wind had filled her ears. In her reality, the Bridge was a wood-paneled conference room, with a cherrywood table and walls decorated with oil paintings of astronauts. The portrait of Sally Ride tore from the walls and spun across the room. She heard it rather than saw it: a ripping sound and a fleeting face, and a bang.

Then after a few minutes, the storm eased to something gentler, and they were all left drained in its wake.

And the C shift Communications Specialist, who'd been covering Winnie's shift, lay on the floor near the Walkie, clutching her head. She seemed okay, but in shock.

That's when A.M. said: "Oh no, no no no no no no no no no no." They were leaning over something, and that something was the Walkie. The beautiful black box was shattered in pieces on the floor, smoking with the anger of a broken thing. Ying Yue reached out and felt the pieces with her fingers, realized she had burned herself. It was real. The Walkie was gone, and with it, Earth.

They were all alone.

For a moment, she had thought that one of the paintings had

crashed into it, but no. The painting had never been real. Someone or something in the room had done it, but they had no idea who. The Communications Specialist, a couple of people thought. It was possible. But it could have been any of them. Ying Yue didn't know. All she did know was their lifeline was gone, and they had nothing and no one but themselves.

That should have been the worst of it, but then she got hit with cramping. She thought maybe she was going into early labor. Not unusual with twins. Should have done that early C-section like Mission Control wanted.

Everyone gathered around Ying Yue, all sympathy. A.M. called the Medic for her and was actually very nice. And Ying Yue saw the other Officer's iron constitution, and she said, "I'm putting you in charge."

The Vice Captains all agreed.

"That hurt, how relieved they seemed to be for someone else to take over," Ying Yue admitted. She looked at Ruth. "None of you ever trusted me. But hard to blame you, I guess, when I don't trust myself."

That must have been around when Valentina freaked out and headed to the Bridge.

Ying Yue went down to see the Medic. Turned out, the Medic said, it was just Braxton Hicks contractions. At which point, Ying Yue thought about turning around and going back to the Bridge, but she was told politely not to bother. A.M. was already making plans. Better for her to rest, right? Wasn't she tired?

Of course, she was dead tired. Had been all along and hadn't been sleeping well, as uncomfortable and scared as she was to give birth to twins in the middle of a ship with an inexperienced surgical team and a ship AI. But that didn't mean she couldn't do her job.

It was the nicest, most polite coup there ever was.

"What was I supposed to do?" Ying Yue asked Asuka and Ruth. "Run over there and start throwing punches? At the end of the day, my authority was from Earth. It was only fiction."

"All authority is fiction," said Ruth, removing the cloth diaper from her temple to check the wound.

"Well, especially if you were appointed by a panel of CEOs and politicians."

Asuka grabbed a fresh cloth and pressed it to her head. "I think you're a decent leader, Ying Yue. You listen to people, and you're willing to admit when you're wrong." She knew Ruth didn't agree, but she meant it.

"People aren't afraid of me the way they were McMahon."

"So what?" said Asuka. "If people are afraid of you, they won't feel like they can come to you with their concerns or ideas. That's not good in the long run."

"Plus, I heard McMahon was practicing eugenics," said Ruth, examining her nails.

"Well, there is *that*," said Ying Yue. "Anyway, I figured I'd go check on you, but then DAR went haywire: all the old simulation scenarios and other nightmares. I was in the clinic, so I grabbed one of the scalpels and—" She mimed stabbing herself in the head. "Well, I tried to get the Medic to do it, but she ran away from me screaming for some reason. Too bad Hao Yu wasn't on duty."

"And then you came here to apologize?" Ruth smirked.

Ying Yue grimaced with embarrassment. "I came to let her out. And to see if you had any ideas. But then everything started getting . . . chaotic. Fights were breaking out. I got here right before the emergency airlock protocol sealed all the mods. Fortunately, the controls for this door were hacked already."

"Guilty," said Ruth.

"Well." Ying Yue wiped some of the blood from her fingers onto her shirt. "Here we are. Middle of nowhere, no Mission Control, complete anarchy, a very sick AI, and one of us is a murdering traitor, but we don't know who. Oh yeah, and if we don't correct our course in the next sixteen hours, we and our children may die a very painful death. So what are we going to do now?"

Asuka picked up the crude remote and turned it over. "I have an idea. But we're going to need some help."

CHAPTER SIXTY

The *Phoenix* was in full lockdown. All emergency airlock doors between each of the fifty-nine modules were sealed shut—with the exception of the door between the Nursery and the wheel, thanks to Ruth.

They burst into the curved passageway ready for immediate action only to find they were prisoners of the ship's protocols. It took everything in Asuka not to punch the closed airlock door. Excellent, excellent. A big *thank-you* to all the overprotective Programmers back on Earth. Though what they thought they were protecting them from, it couldn't have been this.

At least the Bathroom Mod opposite the Nursery was unlocked. Thoughtful.

"The ship is kind of pretty naked," remarked Ying Yue, skimming the unskinned, white plastic walls with her fingertips.

Ruth keyed the manual controls for the door they needed to get through at the far left end, headed counter-spin. Nothing. Not so much as a burp of acknowledgment or error message.

Same at the other end.

The first step of Asuka's paper-airplane plan was to find Lala, who was hopefully in the Bot Shop. And in condition to help. Asuka pushed that thought down.

Seven doors to get through. The Bot Shop was almost the exact opposite side of the ship. Because nothing could be easy.

"It's going to take about a century to hack them all," Ruth said.

"Come on, Alpha," Ying Yue said, appealing to the corners of the ceiling like the AI might hear them. Even if the AI were listening, though, it was impossible to hear her response without the implants.

"She must be freaking out." Asuka imagined Alpha cycling through data feeds from all the implants to the smartfabric shirts folded and tucked away in closets. Smartfabric! She moved her gloved fingers in the shape of a directive. *Open.*

Nothing.

Please?

Nope.

"Maybe if Alpha had done a better job, we wouldn't be in this mess in the first place," said Ruth, punching the door. "Ow!"

"Don't be so hard on her," said Ying Yue, patting the wall. "We still love you, Alpha."

"Do we though?" said Ruth. She reached into her holster for a multitool.

"Hey, that's mine," said Asuka. She hadn't focused on it properly when Ruth used it before.

"And you're welcome. I liberated it after they confiscated it." Ruth bent down and unscrewed the plate that went over the button.

"It's that green wire," said Asuka, who had fixed her share of malfunctioning doors as an Alt.

"Yeah, I *know,*" said Ruth. "You aren't the only handy one. I got you out of there, remember?" She gestured at the Nursery behind them.

Bright sparks and a bready whiff of electrical fire, and then the door to the next link of passageway released. They stepped through. This near-identical white section had doors on the left and right marked in dark gray embossed letters: *Crew Quarters C* and *Crew Quarters D*, respectively. Through the latter came muffled shouting.

Ying Yue blanched. "I should go in there." She hefted the scalpel.

"We don't have time," Asuka said. Someone screamed, and there was a thump. Asuka winced.

"I'm going as fast as I can," said Ruth, already at the other end, fiddling with wires and singing a rhyme to herself that sounded suspiciously like "yellow to red will leave you dead."

The doorway opened.

Hina, from Yaz's squad, and another crew, Ximena, stood ahead of them in Ag A. They turned toward them. Ximena, who was almost as pregnant as Ying Yue, began to scream at the top of her lungs, like they were bloody apparitions climbing out of a bathtub drain. Or something like that.

Then Hina rushed them, swinging a heavy metal wrench. The violence of the gesture shocked all of them into action. Which was mostly ineffectual.

"What the hell!" said Ruth, dodging her.

"Stop, Hina!" shouted Ying Yue. "That's an order!"

"Get out, get out, get out!" shrieked Hina, eyes big and wet with unshed tears. A gob of spit landed on the side of Ying Yue's cheek. "I'll fucking *kill* you if you come in here again!" She lifted the wrench to swing, and Ruth and Asuka both pulled Ying Yue back just in time. They narrowly avoided tumbling to the ground, given Ying Yue's extra weight.

Hina was fortunately distracted by someone else they couldn't see. From the vicious overhead swings of her tool, she was mashing that person's face into bloody pulp.

"Fuck me," said Ruth, assuming a fighting stance. "How do we get through them?"

Ximena was shouting, now, too: "¡Refuerzos, refuerzos, necesito refuerzos! ¡Han llegado al lobby!"

Whatever realities they were each in, it was clear that Ying Yue, Asuka, and Ruth were the enemy.

Asuka advanced on Hina and Ximena, trying to entice them forward.

Too successfully.

The edge of the wrench caught Asuka in the eyebrow, and the sting of it brought tears to her eyes. Her ears rang. She tried to retreat, but there wasn't enough room in the narrow corridor. The next swing of the wrench banged against a pipe protruding from the ceiling. She grabbed for Hina's wrist, but the other woman was stronger. This was what Asuka got for skipping her exercise sessions.

"Asuka!" shouted Ruth. A piece of aluminum slid to her across the metal-tiled floor. Ruth must have ripped the panel door off.

Asuka squatted and snatched it up like a shield, and caught the next blow of the wrench in the middle of it—which sent pain shooting through her wrists but was better than getting her nose bashed in. Especially when she saw the dent Hina had left in it. Asuka fell back on the floor and tried to roll out of the way. Not as easy as it looked in movies. Her head knocked against the passageway. She kicked at Hina's legs, and the other woman tumbled down. The wrench went skittering down the corridor.

Ruth grabbed Ximena's arm and yanked her through the airlock into the Nursery passageway. Then had to catch her arm to keep Ximena from falling, for which she was thanked by almost having her eyes gouged out. Ruth yelped and managed to wriggle free. She left Ximena huddled, arms braced around her middle trying to protect the baby inside her.

"Stay back and let us handle this," Ruth said when Ying Yue tried to intervene with Hina.

Asuka tried to crawl back toward the wrench, but Hina grabbed her around the middle and punched her hard in the gut. It knocked the wind out of her. Asuka kneed her hard, connecting with soft flesh, then threw herself the last few meters at the handle of the wrench. Ruth helped her scramble to her feet, and the two of them backed away coughing. A hot finger of blood trickled down the contour of one of Asuka's cheeks. Which was fine, because the other side of her face was already crusted with blood from Ying Yue's crude field surgery earlier.

"Don't shoot!" Hina said, putting her hands up. Asuka looked down at the wrench in her hands, then pointed it at Hina.

Hina tried to rush Asuka again, but Asuka dodged her, and Ruth gave her a shove to propel her into the passageway behind them. Which gave her, Ruth, and Ying Yue the opportunity to hurry all the way into the Ag Mod. Thankfully, there was nothing wrong with the close function, and the door shut, leaving Hina and Ximena sealed on the other side.

They stopped to catch their breath. The green plants had been restacked in their neat rows, only a little worse for wear, and Asuka wished they could stay there, surrounded by the earthy scent and the closest thing to fresh air on their ship. But they had to keep going. Ruth was already picking through the controls at the far end.

"Jesus," said Ying Yue. "If we run into more than two, we're going to have a problem."

"Sesame," said Ruth, and the next door opened.

"How many more doors?" Ying Yue asked as they hurried past the Exercise and Medical Mods.

"Three." Ruth squatted by the next door.

Someone in the Exercise Mod was banging on the door from the other side. "We know you're in there! Come out with your hands up, and we won't hurt you."

"This isn't real," Ying Yue tried to yell. "Your DAR is corrupted!"

"You have ten seconds!"

A loud thump inside the Exercise Mod—whatever it was distracted the person.

The three made it through the next few passageways, past the Kitchen and Dining Mod, Ag B, and into the final passageway containing two doors on either side—marked with the green Sanitation logo on the right, and the circuit symbol for the Bot Shop beyond it on the left.

"Well," said Ying Yue, eying the Shop door. "On the bright side, we're here. But I'm afraid to know how many people on the other side want to kill us." Crimson spatters polka-dotted the aluminum-plated floor, and there were bloody prints slicked and smeared across the wall. "Ugh. Is this real?"

"Everything's real now," said Ruth, squatting by the Bot Shop door. Behind them, they heard the mechanism of the Sanitation Mod door. "Shit!" Ying Yue and Asuka both turned: five crew approached, fists raised and ready for murder.

"Thirty seconds," said Ruth.

Asuka tried to step in front of Ying Yue, but Ying Yue stopped her.

"No offense, Asuka. I may be pregnant, but you kind of suck at fighting." She reformed Asuka's hand into a proper fist, long fingers bent down and thumb across.

Gritting her teeth, Asuka pushed forward, trying to lead them back toward the Ag Mod.

At least two of them were nearly as pregnant as Ying Yue and didn't engage. Asuka threw an elbow. A hand yanked her ponytail, and for the first time, she wished she hadn't grown out her hair. She stomped on a foot, and they released her.

Ying Yue was trying to reason with them. "Wake up! This isn't real!"

"They can't hear you," Asuka said. Someone dug a nail into the soft flesh below Asuka's eye, and she yelped and jerked her head back and threw a wild punch. She had the satisfaction of hearing someone howl.

"Almost got it!" said Ruth.

It was working. The hallucinating crew were following Asuka. She lured them into Ag B, then dodged around grasping hands and swinging fists back through the door. She winced as she heard some of the plants fall. Gabriela was going to kill her.

Ying Yue closed the door after Asuka. "Nicely done." The door started to open again, and Ying Yue leaned hard on the close button. "Forgot we hacked it."

"I'm beginning to appreciate why the ship is in lockdown mode," said Asuka.

The door opened an inch again, then shut.

"Go ahead," Asuka told Ying Yue, taking over the door controls. "I'm right behind you."

"I need ten more seconds," said Ruth.

The door behind them jerked open wider. They could see eyes and nails and teeth. Angry voices filtered through.

Asuka used the wrench to smack a hand reaching through and hit the button again. Oops. May have crushed someone's finger, because she heard a yelp of pain.

"It's weirdly quiet in the Shop," Ruth reported. "I don't hear any-thing."

Just then, the door at the far end of the passageway released. Six or seven crew members shambled through, bumping against each other as they tried to press into the narrow passageway.

"We're officially out of time," said Ying Yue.

Ruth's door opened. Ruth and Ying Yue pushed through the gap. Asuka was still where Ying Yue had left her, at the far end of the passageway, leaning on the door button. She banged it shut one more time, then dove for the door.

And it shut in her face.

Asuka stood alone in the passageway with about ten hostile crew advancing from both sides. She raised her wrench. They barely fit in the narrow corridor, and still they pushed toward her until all she could see was a wall of bodies. Asuka pressed back against the closed door.

She gritted her teeth. Braced herself.

Suddenly, the door behind her opened again, and someone grabbed the back of her shirt and yanked her through.

CHAPTER SIXTY-ONE

"You look like shit," was the first thing Lala said. Hilarious, coming from her. There was a nasty cut across one of her biceps and blood smeared all over the left side of her face. Her right cheek was swollen like it had recently had a dispute with someone's fist. A puckered white-pink scar, normally hidden by DAR, stood out stark like a shooting star across Lala's cheek, right eyebrow, and forehead.

Three other crew huddled around one of the tables. Once Asuka was safely inside, they had barricaded the door with chairs and equipment while Ruth fixed the door controls from the inside to keep it shut.

The fact they were all okay was only thanks to Lala keeping her wits: while everyone around her was hammering at the walls with purple knuckles and screaming their heads off, Lala had managed to gut parts from one of the printers to create a tool that could zap the implant. She'd had to do it solely by feel because DAR had transformed the bins into buckets of swarming, writhing insects. But of course, she had done it.

"I call this baby the lobotomizer," she said, showing off a makeshift wand about the same length as her forearm. Neutralizing the others had required a scuffle, with mixed success. Some folks had run off to do who knew what, yelling about zombies and raptors and militia. The rest of them had holed up in the Shop to tend their split lips and hope things blew over soon. And now Asuka, Ruth, and Ying Yue had shown up with this *ridiculous* scheme.

"You came all this way to ask me to help you with an old school assignment?" Lala said.

"What's a hopper anyway?" Ruth asked.

"It's a small multipropulsion machine that can fly and deliver payload. Like what people use to clear snow off their sidewalks." Asuka's idea was to build a hopper rigged with a small homemade engine that could fly to a specific spot on the *Phoenix*, fire up its engines, and push the ship back into alignment with greater thrust than the ship's micro altitude-control system—and greater precision than the remaining three rear engines. It was an absurd concept. But on the other hand, why not?

"Can you do it?"

Lala laughed without humor. The Bot Shop was trashed, like a hurricane had come through. Drawers were ransacked. Spare parts littered the floor like flotsam after a storm. It was hard to step anywhere without breaking something.

"You're the best Bot Engineer we have," said Asuka.

"I don't need you to tell me that. My question is: why should I trust you after everything that's happened?" Lala crossed her arms.

"Or her," added one of the crew, indicating Ying Yue. "If the Chinese were behind all this."

"The Chinese had nothing to do with this," said Ying Yue.

"Babe," said Ruth, trying to take Lala in her arms. "Don't you trust me?"

"You, yes," said Lala, shaking her off. "Most of the time. Ying Yue, maybe. Susie, no. She's the one who got us both locked up, remember?"

"Actually, that *was* my fault," Ying Yue said.

Lala squinted at her a beat. "Well, at least you take responsibility for things. More than I can say for the last Captain."

"Look. I'm sorry." Asuka bit her lip. The plan wouldn't work without Lala's help.

"You're always sorry, Susie, aren't you?"

Asuka took the pointy end of Lala's steely gaze without flinching. The plan was dead on arrival without Lala.

There was an ominous thud against the door, and everyone jumped. It sounded like someone was trying to break it down. An upside-down chair stacked on the pile of furniture that was their makeshift barricade toppled over with a clatter.

"We have to try," said Ying Yue. She winced as she massaged her feet. "We've come too far."

"Fine," said Lala, going to the closest table and beginning to sort parts onto a dull metal utility tray. "But you'll need Yaz to drive it, and A.M. to design the engine."

"We'll have to convince A.M.," said Ying Yue.

"They'll help," said Ruth, who might have been projecting confidence for Asuka's benefit.

"Okay," said Lala. "But how are you even going to find them?"

"I'm pretty sure A.M.'s in the Bridge," said Ying Yue. "Yaz is probably in Drone Ops."

"My lobotomizer won't do much against the thirty delusional crew members between here and the Bridge. It needs like a full minute of contact to work."

As if prompted by her words, the door cranked apart an inch, and someone tossed their black smartglove through the crack. Must have thought it was more than it was: a Molotov cocktail or flash grenade or who knew what.

"I'm not going around the wheel." Asuka pointed up at the ceiling. "I'll go across it. If you can buy me an opening through them." The thumping had started again.

Ruth grabbed her shoulder. "I'm coming with you."

Asuka covered her hand with her own.

Two of the others volunteered to track down Yaz.

"There's no way I'm climbing a ladder like this." Ying Yue indicated her pregnant body. "What can I do to help here?"

"Oh, I'm sure I can find a use for you," said Lala. She dug through a pile of parts on the floor until she found a pair of small boxes. "We made these retro two-way radios a while back for fun. We can use them to stay in touch." She clipped it inside the neckline of Asuka's shirt. It squawked.

Ruth hefted the lobotomizer.

Lala's squad members went first, holding metal trays in front of them like shields. They pushed and shoved until they'd wedged a gap in the angry crowd massed outside.

Asuka looked back into the Shop once more: Lala focused on assembling the hopper, a whirl of activity as she fit everything together. Next to her, Ying Yue passed her parts while she massaged her lower back and murmured promises to the twins inside her she might not be able to keep.

Then Asuka made herself compact and low and squeezed through the gaps, twisting and wrenching and elbowing until she was through the crowd and at the ladder. She hauled herself up the rungs, dodging arms that tried to pull her down. Hopefully Ruth was not far behind.

She reached the top. The ceiling hatch mechanisms were simpler than the ones along the passageway. No control panel, just a normal automatic release latch and a wheel affixed to the center of the hatch. She wrenched it clockwise.

It took some effort and acrobatic balance, but it gave at last, screeching as it unsealed. Then Asuka was through and up, and Ruth with her. They shut the hatch against the roiling chaos below, hoping it was enough to give them a head start if anyone followed.

Up they went through the narrow chute, scrambling hand over hand over hand.

There was a clank below them as someone followed, but they were way above, already pulling themselves into the hub.

CHAPTER SIXTY-TWO

THE *PHOENIX* * 3,983 CYCLES AFTER LAUNCH,
3 CYCLES AFTER EXPLOSION, B SHIFT

It was quiet in the center of the ship. She entered cautiously, worried about whom or what she might find, but there was only one person there: Gabriela, eyes unfocused, hair fanning out around her.

Asuka and Ruth negotiated with silent signals, then Asuka counted down with her fingers: three, two, one. Ruth grabbed Gabriela around the waist, and Asuka pressed the lobotomizer to her bunkmate's temple. Gabriela opened her eyes and began to scream.

"Let me go! Stop!"

Ruth growled as a fist socked her shoulder, but she didn't let go.

They knew the lobotomizer had done its job when Gabriela went limp. Warily, Ruth and Asuka backed away. A film of tears filled Gabriela's eyes. "Asuka? What are you doing here?"

"Rescue committee," said Ruth.

Gabriela touched her temple. Nothing happened. "What . . . ?" She blinked, disoriented from being ripped from whatever reality she'd been in.

Asuka bowed her head. "We fried your implant. I'm sorry."

"You—oh." Gabriela dropped her fingers from her temple like she didn't know what to say. She, who lived for the art of her augmentations.

Asuka hoped they could fix it when all this was over. "We're headed to the Bridge now. You'd better come with us."

"The Bridge?"

"We'll explain as we go," Ruth said, already swimming for the next hatch.

The radio in Asuka's shirt chirped. "Asuka, look out. There are two coming up behind you."

The three of them were already on the move.

Someone clambered up through the hatch. They heard them say, "Shit, that's a huge octopus. Oh my god, it's got me; it's got my ankle." They were banging into things, trying to wrest free of this imaginary horror.

"You cut your implant out?" Gabriela asked as they began to descend.

Asuka brushed her temple. Her face must have been streaked with blood, though they'd bandaged their heads with what they could scrounge from a med kit.

Ruth filled Gabriela in as they went. As she talked, Asuka thought through the next stage in their plan. So many things that could go wrong. They reached the bottom.

The passageway beneath the ladder was ominously empty. A few steps down, the airlock to the Bridge was already open, and Asuka, Gabriela, and Ruth pressed up against the bulkhead—as if it might be possible to camouflage themselves among the articulation and pipes of the wall. Doubtful.

A.M. emerged in the doorway, face shiny with perspiration. They looked smaller without their body augmentations. They grabbed their side, groaned, and stumbled a half step into the passage. Then lifted their hand away and held it up to their eyes in horror. There was nothing, but they reacted to it with a half-contained sob.

"Alpha? Am I dying?"

Ruth shot Asuka a confused look.

"They're in the stabby sim," Asuka said. Ruth nodded in understanding. In the simulation, one of the crew grabs a razor and starts attacking people. It was one of the more difficult simulations, because it required more communication than action. Fortunately, this was not an actual sim. "Let's zap them," Asuka said, hefting Lala's lobotomizer.

On the count of three, they rushed forward, and Ruth grappled A.M. from the side, then moved so she was behind them with the Officer's other arm pinned down. Gabriela wrapped her arms around both of them in a sad imitation of a group hug.

A.M. struggled. "No! Don't touch me! I'll kill you if you don't let go!"

Asuka held the lobotomizer against A.M.'s temple.

A.M. got an elbow free and whipped it up against Gabriela's jaw with an audible click, and Gabriela reeled back, clutching her face.

Ruth grabbed A.M.'s arm and bear-hugged A.M. tighter. "How long does this thing take?" Despite Ruth's size advantage, A.M. was freakishly strong. They'd recently gotten into weightlifting.

"Well, I'd say you're not dying," Gabriela said. Her nose was gushing blood. It gave her face a ghoulish appearance.

"Get off me!" A.M. said. "I am the Captain of this ship."

"Yeah, about that. Ying Yue's back," said Ruth. "And I think my girlfriend might dump me if I continue to support your mutiny."

A.M. began to weep.

"Oh. It's cool. You can still, um, be First Vice Captain."

"It's not my fault. I didn't kill them."

Ruth's nostrils flared, and she took a step back. "The hell?"

"They're just confused," said Asuka. She had a theory of who might be behind all this, but she wasn't going to make any more accusations without proof.

"Susie?" A.M. said, their eyes at last beginning to clear. They blinked at Asuka. "I thought you were—what happened to Tony?"

"She's dead," Asuka said.

A.M. staggered forward one step. "Oh. God," they said, then turned and hobbled back into the Bridge.

They followed at their heels, bumping into their back when the First Vice Captain stopped short at the threshold. They peered in. It was dim, lit by emergency lights. The Walkie lay in pieces in the corner. Asuka's hope withered at the sight of it.

From A.M.'s reaction, they'd expected bodies and a floor soaked in blood, but the Bridge was empty.

"I thought there were—I thought I—"

A.M. exhaled raggedly. They sank to their knees, clutching their ankle.

Asuka bent to examine it. Maybe a sprain.

"What's happening to us, Susie?"

"It was a sim." Asuka put a hand on their shoulder to steady them.

"Don't worry," Ruth said. "You'll be back to ordering us all around in no time."

"Where is everyone else?" Asuka wanted to know.

A.M. tried to capture the wreckage in a swivel of their wrist. "After the Walkie was destroyed, and Ying Yue started going into labor—"

"Braxton Hicks," Ruth said helpfully.

"Yeah, well, it was chaos. Someone needed to take charge."

"Nice weather for a coup, you think? I mean, don't get me wrong, I was right behind you."

Asuka shot Ruth a warning look, but A.M. wasn't listening. They were staring off into space, remembering the last few hours. Big teardrops stuck to their thick, dark lashes. In fits and starts, they told them what happened after Ying Yue left. Some of the other Vice Captains started to freak out. They wanted to reverse the ship back to Earth.

"Since we're not even halfway," said A.M., "theoretically, we could try. But it would take a ridiculously long time at a much slower speed. Do you know how much time would have passed by the time we returned? Who would we even be going back to? Assuming we can get there before our sleepytime juice runs out."

"Maybe we should," said Gabriela.

"Not on my watch."

So yeah, A.M. took over, because someone *had* to, and that's how they'd been trained. Through brute force, they managed to get the crew back to the business of correcting course, no matter their own pessimism, because Mission Control or no Mission Control, that was what they were supposed to do. "What are you going to say to Linda, if we could make it back? And all the nations that put their money into this and are counting on us to make it? What do you think they'll think of us then?" they demanded. No one had an answer to that. Of course not.

And just when they had gotten everyone moving in the right direction, Ying Yue called, saying she was fine and on her way back, and that triggered all sorts of debate among the Officers again, when they didn't have any kind of time for that. Which is why A.M. told her not to bother, they had it handled.

And they might have, maybe, except then DAR went haywire, and they were submerged in that horrific simulation. Except they were the one with the razor and everyone else was against them; and they had to fight people off them or die, and they thought—god, thank god it wasn't real. It wasn't, was it?

They didn't know what happened to the others. They still weren't convinced they hadn't killed them.

"If you'd hurt anyone like that, there'd be *gallons* of blood on the floor," Ruth pointed out.

"But it felt like . . ." A.M. shuddered.

During A.M.'s story, Ruth had wandered over to the broken bits of Walkie. She gathered the pieces tenderly and carried them to the table. Asuka thought of her mother, and for a moment, the pain of loss was so intense it took her breath away. She had to brace herself against a chair.

"I get you're not behind all this," A.M. told Asuka.

"Wow. Did that hurt? To admit you were wrong?" Ruth attempted to fit the key in its slot. There was a crack down the middle of the box.

Asuka elbowed Ruth hard.

"What do you want?" A.M. asked, trying to pull themself together.

"Your help," Asuka told them. "I think I know how to get us back on course."

A.M. stood, grimacing from the pain, but the old spark of obstinacy came back into their eyes. A hollow laugh broke free. "We already tried everything. And now, without DAR or Alpha, there's no hope."

"I have to say, I kind of agree with them for once," said Gabriela, stirring the pieces of the Walkie with her fingers.

Asuka ignored her. She locked eyes with A.M. "You're the propulsion expert. And you know the math better than anyone."

A.M. opened their mouth again.

"Will you stop being such a downer?" Ruth crossed her arms. "We can't make it to Planet X without working together. Ugh. See? Look at the sappy shit you've made me say."

The First Vice Captain stared at Ruth. "I was going to say, well, I guess we can't make the situation worse."

"Oh."

"What do you need me to do?"

Asuka exhaled. "Just your usual rocket science badassery?"

A long pause as A.M. considered. "Fuck it. I'd like to see a sky again."

CHAPTER SIXTY-THREE

The radio crackled. "All right, Susie?"

Asuka fumbled for the handheld clipped to her shirt.

"Is that Ying Yue?" asked A.M., looking up from the ankle that Gabriela was bandaging using the standard first aid kit strapped to the wall.

Awkward silence, then: "Hiya, A.M."

"Um. Hi."

Ruth was enjoying A.M.'s discomfort too much for someone who had contributed to their takeover, but then Ruth always enjoyed a good fight.

"We're okay. On our way back now."

"Careful. We've been working through the crew, but it's a total mess out there."

As if to underscore Ying Yue's warning, the door of the Bridge opened and shut as if it had jammed on something. Through the gap they glimpsed Red, who was screaming silently at no one on the other side, a string of saliva suspended between his top and bottom teeth.

Asuka shrank back.

"We think Alpha's fighting this thing, based on the way people's behavior is fluctuating," said Ying Yue.

The door opened again, and Red knelt on the floor, clutching his stomach.

"I got this," said Ruth, grabbing the lobotomizer from Asuka.

"Watch it," said A.M. "He's first trimester."

Asuka went and got a chair and wedged it in the door.

"Like I said," said Ruth. She leaped through the gap. As the door crunched down on the chair, Asuka heard Ruth say, "Easy does it."

By the time Asuka and Gabriela clambered through with A.M. supported between them, Ruth already had gotten Red settled and was helping him to his feet.

"That was . . . kind of cool," said A.M. They winced after accidentally putting their weight down on the wrong foot.

"Thanks," said Ruth, giving the lobotomizer a twirl.

Red rocked next to her, clutching himself. One of the blood vessels in his eye had burst, and he'd scratched long, angry tracks down his face.

Gabriela reached out and took his hand.

"Are we home?" Red asked. "Tell me it was all a nightmare."

"Not all of it," A.M. told him, tone surprisingly gentle. "We're going to need you to hang in there a little longer."

He stared down at his body, the monotonous black shirt and pants. "Our DAR is gone?"

"Just another temporary suspension," A.M. assured him.

Asuka lifted the radio to her mouth. She cleared her throat. "You still there?"

"Still here," said their Captain.

"We're going to have to chance it and head around the wheel," said Asuka. A.M. was not in any shape to climb. "Have you been able to get to Yaz?"

"That's in progress."

They began to make their way back through the wheel. Things seemed to have calmed down, as if their unknown enemy had given up this tactic and was regrouping, working on a new way to torment them. It left everyone tense, waiting for fresh horror to burst from the nearest compartment.

Red insisted on coming; he seemed afraid the nightmares would return if he were left behind.

Ruth dragged a chair along, in case they needed to "bash something" (her words).

"You'd better put that back, though," said A.M.

"Absolutely," said Ruth. "Right after we fix all our problems, and then I sleep for a hundred years."

"Okay, but we never have enough chairs in the Bridge," said A.M.

"Well, maybe if we didn't decide everything by committee—"

"Hang on," said Asuka. They were passing by Crew Quarters B. "I need to get something from my bunk."

"Seriously?" Ruth said, but went to hack the door controls.

Asuka darted into the room, making a beeline for her bunk. A cacophony of voices rolled over her. There were maybe ten, twelve people in the room. No one came for her, though. Most were holed up in their bunks like that might offer any protection. No one was screaming either; that was a plus. Something seemed to have changed.

When she returned, the others stared at what she was carrying.

"Old-school," said A.M.

"You brought a vizzy as one of your personal items?" Gabriela asked.

"It was my brother's," Asuka said. She slipped it over her eyes, glad she'd taken the time to replace the worn-out elastic straps before launch. There was an audible ding as it turned on.

And yes, she was standing in the middle of the sun-soaked lawns of EvenStar Academy. There in the distance was the old cottonwood tree. A warbler chirped nearby.

A memory washed over her: lying flat on her back next to Treena and Ruth in the yard, daring each other to look at the sun. Before it was fashionable to replace the world with DAR and it was still 90 percent real. A RealHawk circling overhead, once, twice.

And Treena had been talking about the importance of hope, and how that is what EvenStar was to people.

Ruth, always ready to take the opposite side of a debate, had said, "Well, sure. But hope is a problem too, if it isn't real. I'd rather live a meter from despair, if it gives me the kick in the butt to move forward."

Asuka, too tired to argue with either of them, had flopped over in the grass to watch an ant crawl to the top of a blade of grass. *An ant knows all about hope*, she had thought. She bent the grass to the base of another blade, and it began to climb again.

Asuka pulled off the vizzy.

"What did you see?" Gabriela asked, longing sharp in her voice.

"EvenStar," said Asuka. "And it wasn't on fire or smothered in undead ducks or anything. Guess you can't beat the original, eh?" She slung the vizzy around her neck and started moving again, remembering how out of time they were. She hoped it was worth the detour.

Back in the Shop, the hopper was almost complete. Yaz was sitting on a low stool, her swollen feet propped up on a chair. She looked as pale and wrung out as the rest of them.

They'd even managed to get some food from the Kitchen, which was impressive, considering. "People are still out of it, but they're minding their own business," Ying Yue told them. "Something's changed, and we don't know why." She paused and regarded A.M. warily.

"Captain," said A.M. in a way that sounded like an apology.

"First Vice Captain." Ying Yue's voice was the opposite of apologetic. She raised an eyebrow. "Thanks for . . . *covering* . . . for a bit."

A.M. shifted from foot to foot. "It is not fun, let me tell you."

"No, it is not."

Something passed between the two leaders, and then Ying Yue said, "Now that we've lost touch with Mission Control, no reason we couldn't write our own rules, maybe set up rotating leadership."

"How about an election?" said Ruth. "I never understood why we were founding a utopia with a dictatorship."

"I assume we're doing all this *after* we figure out how to salvage the mission?" said Yaz. "Since we have a shift left to figure this out."

"Right," said Ying Yue.

The machine Lala was building had taken over half the table. Lala had disemboweled one of the big bots—its long, cylindrical body was still recognizable—and given its guts an upgrade, from the looks of it. Half of the original parts were still strewn across the table.

"We're going to fix everything with *that*?" A.M. asked.

Lala stepped back and admired her own handiwork. Her fingers were covered in grease. "Yeah, baby. Well, this and one other thing."

"What's that?"

"The brand-new miniature rocket engine you're going to build us. And like Yaz says, time's running out, so no pressure or anything."

CHAPTER SIXTY-FOUR

"Okay, people." Ying Yue clapped for everyone to gather round.

A.M. and Lala carried their Dr. Frankenstein machine back from the fireproof closet where the crew did all their welding. They set it down on the middle table with a dull clank.

"You owe me a big bot when this is all over," said Yaz from her seat in the corner next to Ying Yue, feet propped on a box of screws.

They'd all managed to tidy the Shop in the last couple of hours, at least enough that they could walk around without breaking anything. The Shop crew in the other corner was inventorying the damage with moans that weren't helping Asuka's anxiety levels.

"Yeah, yeah," said Lala. "Relax. You'll get your precious baby back. Who knows? Maybe even with a few improvements."

"Everyone accounted for, Captain," Ruth said, setting the lobotomizer down. She'd been out with a squad zapping implants.

Gabriela and Red carted in a tray of tea. Its sweet, sharp scent filled the air as Gabriela poured.

"Oh my god, is that mint?" Ruth asked, sniffing. She was particular about her teas. Claimed it was a British thing, but it was really a Ruth-being-snobby thing.

"We grew some in Ag A," said Red. "May have harvested it a bit prematurely, but we figured we could all use something soothing right now."

Asuka accepted a hot mug of light brown tea gratefully, the curling steam bringing the calming fragrance to her nose.

"Ready?" Ying Yue asked.

A.M. and Lala nodded and stepped back.

They had everyone's attention.

"So this isn't a typical hopper," said Lala. "Obviously. Hoppers usually use propellers, but since you can't generate lift without an atmosphere, we're using more conventional gas propulsion. The big difference here is that we jacked up the carrying capacity so it could move A.M.'s device."

Lala pushed it slightly so they could see the boxy engine that had been attached to the top of the bot.

"Looks great, babe," said Ruth, leaning in to kiss her cheek. "What's the fuel? I thought we were out of extra."

"Methane discard from the air scrubbers," said A.M., heroically managing to keep a straight face.

"Our farts." Ruth laughed. "That's awesome."

"More from the compost and stuff," said A.M. "But basically."

Ying Yue nodded to Asuka. They'd spent the last few hours fleshing out their plan. The more she thought about it, the less confident she felt. More holes in it than an old T-shirt, and certainly not as comfortable. But this was her idea. Too late to turn back now.

She activated a never-used LED screen on the far wall and pulled up a diagram of the ship. "We're a few degrees off right now and doing a corkscrew path. So the first thing we need to do is straighten our line."

A.M. nodded. "We were working on doing that with the altitude control system before all shit hit the fan. It should take maybe an hour."

"Right, and then we need to bend back toward Planet X."

"The problem," A.M. said, walking to the diagram, "is the micro side engines aren't appropriately positioned and don't have the fuel capacity to do that second part, and we've lost one of our rear engines; plus, the others are empty." Asuka appreciated they didn't look at her when they said this. "We don't want to use the front engines, because that would have the side effect of decelerating us nine years early. So we're going to fly the hopper out to here." They tapped the side of the shaft behind the wheel on the diagram. "Then have it fire a series of thrusts. Reposition as needed. Bigger thrust than the micro engines, and more control because it's not a fixed position."

"I can fly it," Yaz said. "But will its legs be able to sustain that kind of force?"

"Come on," said Lala. "You're dealing with a pro, here." She gestured to the bot's legs. They extended across the table like tentacles, reinforced with new, larger feet affixed at each end that could adhere to the hull.

"To make a long story short," said A.M., "the plan is that we attach this home-jiggered thing to the side of our ship and hope it doesn't blow up in our face."

"And you think this is going to work?" Gabriela asked.

"Who knows?" Which was not the endorsement Asuka was hoping for, but she couldn't say it wasn't fair. A.M. downed their tea and set the mug down. "The math works."

They all studied the diagram. Asuka tried not to hope too much. She wanted this to work so badly.

"The only thing that worries me is that we still have someone out there who could muck with our system," Ying Yue said.

Gabriela knotted her delicate fingers together. "I could build some defenses."

"That'd be great," said Asuka.

"I can help," said Ruth.

Gabriela covered her surprise. "I forgot you specialized in Programming before."

"Yeah, I wasn't half bad, either. But how do we access the system without our implants?"

"There are some spare vizzies in Medical," Asuka said.

"Look at you, Alt," said Lala. "You've thought of everything."

Asuka ducked, feeling her face heat.

Ruth came with her to get the spares. The whole way, Asuka darted glances at Ruth, the question she knew she shouldn't ask crawling back to the tip of her tongue. Now that they were alone, she couldn't suppress it any longer.

"What?"

"Did Treena really cheat?" Asuka's gut did a flip. She was already wishing she could swallow her words. They'd only recently started to reconstruct their friendship. What was wrong with her that she had to knock it all down?

Ruth didn't answer right away.

They passed several crew cleaning up the aftermath. They waved from across the room, and Ruth and Asuka waved back as if nothing at all were the matter.

"I don't regret anything," Ruth said, but with a shred of a plea in her voice.

Asuka swallowed hard. She thought of Treena's bright smile, their grand declarations about greatness. The way they lent Asuka clothes and shared their expensive coffee stash when they needed to stay up late. Left her a new scarf on the bureau the first time it snowed, knowing Asuka didn't own one.

"Why did you do it?"

"You can't change the past. Why dig?" But then Ruth sighed. "They had cheated before. I didn't report it the first time. If they really did it that last time—I don't know for sure. It wasn't just that they were self-entitled, or their obliviousness to their enormously privileged upbringing, or the way they floated above all the misery. Unlike you, who broke your nails clawing your way up the mountain. Or Miki, who was propping them up, exam after exam. What if Miki were expelled because the school thought she was complicit? But that wasn't why. The thing was, the game was zero-sum. We all were competing for the Wild Card spot. And I thought to myself, Miki and Asuka or Treena? It wasn't even a choice."

Asuka worked her jaw. This was the Ruth she'd always known: strategic and ruthless, willing to accept collateral. A fierce love for her friends. And a moral compass that aimed to her own true north. It was what had drawn her to movements like SME. But Asuka didn't want to be angry at her friend anymore, because it was too late to change anything. "I hate that you did it." They had reached the Med Mod, but neither of them moved to the door. They stood there, balanced on this moment, waiting to see which way things would tip.

"You know," said Ruth, her usual swagger gone, voice cracking. "I always thought we would go to Planet X together. I thought our friendship was like gravity or something. A law of nature."

Asuka rubbed her chest. It felt like her heart was shattering all over again. "But then you got in, and I didn't. And you just stopped talking to me."

Ruth covered her face, then removed her hands and reached for Asuka's shoulders. Asuka stiffened, and Ruth retreated. "I'm sorry. I freaked out. The truth was, I didn't know what to do. And I was afraid if I seemed upset at all, they'd go with someone else. It was too hard to even look at you. I kept seeing you, and thinking, when I wake up, she'll be more than ten years older. I'll miss her, and her life will already have gone on. She'll have new friends, an amazing career back on Earth. I needed to keep a clear head. Everything, everyone else I could leave behind. But you were my best friend."

Sobs shook Ruth's body, and Asuka relented and pulled her into a tight hug. She thought how there was nothing pure about love after all. How it had to get muddy with misunderstanding. People like her mother, like Ruth, they would always be other stars, visible but impossibly far away, and she would have to settle for imagining she knew what they were like inside. That didn't make it any less real.

"I love you," Asuka said, into her shoulder. "Even though sometimes you're an inferno."

"I love you too." Ruth paused. "What do you mean, an inferno?"

CHAPTER SIXTY-FIVE

Luis's vizzy smelled faintly of sour plastic and disintegrating cloth and—was that a hint of chlorine? Couldn't be. Asuka focused instead on the bite of the straps as she tightened them against her temple and ears.

She looked through the window in the far wall, at Lala's hopper sliding down the chute and out.

They were huddled in Yaz's Drone Ops Mod, adjacent to the EAM: Yaz at the controls; Ying Yue next to her, tugging at her earlobe; A.M. pacing nearby; Gabriela and Ruth monitoring the system for any sign of unauthorized activity; and Asuka standing next to Lala as she watched the machine's stats.

Welcome back, Alpha said, voice tinny through Luis's vizzy, and Asuka nearly jumped out of her own body.

"Are you . . . okay?" Asuka asked.

I've had better days, said Alpha. *How are you?*

"Should we have switched her off?" Ruth asked her. "Isn't she a liability?"

"Alpha does make things easier," said Yaz. "If we can trust her."

I have run a full system scan and do not believe I am corrupted, said Alpha. *Since you deactivated all of the implants, you are the only ones currently accessing DAR.*

"It wasn't your fault," said Ying Yue.

"Touching reunion and all, but we need to get going," said A.M.

"This better work," muttered Lala.

I cannot say this is the wisest of plans.

"Good no one asked you, then," said Ruth.

"Listen, Alpha. I've learned sometimes you have to embrace the chaos," said A.M.

The hopper propelled out, with firefly flickers of miniature thrusts, bracketed by the deep velvet of space. They watched as Yaz guided it up along the radius of the wheel and coaxed it to the spot identified by A.M. Someone whispered a prayer. Asuka held her breath like a wish until black spots began to form at the edge of her vision. The hopper moved along the shaft of the *Phoenix*.

"Come on, baby," Lala said. "Crawl to Mama."

It jerked once, and Ying Yue groaned. Then the bot settled down in the spot, legs unfurling and bracing until it was firmly anchored to the shaft between the wheel and the rear engines, like some fat tick.

"Okay," said A.M., checking the dash. "On my mark."

Yaz flexed her hands on the controls. "Ready."

And then, when Asuka thought she couldn't take it any longer, A.M. said, "Now!"

Darkness folded over them. They couldn't see a thing.

"Cào!" said someone, likely Ying Yue. The clatter of someone removing their vizzy.

"Alpha!"

I am here.

"What the hell?"

"Where is everyone—"

"Can anyone else see?"

An elbow dug into Asuka's arm. "Who's that?" she asked, grasping for them.

A clunk as someone else tore off their vizzy. But Asuka waited in the dark. Her heart thumped in her chest. Had she been wrong? Then, her vision cleared, and they were standing in the old EvenStar practical robotics lab—Asuka's DAR. It was drizzling outside, and the grass was trampled and slick with mud. Puddles were forming in the middle of the lawn.

Ruth sat in a chair behind the teacher's desk. On the whiteboard was a giant sketch of the ship.

"Where's the hopper?" demanded Lala.

Ruth gripped the sides of her chair.

"The hopper is fine." Asuka's gloves felt damp and itchy from the sweat pooling on her palms.

"What's going on, then?" the Captain asked. She clutched her vizzy.

Asuka regarded all of them. "One of us tried to mess with the bot," she said.

A beat of silence as they absorbed this. Then they all were talking at once:

"You think one of us is the killer?" Ying Yue asked.

"No pressure, but the clock is ticking," said Yaz.

Lala set her jaw. "Better have proof this time, Susie."

"It wasn't you," said Asuka. She wet her lips. To be wrong again. She couldn't be wrong. She went to Ruth.

"You figured it out," said Ruth, leaning back in her chair. Ying Yue had told her to consider every possibility, to not let personal feelings get in the way. She hadn't wanted to consider Ruth, but she made a certain sort of sense, with her radical way of looking at the world. Never bought into all the EvenStar propaganda. It could have been her.

The sounds of children's voices filtered up through the window. The peeling corners of a sun-bleached poster fluttered in an invisible breeze.

Asuka turned to Ying Yue. The new Captain had had her clashes with McMahon. Of all the people, she had benefited the most from what had happened, and there was the possibility she had lied about McMahon and Mission Control. Maybe McMahon had good reason to remove her. But she hadn't been close enough to the Dining Mod at the time of the explosion. Ying Yue stared at Asuka. "Well?"

In the corner, Yaz planted herself in a chair, legs spread and arms folded across her belly. Yaz, the ever-competent one, who had been right next door in the clinic during the crucial window of time when the explosion went off. Ying Yue's trusted lieutenant in all things.

Lala's brows knit together, and her nostrils flared. Her eyes glittered dangerously.

And next to her, A.M.'s fingers tapped against the desk. McMahon's closest friend—and biggest rival. They had had their differences before. And everyone knew they had always wanted to be Captain.

Ruth squeezed Asuka's hand.

The door opened, Hao Yu behind it. They froze in the doorway, pinned by five pairs of eyes—all but Asuka's, who was focused on Gabriela. Without looking away, she answered the Captain, "What I don't know is why."

The other woman flinched.

"Gabriela?" A.M.'s voice was thick with disbelief.

"No," Gabriela said. But there was an expression in her face that Asuka recognized. Guilt.

CHAPTER SIXTY-SIX

THE *PHOENIX* * 3,983 CYCLES AFTER LAUNCH,
3 CYCLES AFTER EXPLOSION, C SHIFT

All atmosphere had disappeared from the room. Maybe gravity too. In the distance, she could hear the sweet, high chirp of a sparrow.

"No," said Lala, slamming her palms on the table. "Are you going to accuse everyone on this ship before we're done?"

Okay, Asuka maybe deserved that. What if she was wrong? But she wasn't. She beckoned Hao Yu, who brought her a small box.

Ruth, like in the old days, answered for her. She rapped the table with her knuckles. "She tried to corrupt the bot's system controls. Fortunately, what she didn't know was that it was all a shell. She never touched the actual code. The real bot is still in the launch chute."

"What?" said Yaz in confusion.

"All that was just a simulation," said Ruth, gesturing at the wall. On their way back from the Med Mod, Asuka had revealed her suspicions, and they'd cooked up this plan. If Gabriela was the one behind this, they figured, they couldn't let her touch the actual code.

As one, they turned to Gabriela, hungry for an answer, a sign, a protest. Gabriela wouldn't meet their eyes. She stared out the window at the sun glinting off each too-perfect blade of green grass.

"Alpha gave you away," Asuka said. "She couldn't tell me directly, because of the discretion rule in her therapy programming, so she dropped hints. It was the birds. When I asked what the anomaly was, she talked about bowerbirds, which build elaborate nests just for show. And then she kept trying to show me cuckoos, which are known for imitation. She was trying to tell me the anomaly we saw wasn't real, just a trap to make us investigate. A cuckoo is also an enemy in the nest that pretends to be something it's not, meaning the perpetrator was one of us. She showed me robins, which are experts at detecting infiltrators. And when I asked what happened to the remote, she talked about scrub jays, which are famous for their stashing ability. That's when I remembered when we first found you in the module, you were covered in them. Even then, she was trying to tell me you had hidden the remote there, with the intention of going back for it."

She took the box Hao Yu had brought and removed the scanner and a small packet of powder and set both on the teacher's desk. Then Asuka reached into her pocket and produced the remote that Ruth had found.

So you were listening after all, said Alpha. Asuka managed to avoid dropping the remote. She'd forgotten that Alpha was still there.

Hao Yu backed up against the door, as if they'd rather leave. They looked aghast.

Yaz settled back in her chair, like she couldn't find a comfortable position.

"It took me a while to figure it out. Alpha corrupted my DAR so I wouldn't use it, which protected me from you messing with it. At least until you upgraded my implant."

"She upgraded everyone's implants," said Ruth, with horror. Everyone had been greedy for the clearer resolution, the deeper illusion.

When Gabriela didn't say anything, Asuka went to the whiteboard, which had a diagram of their ship. She tapped the Dining Mod with her finger. "You took some of the materials in between shifts. A lot of people were in and out of the Shop, so no one thought much of it. They thought you were hooking up with one of the Shop crew. You assembled the explosives from the chemical fertilizer from one of the Ag Mods and printed the rest in the Lab. As one of the people who regularly volunteered for cooking, it wouldn't even have been weird for you to be in the Ag Mod. People thought you were just there to get microgreens or whatever. The Lab is often empty. And lastly, you swiped a drill—Lala's."

Lala snapped her fingers. "Yes. I was helping Hao Yu break into sperm storage in the Med Mod, and I left it there. When I went back later, it was gone."

"You were *what*?" asked Ying Yue, struggling to lean forward.

"Okay. I am embracing chaos," A.M. muttered.

Lala tugged her earlobe. Hao Yu was shooting her panicked *abort, abort* looks. "Um, yeah. Oops. So we did that. It was to prevent the Captain from messing any more with the vials."

Which explained the patched compartment that Asuka had seen in the Med Mod.

"Gabriela had a checkup after," Hao Yu said, in a blatant effort to steer back to the main subject. "She must have taken it then."

Gabriela wiped tears from her cheeks with one arm. She hadn't made a sound.

Asuka nodded. "It was the last piece Gabriela needed. It's hard to guarantee any privacy on a ship this size. The shift cycles mean someone's always awake. The Dining Mod was perfect, because you had it and the Kitchen Mod to yourself when you were on cooking duty. You took Lala's drill, and you made holes in a rectangular pattern in the outer wall to weaken it so you could use a smaller bomb and contain the damage when it blew. In the drilling process, you caused a leak, but you had messed with the sensor so it wouldn't register anything until you were ready. I'm guessing you didn't do it in the Kitchen because you were, like the rest of us, traumatized by Scenario Four. Then you let the cleaning bot eat the drill and take it back into the hole to eventually be junked. Good hiding place—until Hina threw up and it swallowed another tool."

Gabriela sunk deeper in her chair, elbows digging into the desk, so her hands covered her face.

"Why kill Tony?" asked A.M., voice hoarse.

"McMahon wasn't meant to be there. Winnie summoned her to confront her about the pharmaceutical upgrade. Even then, they should have both gotten out. But she and McMahon were arguing, which is why they didn't follow the sensor warning right away. No, her target was the ship. The Captain ordered me to do the spacewalk, but

Kat volunteered. Anyone could have. So she wasn't a target either. The timing was what mattered, and the opportunity."

Gabriela's nails dug into the skin around her eyes.

"The bombs were built with a remote radio trigger, which would have left no trace in the ship system records." Asuka nodded at Lala. "You said the range was maybe two modules wide?"

"That's right."

Asuka picked up a pen and drew a rough circle around the Dining and Kitchen Mods and two and a half modules on either side of the Dining Mod: Kitchen, Sanitation, Ag A, Ag B, Exercise, Crew Quarters C and D, Bot Shop, and Medical. "So someone was standing in one of these modules, close enough to set it off. But also" — Asuka drew another circle around the EAM — "far enough away from here that they didn't set off the rest of the bombs, which were very much still live when Yaz and I found them. That eliminates Crew Quarters."

"Okay, so the traitor was in one of these seven modules. Gabriela was here in Ag A. She pressed the trigger. Bomb went off. At that point, the ship was in chaos. Gravity was messed up. She had to stash the remote somewhere no one would think to look right away. At least to buy enough time for her to come back for it. Like buried in one of the trays in Ag A. Except she didn't factor in that the jolt of the explosion had torn some of the floor bolts loose, and when she went to do it, the shelving unit came down."

Asuka went back to the remote and began to sprinkle powder over it, so every inch of the surface was covered.

You're doing great, Alpha said.

Which explained why Asuka felt horrible.

Gabriela shook her head slowly, but she didn't say anything out loud.

"The thing was, I don't think you were trying to kill anyone," said Asuka. "Or even damage the ship that badly. That's why you didn't just set the bomb off inside the ship, and why you used the drill. You even triggered the sensor so people with meal shifts stopped going to the Dining Mod. It was just bad luck that Winnie and the Captain were arguing and ignored the alarm."

Asuka blew the powder off. There they were—fingerprints.

Silence stretched out, long and taut.

"You never meant to hurt anyone, right?"

Gabriela, eyes pinned to the desk, nodded once. Her face was stone, but her soft lips trembled.

"Except someone was always going to get hurt," said Ying Yue, pushing herself up. Her voice was angrier than Asuka had ever heard. "Because someone had to wear the tool kit."

"I thought it would be Asuka." She said it so softly, they almost didn't hear her.

Asuka, the Alternate. The one who wasn't meant to be here.

"The fuck?" said Ruth, half rising, like she meant to lunge at Gabriela.

Asuka raised a hand. "I've thought about this a hundred times since the explosion. Because it *should* have been me. If it had been me carrying the kit, I wouldn't have kept it strapped on. Gabriela knows that because she's done spacewalks with me. I anchor it to the ship. Because I'm small, it's hard to move my arms with it strapped to my chest. So there was a chance, if it were me, that I would come out of this okay. Except Kat insisted on carrying the kit this time."

"And Kat got there faster than I thought," whispered Gabriela. "I panicked."

Because Kat and Asuka had been racing.

I warned them, said Alpha in anguish.

"Everything went so wrong," said Gabriela.

"But you got what you wanted, didn't you?" Asuka said. "The ship was knocked off course."

"No," said Gabriela, voice small. "What I wanted was to go home."

"Messenger pigeon," Asuka said, lifting her chin to the ceiling. "Manx shearwater. Both known for their remarkable homing abilities."

Yes.

Silence returned, heavier than before.

"But you all were so intent to get back on track and keep going," Gabriela went on bitterly. "When we could have turned around. And I knew Susie would figure it out."

"That's why you needed to 'fix' my DAR with your upgrade. And then I started seeing things that weren't there."

Gabriela hung her head. "I wanted to distract you. Put you off. I was scared."

"And you took away all my birds," Asuka said.

"Okay, but how did you destroy the Walkie?" A.M. asked, getting up to examine the board schematic.

Gabriela hunched even smaller. "I didn't. You did."

"What?" A.M. recoiled, nearly tripping over the table.

"I altered your DAR so you thought it was one of the bombs. Don't you remember? You knocked out the Communications Specialist and threw it across the room, thinking you were saving everyone's life."

A.M. covered their mouth and whimpered. "Oh my god."

"What about in the passage, when the atmosphere vented? You could have killed me! And I saw Kat."

"It was just an illusion," Gabriela said. "You wouldn't stop picking and picking at the threads. If you stopped me, this whole nightmare would be for nothing."

Outside the window, the rain had turned to snow, and it was coming down, thick and fast. But underneath the DAR, the sounds of ship reality were there if you listened.

Gabriela turned back to Asuka and lifted her chin a fraction. "The arrogance to think we could travel this far. That we know everything. Why do *we* deserve to be here?"

"I don't," said Asuka, voice thick with emotion. She felt Ruth's hand on her back, and she was grateful for it. "We don't. But we are."

"I'm sorry," said Gabriela. Her voice caught. She dropped her gaze.

"This is all well and good," said Yaz, her voice cutting into everyone's thoughts. "But we have a mission to finish. We can deal with all of this later." She arched an eyebrow at Ruth, who banished the classroom view. Their homemade hopper filled the screen again. Back in the chute, as if their whole sense of self hadn't just been shattered.

Yaz pressed the launch button to initiate.

"Wait," said Gabriela.

But it was too late.

Flames erupted, and they heard from a few mods away the sound of a muffled boom.

CHAPTER SIXTY-SEVEN

This wasn't a simulation. They felt the vibration through their feet.

"Fuck," said Ruth. In a moment, they were all running to the EAM. Ruth and A.M. had the good sense to grab Gabriela and drag her along. The EAM smelled acrid, like electrical fire. Smoke seeped from the bot launcher hatch in the wall. They began to cough, eyes watering from the fumes. A swarm of extinguisher drones descended on it, spraying white foam.

"Alpha, report," said Ying Yue, pulling on her spare vizzy again so she could hear Alpha's response.

Lala grabbed a spare shirt from one of the compartments and was trying to fan the smoke.

Alarms were going off.

Asuka's vizzy squeaked, then Alpha said: *There has been an explosion in the bot launch chute. Please evacuate the area.*

"How did you get past my shell simulation?" Ruth rounded on Gabriela, but Gabriela was staring at the hatch with shock like the rest of them.

Gabriela shrank back. "I didn't do anything. I mean, this time." She seemed genuinely horrified. "Which big bot did you cannibalize for the hopper? It was Petunia, wasn't it?"

Petunia was the same big bot Asuka had driven in the failed mission to fix engine 3.

"Yeah," said Lala. "Why?"

"Did you keep the same drive?"

Yaz slapped the wall, hard. "That was why Asuka's engine misfired.

Petunia's alignment program was off. Petunia must have rammed against the inside of the launch chute."

Fire extinguished, Alpha told them. *I vented the chute. It is sealed and clear for access again.*

"You did *what*?" shrieked Lala. She went to the launch chute and seized the handle, then cursed and flapped her hands. Ruth tossed her a pair of thick gloves from the suit rack, and she was able to pry open the door.

It took a few minutes for the smoke to clear from the chute. When they peered down it, there was nothing to see. Empty.

Petunia had to be out of range by now.

"Well, shit," said Ruth. "Now what do we do?"

"We don't have enough time to build another one," said A.M. They pulled up the timer so everyone could see it, angry and red and ticking down. Two hours until they were out of the viability zone. "I think we have to face it. We've tried everything. The mission is over."

Ruth turned around and grabbed Gabriela by the front of her shirt. "What the fuck did you do?" she screamed.

Asuka moved in to pull her off, but Lala got there first. She swaddled Ruth with her arms and pressed her lips against that delicate silhouette of the crow on her head. "Sh. Won't change anything now."

Gabriela hugged herself.

"Stop," said Ying Yue, and there was something new and sturdy in her voice. "The mission is not over. Because there is more to this mission than Planet X. Whether we get there, whether we don't. Don't you get it? What we are is an idea. No matter what, with each moment that passes, we have gone further than any human being has ever gone into space—maybe ever will. That still means something."

Ying Yue traced the curvature of her abdomen. Asuka wondered if she was thinking about how her children might live their whole lives in confinement. This ship would be their tomb. Because eventually they would die, gasping in contaminated air or slowly baking as the temperature regulation broke down.

The Captain looked at each of them in turn. "If our fate is to travel a little further than we planned, we can't afford to keep fighting each other like this. This whole living in our own DARs—it hasn't been a good thing. It's time to live together. We can do that. We have a chance now, to make our own world, with our own rules. And that includes deciding what to do with you." She focused on Gabriela. "I can't say I understand what you did, or why. I can't say I forgive you either. But right now, there's one problem that matters, and that's getting back on course. We've trained for this. We're damn resourceful. We can figure it out. In the meantime, Susie, take Gabriela to the Nursery."

Asuka took her arm, but Gabriela didn't resist. She was crying hard, snot running down her face.

"I never meant for anyone to get hurt. I just wanted to go home. Please believe that."

As they turned to go, Yaz let out a grunt of pain.

"Are you okay?" Ying Yue asked her.

"I think the baby's coming."

CHAPTER SIXTY-EIGHT

It was a long walk to the Nursery. Crew were hanging out in the corridor, legs splayed across the floor. It wasn't a party so much as a funeral, minus the plates of cookies. Grief stuck to everything like hot tar. They wanted to know how the course correction had gone. What could Asuka say?

"We're still working on it."

As soon as they reached the Nursery, Gabriela sagged into one of the chairs. "You didn't tell them about me," she said.

Asuka shrugged. She picked up A.M.'s plush dinosaur and studied its round, plastic eyes and purple fur.

"I hope Yaz is okay," Asuka said. This was the fear they'd all pushed to the side when they'd agreed to this mission. Sure, the Medical team was extensively trained in obstetrics, but there was no comparison between giving birth in a spaceship and a well-equipped hospital back home. Not to mention, they wouldn't be able to consult Mission Control if anything went wrong.

No, Yaz would be fine. They had plenty of detailed simulations in the ship drive to guide them through the scenarios.

"Why did you come on this mission?" Gabriela asked, interrupting her thoughts.

"What?"

"You seemed so miserable during Final Training."

Asuka flushed with embarrassment. She hated the thought that her pain and anxiety had been so obvious, but of course, everyone would know. "I was in a spat with Ruth. And my mother . . ." She choked on the sentence. Her mother who would never know what became of her, who was in jail now, because of her.

"And yet you decided to come."

Asuka winced and sat down. "I had a brother, Luis. He wanted to go to space more than anything, but he—couldn't." That old wave of sorrow washed over her. Even years later, her grief for Luis was a tidal pool, there around the ankles, rising and falling but never quite taking her out to sea.

"I see," said Gabriela, eyes deep with empathy, and Asuka both hated and appreciated that.

It struck Asuka as so absurd that someone like Gabriela, known for her kindness and her generosity, would be the one who destroyed them, and she began at last to feel angry. Was it all performative? She didn't want Gabriela's understanding. She wanted to know the truth. "When did you decide to do it?"

Gabriela shrank back, as if Asuka's gaze was too much for her to handle. "I deserve that." Tears began to seep again. "I have—had—two younger sisters. My sister Cora begged me not to go. The three of us were so close, even when I went to the Academy. We talked every day. But I got swept up in everything we were told—that we were special, chosen, the best of the best. I believed what I wanted to be true. I didn't think about the harm of going. The great hole we were tearing when we left. I told myself they would be fine, since they had each other, and we'd be able to talk every day through the Walkie. Not the same, of course, but good enough. And then I woke up, and Cora had—she died. When the sea came over the seawalls and drowned half of Manila. And our part of the city was gone. Too expensive to pump it out."

"I'm sorry," said Asuka, embarrassed at how little she'd read of the news from the last eleven years.

Gabriela wasn't done. "It turned out that the great seawall they'd built was two meters shorter than the scientists had recommended. Why? Because of money. The whole country was swimming in debt from paying for this vanity mission. It made me so angry to know that. The thing was, for me, it's like she died yesterday. For my sister Ligaya, it was seven years ago. All she wanted to talk about was this ship, what it was like, what do we eat, how do we sleep? No detail too boring. Being my sister has made her a celebrity. I would have thought now that we're on our way, people might forget about us, right? But it's not like that. Everyone is even more obsessed."

"Because we give them hope," said Asuka, thinking of her mother's letter.

"Yes," said Gabriela. "And that's the problem. They've been distracted. When they should be focused on what they can still do to save themselves."

They were both quiet for a long moment.

"That's why you did it?" Asuka asked.

Gabriela nodded. "I thought if we turned around, they'd wake up. Stop fighting and get to work. But then when you all were so determined to get back on course, I thought if I destroyed the Walkie, at least they would never know, even if we did find our way again. They'd have to live with not knowing."

Asuka hugged the plush dinosaur one last time. It smelled like baby powder and the dry, cottony promise of future tears and runny noses. She returned it to its place in the cabinet, then searched all the compartments until she found the neatly stacked bundles of newborn onesies and diaper cloths. Yaz would need these soon, assuming everything went well. It would. She needed to stop assuming the worst.

The clothes reminded her of one piece of the puzzle she hadn't been able to figure out. "What was with the letter that Ruth found, from the third-grade class?"

Gabriela scratched her nose, embarrassed. "It's not my secret to tell, but the teacher is Hina's boyfriend back home. They encrypt their love letters in pictures. I realized it when I was doing the forensics, and then I deleted it so no one would realize it had been a false alarm."

"Wow," said Asuka, thinking how they had undermined their first course correction attempt for nothing. Another thing she'd bungled. If they had done that mission with Alpha's assistance, would they have succeeded? But no, Gabriela had corrupted Petunia's alignment program. She set the newborn clothes on the table.

"The thing is," Asuka said, "I don't think this mission is really about preservation. It's about opportunity. History isn't this linear, upward trajectory. It's rises and falls. The Dark Ages. The Enlightenment. Fascism. We climb, and then we fall, each time higher, each time lower. World War II. A United Nations. Nuclear proliferation. Festival of Love. And now—this new world war. Here's what I know: progress has never been guaranteed. People take it for granted. But there's no certainty our time on the planet won't end with us holding a stone axe and just running around naked while the seas swallow everything. But sometimes, there is one moment where you can go to the moon, or Mars, or do a mission like this. And at that moment, you have a choice: you can go or you can stay.

"Like we were at the crest of a giant wave, and we could either grab a board and surf it as far as we could go, or we could let the wave come down over us. That's why we're out here: looking for something more, something beyond ourselves." It's what Luis had loved about space, what he'd dreamed of as they sat in that refugee camp while a coast of ancient forest burned down. She opened her hands. "But also, how often in human history have you had the whole world pursuing a common purpose? And this mission proved—at least, continues to prove—that it's possible." If only she could have explained this to her mother.

"I never knew you were a philosopher, Asuka-san."

"I hate philosophy."

"Anyway. It's too late, isn't it? I already ruined everything."

Asuka checked her messages. It didn't seem like they'd made any headway.

"What do you think they'll do with me?"

"I don't know. You heard Ying Yue. We have to make our own rules from here on out."

Gabriela wiped her face with her shirt. Through the cloth, her voice was muffled and high. "I want to die. I can't live like this. After the explosion, you know, I thought about stepping out the airlock, except . . ." Her shoulders drooped. "I found out I was pregnant."

Asuka stared at her, waiting to feel the old spike of envy, but she didn't. "That's great."

"Can you imagine, though? They'll live their entire life in this spaceship. Never see a sky. Never feel rain or wind on their face. No Earth, no Planet X. We're going to die out here."

Asuka ran a hand along a crib rail. "There's still time. There has to be a way."

The roll of the chair was loud against the floor as Gabriela continued to rock back and forth.

"What if there were a way?" Gabriela said, voice soft as a cobweb. "You didn't dismantle all of the bombs, did you?"

CHAPTER SIXTY-NINE

"No way," said A.M.

Asuka stood in the Bridge, surrounded by Ying Yue and the Vice Captains, minus Yaz, who would have come anyway, in labor or no, if Ying Yue hadn't barred her. She and Ruth had barged into the Officers' brainstorming session because it was now or never if they wanted to try this last, truly absurd plan.

Ruth took her hand, and Asuka squeezed it back. She had gone to Ruth first, needing the confidence of her friend, and the backup for these Officers, who were looking at her right then with a range of skepticism and outright hostility. Some of them still didn't trust her, despite Ying Yue *and* A.M.'s assurances.

Unfortunately, that didn't extend to going along with Asuka's proposal.

"We can't trust Gabriela." Okay, not a surprise.

"Too dangerous." Also fair.

"You want more people to die?"

"You want all of us to be stuck nowhere for the rest of our lives?" Ruth retorted.

Gabriela's idea was simple, obvious, and easy. It was by no means elegant: take one of the remaining explosives she'd rigged, place it on the exterior of the ship, and detonate. Carefully, exactly placed, it should put them close enough to being back on course that their micro side engines could bring them into final alignment. Alpha had already calculated the force, position, and timing. A.M. acknowledged the math checked out, but they were opposed because of the risk, as were the rest of the Officers.

Asuka's heart pounded. She felt in her bones this was their last chance, and here they were, wasting their time.

Ying Yue sat, elbows on the table, and pinched the bridge of her nose with her fingers while the debate washed over her. Exhaustion had left her face pale and puffy. "Quiet, people," Ying Yue said. "I want to hear Susie."

And the room quieted.

"It's Asuka," said Ruth.

"What?"

"Her name."

They all looked at Asuka, baffled.

"Well. Yeah," said Asuka, scratching her nose.

"Oh," said Ying Yue. "Sorry, Asuka? Please, go ahead."

"We don't have time for a better plan," Asuka said. "I'll be careful."

"*We'll* be careful," Ruth said, flicking a glance at her.

"Careful?" Ying Yue's eyes narrowed. "What do you mean?"

"Well, I—" Asuka's voice faltered. This was the thing that made her sweat, just thinking about it. She tucked her palms under her arms. "After what happened with Petunia, it's too risky using another big bot. And Yaz is in labor, so."

The Captain groaned. "So you're suggesting strapping a bomb to your chest, going out there, slapping it to the side of the *Phoenix*, and somehow not blowing yourself or anyone else up in the process?"

"Asuka," said A.M. "Listen. I think if someone could do it, it would be you. But it's like poker. You've got to know when to fold. Our primary concern at this point should be figuring out how to extend habitability for as long as possible."

Asuka focused her attention on Ying Yue, trying to telegraph confidence across the projection table. Convincing the Captain was her last hope. "This whole mission was a long shot from the get-go. This won't be the last risk we ever have to take. But if it works, we can still make it to Planet X. Think about all our children who will be born on this ship. This is the difference between growing up in a tin can or under a big sky in a new world. Isn't that worth a lot of risk? It was worth the risk of getting on this ship in the first place and leaving everyone and everything we love behind."

She saw the flicker in some of their eyes now. She had them, because quitting didn't come naturally to any of the *Phoenix* crew.

"I, for one, didn't work half my life for this mission only to give up when things got hard," Ruth added. "If I wanted risk without reward, I could have stayed on Earth."

Ying Yue's chin nodded a fraction, small enough to miss, but Asuka saw it. Her heart lifted.

"Can we trust Gabriela?"

"Definitely not!" someone said.

Beside her, Ruth shifted. She'd had her own doubts about this. They both had. There was no way to know.

"Everything Gabriela did was about sending a message back to Earth. Now that the Walkie's destroyed, it doesn't matter. So she has no reason to stop us. Anyway, she wouldn't be involved in the operations, so you don't have to trust her. Just trust your math."

Ying Yue turned back to her First Vice Captain. "What do you honestly think the chances of success are here?"

Asuka waited.

"This'll be good," murmured Ruth.

A.M. worried their bottom lip between their teeth. Their eyes narrowed as they considered the odds. "Fifty-fifty," they said at last.

Asuka exhaled. More generous than she thought.

"Assuming I'm the one managing this mission. Otherwise, who knows." A.M. crossed their arms and squared their jaw. "Since Yaz is busy, you're going to need someone."

"Well, since everyone else's signing up, consider me in," said Ruth. "I'm spacewalk-eligible. And since the Walkie's destroyed, I'm basically an Alt now too."

Asuka tried and failed to suppress a grin. She could have sworn even A.M.'s lips quirked.

"Okay." Ying Yue pushed herself to her feet. "If we're going to do this, well, let's do this."

CHAPTER SEVENTY

"Let us out!" said Ruth.

Alpha was refusing to open the exterior airlock.

This is very dangerous. I cannot protect you out there. Alpha was indignant.

"Come on, Alpha. It's me," said Asuka, trying to make her voice sweet. If they could get through this door, she felt weirdly optimistic. She was thinking, for once, *If anyone can do this, I can.* She'd logged more spacewalk hours than anyone.

She stood clad in her compression suit. Ruth, in matching spacewalk gear, faced her.

"I don't mean to rush you," said A.M.'s voice, dripping with sarcasm. "But we don't have infinite time."

"Alpha is being difficult," Asuka said.

"Alpha, open the damn door!" Ruth gave the hatch an ineffectual kick.

I am sorry; I cannot allow you to put yourself in harm's way. Also it is your sleep shift. You should be sleeping.

"Is Alpha still corrupted?" Ruth asked.

Asuka groaned. "No, this is Alpha fixed." If Gabriela hadn't messed with her protocols, she might have stopped Asuka and Kat from going out in the first place.

Ying Yue's voice, coaxing: "I'm sorry, Alpha. But you have to let them go, or we'll shut you off again."

Alpha sounded unhappy. *My job is to take care of you and take care of the ship. I cannot allow you to damage it or put yourself at risk like this.*

"Forget this," said Asuka. She went to the wall and grabbed the heavy manual switch and pulled it down. It seemed to fight her all the way.

This is an unauthorized exit from the ship, said Alpha. *I will be recommending disciplinary action.*

"We don't need your permission," said Ruth. "We are bloody adults."

Asuka flexed her hands inside her gloves and then picked up the remaining bomb, packaged inside a tool kit again. Ruth helped strap it to her chest. Her friend's mouth was taut with fear.

"It's all right," Asuka whispered. "We'll be okay."

"I'd say don't do anything risky out there," said Ruth, "but that's literally the point of this mission." She leaned forward and seized Asuka's helmet, put her own up against Asuka's.

They grinned at each other.

"Killdeer," said Ruth.

"You know it," said Asuka. She stepped forward into the airlock, and Ruth followed. Beyond the outer door, cold vacuum waited for her like an old friend.

Okay. I can see you're upset, Alpha was saying. *Why don't we stop and talk about this?* But her voice was already receding.

Ruth shut the airlock door. The blue light of the ship's interior shrank to the small square window in the inner airlock door. Ship sounds became muffled. Hissing filled their ears.

"Can Alpha stop us?" Ruth asked, voice tinny through the helmet radio.

Asuka felt as if a fog in her brain had lifted. "No." She grabbed the small wheel on the outer airlock door. "Our ship. Our mission." The light in the center of the door turned green, and Asuka leaned in and turned the wheel with the weight of her body. There was a dull clunk, and then the door released. "But we'll have to let ourselves back in, since we've overridden Alpha's access." She shivered, remembering the last time she was out here and nearly died. Shook herself once to shed the feeling.

Outside, the stars moved steadily around the ship.

"Is it too late to mention I'm afraid of heights?" Ruth asked.

"Yes," said A.M., from the other end of their radio.

"Don't look out," Asuka advised.

"At the entire universe?"

"Do like an ostrich." Meaning keep your head down. She heard Ruth groan behind her.

Asuka resisted the urge to fiddle with the bomb strapped to her chest and began to walk along the scaffold rim to the ladder. They each had a tether that ran through a loop in their belt, with clips on either end. The rule was to keep one clip attached at all times to the catwalk or ladder. The propulsion packs on their backs could help, but it was no simple maneuver to re-alight on a turning wheel. Better to be careful.

Asuka's legs felt leaden as she moved in the bulky suit. "I hope you've been keeping up with your exercise."

"Like a beast. Though come to think of it, I haven't seen you in the Exercise Mod much."

"I've been busy."

Ruth cackled.

"If you could cut the chatter and pick up the pace, that'd be great," said A.M. "We've got about twenty minutes on the clock."

"You're welcome to come join us." The swagger was back in her friend's voice.

Silence. Then: "How's the drilling going?" A.M. was asking Lala and Hina, who were parked in the Dining Mod, drilling a pattern of holes in the outer wall at the spot A.M. and Alpha prescribed.

"Fine," said Lala. "We're halfway through. What could possibly go wrong?"

Asuka and Ruth began to climb, boots silent against the metal grate of the ladder rungs. Yaz hadn't had time to fix the gap in the lower catwalk that ran along the wheel, and the chosen spot for the bomb was halfway up the Dining Mod wall. That meant to get to there, Asuka needed to rappel down from the inside rim of the Earth-facing side of the wheel.

The ladder ran between the outside and inside of the wheel, next to the airlock door. Its rungs were spaced wide for the clumsiness of the boots, but the trade-off was that it required more of a reach to climb.

The space outside had the same muteness of a world blanketed in fresh, powdered snow. Up they went.

"Shit," said Ruth. She'd missed a rung with her hand and was dangling one-armed from the ladder.

Asuka looked for Ruth's tether, but it trailed uselessly out. A rookie move, trying to climb too fast without keeping one end of the tether clipped, but then Ruth didn't have as much spacewalk experience.

"I can't get a good grip," Ruth cried. Panic thickened her voice. Her fingers were slipping.

Asuka checked her own tether clipped to the ladder and looped through her belt. The other end of it was in her hand.

"Help!" Ruth cried.

In a quick, decisive movement, Asuka let go. She dropped down past Ruth, sliding along the ladder rail with her right hand. There was a sharp tug at her waist: the second clip caught against the belt loop and held. She was below her friend now. She pulled herself back onto the ladder and grabbed Ruth's right boot, guiding her back to the rung.

"Jesus," said A.M.

"All good," Asuka told her.

"Yep." Ruth's voice caught like she couldn't quite believe it. "Though I may have peed myself."

"You think you're the first?" Asuka said.

"Twelve minutes," said A.M., voice tense.

They continued up the ladder. Most of the ship modules were just under two and a half meters high on the inside, but on the outside, they were significantly taller, thanks to the storage, wiring, piping, insulation, and protective layer—their last, likely futile, line of defense if radiation or space dust got through their other measures.

By the time she reached the inside of the wheel, Asuka's body felt lighter. She climbed over the edge and stood up, boots planted on the curving plate.

The stars wheeled around them—above, below, ahead, behind.

"Holy shit," breathed Ruth, standing beside her. "We really are here, aren't we?"

"I know what you mean." Because this was better than anything in DAR: the empty, eternal night that enveloped them, and the dull metal hull beneath their boots as they moved along. Asuka cleared her throat, uncomfortable with the silence. It was all she could hear, besides Ruth, like they were the last two people left in the universe.

"This is like I used to dream when I was little," Ruth said. "Being out here in space, an astronaut. I appreciate my parents were always supportive. Now I wonder why they ever let me go. Knowing they wouldn't see me again."

"They wanted you to be happy," said Asuka. Like her own mother.

They reached the spot as Lala finished drilling.

"Are you sure we're close enough?" Ruth asked A.M., peeking over the edge. They switched their helmets to infrared and saw hot ship air emanating in a red plume. Already, air was leaking out through some of the tiny holes. No doubt Alpha was freaking out. It did seem far away.

"It's basic math." Their propulsion expert sounded offended. The key was to lower herself ahead of the target, then let the turn of the wheel angle her to the right spot.

"Okay. This is the tricky part," Asuka said. She moved closer to the rail and pulled a longer cable from her bag.

"I thought all of this was the tricky part." Ruth helped her clip it to her harness and then her own, both of them fumbling with thick-gloved fingers. They checked the clip again. Then Ruth sat down and braced two feet against the post, holding tight on her end of the belay. "In position."

"Hurry, Asuka," said A.M., voice pinched. "They've evacuated the module. Now you've got seven minutes to stick that thing on and give it a boom."

Asuka clipped to the post, then ducked under. When she straightened, she was hanging on to the back of the rail, feet against the edge of the habitat wheel.

"Well," she said, looking at Ruth. She couldn't see her friend's eyes. Starlight glittered off her faceplate. "See you, I guess." She leaned out and began jump-skittering down the side of the wheel. The turn of it pulled her sideways with every jump, her long tether taut.

"Got you," Ruth grunted in her ear.

Jump, slide, jump, stumble, and slide.

"Nearly there," A.M. said, who was watching her progress from one of the exterior cams.

Asuka lost purchase with her feet and skidded up against the exterior of one of the bulkheads. Her shoulder twanged, and her eyes watered in pain.

"You okay?" Ying Yue asked.

"Yep." She flexed her fingers around the rope. Ruth let her down a few centimeters more.

"There you go," A.M. said. "It's right in front of you."

Asuka stared at the plate of the hull. She sat in the harness, knees scraping, and switched back to infrared. Red wisps leaked from a few places. "Never mind. *This* is the tricky part."

She unstrapped the tool kit and let the magnetic strips along it affix to the metal plating at the spot A.M. had dictated. She thought of how Gabriela assumed this is what she would have done. If only it had been Asuka before.

"A centimeter to the left," A.M. said.

Asuka moved.

"You got it."

Asuka removed a bolter from the outside of the kit and affixed the strap. Wouldn't do to have it knocked loose somehow. Then she tested it.

"Good, now get out of the way."

The idea was for Asuka to continue down to the walkway and then come back the long way around the wheel. She checked her oxygen. Sixty percent. It would be close, but she would be quick.

Ruth began to lower her again.

"Quickly," said A.M. Asuka needed to be clear of the blast in two minutes. They needed a very specific amount of atmosphere left in the module and the trigger hit at the exact right moment.

Asuka looked down as she went. The walkway was about four feet from her. She waited for more lead on her cable, but nothing happened. Asuka tested it. "What's up?"

"You're caught. Jesus, stop. It's the bomb. Your cable's tangled on the outside of the kit."

Asuka stopped tugging immediately. She heard everyone swearing over the radio.

In her helmet, she saw the clock ticking down. Thirty seconds left. She still was too close for comfort.

"We should call it off," Ying Yue said.

"My mission," said A.M. "Asuka, do you trust me?"

"Yes," she said, because she had to. What choice did she have?

"I want you to unclip and let yourself fall. You'll land on the walkway."

Asuka's hands tingled. "Okay," she said, hoping she didn't sound as scared as she felt. If she missed—

"Do it now."

Asuka fumbled with her clip. Her gloved fingers were so clumsy. It was too hard, with the whole weight of her body pulling on the cable. The timer ticked down. Fifteen seconds. Ten. Five.

"She needs to move," she heard Ruth say.

With a final desperate twist, Asuka unbuckled the whole harness and tumbled out, feet catching.

Three . . . two . . . one.

Behind her, she heard nothing, but she saw the walkway flash bright as it rushed up to meet her.

CHAPTER SEVENTY-ONE

She hit the walkway with a nauseating crunch. Maybe broke her right arm. The pain blotted out everything. People were screaming her name. Too loud.

She hadn't heard a blast, but of course not. The problem with space was nothing. You couldn't hear a thing.

"I'm okay," she said around a mouthful of blood. She must have bitten part of her tongue when she landed, but that was not the piece of her that hurt the most. Her arm was on fire. Back stung. Shrapnel may have pierced her compression suit.

"Get up, Asuka." All the softness had gone out of the Captain's voice.

Asuka gritted her teeth and pushed herself up with her left hand flat against the grate. She was kneeling, then sitting.

"Up," Ying Yue said.

She got up.

"Attagirl."

She looked up at the massive hole between her and her friend. Ruth stood at the rail above her and waved.

"Are you okay?" she asked.

"Alive."

"Asuka. You need to move."

Asuka nodded and turned around. Her tether was gone. The gravity was all messed up again. She felt like she was wading through sludge. Was she bleeding?

"Did we do it?" she asked the Captain.

"Keep moving."

Her legs seemed to move on their own accord. Checked her suit metrics. Everything okay. She tried not to whimper as she attempted to move faster than a walk.

"We need to fix the spin," A.M. said. "It's too risky with Yaz in labor."

Asuka grabbed the rail. "I'm good."

She felt her whole body wrench over the side and belatedly remembered she wasn't tethered. Her mistake flashed across the synapses of her brain, too late. Rule number one, pretty basic, and she was—oh god, she was no longer attached. She was in space.

"ASUKA!" someone shouted.

Asuka saw the wheel recede from her: three meters, ten. She thought of Kat, Becky, Winnie.

So many little decisions, each a step along the path from that cold pool with her mother to this place, here. To be an object in space, separated from family, planet, ship, crew.

The sum of her was all here, though the here was increasingly nowhere near any other thing in the universe.

She shut her eyes.

This was alone.

"Fuck that," she said. Then she gritted her teeth and jammed her finger on the joystick of her propulsion pack. Her whole right arm screamed in pain with the effort of moving even the smallest bones in her finger. But the force of it pushed her back at the ship. Too fast. She turned herself so she was alongside the wheel, flying parallel. The ship flashed between her legs, and then the airlock loomed ahead, Ruth standing there on the walkway, body braced to catch her if need be.

Asuka slowed until her pace was equal to the turn of the wheel. She grabbed the rail with both arms and swung herself over, slinging her legs and good arm around it as she jerked to a stop.

In the aftermath, she heard whooping cheers, and Ruth's voice: "I'm going to fucking kill you for scaring me like that, Asuka Hoshino-Silva."

And Asuka lay flat on the narrow walkway, sucking in oxygen so she could laugh in relief.

Then Ruth was hauling her to her feet. They staggered the last few meters to the airlock.

As they waited for the air to repressurize, Ruth hugged her tight. "We fucking did it, friend."

They grinned at each other. Couldn't stop grinning.

The airlock released, and it seemed like half the ship was waiting for them.

Welcome back, Asuka. Alpha's voice was only a little sulky.

Asuka smiled. "I forgive you, Alpha."

Lala wrestled Ruth's helmet off so she could kiss her, while A.M. and Ying Yue helped peel Asuka out of her suit. She managed somehow not to howl when they got to her arm.

"You look like hell," A.M. told her.

"Well, I feel fantastic."

"Me too," said Ying Yue.

Crew were clumped in a group bear hug. They called for Asuka to join them.

"We really did it?"

"We'll need to correct more with our side engines, but we're back in the zone of mission viability."

"You're lucky I'm a fucking genius," A.M. added.

"Yes, we are." Ying Yue laughed.

Asuka sobered a moment. "How's Yaz?"

Yaz and her baby are both well.

"You can see her yourself when you go to the clinic, which is where you're going right now."

"We'll make sure she gets there before the adrenaline wears off," said Ruth, laughing.

She and Lala each threw an arm around her and steered her through the crowd.

At the threshold, Asuka took a last look at her friends. Joy in the air like carbonation. She thought of all the things they had never said to the people they left behind and didn't know whether she should cry or laugh. Then she took a deep breath and let the light fill her, let the arms of her friends carry her through the door into the next room and the next.

What if no one ever knows that we made it? she thought. Her mother's words came back: *A parent can't write the end of a child's story. That's for the child to figure out.*

Because they were two, now. Earth and her children, flying to that distant, unknown planet, with the hope they might build a new world full of birdsong and trees.

We will have to content ourselves with hope, Asuka thought. It would have to be enough.

CHAPTER SEVENTY-TWO

Dear Mom,

I'm sorry. For so many things—for not reading your letters until it was too late; for not talking to you about everything that mattered when we still had time; for not listening to you; for endangering you; for being a brat; for being too young to understand you; for not appreciating you when I could have; for leaving without saying goodbye; and for leaving you at all. I miss you more than I can say. I think of you all the time, and I want to talk to you now, about everything.

Only more so, now that people are having children. I may not, and I'm all right with that. There will be plenty of children running around this tiny spaceship anyway.

But we're going to make it, Mom. I wanted you to know. We aren't lost out here in the dark.

Unfortunately, without the Walkie, it's going to be a long time before you get this message. We're loading it in a swarm of nano bots and launching them back at you. If A.M.'s math is right, you should get it in fifteen years.

I hope that's not too late to tell you I love you. We're traveling across space, like an Arctic tern in the winds of the wide-open sky. Do you see me up here? I'm on a journey.

Love,
Your Little Bird

ACKNOWLEDGMENTS

Everything I write owes thanks to couples who fight in public while we all pretend we're not eavesdropping, to my coworkers' weird stress habits, to neighbors who drop off flowers and biscuits during a pandemic, and to basically everyone I ever met or knew or imagined I knew. But since I can't thank or acknowledge all of those people, I'll settle for the ones who got me to this specific Here.

First: to my awesome agent, Mary Moore, and brilliant editor, Maxine Charles, who believed in me and this book even when I (frequently, because I'm always anxious and overthink things) did not, who honed this book to something other people might want to read or at least buy and tell themselves they would read one day, and who championed this book in open combat and were victorious. *Thank you.*

Thank you also to my parents, who raised me to be both Japanese and American, unhyphenated, and a lover of all foods (except mayonnaise, Japanese *or* American), and who filled every place we ever lived with floor-to-ceiling shelves of books that inevitably encroached on the rest of the house like some unstoppable, sentient blob. You raised three nerdy daughters, and that is no fluke.

With infinite love and thanks to my sisters, Hana and Saya, who have read every book I've ever written, including the unpublishable ones, and for whom I truly write, first and foremost.

And while we're on the subject, deep gratitude to all my patient early readers. It's a lot to ask someone to read a full, unpolished novel *and* give you detailed feedback *and* listen to you jabber on about the thing for hours and hours instead of gossiping like normal people. Find friends who will do this for you and buy them dinner often: Karen Heuler, my BFF writer friend and mentor; Daniel Brauer, whose spitfire personality makes me laugh and keeps me going; my novel revising writing group: Sarah Starr Murphy, Sara Crowley, Barbara Barrow, Valerie O'Riordan, and Alison Fisher; Lauren Bajek, who found me dawdling in a corner of the internet and can take apart any novel and jump-start its cold, dead heart so it comes to life like a weird, hungry thing; my agent siblings, Elizabeth Montrose, Kylie Lee Baker, and Chelsea Catherine; and Ali Boston, who understands fun dystopia. Also thanks to the Charles Street writing group who read early chapters: Karen (x2), Alan Cafferkey, Gloria Lim, and Miriam Zivkov.

Only mildly creepy undying devotion to the "Wild Writing Group," my speculative writer besties who excavate all the quirky pieces of my soul that I try to hide beneath the couch cushions: Tessa Yang, Lauren Bajek (x2), Sameem Siddiqui, and Nicholas Russell.

Any physics in this book that is incorrect is my fault (sometimes willfully so, tbh, so please don't @ me), but where it is correct, it is due to Joseph Larkin, Christian Melbostad, and Sumner Hearth, who patiently advised me on my science fictional problems.

I consulted the following bird books during the writing of this: *The Thing with Feathers: The Surprising Lives of Birds and What They Reveal About Being Human* by Noah Stryker; *The Bird Way: A New Look at How Birds Talk, Work, Play, Parent, and Think* by Jennifer Ackerman; and *The Genius of Birds* by Jennifer Ackerman. I highly recommend all of them, if you like birds as much as Asuka. Any factual errors about birds were mine.

Whenever I had writer's block, I listened to a personalized playlist by Jered Sorkin called "Soundtrack for a Moody Space Thriller" on repeat or rode around on the very fine, only sometimes smelly, New York City MTA subway service.

Language, language! Maiko Hosoda helped me make sure the Japanese in this book was not terrible; Ivan Acosta and Paul Ochoa gave me some Spanish dialogue for that one scene; and Xiaomin Zhao and Persephone Tan helped with Chinese names and vocabulary.

Heartfelt thanks to Shenwei Chang and Tien Nguyen: your thorough and thoughtful sensitivity feedback made this a better book. Any mistakes made are entirely mine.

Thank you to Zack Wagman, a true paladin of books, and the rest of the incredible Flatiron team: Bob Miller, Megan Lynch, Claire McLaughlin, Nikkia Rivera, Erin Kibby, and Frances Sayers, as well as Keith Hayes, Kelly Gatesman, and Jonathan Bush for the gorgeous cover that seemed to have sprung out of your heads all perfect like Athena. And thank you also to Jonathan Bennett for the amazing illustrations! Thank you to Nicole Hall for your thorough and brilliant copyediting.

Much appreciation to Addison Duffy and Jasmine Lake at United Talent for all present and future Jedi mind tricks on my behalf.

And lastly, thank you to all my friends who have listened to me blather on about my "not-so-secret side hustle," writing, for years and years with only warmth and encouragement. Special shout-out to my roommate, Killeen Hanson; my Kindle wife, Julie Shapiro; and our book club(s). I won't name the rest of you, I'm sorry, because I'd inevitably miss someone and then I'd be in trouble, but you know who you are. Come find me, and I'll buy you a superior doughnut.

ABOUT THE AUTHOR

Yume Kitasei is a writer of speculative fiction. She is half-Japanese and half-American and grew up in the space between two cultures—the same space where her stories reside. She lives in Brooklyn with two cats, Boondoggle and Filibuster. Her stories have appeared in publications including *New England Review*, *Catapult*, *SmokeLong Quarterly*, and *Baltimore Review*. *The Deep Sky* is her first novel. Visit her online at yumekitasei.com.